RAVES FOR JAMES PATTERSON'S SIZZLING NEW SERIES!

NYPD RED 2

"THE SECOND BOOK IN THIS FINE SERIES SHOWS PATTERSON AND KARP AT THE TOP OF THEIR CREATIVE GAMES, PRODUCING AN EXCITING STORY THAT TWISTS, TURNS, AND SHINES FROM FIRST PAGE TO LAST...The action never really lets up, even when the characters stop to take (or steal) a breath. This is one of the better police procedural series out there today. Long may it run."

—BookReporter.com

"THERE ARE THRILLS GALORE, ALL PUNCT-UATED BY KARP'S ACIDIC WIT AND SPOT-ON DIALOGUE. OR IS IT PATTERSON'S? IN THE END, IT SCARCELY MATTERS WHEN A BOOK IS THIS ENJOYABLE." —*Louisville Courier-Journal* (KY)

"Patterson and Karp spare no plot twist in this page-turning thriller...Love triangles, mafia ties, and political entangle-ments abound, expertly layering this character-driven mys-tery in such a way that no dull moment ever arises...*NYPD RED 2* IS JUST ONE MORE TRIUMPH FROM PATTERSON'S LITERARY EMPIRE, AND CLEARLY WE CAN'T GET ENOUGH."

—*Hampton Sheet* magazine

"PATTERSON AND KARP ONCE AGAIN PROVE THAT THIS IS ONE CRIME SERIES THAT'S NOT TO BE MISSED...Whether you're packing for a poolside getaway or planning a short staycation in your favorite reading chair, it's the perfect pick for literary thrill-seekers."

—NightsandWeekends.com

NYPD RED

"WITH *NYPD RED*, THIS DYNAMIC DUO HAS ONLY GOTTEN BETTER...CRIME THRILLERS DON'T GET A WHOLE LOT MORE ENTERTAINING THAN *NYPD RED*...WITH ITS NONSTOP ACTION AND ITS WICKED WIT, IT'S AS MUCH FUN AS YOUR FAVORITE SUMMER BLOCKBUSTER—BUT IT'S STILL CHEAPER THAN A TICKET AND A TRIP TO THE CONCESSION STAND."

—NightsandWeekends.com

"[PATTERSON AND KARP] REACH NEW HEIGHTS WITH *NYPD RED*, A GREAT THRILLER...THE PLOTTING AND PACING ARE SPOT-ON...It is bravura storytelling, a grand example of the best the genre has to offer." —*Louisville Courier-Journal* (KY)

"IN THE CASE OF *NYPD RED*, THERE IS SIMPLY TOO MUCH FUN—IN THE FORM OF INVENTIVE MURDER, SEX, CHEMISTRY, INVESTIGATION, MORE MURDER, MORE SEX, AND THE LIKE. POTBOILER? YES. WONDERFULLY TOLD? INDEED." —BookReporter.com

ALSO BY JAMES PATTERSON
FEATURING NYPD RED

NYPD Red

A complete list of books by James Patterson is at the back of this book. For previews of upcoming books and information about the author, visit JamesPatterson.com or find him on Facebook or at your app store.

NYPD RED 2

JAMES PATTERSON
AND MARSHALL KARP

GRAND CENTRAL
PUBLISHING

NEW YORK   BOSTON

NYPD Red 2 copyright © 2014 by James Patterson
Excerpt from *NYPD Red 3* copyright © 2014 by James Patterson

Grand Central Publishing
Hachette Book Group
1290 Avenue of the Americas
New York, NY 10104

www.HachetteBookGroup.com

Printed in the United States of America

RRD-C

Originally published in hardcover by Hachette Book Group.

First Target trade edition: December 2014
10 9 8 7 6 5 4 3 2 1

Grand Central Publishing is a division of Hachette Book Group, Inc.
The Grand Central Publishing name and logo are trademarks of Hachette Book Group, Inc.

The Hachette Speakers Bureau provides a wide range of authors for speaking events. To find out more, go to www.hachettespeakersbureau.com or call (866) 376-6591.

The publisher is not responsible for websites (or their content) that are not owned by the publisher.

Library of Congress Cataloging-in-Publication Data
Patterson, James
   NYPD red 2 / James Patterson and Marshall Karp.—First Edition.
     pages cm.
   ISBN 978-0-316-21123-9 (hardback)—ISBN 978-0-316-21126-0 (large print)
   1. Detectives—New York (State)—New York—Fiction. 2.
Murder—Investigation—New York (State)—New York—Fiction. 3. Motion pictures—Production and direction—New York (State)—New York—Fiction. I. Karp, Marshall. II. Title. III. Title: NYPD red two.
   PS3566.A822N97 2014
   813'.54—dc23   2013028868

ISBN 978-1-4555-8813-8 (Target pbk.)

For my other coauthor, my grandson, Zach.
Write on, kiddo.
—MK

GIDEON AND DAVE

ONE

October 31, 2001

"WERE YOU REALLY serious about the Hitler thing?" Dave said, dousing Meredith's jeans and sweater with lighter fluid.

"Easy on the rocket fuel there, pyro," Gideon said. "We're just torching her clothes, not trying to burn the house down."

"I tried to stop her," Dave said, throwing her bra and panties on top of the pile. He tossed them on casually—a teenager disposing of his big sister's underwear. To Dave they were just rags to be burned. But to Gideon the lacy black bra and wispy matching thong were fuel for his sixteen-year-old fantasies.

Meredith was twenty-one, a college girl—red hair, green eyes, creamy white skin. As far as she was concerned, Gideon was just another one of her kid brother's geeky friends. She had no idea how much further his imagination had taken him.

Dave added a few more generous squirts of accelerant to the mound of clothes. "You saw," he said to Gideon, looking for validation. "Didn't I try to stop her?"

"You always try to stop your sister from doing stupid shit," Gideon said. "But she's five years older than you and fifty times more stubborn. Stand back."

Dave stepped away from the crusty old Weber kettle grill.

"And yes," Gideon said, striking a wooden match. "I'm dead serious about the Hitler thing." He tossed the match onto Meredith's tattered sweater, and as blue-orange flames shot into the air, he allowed himself to relive what had happened that evening....

It was the night of the Salvis' Halloween beach party, and Dave did his best to convince Meredith not to go. "What's the attraction?" he asked. "The clams, the cannoli, or just hanging out with a bunch of drunken greaseballs?"

"No, David," she said, which is what she always called him when she was pulling rank. "I'm going because they've got a kick-ass band, fireworks like it's Chinese New Year, and because my brain is fried from burying my head in a macroeconomics book for four hours. Why don't you and Gideon go?"

"To a Mafia party?" Dave said. "No. You know how much Dad hated the Salvis."

"Everybody hates them, but everybody still goes. So what if they're Mafia? The beer is free, and you know for sure they're not going to check your ID." She opened the front door. "What time does Mom get off work?"

"The bar will be packed tonight. She won't be home till after three."

"Then I'll be home by two fifty-nine." She blew them both a kiss and left, laughing.

Two hours later she was back, her jeans and sweater torn, her face streaked with dried blood, her hair matted with wet sand.

"Enzo," she said, struggling to hold back the tears. "Enzo Salvi."

"He hit you?" Dave said.

She wrapped her arms around her kid brother and sobbed into his chest. "Worse."

"Don't shower," Gideon said. "The police have rape kits."

"No cops," she said, breaking loose from Dave. She locked the bathroom door and spent the next thirty minutes in the shower, trying to wash away the dirt, the smell, and the shame.

She joined them in the kitchen, wearing baggy gray sweats and a Mets baseball cap that concealed half her face.

"We made you hot cocoa," Dave said.

"You want marshmallows?" Gideon asked, holding a bag of Jet-Puffed minis.

"It's not exactly a marshmallow kind of night," she said, pouring half the cocoa into the sink. She pulled a bottle of Jameson Irish Whiskey from the kitchen cabinet and topped off her cup.

"I'm serious. No cops," she said. "And definitely you can't tell Mom."

Dave shook his head slowly. "I don't know, Mer, don't you think Mom should—"

"No!" Meredith screamed. "No, no, no!" The tears started to flow again, and she wiped her face in her sleeve. "He said if I tell her..." She fortified herself with the cocoa. "He said if I tell her...she's next."

Two more shots of Jameson later, Meredith was ready for bed. "Thank you," she said. "I don't know what I'd have done without you guys." She hugged them both and gave each one a soft kiss on the cheek. A kid brother kiss. Not nearly the one Gideon had been dreaming of for years.

"One more favor," she said, tossing her clothes on the floor. "Burn these."

The stretch jeans burned slowly. "I wish Enzo Salvi's balls were in there," Dave said, finishing off his third beer as the flames crept up the denim crotch.

For more than a year, the Hitler thing had been Gideon's favorite argument. "Do you think Hitler was a nice guy when he was in high school?" he would ask Dave. "No—he was an evil, crazy fuck," he'd say, not waiting for an answer, "and he got worse and worse. Don't you think the world would be a better place if someone whacked

Hitler when he was still young? Because Howard Beach sure as hell would be a better place if someone killed Enzo Salvi."

Dave's standard response was always, "You're crazy." But tonight, as he watched his sister's clothes turn into ashes, it no longer sounded so crazy.

"It's my fault," Dave slurred. "I'm three payments behind."

"Bullshit," Gideon said. "Nobody rapes a guy's sister over sixty bucks. Enzo Salvi is a psycho."

Dave popped the top on another Bud Light and finally asked the question Gideon had been waiting to hear.

"How would we do it?"

TWO

THE NEXT AFTERNOON, Gideon went to the comic-book store and sold his *Spawn* collection at a painfully cheap price. "Thanks," Dave said, knowing he had no other way to get the money to pay off Enzo.

"Killing this prick is expensive," Gideon said. "But it's worth it."

For the next three weeks, the two boys thought, rethought, and overthought the murder, watching episodes of *CSI* and renting as many movies as they could find starring Jet Li, Jackie Chan, and Jean-Claude Van Damme. They jogged on the beach, lifted weights, and tried to bulk up on Joe Weider's Mega Mass 4000.

"Enzo's been on steroids since freshman year," Dave said as the two of them downed one of their three daily protein shakes.

"That means his balls are shrinking," Gideon said.

"No, it means we could drink this chocolate shit forever, and he'd still have twice as much muscle as the two of us put together."

Gideon raised his glass in a toast. "Who gives a shit?" he said. "We'll still have bigger balls."

It didn't feel really real until they decided on a weapon. They put together a list of possibilities with the pros and cons next to each one. A gun had the most pros. It was almost guaranteed to do the job. But it also had the most cons. Guns were hard to come by and easy to trace. In the end, they decided on the oldest weapon in the world and the easiest to get their hands on. A club.

"It worked for the cavemen," Dave said.

They took the subway to Royale Sporting Goods in Brooklyn and paid sixty-two dollars for a thirty-four-inch Brett Bros. Stealth bat in black. Next they headed over to AutoZone for a box of Diamond Grip latex gloves.

Then they waited.

It had to be a Friday night. Most of the kids at John Adams High paid Enzo off in cash, but Gideon worked in the stockroom at Tonello's Liquor Store and had to steal a bottle of vodka every week. Every Friday after work, he would trudge out to the dunes across from the Salvi house on 165th Avenue and hand over the booze to Enzo.

They zeroed in on the day after Thanksgiving. There was no school that day, and if they were lucky, Enzo would be drunk by the time he showed up.

As always at this time of year, the dunes were damp and cold, but Gideon was dressed for it—Carhartt waterproof gear, ski cap, Timberlands. Enzo, as usual, didn't show up on time. Five minutes. Ten. At fifteen, the mind games started. *He knows. He's not coming. He's going to let me freeze out here, and then when I finally give up, he's going to kill—*

"Where's that faggot with my vodka?" Enzo yelled, tromping through the tall grass. There was a half moon, and Gideon could make out a shadowy figure in the mist with the massive neck, arms, and chest of a steroid abuser.

"Yo," Gideon said.

"What the hell are you doing so deep into the dunes?" Enzo said. "I'm not here for a blow job. Just a bottle of booze."

Gideon held up the liter of Absolut. "Here it is."

That was the signal, and what was supposed to happen next had been modeled after a scene from *Fist of the White Lotus.* Dave, who had been hunkered down in the wet grass, jumped up behind Enzo and brought the maple/ash-wood bat down hard.

But real life doesn't play out like kung fu movies, especially when the victim has the street smarts of a Mob boss's son, and the attacker—who had taken countless practice swings—chokes at the moment of truth.

Aiming for the back of Enzo's head, Dave managed to hit only his right shoulder.

Enzo exploded. In a lightning move, he wheeled around and kicked Dave's arm, sending the bat sailing. A split second later, Enzo pulled a Smith & Wesson Extreme Ops knife from his pocket, flipped open the business end, rushed Dave, and shoved him to the ground.

"You dickless Mick bastard. I'm gonna cut your fucking heart out and shove it up your bitch sister's skanky Irish ass." He straddled Dave, drew his arm back, and was about to plunge the serrated steel blade into Dave's chest when Gideon brought the bottle of vodka down on Enzo's head.

The knife fell from his hand, and then the rest of Enzo Salvi toppled face first into the sand.

"I'm sorry. I'm sorry," Dave said, crying for the first time since his father's funeral when he was twelve. "I blew it. Thank you, Gid, thank you. He was gonna kill me. Is he dead? Is he dead?"

The answer was clear as Enzo flailed at the grass, cursing incoherently, his mouth spitting sand and saliva, his brain and his coordination misfiring.

This wasn't the plan.

"What'll we do, what'll we do?" Dave asked.

"Grab his other side," Gideon yelled, yanking hard on Enzo's already damaged right arm.

"What are we doing?" Dave said. "Where are we taking him?"

"Just shut up and do what I say."

Dave locked on to the left arm, and Enzo howled in pain as the two boys dragged him through the dunes to the water's edge.

After wading into the bay up to his thighs, Gideon shoved Enzo's head under the water. Enzo's feet thrashed wildly.

"Grab his legs! Don't let him kick loose!" Gideon yelled.

Dave fought to grab Enzo's feet.

"Hold them as high up as you can," Gideon said. "It'll force his head down more."

Dave followed orders, and thirty seconds later Enzo's body went limp.

"We can't take a chance," Gideon said. "Come around here."

Dave dropped the legs, and they both held Enzo's face down underwater.

"This is for my sister, you Guinea fuck!" Dave screamed, punching through the water and connecting with Enzo's pulpy skull. "And this is for all the money you took from me, and this is for all the years you beat me up, and this is for that time you threw my books and all my shit in the bay, and this is for..."

He continued to rant and drive his fist into the water.

"Enough," Gideon finally said.

"Is he dead?" Dave asked, pummeling the bloody, submerged figure one last time.

"He's been dead about two minutes."

"We...killed...Hitler," Dave said, panting, crying, and laughing at the same time. "We killed...Hitler...."

They dragged the waterlogged body to the shore and then went back to the original plan. Gideon ripped the gold chains from Enzo's neck, took his watch and the money from his wallet.

Dave spat on Enzo's face. "Let's get out of here," he said, ready to bolt.

"Not so fast," Gideon said. "The collection book—our names are in it."

Enzo Salvi kept detailed records of his burgeoning

criminal career in a most unlikely place—a dark red Moroccan leather journal, bordered in gold filigree, with a magnetic flap closure to protect the inside pages.

Gideon fished the four-by-six diary out of Enzo's jacket pocket. It took another ten minutes to find the bat, the knife, and the Absolut bottle, which remarkably was still intact.

"Rot in hell," Dave said, spitting on Enzo's remains one last time.

Nobody was in sight as they stepped out of the dunes onto 165th Avenue. They walked silently through the cold November night, past the honeycomb of middle-class homes, swigging vodka from the murder weapon as they went.

THREE

IT WAS EVERY florist's dream. A Mafia funeral.

As fate would have it, Gideon's mother and father owned the local flower shop and had been the beneficiaries of the outpouring of condolences from friends, relatives, and business associates of the Salvi family.

"It's like my parents found a winning lottery ticket in their pocket," Gideon told Dave, "and they have no idea I'm the one who put it there."

The two boys, along with Meredith, walked solemnly past the line of thirty-two flower cars and up the stairs of St. Agnes. A white hearse was parked in front, and behind it a caravan of black limousines stretched for three city blocks. Media vans jammed the opposite side of the street, and a frenzy of photographers pressed against the police barricades, all hungry for the money shot that could make the front page of tomorrow's *Daily News*.

And cops. Cops everywhere. Beat cops, sergeants, and brass all the way up to deputy chief. The Feds were there, too, filming every move, every detail, every face. Grief and privacy be damned. There's nothing like a Mafia funeral to fill the Bureau's archives with valuable footage of "known associates."

Gideon, Dave, and Meredith were ushered into a pew, and Meredith immediately knelt to pray.

"How could you pray for him?" Gideon whispered once she took her seat.

"I didn't. I prayed for forgiveness."

"For what?" Gideon asked.

"I've been praying to the Holy Mother to punish him, and now I feel guilty."

Gideon wished he could tell her the truth. "Don't take all the credit," he said. "A lot of people were praying for Enzo to die."

By 11:00 a.m., every seat in the church was filled. A side door opened, and the crowd rose. Father Spinelli led the family into the chapel. First, Teresa, Enzo's mother, wearing an elegant black silk designer suit and a simple gold cross around her neck. In lieu of a veil, she was stone-faced behind oversized dark glasses. Jojo, the surviving son, escorted her to the front pew.

Meredith squeezed her brother's hand, knowing what was next. Joe Salvi, the silver-haired spitting image of his late son, entered arm in arm with his eighty-five-year-old mother, Annunziata, who was in the black mourning dress she had worn since her husband died decades ago. She let out a wail as she cast her eyes on the coffin.

The priest began. "For over eighty years, the Salvi family has made Howard Beach their home."

Not their home, Gideon wanted to scream out. *Their territory.*

"And it is clear by the outpouring of love from this community..."

They're only here because they're too scared to stay away, or they want to enjoy the family's misery.

"...that Joe and Teresa Salvi's generosity is legend. Food baskets for the poor at Thanksgiving, toys for the children at Christmas..."

A fully stocked wine cellar for the rectory.

"...and just last month, their annual Halloween beach party. This year it was especially meaningful because it was the first time many of you were able to let yourselves have fun since the towers fell in September."

Enzo had fun. Meredith didn't.

"I know that the New York City Police Department is working hard to bring the person or persons who cut Enzo's life short to justice, and—"

Without warning, Annunziata Salvi rose from her seat and lurched toward the coffin. "*No polizia. La famiglia fornirà giustizia. La famiglia fornirà giustizia!*" she screamed, throwing herself onto her grandson's casket.

It was old country funeral theatrics, and Joe Salvi let his mother wail until she sank to her knees, sobbing. Finally, he went to her, helped her back to her seat, and stood facing the crowd.

Twelve hundred people held their breath as the Mafia boss cast his cold, dark eyes across the room, a message to one and all that despite their loss, the family was none the weaker.

Gideon and Dave, hearts pounding, lips sealed, dared to stare back. They knew what Joe Salvi was looking for. Them. And his eyes made it clear that he would keep looking for them as long as he lived. *La famiglia fornirà giustizia*, the old lady had proclaimed.

The family would make its own justice.

PART ONE

THE HAZMAT KILLER

CHAPTER 1

THE TWO HOMELESS men were sitting on the cobblestones in front of the World War I memorial on Fifth Avenue and 67th Street. As soon as they saw me heading toward them, they stood up.

"Zach Jordan, NYPD Red," I said.

"We got a dead woman on the merry-go-round," one said.

"Carousel," the second one corrected.

His hair was matted, his unshaven face was streaked with dirt, and his ragtag clothes smelled of day-old piss. I got a strong whiff and jerked my head away.

"Am I that bad?" he said, backing off. "I don't even smell it anymore. I'm Detective Bell. This is my partner, Detective Casey. We've been working Anti-Crime out of the park. A gang of kids has been beating the shit out of homeless guys just for sport, and we're on decoy duty. Sorry about the stink, but we've got to smell as bad as we look."

"Mission accomplished," I said. "Give me a description of the victim."

"White, middle-aged, and based on the fact that she's dressed head to toe in one of those Tyvek jumpsuits, it looks like she's the next victim of the Hazmat Killer."

Not what I wanted to hear. "ID?"

"We can't get at her. The carousel is locked up tight. She's inside. We would never have found her except we heard the music, and we couldn't figure out why it was playing at six thirty in the morning."

"Lead the way," I said.

The carousel is in the heart of Central Park, only a few tenths of a mile off Fifth, and unless a Parkie showed up in a golf cart, walking was the fastest way to get there.

"Grass is pretty wet," Bell said, stating the obvious. "I thought NYPD Red only got called in for celebrities and muckety-mucks."

"One of those muckety-mucks went missing Friday night, and my partner and I have been looking for her. As soon as you called in an apparent homicide, I got tapped. We work out of the One Nine, so I got here in minutes. But if this isn't our MIA, I'm out of here, and another team will catch it."

"Casey and I volunteer," Bell said. "We clean up well, and if you really twist our arms, we'd even transfer to Red. Is it as cool as they say?"

Is it cool? Is playing shortstop for the New York Yankees cool? For a cop, NYPD Red is a dream job.

There are eight million people in New York City. The department's mission is to protect and serve every one of them. But a few get more protection and better service than others. It may not sound like democracy in action, but running a city is like running a business—you cater to your best customers. In our case, that means the ones who generate revenue and attract tourists. In a nutshell, the rich and famous. If any of them are the victims of a crime, they get our full attention. And trust me, these people are used to getting plenty of attention. They're rock stars in the worlds of finance, fashion, and publishing, and in some cases, they're actually rock stars in the world of rock.

I answered Bell's question. "Except for the part where I ruin a good pair of shoes tromping through the wet grass, I'd have to say it's pretty damn cool."

"Where's your partner?" Bell asked.

I had no idea. "On her way," I lied.

We were crossing Center Drive when I heard the off-pitch whistle of a calliope.

"It's even more annoying when you get closer," Bell said.

The closest we could get was twenty feet away. We were stopped by a twelve-foot-high accordion-fold brass gate. Behind it was a vintage carousel that attracted hundreds of thousands of parents and kids to the park every year.

It was hours before the gate would officially open, but the ride was spinning, the horses were going up and down, and the circus music was blaring.

"You can't get in," Casey said. "It's locked."

"How'd she get in?" I asked.

"Whoever put her there broke the lock," he said. "Then they replaced it with this Kryptonite bicycle U-Lock. It's a bitch to open."

"They obviously didn't want anybody to wander in and mess with their little tableau," I said.

"We kind of figured that," he said. "Anyway, ESU is sending somebody to cut it."

"Not until the crime scene guys dust it for prints," I said. "I doubt if we'll find anything, but I don't want it contaminated by some cowboy with an angle grinder."

"Detective Jordan…" It was Bell. "You can get a good look at the body from here."

I walked to where he was standing and peered through an opening in the gate.

"Here she comes," Bell said, as though I might actually miss a dead woman in a white Tyvek jumpsuit strapped to a red, blue, green, and yellow horse.

"Damn," I said as she rode past us.

"Is that your missing muckety-muck?" Bell asked.

"Yeah. Her name is Evelyn Parker-Steele."

Both cops gave me a never-heard-of-her look.

"Her father is Leonard Parker," I said. "He owns about a thousand movie theaters across the country. Her brother is Damon Parker—"

"The TV news guy?" Casey said.

"The bio I have on him says he's a world-renowned broadcasting journalist," I said, "but sure—I can go with TV news guy. And her husband is Jason Steele the Third, as in Steele Hotels and Casinos."

"Holy shit," Casey said to Bell. "We stumbled onto the First Lady of rich chicks."

"She's a lot more than that. She's a high-paid political operative who is currently the campaign manager for Muriel Sykes, the woman who is running for mayor against our beloved Mayor Spellman."

"Rich, famous, connected," Bell said. "Six ways to Sunday, this is a case for Red. I guess we better get out of here before we blow our cover. Good luck, Detective."

"Hang on," I said. "My partner is running late, and I could use your help feeling out the crowd."

Casey instinctively looked over his shoulder at the deserted park.

"They're not here yet," I said, "but they'll come. The media, the gawkers, people in a hurry to get to work but who can always make time to stop and stare at a train wreck, and, if we're lucky, the killer. Sometimes they like to come back to see how we're reacting to their handiwork. You mind helping me out?"

The two cops looked at each other and grinned like a couple of kids who just found out school was closed for a snow day.

"Do we mind helping Red on a major homicide?" Bell said. "Are you serious? What do you want us to do?"

"Throw on some clean clothes, get rid of the smell, then hang out and keep your eyes and ears open."

"We'll be cleaned up in ten," Bell said, and they took off.

The calliope music was driving me crazy, and I walked far enough away from the carousel so I could hear myself think. Then I dialed my partner, Kylie MacDonald. For the third time that morning, it went straight to voice mail.

"Damn it, Kylie," I said. "It's six forty-seven Monday morning. I'm seventeen minutes into a really bad week, and if I haven't told you lately, there's nobody I'd rather have a bad week with than you."

CHAPTER 2

I FINALLY GOT a text from Kylie: Running late. Be there ASAP.

Not ASAP enough, because she was still among the missing when Chuck Dryden, our crime scene investigator, let me know he was ready to give me his initial observations.

They call him Cut And Dryden because he's not big on small talk, but he's the most meticulous, painstaking, anal-retentive CSI guy I know, so I was happy to have him on the case.

"COD appears to be asphyxiation. TOD between one and three a.m.," he said, rattling off his findings without any foreplay. "There is evidence that the victim's mouth had been duct-taped, and the marks on her wrists indicate she was handcuffed or otherwise restrained."

"Talk to me about the jumpsuit," I said.

Dryden peered at me over rimless glasses, a small reprimand to let me know that I had jumped the gun and he wasn't ready for Q&A. He cleared his throat and went on. "The inside of the victim's mouth is lacerated, her tongue and the roof of her mouth are bruised, some of her teeth have recently been chipped or broken, she has fresh cuts on her lips, and her jaw has been dislocated. It would appear she was tortured for several days premortem. Indications are that death occurred elsewhere, and she was transported here." He paused. "Now, did you have a question, Detective?"

"Yeah. Love that little white frock she's wearing. Who's her designer?"

"Tyvek coveralls," he said, not even cracking a smile. "Manufactured by DuPont."

"So we're looking at the Hazmat Killer," I said.

Dryden rolled his eyes. *A different shade of reprimand.* "What a God-awful name to call a killer of this caliber," he said.

"Don't blame me," I said. "That's what the tabloids are calling him."

"Totally unimaginative journalism," he said, shaking his head. "This is the fourth victim. All kidnapped, all dressed alike, and all bearing this oddly curious pattern of facial injuries. A few hours after the body is found, a video goes viral on the Internet where the victim confesses to a heinous crime of his or her own—and the best the New York press can come up with is the Hazmat Killer?"

I shrugged. "It's pretty descriptive."

"And highly inaccurate," he said. "Technically, it's not even a Hazmat suit. It's a pair of hundred-dollar Tyvek coveralls. What's more intriguing is that in the three previous cases the bodies were all scrubbed down with ammonia, which makes it almost impossible to process any of the killer's DNA, and that the Tyvek further prevents other traceable evidence from getting on the victim. At the crime lab, we call him the Sanitizer."

A satisfied smile crossed his face, and I was pretty sure that he was the one who came up with the catchy handle.

"So you worked the first three cases?" I asked.

Dryden nodded. "The lead detectives are Donovan and Boyle from the Five."

"The Five?" I repeated. "Chinatown?"

"The first victim was an Asian gangbanger," he said. "The second body turned up in the One Four, and the third—a drug dealer—was dumped in Harlem, but Donovan and Boyle caught *número uno*, so they've stayed with the case. However, I imagine that Mrs. Parker-Steele, with her blue-blooded heritage, will go directly to the top of the homicide food chain, and she'll be turned over to the Red unit."

"Her blood may be blue," I said, "but her brother is famous, her husband is a billionaire, and her father is a zillionaire, so the operative color here is green. Mrs. Parker-Steele will definitely get the same five-star service in death that she was used to in life."

"So then, I'll be working with you and your partner..." He paused, trying to remember her name.

He was full of shit. Chuck Dryden's brain operated like

a state-of-the-art microchip. When he examined a body, he processed every detail. And when the body was accompanied by Kylie's sparkling green eyes, flowing blond hair, and heart-melting smile, it was forever stored in his highly developed memory bank. He knew her name, and like most guys who meet Kylie, he'd probably given her a starring role in his fantasies. It happened to me eleven years ago, only in my case, Kylie and I took it beyond the fantasy stage.

Way beyond.

But now she's Mrs. Spence Harrington, wife of a successful TV producer with a hit cop show shot right here in New York. Spence is a good guy, and we get along fine, but it gnaws at me that I get to spend fourteen hours a day chasing down bad guys with Kylie while he gets to pull the night shift.

"Her name is Kylie MacDonald," I said, playing into Dryden's little charade.

"Right," he said. "So this will probably wind up in her lap. I mean yours and hers."

Her lap? What are you thinking, Chuck?

"Yeah," I said. "I'm pretty sure Detective MacDonald and I will be tapped to track down this maniac."

Assuming Detective MacDonald ever shows up for work.

CHAPTER 3

"TAKE HER DOWN," Dryden ordered as soon as his team had clicked off a few hundred pictures of Evelyn Parker-Steele in situ. As macabre as it was, I imagined that the twinkling lights and brightly colored horses would make her crime scene photos more festive than most.

They lowered the body to a tarp near the base of the carousel, and I knelt next to her to get a closer look.

"Looks like you found your missing person," said a familiar voice.

"You mean her or you?" I said, too pissed at Kylie to look up.

Kylie MacDonald is not big on apologies. That's because in her worldview, she's never wrong. "Hey, I got here as soon as I could," she said, stretching out the word *could* so that it sounded more like *back off* than *I'm sorry*.

Now I definitely wasn't going to look up. "Did you happen to get a message that said we have a murder to solve?" I said, staring intently at the corpse.

"Yeah, I think you left that one about twenty-seven times."

"Then your phone works," I said. "So the problem must be with your dialing finger."

"Zach, there are about a hundred rubberneckers watching us from the other side of the yellow tape. Do you really think this is the best time for me to explain why I was late? How about you just fill me in on what I missed."

"Small update on that 'we have a murder to solve' message. We now have four."

She knelt beside me.

"This is the late Evelyn Parker-Steele," I said. "Evelyn, this is my partner, the late Kylie MacDonald."

I glanced over so I could catch her reaction. It's almost impossible for Kylie to look anything but beautiful, but this morning she was one hot mess. The mischief in her eyes, the sexy wiseass grin—gone, replaced by puffy eyelids and a tight-lipped frown. All the usual magic that made heads turn was now cloaked in gloom. Whatever had made her late wasn't pretty.

I felt rotten for coming down so hard on her. "Sorry I got pissy," I said. And just like that, I was apologizing to her. "Are you okay?"

"Better than her," she said, examining the victim's mangled teeth and disarticulated jaw. "This is nasty. She was alive when they did this. Were you serious about four murders? Where are the other three?"

"Dead and buried," I said. "The previous victims of the Hazmat Killer."

She already had latex gloves on, and she touched the Tyvek suit. "Anyone can buy one of these Hazmat outfits. How do we know it's not a copycat?"

"Chuck Dryden worked the others, and he says the forensics on this one have the earmarks of number four."

"He's probably right. The carousel fits the pattern too. When Hazmat Man dumps his victims, he likes to pick a spot that makes a statement. It's like his little touch of poetic justice."

"So what's the metaphor here? Parker-Steele's life was a merry-go-round?"

She shook her head. "Horses. Evelyn grew up on them. Show jumping, dressage, all that rich-girl equestrienne shit. She and her husband have a big horse farm up in Westchester County."

"So maybe he's just saying, 'Screw you and the horse you rode in on.'"

"Let's go find him and ask. There's no question that this is our case. If anybody fits the Red profile, she does. You think Cates is going to ask us to work the other three?"

"Can you think of any other reason why she called and said the mayor wants to see us at Gracie Mansion?"

"The mayor sent for us?" Kylie said, smiling for the first time since she showed up. "When are we meeting him?"

I looked at my watch. "Twenty minutes ago. But, hey, he'll understand. He keeps people waiting all the time."

"Damn," she said. "Why didn't you just go without me?"

"Cates is there," I said. "If we're both late, we can tell her we got jammed up at the crime scene, and she'll let it slide. But if I showed up on my own and told her my partner was MIA, she'd find a new team in a heartbeat."

Kylie took a few seconds to process what I'd said, and I could see that familiar look of appreciation in her eyes.

"Thanks," she mumbled.

Knowing Kylie, that was about as close to an apology as I was going to get.

CHAPTER 4

THE SQUAD CAR Cates sent for us was parked in the bike lane on Center Drive, lights flashing.

"Oh shit," Kylie said as we hiked across the lawn.

"What now?"

"Timmy McNumbnuts."

"I need another clue," I said.

"Our ride. The driver's waiting in the car like he's supposed to, but his partner who's out there chatting it up with those three women is Tim McNaughton."

"I've met him," I said. "Cocky son of a bitch, but so were we at that age."

"Zach, there's a difference between self-confidence and being an asshole who hits on anything with tits. His picture is on the bulletin board in the ladies' room with a circle/slash symbol over it. On the bottom somebody wrote,

'His pickup lines have all the subtlety of a chloroform-soaked rag.'"

"You always had a way with words," I said.

"Thank you," she said as a hint of the missing mischief crept back into her eyes. "Somebody had to warn the newbies."

As soon as McNaughton saw us, he turned back to the women he was yakking with. On cue, the three of them yelled out "Go, Red, go!" and pumped their fists in the air.

"You guys deserve a cheerleading squad," he said, proud of his handiwork.

"Not at a homicide scene," I said, hoping there were no video cameras around to capture the moment.

"Oops!" He laughed. "My bad."

"Gracie Mansion," I said. "Lights, hold the sirens."

The backseat of a cop car is not designed for comfort. It's cramped, made of hard plastic for easy cleaning of body fluids, and slung low to make it tougher for the occupants to get any leverage should they try to attack the good guys on the other side of the steel mesh cage and bulletproof glass.

The driver pulled away and headed east out of the park. McNaughton twisted around and flashed Kylie his best game show host smile. "It's a tight squeeze back there, Detective. Just wondering if you had enough room for those legs?"

"I am more uncomfortable than you can possibly imagine," she said.

He laughed as if he actually got the joke. "How's your husband doing?" he asked.

"My husband? What the hell are you talking about?" Kylie snapped.

"Hey, no offense. I read the whole story in the *Daily News.* Big-shot TV guy who makes cop shows becomes crime victim."

Kylie's husband is one of the more visible TV producers on the East Coast, which made him a prime target for the nut job who almost crippled the film business in New York. Kylie and I took the maniac down, but not before he put Spence in the hospital.

"So, how's your old man doing?" McNaughton said.

"My old man?" Kylie repeated. "My old man is doing *turn around and shut the fuck up, McNaughton*—that's how he's doing."

Timmy McNumbnuts slunk around in his seat, and nobody said a word till we got to 88th Street and East End Avenue.

Kylie bolted from the car and marched up the walk toward the mayor's residence without looking back. I hung back and thanked the driver for the lift.

McNaughton put his hand on my arm. "What's her deal?" he said. "Is she like this with everybody?"

"No," I said, removing the hand. "Just child molesters and assholes. Have a nice day."

CHAPTER 5

GRACIE MANSION WAS two centuries old, but it wasn't until World War II that it became home to anyone crazy enough to want to be mayor of New York. The current occupant, Stan Spellman, desperately wanted to renew his lease for another four years, but if you believed the pollsters, he was eight days away from being replaced by Muriel Sykes.

As mansions go, it's pretty low-key. No commanding porticos or marble columns—just a simple two-story, yellow-and-white Federal house with five bedrooms and a better than average view of the East River.

Kylie was at the top of the steps, fuming. "What is this—No Personal Boundaries Day?" she said. "Why is everybody invading my private space?"

"*Everybody?*" I said, trying not to shout on the mayor's

front porch. "That sleazebag would *love* to invade your private space. That's why he's asking 'how's your husband.' All I want to know is why you fell off the grid this morning. How the hell can you lump me and him in the same category?"

"Because you're asking different questions, but they have the same goddamn answer. Spence fell in the shower this morning. Hit his head. I took him to the ER. He's okay now, but he's upset that he's still wobbly on his feet three months after the Chameleon incident. That's why I was late. You happy now?"

I felt like a jerk. "I'm sorry," I said—my second apology in less than twenty minutes. "Why didn't you tell me?"

"Because I thought our main priority was to find a killer. Now, can we get on with it?"

She pushed open the front door, and we entered the foyer. I get my furniture from IKEA. The mayor gets his from the nineteenth century. But I'd been here before and picked up a few factoids. I pointed at the floor, a vast expanse of black and white diamond shapes that led to a winding staircase thirty feet away.

"Faux marble," I said, trying to soften the edge. "It's painted wood."

"I know, Zach. I've been here."

Draped on Spence's arm was left unsaid.

"Detectives!"

It was our boss, and all I needed was that one-word clue to know her mood. She stormed down the stairs.

Captain Delia Cates is one of the rising stars in the department, black on the outside, true blue on the inside—a third-generation cop. While she can barely tolerate the politics that comes with her job, she plays them well. And when a woman finally crashes through the Y-chromosome ceiling at NYPD, the smart money is on her. Her reputation is "Always tough, sometimes fair," and I braced myself for a serious dose of verbal bitch slapping.

"You're late," she said, "and the mayor is six degrees beyond batshit."

"Sorry," I said. "We were working under the theory that homicides take precedence over political hissy fits."

"You think I like pulling my lead investigators off a major crime scene? This is not your run-of-the-mill hissy fit. It's as big a political clusterfuck as I've ever been in the middle of. What's the story on our VIV?"

VIV is Red jargon for "very important victim." I filled Cates in on the little I knew so far, ending with, "And Chuck Dryden is convinced that she's the latest victim of the Hazmat Killer."

"He's probably right," Cates said. "Someone just uploaded an online video of Parker-Steele confessing to the murder of Cynthia Pritchard. That's the Hazmat's MO—kidnap, kill, then go viral to let everyone know that the innocent victim isn't so innocent."

"Who's Cynthia Pritchard?" I said.

"An event coordinator who worked with Parker-Steele two years ago on the campaign to reelect Congressman Winchell. A month before the election, Pritchard fell fourteen stories from the terrace of Evelyn's apartment."

"Fell?" I said.

"That's what she told the DA. She changes her tune on the video."

"I never even heard about this case," I said.

"You didn't hear about it because Leonard Parker has enough lawyers to squelch the sinking of the *Queen Mary*," Cates said. "The autopsy showed that Pritchard was drunk. Parker-Steele was wasted herself, passed out on the floor when the cops arrived. The coroner's conclusion was that Pritchard leaned too far over the terrace railing and fell. He ruled it an accident."

"Medical examiners make mistakes all the time," I said. "Didn't the department ask for a follow-up investigation?"

"Yes, but the lawyers cut it off at the knees. They said the two women were co-workers, got along well, and there was no motive. They also stated loud and clear that if *an unwarranted departmental witch hunt*—their words—was leaked to the press and in any way damaged the reputation of Evelyn or any member of one of the city's most prominent families, there'd be repercussions."

"Financial repercussions," I said.

"Right. They'd sue the city's ass, and they'd probably win. So—no investigation, no press, case closed," Cates said. "Money buys anonymity, Zach, and a lot of money buys total silence."

"Only now some vigilante comes out of the woodwork and gets Parker-Steele to confess to murder," Kylie said.

"Yes, and Muriel Sykes is already firing off tweets that say it's a crock of crap. If you torture somebody long enough, they'll tell you Jimmy Hoffa is buried in their basement. She's screaming that Parker-Steele is not a killer, she's a victim. And this city needs a mayor who can lock criminals up, not have them run loose so they can pin murders on innocent citizens."

She turned and headed toward the carpeted staircase, talking as she went. We followed. "The mayor has been plunging in the polls, and with a serial killer on the loose and an opponent who's bashing him for being soft on crime, unless we catch this Hazmat Killer, his reelection campaign is going to plunge right into the toilet."

We were at the top of the stairs, and Kylie stopped. "Captain," she said, "can I be brutally honest with you?"

Cates turned around. "With me, yes, but not with the mayor. Speak."

"If you told us the Loch Ness monster was seen in the subway system, Zach and I would walk the tracks from the Bronx to Far Rockaway till we found it. I don't know how long it would take, but we'd get it done. Now we're chasing down a painstakingly smart serial killer who has eluded the cops for four months, and the mayor wants us to solve it in a week?"

"You got it, MacDonald," Cates said.

"We're cops. Our job is to nail this bastard before he kills someone else, not to save the mayor's sorry political ass."

Cates laughed. "You sound like me back in the day when I didn't have to worry about being politically correct. But the mayor asked for you two by name. You want the job?"

"Totally. And we're flattered that he sent for us," Kylie said. "But he might want to hedge his bet and send for a moving van."

CHAPTER 6

STANLEY SPELLMAN STARTED his law career with the Legal Aid Society in New York City forty years ago. His insightful logic, compassion for others, and personal charisma propelled him from his small office on Water Street to Congress and eventually to Gracie Mansion.

None of those sterling qualities were in evidence this morning. He was in a full-blown panic.

"It's about bleeping time!" he bellowed as we walked through the door. He wanted us to know he was mad, but he was old school and preferred *bleeping* over F-bombs when he was in mixed company.

The man sitting next to him stood up and crossed the room to greet us.

It was Irwin Diamond—Spellman's oldest friend and most trusted adviser. The mayor could go off the tracks—

especially in times of crisis. Diamond kept him grounded. His unofficial title at City Hall was deputy mayor in charge of damage control.

"Detective Jordan, Detective MacDonald," Diamond said, shaking our hands. "Under the circumstances I can't say I'm happy to see you again, but I'm reassured that we're putting our trust in the best law enforcement officers this city has at its disposal. Thank you for coming."

"Get on with it, Irwin," the mayor said, waving a hand at him.

"The mayor has been running the city and campaigning hard," Diamond said. "He's spread a little thin, so he's not his usual charming self."

"If it's any consolation, neither are we," Kylie said. "Crime scenes tend to bring you down."

"Understood. First order of business: Everything you hear within the confines of this room is confidential," Diamond said, speaking slowly and enunciating each word like a teacher laying down the ground rules on the first day of school. "It is not to be repeated to anyone or referred to in any written reports. Do you both accept and agree to that?"

Accept and agree? Were we kicking off a homicide investigation or downloading software? At least he didn't ask us to solemnly swear. Kylie and I quickly accepted and agreed.

"We made some mistakes," Diamond said. "The Hazmat Killer's first three victims were hardly a loss to the city. They were all criminals themselves. And while we abhor vigilantism, we may not have been aggressive enough in tracking him down."

"May not have been aggressive enough?" Spellman echoed. "It wound up being dumped on two gang cops from Chinatown."

Diamond ignored the comment. "The murder of Parker-Steele changes everything," he went on. "Hazmat is now our number one priority, and the case is assigned to NYPD Red. You two will head up the task force."

"What about the two detectives who are handling it now?" I said.

"They're under you. And we're streamlining the chain of command. You report directly to Captain Cates, and she'll have a straight line to Commissioner Harries's office."

"Irwin, the video," the mayor said, his agitation level up a notch. "They should watch the damn video."

"Excellent idea," Diamond responded as if his boss had made a major contribution. He turned to Cates. "Please put it up on the big monitor, Captain."

Cates queued up the video on a laptop, and we all took seats facing the flat-screen on the wall.

The mayor turned to me and Kylie. His shirt was stained with flop sweat. "I'm sorry," he said. "I didn't mean to yell at you when you came in."

"No apologies necessary, sir," Kylie said. "We're here now, and we'll do everything we—"

"This Parker-Steele," Spellman interrupted, raising his voice. "She admits to murdering an innocent young woman. You would think that would reflect negatively on Muriel Sykes, who picked her as a campaign manager. Am I right?"

"Stan," Diamond said, "they're cops, not politicians."

The mayor ignored him. "But no," he went on, his finger shaking as he pointed it at us. "Sykes says the confession was forced. She says that NYPD didn't take the first three murders seriously, so it's all my fault. She's saying if I were tougher on crime, Parker-Steele would still be alive. And *then* she does a one-eighty and goes after me for the Pritchard murder—claiming that I allowed Parker-Steele's family to strong-arm me into dropping the investigation."

"Stan, you've gone through this before," Diamond said, pouring a glass of water from a chrome pitcher on the desk. "It's politics. Get a grip. What did you think she would say? 'I'm an idiot for hiring a murderer to run my campaign'?" He crossed the room and handed the water to the mayor.

"This is different," Spellman said. "She's got Leonard Parker and Jason Steele behind her. They want me out of office, and they have the money to do it. Plus she's got Evelyn's blowhard brother, Damon Parker, and you can pretty much guess what he's going to say on TV."

"He'll probably say that his sister is an innocent victim," Diamond said, "and lay the blame squarely on you."

He offered the mayor two small pink oval pills. Xanax—the anxiety killer of choice for panic-riddled city fathers and stressed-out soccer moms.

"Parker-Steele isn't a victim," the mayor shouted, grabbing the pills from Diamond's hand. "She's a murderer. I'm the bleeping victim!"

He popped the pink footballs as if they were M&M's and washed them down.

Diamond looked at Kylie and me and shook his head, an unspoken apology for his candidate's unmayorlike behavior.

I now understood why he'd insisted we take that vow of silence.

What happens in Gracie stays in Gracie.

CHAPTER 7

THE VIDEO WAS queued up on LiveLeak.com, ready to be played. The bar at the bottom let me know it was four minutes and seventeen seconds long. I wondered how many times I would watch it before the case was closed.

Cates clicked Play, and the picture came up on the big screen.

Evelyn Parker-Steele was seated in a metal folding chair. Her white Tyvek suit was a stark contrast to the black background.

Her hair was bedraggled, she had on no makeup, and the harsh lighting made her look more like a member of the Manson family than a woman at the top of New York society's pecking order. "My name is Evelyn Parker-Steele, and two years ago I killed Cynthia Pritchard," she said, lisping the name through broken teeth. "Cynthia was my co-worker, my friend, and my lover. She was open about her sexuality. I was not."

Her eyes were empty, her voice a monotone. It reminded me of al-Qaeda hostage videos I'd seen, and I wondered if she was reading from a script.

"I grew up in a household that considered homosexuality as Satanic. They would never have accepted me as I am, so I pretended to be something else. When I married my husband, it was a marriage of convenience that suited both our needs."

"Translation: Jason Steele is gay," the mayor said. "As if you couldn't tell."

"Stanley!" Diamond yelled, pointing at me, Kylie, and Cates to remind the mayor that he was being very un-PC. Then he ran two fingers across his mouth—the universal sign for *zip your lips*.

"Sorry," the mayor grumbled, clearly not sorry.

"Most of my sexual encounters were discreet, even anonymous," Evelyn went on, "but when Cynthia joined the campaign team for Elliott Winchell, I fell in love with her, and we were together day and night. I was happy to continue on in secret, but Cynthia refused to live a lie.

"The night she died, we were on my terrace. She was drinking heavily and begged me to leave my husband. Same-sex marriage had been legalized in New York. Everyone was talking about it, and she wanted me to tell the world that we were in love. I told her I couldn't even tell my father, how could I tell the world? She said, 'If you won't, I will.' And then she walked to the edge of the terrace, stood up on a planter, and started screaming.

"We were fourteen stories over Park Avenue. It was dark. Probably nobody would hear her. Even if they did, I thought she'd just yell something like 'Evelyn Parker-Steele is gay' and that would be it, and we'd laugh about it in the morning. But that's not what she did.

"She screamed, 'Leonard Parker cordially invites you to the wedding of his gay daughter, Evelyn, to Cynthia Pritchard, a beautiful and talented young lesbian. Mr. Parker deeply regrets his narrow-minded, homophobic behavior that fucked up his daughter's life and—'"

There were several seconds of silence as Evelyn just stared into the camera. "And that's when I pushed her. It all happened in an instant. I didn't want to kill her. I just wanted to stop her.

"I panicked. I picked up the phone to dial 911, but I knew if I called just a few seconds after she hit the ground, they'd know I was right there with her. I had to be *not* with her if they were ever going to believe that she fell. I couldn't leave the apartment. People knew I was home. And then I had an idea. I went to the bar and grabbed a bottle of vodka. I took a big gulp, then another, and another. I was gagging with every swallow, but I just kept drinking.

"The cops found me passed out on the floor in a pool of vomit, drunk, incoherent. It wasn't an act. My blood alcohol level was three times the legal limit. They took me to the hospital. When I finally could focus, they told me Cynthia was dead, and I cried. I was so sick they couldn't interview me till the next day. By that time, my father had a wall of lawyers around me. I told the police that I had passed out early in the night, and the last thing I remember was Cynthia sitting on the terrace, drinking. The DA bought my story. It didn't hurt that my father plays golf with him and supports his reelection campaigns.

"I want to apologize to Cynthia's parents and her two brothers. I killed her because I didn't want the world to know how I felt about her. But now I do. She was the free-spirited young woman I always wished I could be, and I loved her more than I ever loved anyone in my life. I didn't mean to kill her, but I did. I'm sorry. I know what's going to happen to me next. No trial, no judge, no jury. By the time you see this—"

The counter on the video read 4:17, and the screen went dark.

Nobody said a word. Even the mayor was silent. The Xanax had kicked in.

CHAPTER 8

NICE TURNOUT, GIDEON thought as a steady stream of voyeurs blew off their Monday morning plans and made a beeline for the carousel.

That's the thing about New Yorkers. They have five hundred homicides a year to choose from. Shoot an old lady getting out of a taxi on Madison Avenue, and people will step over the body to grab the cab. But put a dead rich bitch in a Hazmat suit on a painted horse in the middle of Central Park, and they'll call in late to work and crane their necks to get a better view.

He smiled. *Give the people what they want, and they will flock to your door. You're welcome, people.*

A hand tapped him on the shoulder. "So are you pro-Hazmat or anti-Hazmat?" asked a female voice behind him.

Gideon froze. The park was lousy with reporters shoving cameras and microphones in front of the gawkers, hoping to catch sound bites for the next newsbreak. Returning to the scene was crazy enough, but doing an on-camera interview would be insane.

He turned around slowly. *Definitely not a reporter. Reporters don't usually wear black sports bras on the job.*

"I'm sorry," Gideon said. "Were you talking to me?"

"Only if you feel like talking," she said. "I'm Andie."

She was at least five years older than him, brown eyes, brown hair scrunched up and tucked through the back of an FDNY baseball cap. She was just shy of being pretty, but she knew her best asset, which was why she had nothing on over the sports bra this late in October.

He pointed at her hat. "You a firefighter, Andie?"

"It belonged to my *ex*," she said, rolling her eyes to let him know she was glad the creep was out of her life. "Me? I'm much better at starting fires than putting them out."

Gideon was six two, with thick dark hair, full lips, and a hint of a bad-boy smile. He was used to getting hit on. And Andie was a pro. She positioned herself in front of him so he couldn't talk to her without looking down at her world-class rack.

Damn it, honey, your timing sucks. As much as I would love to take your hot, sweaty body home and drill you senseless, this morning the only aphrodisiac I need is this crowd.

"Can you repeat the question?" Gideon asked.

"I asked how you felt about the Hazmat Killer. From the way you were smiling, I figured you for a big fan."

I was smiling? Dumb. Thanks for the heads-up, Andie.

"You think this guy has fans?" Gideon said.

"Thousands, and I'm at the top of the list. You might think a nice Jewish girl from Queens would be a bleeding heart liberal, but you'd be wrong."

"Doesn't it bother you that he's a vigilante?" Gideon said.

"No. What this city needs is a couple of hundred more just like him."

"Wow," Gideon said. "What happened to the nice Jewish girl?"

"Date raped in college. Rich kid. Daddy bought off the cops, the judge, and the school. That's when I changed my politics. Y'know, sometimes a staunch conservative is just another schmuck liberal who's been mugged."

She held up her cell phone. "Did you see the video— the one Hazmat posted?"

"Not yet," Gideon said.

"Get on it, man. It's got like fifty thousand hits already."

Eighty-nine thousand last time I looked.

"The victim's name is Eleanor something," Andie said. "She killed her girlfriend in cold blood, but she got away with it because she's rich and her family knew how to play the system. But Hazmat gave her exactly what she deserved. I only wish I could shake his hand."

Gideon was breathing hard. *Shake his hand? Hell—this girl wouldn't be satisfied with a handshake. Any other time, Andie. Any other place...*

"It's nice talking to you," Gideon said, "but I have to run."

Andie wet her lips and lowered them into a pout. "Too

bad you're not running my way," she said. "What's your name, anyway?"

"Brian," Gideon said.

She held out her hand. "Nice to meet you, Brian."

He took her hand and shook it.

There you go, Andie. You got your wish.

CHAPTER 9

CATES'S CELL RANG. She checked the caller ID. "Matt Smith," she said to us, and took the call.

"This is Captain Cates. What did you come up with, Matt?"

She listened for twenty seconds, her expression never changing. She thanked Matt and hung up.

"It was our IT officer—our computer guy," she said, simplifying it for the mayor. "He tried to trace the source of the video, but it was uploaded using VPN—that's a virtual private network, sir. It masks the location of the originating IP address."

The mayor threw up his hands. "Of course it's masked. But we've got millions of dollars' worth of equipment and all these computer geniuses running around. Are you telling me none of our people can unmask it?"

"Sir," Cates said, "all of the uploaded data is encrypted. Whoever posted these videos creates a different user name and a different throwaway email address every time. So yes, we have a lot of equipment and a lot of smart people, but the killer knows how to hide his tracks. Hacking and tracing isn't an option."

"Fine," the mayor said. "So you can't find this guy with all that technical mumbo-jumbo. Catch him the old-fashioned way. Legwork." He stood up. "Irwin, do you need me anymore?"

"No, and I know you have a busy day ahead of you," Diamond said. "Give me a few more minutes, and I'll catch up."

The mayor went through the motions of thanking us and left the room.

"Detectives," Diamond said, "I don't have to tell you that this could be a deathblow to the mayor's reelection campaign."

"Sir, I don't know much about politics," I said, "but Parker-Steele's video is filled with damning details. I believe she killed Cynthia Pritchard."

"Of course she did," Diamond said.

"Then why doesn't this hurt Muriel Sykes? First she says it's a bogus confession. Then she flips it and says if Parker-Steele *is* a murderer, it's the mayor's fault that she got off. She's talking out of both sides of her mouth."

"You're right, Detective," Diamond said. "You don't know much about politics. Rule number one: Whoever speaks out of both sides of their mouth the best wins the election."

"With all due respect, Mr. Diamond," Cates said, "unfortunately, I do know a little about politics, and as long as we're sworn to secrecy, can we put it all on the table? Information is currency, and the more Detectives Jordan and MacDonald know, the better their chances of solving this."

Diamond weighed the question in his head. "All right, Captain," he finally said. He turned to Kylie and me. "Muriel Sykes makes one undisputable point. It *was* the mayor's fault that Evelyn Parker-Steele went scot-free. Commissioner Harries wanted a thorough investigation, but Evelyn's family convinced the mayor to stand behind the coroner's ruling that it was an accident. He agreed, and the case went away."

"*Convinced?*" I said.

"You don't need to know the details," Diamond said. "What's important is that right now the mayor is in a deep hole. And the worst part about it is that he dug it himself."

CHAPTER 10

YOU CAN NEVER go wrong buddying up to the precinct desk sergeant. One call to Bob McGrath at the One Nine and there was a brand-new Ford Interceptor waiting for us outside the mansion. Keys in the ignition, no numbnuts driver.

I got behind the wheel and turned left onto East End Avenue.

"You think we can nail this guy in a week?" Kylie asked.

"Maybe," I said. "If we work together as a team."

Her head snapped around. "What is that supposed to mean? Are you still ragging on me because I didn't show up the minute you wanted me? Look, I'm sorry I made us late, but give me a break, Zach, we're still partners."

"Did you just say you're sorry you made us late?"

"You heard me. I am sorry, and I appreciate that you covered for me."

I made a right turn onto 86th Street and pulled the car into a bus stop. I turned in my seat so I could look Kylie in the eyes.

"I don't know if you're lying to me," I said, "or just holding back a big chunk of the truth, but you saying you're sorry is the same as some guy bringing flowers home to his wife after he spent the afternoon banging his secretary. 'Sorry I'm late, honey. All kinds of crazy shit happening at the office.' Look, Kylie, I'm a detective, and I know half a story when I hear one. You've been late or off the grid three times in the last month, so either tell me what's going on, or tell me that the person I trust my life to doesn't trust me enough to tell me what the hell is going on in hers."

To her credit, she didn't waffle. "It's Spence," she said. "He really did fall in the shower this morning. He was high on pills."

She paused to let it sink in. I didn't change my expression or say a word.

"It's been three months since...since the incident with The Chameleon," she said. "The surgeon wrote him a scrip for one Percocet every six hours, but he's popping them like Tic Tacs. Oh, he's cagey—the bottle on his dresser goes down a few pills a day as prescribed. But he's stockpiled them, and has them stashed all over the apartment. Last night, I found fifty of them wrapped in tinfoil inside a sock in his gym bag."

"Where does he get them?" I asked.

"Dr. Feelgood or any one of those quacks on the Internet who writes scrips from Bolivia," she said. "Anyway, after they stitched him up at the ER this morning, I confronted him with it. I told him if he weren't my husband, I'd bust him."

"What did he say?"

"He just stood there with his glassy eyes, his puffy face, and his gym bag full of oxy, and he told me I was wrong. He said he may have upped his dosage a little, but he has it under control, and as soon as his feet get a little bit better, he'll switch over to Advil. He's in total denial, and at this point I just don't know what to do."

"There's nothing you can do," I said. "He's a recovering drug addict. He's been clean for a long time—"

"Eleven years," Kylie interjected.

"So he knows what to do," I said. "Go to meetings, call his sponsor, even check into rehab if it's that bad. But he's the one that has to do it. You can't pull him out of the gutter."

She took in a long, deep breath and let it out slowly. "Zach," she said, "I'm a cop, and right now I'm afraid that if anyone finds out I'm married to a drug addict, he'll pull me down into the gutter with him."

"Nobody is going to find out," I said. "Your secret is safe with me."

"Thanks," she said, her eyes welling up. "Partner."

I put the car in gear and headed west on 86th.

I fell in love with Kylie the first time I met her at the academy. She had recently dumped her drug addict boyfriend, and I was happy to be the guy who caught her on the rebound. But Spence wanted her just as much as I did. He went to rehab, came back clean twenty-eight days later, and begged her for one more chance.

She said "yes," and a year later she said "I do."

For the past ten years, I've resigned myself to the fact that Kylie and Spence are rich, happy, and in love—the beautiful couple that everybody who is anybody in New York is thrilled to have over for dinner at their penthouse in the city, their home in the Hamptons, or their yacht.

I probably never fell out of love with her, but at least I moved on, and after bouncing around the New York singles market with one short-term relationship after another, I finally found Cheryl.

Cheryl Robinson was the first woman I ever dated that met the impossible standards I set for myself after I lost Kylie. We'd known each other for a few years, but it began to get serious only three months ago, and I was starting to hope that Cheryl could be the one. And now, suddenly, it was looking like Kylie's relationship with Spence was starting to unravel.

If she were any other partner, I'd be rooting for her to get back together with her husband and get her life back on track.

But Kylie MacDonald wasn't just any other partner. And right now, I had no idea how I felt.

CHAPTER 11

SOMEWHERE BETWEEN 86TH Street and the crime scene, I focused on the fact that, as crazy as I was, there was a guy out there with an unlimited supply of Hazmat suits who was even crazier.

"Screw the election," Kylie blurted out, and I knew that her head had gone to the same place mine had. "Irwin Diamond got it right. We're not politicians. We're cops, and our job is to catch Hazmat before he kidnaps and kills another innocent—correction—not-so-innocent victim. Where do we start?"

"Dryden gave me the names of the two detectives working the case—Donovan and Boyle out of the Five—but I'd rather hold off on calling them. I never got a chance to tell you, but there were two guys from Anti-Crime working the park. They called in the one eighty-seven. I recruited them and told them to do some legwork for us. Let's check in with them first."

"Legwork," Kylie said. "So much more efficient than those newfangled computer machines."

"Hey, give the poor mayor a break. Police work is not his strong suit."

"Then he should never have blocked the department from investigating Cynthia Pritchard's death. If he loses the election, he'll be getting what he deserves," Kylie said. "And as long as I'm sharing all my deepest, darkest secrets with you, there's one I've been holding back."

"What's that?"

"Whether we solve this case by next Tuesday or not, I'm still voting for Sykes."

The area surrounding the carousel looked like ground zero for a flash mob. "Is this our crime scene," Kylie said, "or a Bon Jovi concert?"

As soon as I got out of the car, someone yelled, "Detective Jordan!"

It was Casey and Bell, working their way through the crowd. They had cleaned up from their homeless routine, but they looked frazzled.

"Boy, are we glad you're back," Casey said.

"Sorry to cut and run," I said. "You guys in over your head?"

Bell grinned. "Maybe a little."

"Maybe a lot," Casey said. "This is light-years bigger than anything we've ever worked, but we got some good stuff for you, and one thing you're going to hate."

"First, meet my partner," I said. "Detective MacDonald, these are the two guys I shanghaied, Detectives Casey and Bell."

Head nods all around.

"Okay," I said, "what've you got?"

"We found one of those folding shopping carts in the trees alongside the Sixty-Fifth Street transverse," Casey said. "Those things are valuable commodities around here, so it couldn't have been there for long, or somebody would have scooped it up. You said Parker-Steele disappeared on Friday, so he didn't kill her in the park. He killed her someplace else and dumped her here."

Dryden had already told us that, but I let them go on.

Bell picked up the narrative. "Our best guess is that after he killed Parker-Steele, he stuffed her in a bag, drove her to this neighborhood, and parked his car somewhere nearby."

"Can you guys check with Traffic for any parking tickets that were issued within a ten-block radius of key entry points?" Kylie said. "East and west sides."

"Will do, but I wouldn't get my hopes up," Bell said. "Parking is a bitch during the day, but after ten p.m., there are lots of legal spaces he could have used."

"So he parked his car nearby," I said. "Then what do you figure?"

"He loaded the body into the shopping cart and walked through the park as invisible as any of the homeless guys who roam the city streets," Casey said. "That's the way me and Bell have been blending in. Then he cut the lock on the gate, strapped her on the horse, hot-wired the electric panel to get the music and the carousel going, re-locked the gate, dumped the shopping cart, hopped over the stone wall, and walked along the transverse back to his car."

The two of them stood there looking at us like puppy dogs who had just fetched a stick and were waiting for a pat on the head.

"Good job," I said. "You see anybody that looked suspicious in the crowd?"

They turned to each other and laughed.

"Everybody in that crowd looks suspicious," Bell said. "A dead woman in a Hazmat suit on a carousel is like a magnet for wackos. For the killer to stand out, he'd have to be wearing a sign that says 'I did it.'"

"Hey!...Hey! You!"

I turned around. Two men scooted under the crime scene tape and headed straight for Kylie and me.

"What the hell kind of crap are you guys trying to pull?" one of them yelled.

"Hang on to your hat, Detective Jordan," Casey said.

"You know these guys?" I asked.

"We just met them ten minutes ago. Remember I said there's one thing you're going to hate? Here it comes."

CHAPTER 12

"THEIR NAMES ARE Donovan and Boyle," Casey said. "They're acting like jerks, going around telling everybody that they're—"

"I *know* what they're telling everybody," I said. "Thanks. I'll handle it."

Kylie grabbed my arm. "Zach, I'm in a foul mood. Let me take it out on somebody besides you."

"Be my guest," I said, and stepped aside.

Donovan and Boyle stormed across the lawn and stopped in front of us. Before they could say a word, Kylie went on the attack.

"What the hell do you two clowns think you're doing?" she said. "Back off. This is a crime scene."

One of them was tall, over six feet, with dark hair and a pretty-boy face. The other was shorter, with thin lips and a buzz cut—not nearly as pretty. I still didn't know who was who.

"*Our* crime scene," Buzz Cut said. "I'm Boyle, that's Donovan. We've been running the Hazmat case."

"From what I hear, you've been running it into the ground. Effective an hour ago, it's ours."

"Says who?"

"My boss, Captain Delia Cates, her boss, Police Commissioner Richard Harries, and his boss, the mayor."

"This is bullshit," Boyle said. "Why the hell were we pulled off?"

"You weren't *pulled off*," Kylie said. "The case was reassigned to NYPD Red. I'm MacDonald, that's Jordan, and you've been assigned to our task force."

"We work for *you?*" Donovan asked.

"You have a problem with that, Detective Donovan?" Kylie said.

"You're damn right I do."

"In that case, send everything you've got on the Hazmat Killer to our office. We'll take it from there."

"The hell you will. Nobody at Red gave a rat's ass about the first three victims, but now that Muriel Sykes is involved, the mayor jumps in and moves the case to the top of the dog pile. What's your job? Get as much dirt on Parker-Steele as possible so he can sandbag Sykes's campaign?"

"This isn't about politics," Kylie said. "It's about finding a serial killer."

"What the hell do you think we've been doing for the past four months?"

"Funny, that's what the mayor said. 'What the hell have those two cops been doing for the past four months?' If you don't like his decision, file a grievance with the department."

Donovan looked at his partner. Clearly they didn't want to be second string, but they had zero leverage, and Kylie knew it. Then he looked at me as though maybe I could talk some sense into Kylie. I didn't blink.

"Make up your mind, boys," she said. "You on board?"

"Hey, if they don't want it," Casey said, "me and Bell would be happy to—"

"Back off," Donovan said. "It's been our case since day one, and we're not being squeezed out because of some political bullshit. We're staying."

"You can start by getting the files over to us at the One Nine in twenty minutes," Kylie said, handing him her card. "I'll be sure to tell the mayor how cooperative you've been."

My two puppies looked as if someone had just taken their favorite squeeze toy. "Does that mean you won't be needing us?" Bell said.

"You guys were a big help, and we appreciate it," I said.

"But these guys are in, and we're out," Bell said.

I nodded. Kylie, who always likes to get in the last word, offered up two.

"For now."

CHAPTER 13

"**DID YOU GET** all the nasty out of your system?" I asked Kylie after the two teams went their separate ways.

"I always have a reserve tank," she said.

"It sucks to have to trade off two gung ho cops for two with brooms up their asses," I said.

"Zach, we could have kept all four of them," Kylie said. "A case like this, we have a blank check. Hell, we could pull together a task force of fifty people and spend all our time bogged down in our own bureaucracy. The only thing this case really needs is you and me doing what we do best. I asked Donovan and Boyle to stick around because they have a serious learning curve. But as soon as we get up to speed, I will tap back into my tank of nasty and tell them to go play in traffic."

We spent another hour at the crime scene. Chuck Dryden's people were still combing the area, and except for the shopping cart, nothing new turned up. We drove back to the office.

There's no Red precinct. Like a lot of elite units, we're housed in an existing precinct—in our case, the 19th on East 67th Street between Third and Lexington Avenues. The One Nine is home to more than two hundred uniforms and dozens of detectives, but it's still big enough for Red to set up shop on the third floor, away from the day-to-day madness that goes on downstairs.

But we still have to walk through the tumult on our way upstairs. And you can't get anywhere without being seen by Bob McGrath, the desk sergeant.

"Thanks for the wheels, Sarge," Kylie said.

"Anytime, Detective," McGrath said. "Hang on a sec. I've got something else for you."

He reached under his desk and pulled out a cardboard file box. "This was just delivered. It's your Hazmat files."

I picked it up. It weighed next to nothing.

"Is that all?" I said. "Just the one?"

"That's what they gave me. That's what I signed for," he said. "Want to see the paperwork?"

"No, Sarge, it's just that we expected more."

"Sorry to disappoint you. Some cases we get ten, twenty boxes, and the detectives start moaning that they'll never get through it all. This load's a lot lighter. I thought you'd be happy."

"You know how it is with detectives," I said. "We're never happy."

I carried the box to our office, and Kylie opened it.

"This is four months' worth of investigation?" she said. "There are only four folders. Alex Kang, Sebastian Catt, Antoine Tinsdale, and Donald Li."

"I recognize the first three names. They're victims," I said. "Who's Li?"

Kylie flipped through his file. "He has a master's in social work. He's a detective working gangs in Chinatown. Donovan and Boyle asked him to come up with a profile of the killer."

"Is he a shrink?" I asked.

She took another look. "It doesn't say 'Dr.' Li, so I doubt it."

I pulled the Li file from the box.

"I know a real doctor," I said, "and she's a damn good profiler. I think I'll drop by Cheryl's office and ask her to take a look at this guy's notes. I'll be back in a few."

"I thought she was in Boston," Kylie said as I headed for the door.

"Just for the weekend. She flew back on the early morning shuttle."

"So then you haven't seen her since when—Friday?"

"Thursday afternoon."

"In that case, I doubt if you'll be back *in a few*. But don't take too long. Election Day is a week from tomorrow."

CHAPTER 14

GOD BLESS FRED ROBINSON.

For eleven years he was married to a beautiful, intelligent, self-assured woman. Then he dumped her for someone younger, dumber, and needier.

His loss, my gain.

I met Cheryl four years ago, when I was hoping to get into Red. She was the shrink assigned to probe my brain to make sure I was a good fit.

I was nervous as hell, and she knew it.

She smiled. "Don't worry, Detective Jordan. I won't bite."

And I wouldn't mind if you did, Dr. Moist Red Lips, Inviting Brown Eyes, and Smooth Caramel Skin Framed by Tumbling Waves of Thick Jet-Black Hair. I was only twenty-nine, but I was ready to cross sleeping with a hot Latina psychologist off my bucket list.

A few years later, Cheryl told me she was 90 percent Irish, but thanks to her Puerto Rican grandmother, she looks about as Irish as J.Lo. But back then she was still sporting her wedding ring, and I figured hitting on a married woman during a job interview would be a bad career move.

We chatted about my background, both personal and professional, and then she popped a loaded question: "Do you think rich, powerful people deserve a better class of service from the police?"

"Absolutely not," I said, which sounds like the exact wrong answer to give when you're trying to get into the superelite squad created to serve the rich and famous.

She didn't react. All she said was, "Can you elaborate?"

"The rich don't *deserve* any better police protection than the homeless. What they do deserve, *especially when they're the victims of a crime*, is a cop who is sensitive to their needs, not one who resents them because they're rich or spoiled or egomaniacal."

"You come from a working-class background, Detective Jordan. What makes you confident you know how to deal with someone like Donald Trump?"

"My mother was a makeup artist—movies, TV, fashion shoots. She dealt with them all—the divas, the prima donnas, the rock stars, each one more entitled than the last. She taught me how to handle them."

"How?"

"'Don't try to change them,' she used to say. 'Remember that deep down inside they're as insecure as the rest of us. And the room is never big enough for two narcissists, so check your own ego at the door.'"

"You had a smart mom," Cheryl said. "It sounds like she got along with everybody."

"Almost everybody, except for this one guy she argued with constantly."

Everyone loves show business gossip, and I knew I had her. "You don't have to tell me his name," she said, "but I'm dying of curiosity. Who was it?"

"My father."

I got the job.

Cheryl and I became friends early on, and then, when her marriage started to head south, I became the only friend she wanted to confide in. Two weeks after her divorce, we became friends with benefits. And the benefits have been fantastic.

The door to Cheryl's office was open, and I walked in. As soon as she saw me, she bounded from behind her desk, wrapped her arms around me, and kissed me hard. "God, I'm happy to see you," she said, pressing her body against mine.

And just like that, I went limp in some places, not so limp in others.

Cheryl and I had been together only a few months, and I wasn't ready for this passionate a reunion. But my body kicked into autopilot, and my hips started doing small circular motions against hers.

"Exactly how happy are you to see me?" I said, kicking the door shut and maneuvering her toward the inviting baby-blue sofa that came in handy whenever she had to work around the clock.

"You're crazy," she said, pushing back but not pulling away.

"Crazy? Lousy diagnosis, Doc. Try horny." I started unbuttoning her blouse.

I thought she'd stop me, but she began kissing, groping. "Lock the door," she whispered.

I let her go, turned, and reached for the lock. And then someone on the other side kicked the door. Not knocked. Kicked. Hard.

"Just a minute!" I yelled, and waited for Cheryl to scramble back to her desk and button up.

I opened the door. It was Matt Smith.

"Zach, how are you, mate?" he said. "I didn't know you'd be here, or I'd have brought you a coffee."

A true New Yorker would have said *kaw-fee*, but Matt is a British import, so it came out *kah-fee*.

He had a Starbucks cup in each hand, which was why he'd kicked at the door instead of just opening it and walking in.

"I thought you could use a bit of a bracer," Matt said, setting one on Cheryl's desk. "Soy latte with an extra shot of espresso—right?"

Her eyes lit up. "Thank you, Matt. You didn't have to do that."

"My pleasure. And thank *you* for that book. I read it over the weekend. Quite the eye-opener. I have a few questions, but they can wait. You two look busy. Zach, I heard you're on the Hazmat case. I ran a trace on the latest video he posted and came up empty, but I hope you'll still be needing a tech-head."

Matt is an übergeek who could probably hack the Pentagon if we asked him. He's smart, analytical, and fun to work with. Hands down, he's our best IT guy. There's only one small problem. He doesn't look like a nerd. In fact, he looks more like David Beckham than Bill Gates, and right now that was annoying the hell out of me.

"Oh, I'll definitely be calling you," I said.

"Super," he said, and broke into a wide, perfect smile that totally contradicted everything I'd ever heard about shoddy British dental practices.

He left the room and started to close the door behind him.

"Leave it open," Cheryl said. "Zach and I could use a little air in here."

"I guess this means we're not going to pick up where we left off?" I said as soon as Smith was out of earshot.

"I don't know what happened," she said, "but now that I've had a minute to think, I remembered that this is a police station."

"So? It's not like we were going to commit a crime."

"Get a grip, cowboy," she said. "We'll finish this after hours, and I promise you it will be worth the wait."

I had no doubt that it would.

Like I said, God bless Fred Robinson.

CHAPTER 15

THE FURNITURE IN Cheryl's office was too well designed and too comfortable to be department issue. She had decorated at her own expense, picking fabrics and colors that struck a nice balance between her professional and feminine sides. Her degrees were on the wall, but there were no personal photos. She was, after all, a shrink.

"Have a seat, Detective," she said, sitting down behind the glass-topped table that was her desk.

I sat across from her in a guest chair that was covered in peach fabric.

"So, you and Kylie picked up the Hazmat case," she said, all business.

"His latest victim is Evelyn Parker-Steele," I said.

"I know. I saw the video. That poor woman. How can I help?"

"The case files on the first three victims are pretty slim. Kylie and I still have to go through them. But there was a fourth file—a profile of the killer. I wanted you to take a look at it."

I put the file on her desk.

She looked at it, but instead of picking it up, she slipped the lid off the latte and took a small sip. "Who's the profiler who pulled this together?"

"His name is Donald Li."

"I don't know him," she said.

"I doubt if he's in your league. He's a detective with the Chinatown precinct. He has a master's in social work."

She slid the file back to my side of the desk. "I'm happy to help, but I'm not going to look at this. Just let me see what you've got on the victims, and I'll give you a fresh take."

"That's what I planned to do," I said. "Maybe I came over a little too soon, but I just wanted to get you in the loop."

"I think you just wanted to get me on that sofa," she said, and took another sip.

"Yeah, that too," I said. "I haven't seen you in four days, and I needed an excuse to stop by your office. This file was a lame idea. I'd have been better off bringing you coffee. Soy latte with an extra shot of espresso—I didn't know that was your drug of choice."

"That's because when I see you at night, I prefer Chardonnay, but the department frowns on that during the day."

"And Matt Smith knows what you drink?" I said.

"Yes. He's in the office next door."

"So he does coffee runs for you?"

"No. He brought it as a thank-you. I gave him a book on birth order."

"Why?"

"He has two brothers. One older, one younger—"

"Ah, the old middle child syndrome," I said. "Poor Matt didn't get enough attention from his parents, so now he's looking for love in all the wrong places."

"For God's sake, he bought me a coffee. It's a nice gesture. He's a nice guy."

"Yeah, a nice, good-looking *single* guy. Are you going to tell me that was strictly a thank-you-for-the-book gesture? He wasn't hitting on you?"

"Maybe he was. I'm recently single, and nobody but Captain Cates and Kylie know that you and I are dating. As far as Matt is concerned, I'm fair game. So maybe he was flirting with me. I wasn't flirting back."

"Of course not. I was standing right there."

"Zach, as a woman, I'm flattered at the absolutely insane conclusions you are jumping to, but as a shrink, all I can say is get a grip."

The latte had cooled down, and she sat there staring at me and sipping from the cup.

"Taste good, does it, luv?" I said, putting on my best English accent.

"Quite," she said, trying not to smile.

"Did we just have our first fight?"

She thought about it. "Not a biggie, but yes, we did."

"Good," I said. "Then I have something to look forward to."

"You're looking forward to a bigger fight?" she said.

"No," I said, picking up my file and heading toward the door. "Makeup sex."

I didn't look back, but I could hear the laughter.

CHAPTER 16

"WE'RE IN DEEP doo-doo," Kylie said when I got back to my desk.

"Deeper than when I left ten minutes ago?" I said.

She held up one of the Hazmat files we'd just inherited. "Do you remember whose brilliant idea it was to keep Donovan and Boyle involved in this case?"

"I believe you were dazzled by their scintillating personalities and their—and I quote—'serious learning curve.'"

"I was dead wrong on both counts." She dropped the file on the desk. "There's nothing in here."

"Define nothing."

"Most of it is backgrounder stuff. Bios, ME reports, and rap sheets on the victims. We could get more by reading Pete Hamill's column in the *Daily News*. Three murders,

Zach. These guys investigated three murders and came away with zero leads."

"Then I guess we're in luck," I said. "We've got a fourth murder, and they haven't screwed it up yet. Put those aside, and we'll start with Evelyn Parker-Steele. That's the one where *we* have the learning curve."

"Are you in La-La Land?" she said. "We've got squat. Everything we know we got from a fast-talking politician. And that was *before* Parker-Steele changed her status from MIA to DOA, and *before* she outed herself and confessed to murdering her gay lover. As far as I'm concerned, we're at square one."

"You're right," I said. "So let's start by going through Parker-Steele's emails, phone records, credit card transactions—whatever we can dig up—and see if she knew any of the other three victims."

"Based on their backgrounds, she probably didn't know them," Kylie said, "but let's see if they're connected in any way. Maybe they have a common enemy. Also, let's talk to the family and see what they can give us."

"Good idea," I said. "Because zillionaires are always quick to divulge all their dirty little family secrets to help the authorities bring the truth to the surface. Now who's in La-La Land?"

"Now *you're* right," she said. "Let's call Muriel Sykes. Even if she doesn't know anything, we can at least get our hands on Evelyn's computer."

Sykes had given us her personal cell number on Saturday when she'd called in to report Evelyn missing. Kylie dialed.

"Mrs. Sykes, this is Detective MacDonald. I'm—"

Sykes cut her off. It was at least twenty seconds before Kylie got a word in. "Ma'am, I called you as soon as I could find a minute. We were at the crime scene and—"

Pause. Then: "What do you mean, 'what crime scene'? We were in Central Park with Ev—"

Another interruption. Kylie's expression went from exasperated to confused. "No. Nobody told us. When did you report it?…That's the Seventeenth Precinct. What was taken?"

Kylie turned to me and mouthed a string of silent curses.

"Please don't leave," she said. "We'll be there in—"

A few seconds of silence, and then she exploded. "Then where are you now, Mrs. Sykes?" she demanded. *"Where?"*

She signaled me to get moving, and I followed her toward the door.

"Please don't touch anything," she said into the phone. "And don't let anyone else in. We'll be there in five minutes."

She hung up and flew down the stairs, yelling, "Shit, shit, shit, shit, *shit!* We are a couple of *idiots!*"

CHAPTER 17

THE FORD INTERCEPTOR was in front of the precinct, and Kylie got behind the wheel. I barely had the door closed when she peeled out and sped west on East 67th. She flipped on the lights and sirens and ran the red on Lexington. Then she hung a hard right on Park and blasted her way uptown.

"Are we on a Code Three?" I shouted over the howl of the siren.

Code 3 is for life-threatening emergencies only. We're not supposed to totally disregard traffic laws, but we can muscle cars out of our way. Code 2 is for high-priority non-emergencies. *Must follow traffic laws.*

"Code Two and a Half. I'll try not to kill anyone," she said.

"Then slow down."

She didn't hit the brakes, but she eased up on the accelerator.

"Now, where are we going, and why are we idiots?" I asked.

"What was Mayor Spellman's biggest—no, make that his only—concern?"

"Arrest the Hazmat Killer before next Tuesday, or he'll be former mayor Spellman."

"Exactly," she said. "If we do it on Spellman's watch, he'll hog the glory and tell the world that the tough-on-crime candidate is already in office. If we haven't cracked it by the time the voters go to the polls, Sykes will blast the mayor for being weak and impotent. So what do you think she wants us to do?"

"Shit," I said. "*Not* catch him."

"Bingo. It's in her best interests to slow us down, and she may have figured out how to do it. There was a break-in at campaign headquarters early this morning, and guess what? Evelyn's computer was stolen."

"You're right," I said. "We *are* idiots. We were so busy being cops that we never looked at the big picture. Politics."

Kylie swerved around a cabbie who was either too slow or too arrogant to get out of the way. We barreled across 86th in our race uptown.

"Wait," I said. "Campaign headquarters are on Fifty-Fifth. Where are we going?"

"Ninety-Fourth and Park. Evelyn Parker-Steele's apartment. The same place where she murdered Cynthia Pritchard two years ago."

"What's there?"

"Muriel Sykes. And I'll bet a year's salary on what's not there," she said. "Evelyn's personal computer."

"Son of a bitch," I said, pounding the dash with the flat of my fist. "Screw Code Two. Floor it."

CHAPTER 18

AS PARK AVENUE buildings go, Evelyn's was rather modest. It wasn't one of those grand old dames built at the turn of the last century. It was a 1960s-era redbrick building, and Evelyn probably bought her two-bedroom co-op for a couple of mil, which in this zip code is practically Walmart pricing.

Of course, Evelyn and her husband, Jason Steele, owned an eighty-million-dollar horse farm in Pound Ridge. So for her, 1199 Park was just a simple crash pad, tastefully appointed with a few million bucks' worth of modern art and antique furniture.

We didn't have to wave our badges at the doorman. The flashing lights on our double-parked Ford was all he needed.

"You're here about Mrs. Parker-Steele," he said, holding the door for us.

"That's right," Kylie said. "Mrs. Sykes is upstairs. She's expecting us."

"Fourteen A. The elevator's over there," he said. "Shame about what happened. She was a good tenant. Never any problems."

Except for that one time she tossed her girlfriend off the terrace. It's amazing how much you can block out about someone's past when you've seen them being tortured on the Internet.

The door to the apartment opened before we could ring the bell. Muriel Sykes let us in. She had played NCAA lacrosse at Penn State. Thirty years and four kids later, she still had an imposing athletic physique. Her casually styled chestnut-brown hair and her slate-gray skirt/jacket ensemble were age and image appropriate for a woman who wanted to appeal to voters across a broad economic spectrum.

"Thank you so much for coming," Sykes said as if we had accepted her gracious invitation and not as though we'd bolted out of the precinct when we realized she was trying to undermine our investigation.

Evelyn's apartment was blandly tasteful and remarkably inoffensive. The walls, the furniture, and even the art were all varying shades of beige. The one thing that popped out was the sour-faced octogenarian in the black suit and red turtleneck sitting on a minimalist ecru sofa, a silver TV remote in one hand, a bright green can of Canada Dry ginger ale in the other.

"This is Evelyn's father, Leonard Parker," Sykes said, introducing us.

We did the usual sorry-for-your-loss routine. He thanked us but seemed more interested in the stock ticker crawling along the bottom of the TV screen.

"She's not gay," he said, looking up from the TV. "They tortured her into saying that. Evelyn and Jason were happy as a couple of newlyweds."

He made no attempt to deny the fact that his daughter was a murderer—as long as we didn't walk away thinking she was a homicidal lesbian. What a dad.

"You find this Hazmat bastard for me," he said, forgetting that Kylie and I worked for the city and not him. "We'll get the truth out of him. I have people."

Sykes jumped in before he could spell out his revenge plot. "Leonard," she said, "this is all very stressful. I desperately need a cigarette."

He looked at her as though she'd said she was about to pee on the carpet. "Not in here," he said. "I have to sell this place. Buyers will smell that shit from the lobby. Take it outside."

Sykes walked us over to a sliding glass door and opened it.

This was the famous terrace where Cynthia Pritchard had spent her final moments. Because it had belonged to a wealthy woman, I had always pictured it as a spacious yard in the sky filled with expensive Frontgate patio furniture and lush vegetation. This wasn't that.

This was a balcony. Just another one of those small shelves you see hanging off high-rise buildings where storage-starved city dwellers cram their bikes, rusted-out hibachi grills, and other crap they don't want inside.

There was no place to sit, and we stood there waiting for

Sykes to light up a Capri, one of those ultralong, ultraslim cigarettes preferred by women who want to look sophisticated while they inhale nicotine-infused carcinogens.

"No photos, please," she said after taking a drag. "It's bad for my image."

"Tell us about the break-in," Kylie said.

"All they took was a couple of computers," Sykes said. "I'm sure it was Spellman's people. You know politics. You'd think people would have learned something from Watergate, but desperate times call for desperate measures. I guess the mayor will do anything to save his ass."

"Did you report the theft?" Kylie said.

"Someone from my staff called it in."

"Then why are you here instead of at campaign headquarters?" Kylie asked.

"Leonard is a dear friend. He's trying to cope with his grief, and he asked if we could spend some time here alone. He's a crusty old codger, but Evelyn was his only daughter, and he adored her. I think he wanted to have a quiet moment to commune with her."

All politicians are full of shit. Muriel was fuller than most. From what I could see, her dear friend Leonard was more concerned about her cigarette smoke lowering property values.

"Did you take anything from the apartment?" I asked.

"Detective," she said, "that borders on insulting. You *do know* I was a former U.S. attorney? Taking anything from this apartment could be considered a criminal act—at the very least, it might be considered obstruction of justice. The answer is an unequivocal no."

"I apologize," I said. "Typical cop question."

"Except you're not a typical cop—neither of you are. You people at Red are trained to deal with high-profile situations like this one. You were front-page heroes a few months ago. I expect you to think twice before you ask me any more stupid questions."

The best defense is a strong offense, and Muriel Sykes had just pummeled us.

"Now where are you on Evelyn's murder?" she said.

"We wanted to go through her computer," I said. "Does she have a laptop here?"

"I have no idea. If she does, I can assure you that neither Leonard nor I touched it."

And if there were any lesbian porn lying around, I'm sure you and Leonard didn't get rid of that either.

"Do we need a search warrant, or can we look around?" I asked.

"Of course. I'm here to help," she said, turning on the warm, grandmotherly smile that graced all her campaign posters. But from the neck down, her six-foot body was steeled for battle. As one columnist put it, "Sykes is a political enigma. You're never sure if she plans to beat the daylights out of you or bake you cookies."

"Can you think of anything that might have connected Evelyn to the three previous victims?" I asked.

"No, nothing," Sykes said. "The killer didn't know her either. He killed those three scumbags, but the mayor didn't give him what he wanted. Attention. So he targeted someone in power, beat a false confession out of her, and now he's an international media sensation. If I were mayor, he'd have been locked up before he ever laid a hand on Evelyn."

She stubbed out her cigarette and popped an Altoids. "Now let me get back to Leonard," she said, yanking the handle on the glass door. "You're free to look around all you want."

Kylie and I expected to find nothing, but we went from room to room, going through the motions.

"This is interesting," I said when we got to Evelyn's work space. "No computer, no modem."

"Maybe she was Amish," Kylie said. "Good thing we know Sykes was a former U.S. attorney, otherwise I might suspect her of tampering with evidence."

We went back to the living room, where Leonard was pacing and yelling into his cell phone. "Hold on, Vernon," he said when he saw us. "I'll ask the cops."

"Hey, lady detective—is this a crime scene?" he asked, twirling a bony finger around the room. "The apartment? Is it a crime scene?"

"Technically," Kylie said, "there's no current evidence—"

"Just yes or no. Crime scene? Not a crime scene?"

Nobody, no matter how old or how rich, steamrolls Kylie MacDonald. "Mr. Parker," she said slowly, deliberately, "to answer your question, the New York City Police Department does not currently consider your late daughter's apartment as a crime scene."

"We're good to go, Vern," Parker said into the phone. "List it at one point nine five and see if anyone bites."

And with that, the grieving father hung up, brushed past us, and strode out the front door.

CHAPTER 19

"**WELL, THAT WENT** swimmingly," I said when we were back in the elevator. "I practically accused a former U.S. attorney of tampering with evidence, you came this close to telling the victim's father to take a flying leap off the balcony, and Evelyn's computer, which is probably our best link to finding the killer, is mysteriously missing."

"There's nothing mysterious about it," Kylie said. "Plain and simple. Muriel Sykes took it."

"Try proving that one," I said.

"You think I can't?" she said as the elevator door opened. "Watch this."

She headed straight for the doorman.

"How'd it go up there?" he said, all cheery, as though Christmas were right around the corner and she was the heavy tipper who lived in the penthouse.

"What's your name?" she demanded, all badass cop, no charm.

"Nestor," he said meekly.

"You have video surveillance in this building, Nestor?"

"Just closed-circuit," he said, pointing to the eight tiny monitors on his console. "It doesn't tape anything. It just lets me keep an eye on things as they happen."

"So you're pretty alert," Kylie said.

"That's my job."

"Then you'd remember if you saw Mrs. Sykes go upstairs to Mrs. Parker-Steele's apartment early this morning."

"If she did, I didn't see her," he said all too quickly.

"Nestor, do you know why we're here?" Kylie demanded.

"Mrs. Parker-Steele," he said. "Somebody killed her."

"Correct. We're investigating a murder. So if I ask you a question and you lie to me, you are guilty of obstructing justice, which is a felony. Do you understand?"

He nodded.

"Then let me restate the question," she said. "Did you see Mrs. Sykes go upstairs to Mrs. Parker-Steele's apartment early this morning? And before you answer, ask yourself if whatever she tipped you to keep it quiet is enough to get you through the next two years, because that's the minimum you'd pull for lying to a homicide investigator."

"Mrs. Sykes came by this morning," he said. "A little after seven. I know the time because I start my shift at seven, and I was still drinking my coffee. She pulled up in a town car, and she told the driver to wait for her. She went upstairs—she didn't have anything with her when she went up, but when she came down five minutes later, she had Mrs. Parker-Steele's laptop. I recognized the carrying case. It has one of those Apple stickers on it. She gave me a hundred bucks."

"For what?" Kylie asked.

"She said, 'If anybody asks if I was here, you say no.'"

"And that's what you said, so you earned your hundred bucks. And then you told the truth, so now you won't be getting into the back of that police car with me," Kylie said. "Have a nice day, Nestor."

She grabbed the brass handle on the door and yanked it open. She waved me on through and followed me to the car. Nestor just stood there, shell-shocked.

"As I was saying," Kylie said as she slid into the driver's seat, "there's nothing mysterious about it. Muriel Sykes beat us to the punch. And now that I know she's out to sandbag us, I've changed my mind."

"About what?" I asked.

She eased the Ford into traffic. "Next Tuesday I'm voting for Spellman."

CHAPTER 20

WE WERE BACK in the car, heading downtown. "You realize of course that Evelyn's laptop is only missing temporarily," Kylie said.

"You think it will turn up next Wednesday morning as soon as the election is over," I asked, "or do you think Sykes will keep it under wraps until she's sworn in on January first?"

"Either way, NYPD Red is not waiting. Let's go pay Evelyn a visit. Maybe she can tell us something. Give Chuck Dryden a call and ask if he minds seeing me twice in one day."

"I don't think he'd mind if you moved in with him," I said. "In case your keen cop mind hadn't picked up on it, the boy has the hots for you."

"Oooooh," she said breathlessly, tossing her blond hair

in a spot-on imitation of Marilyn Monroe. "He's so smart and I'm so dumb, I can't imagine what he sees in me."

"My guess is he's smitten by your humility," I said.

The Office of Chief Medical Examiner is on East 26th Street, just around the corner from one of their primary sources, Bellevue Hospital. As expected, Chuck was more than happy to see us, and when I say us, I mean not me. I let Kylie do the talking.

"Chuck, we're running into roadblocks left and right. We definitely need your help," she said.

He smoothed out his white lab coat with both hands. "This way," he said, and walked us into an autopsy room where Evelyn was on a slab.

"We're not usually this fast," he said, "but she went right to the front of the queue. We just finished stitching her back up."

"Tell us what you found," she said.

"This is not a copycat murder. In life, this victim may have come from an entirely different social stratum than the first three, but they all died the same death. Asphyxiation. Probably suffocated by putting a plastic bag over their heads. All four were in captivity for at least seventy-two hours, their bodies were all scrubbed down with ammonia, and they all had the same stomach contents—pizza. And not just any pizza. Same dough, same sauce, same quality cheese. This was authentic, homemade—not commercial like Domino's or Pizza Hut."

"You can tell that?" Kylie said. She looked at me. "He's amazing."

Chuck stood there soaking it up, most likely trying his darnedest not to get an erection.

"What about defensive wounds?" Kylie asked. "Bruised knuckles, skin under the nails—something they might not be able to get rid of with ammonia?"

"Nothing," he said. "It would appear that none of the victims ever got a chance to put up a fight."

Kylie leaned over the table to get a closer look at Evelyn's face. "Why is her mouth all busted up like that?" she asked. "Do you think the killer used a ball gag?"

"No, that would keep the victims quiet, but whatever this was did a lot more damage. Broken teeth, lacerations inside the mouth, and torn jaw muscles. A ball gag wouldn't rip them up like that."

"What would?"

"I don't like to hypothesize," Dryden said with a wry smile.

"But you have an educated guess, don't you," Kylie said.

"Not in the official report. Nothing goes into my reports unless it's completely verified. I deal in facts, not whimsy."

"Then give me thirty seconds of whimsy," she said. "Please."

Dryden smiled as I'd never seen him smile before. "Off the record," he said. It was a statement, not a question.

"Cross my heart," she said, drawing an imaginary X on her left breast.

With a twinkle in his eye, Chuck said, "How familiar are you with medieval sadomasochism?"

"A little," Kylie said, looking at him with newfound respect. "But apparently, not nearly as much as you."

CHAPTER 21

"I THINK WE just saw a side of old Cut And Dryden that very few people get to see," Kylie said as soon as we were back in the car. "That boy knows more about medieval torture devices than Kellogg knows about cornflakes."

"I always figured Dr. Straight Arrow had a kinky side," I said.

"He probably has a rack in his bedroom and a guillotine in his basement," she said, laughing out loud.

And just like that, the glow was back. Whatever shroud of gloom had been hanging over Kylie's head was gone, and she was bubbling with energy.

"I don't care who wins the election," she said. "We are going to nail this Hazmat bastard before next Tuesday and level the playing field."

She stopped at a red light and turned to me, a bloodhound straining at the leash. "First thing we're going to do," she said, "is pull Matt Smith in on this."

It was like a punch to the gut. Before I could spit out *What the hell do we need Matt Smith for?* Kylie explained.

"You heard Dryden," she said. "Most of these contraptions are in museums. If you want to get your hands on one, you can't exactly waltz over to the Torture Department at your local Walmart. It's a very esoteric marketplace, and I thought if Matt could track down whoever sells them, that might lead us to the person who bought it. You agree?"

I couldn't disagree. "It's worth a shot," I said.

"I have to tell you," Kylie went on, "I've worked with a lot of computer guys, but Matt Smith is the world's smartest geek. And not only does he get the tech side, he knows how to work well with people. We're lucky to have him right there in the building."

Yeah. Right there next door to Cheryl.

It was late afternoon when we got back to the precinct, but Matt, as affable and good-looking as ever, was there, and he was thrilled that we could use his help.

"A choke pear?" he said when we told him what Dryden came up with. "I never heard of it."

"That makes three of us," Kylie said. "And Dryden won't go on record saying that's what he suspects. He says it's just an educated guess."

"Where was he educated—Hogwarts?" Smith said. "I don't know much about the torture business, but give me a few hours, and I'll see if I can figure out where the killer did his shopping. Now, what about Parker-Steele's computer?"

"Missing," I said. "Gone like a freight train in the night."

"Oh, bollocks," he muttered. It's a word he trots out all the time that is apparently so flexible, he can use it whether he's pissed or happy.

"Did you find anything on her credit card charges or cell phone records that would connect her to any of the other three victims?" I asked.

"Nothing. She didn't text them, call them, or check out one of their video confessions on her iPhone. And there's nothing in her voice or data charges that gives me a clue to the killer. It's possible she never even knew her kidnapper."

"Then how was he able to grab her without her putting up a fight or raising some kind of ruckus?" I said.

"How do you know she didn't put up a fight?" he asked.

"I don't, and that's been bothering me," I said. "Kang, Tinsdale, Catt, Parker-Steele—none of them are the easiest people in the world to kidnap. If they don't have a common thread, then let's assume that a total stranger grabbed them. If that was the case, surely they would have put up some kind of a struggle."

"Especially Kang and Tinsdale," Kylie said, jumping in.

"And if they did, there might be witnesses who saw them fighting off an attacker," I said. "Let's focus on Evelyn. We know from her credit card charges that she was at Hackie's Pub on Second Avenue Friday night. She never made it back to her apartment, which is only nine blocks away. Matt, maybe if you pinged her phone, you could locate the general area she was abducted from. Then we could—"

"I'm an idiot," said the man who Kylie had just informed me was the world's smartest geek. "I've been so busy looking for something that would connect all four victims that I completely glossed over the obvious. Give me twenty minutes, and I'll have something for you."

He sat down at his computer. "You're bloody brilliant, Zach," he said. "I don't know why I bloody didn't think of it myself."

Bollocks, mate. Maybe you were too busy romancing my girlfriend with your soccer star looks, your annoying Britspeak, and your spontaneous bloody soy lattes.

CHAPTER 22

TWENTY MINUTES LATER, Kylie and I were back in Matt Smith's office. I noticed that Cheryl's door was closed and her lights were out, which meant she wouldn't be going home with either of us.

"What have you got?" Kylie asked.

"Evelyn's last known whereabouts were right here," Smith said, pointing to a Google map of the Upper East Side on his monitor. "Hackie's Pub. Second Avenue and Eighty-Eighth Street. She paid her tab with an American Express card at eleven oh-nine p.m. Her apartment is on Ninety-Fourth and Park, which is maybe a ten-minute walk. It was a balmy night, so she might have chosen to walk. But even if she caught a taxi right away, which isn't likely on a busy weekend, what with traffic and red lights, it would take about the same ten minutes. And since we know she never made it home, she went off the grid not too far away from the bar.

"Working under the assumption that she was on foot, I pulled up traffic and surveillance camera pictures along Second. It must have taken her a few minutes to get out of Hackie's after she paid the bill, but at eleven seventeen a traffic cam catches her at Eighty-Ninth Street walking uptown on Second. We pick her up again at Ninetieth, then Ninety-First, and that's it. Nothing shows up on any cameras above Ninety-First Street and Second Avenue.

"Then I went back to her cell phone records. Her iPhone continually pings her location. I checked with Verizon, and they have her at the bar all night, then the signal keeps refreshing, and they can track her as she walks up Second. At eleven nineteen, she's in the vicinity of Ninety-First and Second. Five minutes later, she's twelve blocks south at Seventy-Ninth Street. Eight minutes after that, she's on the Fifty-Ninth Street Bridge heading for Queens, and then the signal goes dead. Verizon never picked her up again. Either she turned off her phone, or it's at the bottom of the East River."

"So a car or a taxi picked her up near Ninety-First Street," I said.

"That strip of Second Avenue is loaded with bars," Smith said. "There are three of them between Ninety-First and Ninety-Second, which is where we lost her. But none of them have cameras outside on the street."

"Even so," Kylie said, "it's Friday night on the Upper East Side. There would still be plenty of potential eyewitnesses."

"But most of them would be inside one of those bars," Smith said.

"I'm not talking about the people inside the bars," Kylie said. "I'm talking about the ones outside."

She turned to me. "Remember what Leonard Parker did to keep Muriel Sykes from lowering his property value?" she asked.

"He sent her outside to smoke," I said. "Good call, Detective. So now all we have to do is hang outside this strip of bars, find some nicotine addict who was there at eleven p.m. on Friday night and was still sober enough to notice Evelyn get into a car and head downtown on Second."

"Sounds like a plan," Kylie said, more upbeat than she'd been all day. "Let's go barhopping, partner."

CHAPTER 23

THE POST-IT NOTE on Emma Frye's desk said "Call Gideon." The big block letters at the bottom of her grocery list said "CALL GIDEON!!!" But Emma had let the whole day slip away without calling her son. Like a lot of New Yorkers, she'd been glued to the TV set, riveted by the Rachael O'Keefe murder trial.

"Emma," Sherman yelled as he came through the front door, "did you call Gideon yet?"

Emma muted the TV and hurried down the stairs, stopping briefly to check her hair in the hall mirror. "Look at you," she said to her reflection. "Giddy as a teenager."

Sherman was at the kitchen sink, putting flowers in a vase.

After her husband died a few years ago, Emma didn't think she'd ever have another happy day in her life. The

flower shop she and Roy had owned together was successful, but without him, Emma couldn't handle it alone. "I'm
going to sell it," she told Gideon.

Gideon found the perfect buyer. Sherman Frye had
been a history teacher and a track coach at John Adams
High and had just retired after thirty-five years. He offered to buy the shop, but only if Emma agreed to help
him run it for the first year.

She said yes, and after two months they started going
out for the occasional business dinner. Then came week-
ends. Golf, antiquing, road trips to Civil War battlefields,
and marina hopping on *Tecumseh*, Sherman's beautifully
restored thirty-three-foot Chris-Craft cabin cruiser.

The night Emma's year of service was up, the two of
them went to their favorite restaurant, La Nora on Cross
Bay Boulevard. He waited till they were having coffee and
cognac before sliding the envelope across the table.

"Here," he said. "It's a going-away present for my favorite employee."

Emma opened the envelope and read the card. It said,
"Don't go away. Ever."

And then he held up the blue velvet box with the an-
tique diamond engagement ring nestled inside. "I'm sorry
I can't get down on one knee," he said. "You should have
known me before my golf game screwed up my ACL, but
I love you, and you've been working for me long enough.
I'd like to spend the rest of my life working for you.
Emma, will you marry me?"

Once again, she said yes to his offer. Since then, she'd
never been happier.

"Irises," she said as Sherman filled the vase with water. "My favorite."

"No, they're not," he said. "Your favorite are lilacs, but all the lilacs I had in the shop were fresh and extremely sellable. These babies have about twenty-four hours left in them before they crap out. So I figured I'd bring them home to my wife, because by now she's surely called her son like I've been asking her to for the past five days."

He put his big bear arms around her. "So," he whispered in her ear, "did you call him?"

She pulled back so she could look into his magical blue eyes and gave him her sexiest mea culpa pout. "Not yet. I meant to call him yesterday, but it was Sunday, and he's been *so* busy at work that I didn't want to bother him on his day off."

"And today is Monday, but you've been watching that Rachael O'Keefe trial on TV all day," he said.

"Guilty," she said.

"Ha! I knew she was guilty."

"No, no, no," Emma corrected. "I'm guilty for watching. The verdict came in this afternoon. The jury found her not guilty."

"That's crazy," Sherman said. "The woman killed her daughter. How can they not see that?"

"Now you know why I couldn't turn off the TV. I'll call Gideon now," she said, tapping his speed dial on her cell.

He picked up on the first ring. "Hey, Mom, is this important? I'm in a hurry."

"Well, hello to you too," she said. "You're in a hurry for what?"

"I'm meeting Dave and a bunch of people. We're going to a bar downtown to grab a few beers and catch the Monday night football game. Can this wait till tomorrow?"

"I have one question. It'll only take me a half a second. You think your friends and your beer can wait a half a second?"

"Sure, Mom. One question. Go ahead."

"Sherman wants to turn your old bedroom into a little den for himself."

"That's not a question," Gideon said, "but I have one. You remarried less than a year ago, and Sherman is already moving out of the bedroom?"

"Don't be cute," Emma said. "He just wants a nice private place to work on his computer. He's going to write a novel."

"Really?"

"Really. It takes place during the Civil War."

"You mean like *Gone With the Wind*?"

She laughed. "Better."

"I'm in a hurry, Mom. What's your question?"

"I spent the whole day packing up your old stuff," she said. "Clothes, toys, a bunch of papers from high school, all your trophies from Little League. Can you come over and pick up all your things so we can clear out the room?"

"No."

"What do you mean, 'no'? You're a grown man. You can't leave all your stuff here forever. We need the space."

"Then leave it all on the curb for the garbageman. I took everything I wanted to keep when I moved out. The rest of that crap I haven't needed for fifteen years, and I don't need it now."

"Are you sure? You could probably sell some of those old toys and games on eBay."

"Mom, you're a pack rat. I'm not. Sherman's not. Chuck all that crap. Burn it."

"Okay," she said. "I think you're crazy to throw away all that good stuff, but I know Sherman will be happy. And for the record, mister, my new husband and I are very happy in our bedroom."

"Oh God," Gideon said. "I'm hanging up now before you give me any of the details. Love you, Mom."

"Love you too," Emma said, and hung up. She wrapped her arms around Sherman. "Okay, flower man, the room is all yours. Now go upstairs to your new office and start writing that book."

Sherman put his hands on her soft, round butt and pulled her in tight. "How about you walk me upstairs to the bedroom just in case I need a little inspiration before I start writing."

"Oh, crap," Emma said.

"Is that any way to talk to a guy who brought you irises?"

"No, I meant, Oh, crap, I forgot to tell Gideon one thing."

"So call him back."

"Not tonight. He's going out to unwind with his friends. I can tell him another time."

"Tell him what?" Sherman said, maneuvering her toward the stairs.

"When I was cleaning out his desk, I found this red leather notebook wedged in behind the bottom drawer," she said. "It's not Gideon's. I wondered if he knew anything about it."

"Whose notebook is it?" Sherman asked as they headed upstairs.

"Enzo Salvi's."

Sherman stopped in the middle of the stairwell. "I knew that kid from back when I was teaching," he said. "He was a total shit. You know who his father is, don't you?"

"Of course I know," Emma said. "Everyone in Howard Beach knows. We all went to Enzo's funeral out of respect for the family."

"Then do me a favor," Sherman said. "Out of respect for me, don't get involved. The kid is dead. He doesn't need the notebook."

"Well, maybe his mother might want it," Emma said. "She lost a son. This is a connection."

"It's a connection all right. It's a connection to us. I don't want to be connected to the Salvi family. Emma, they're Mafia. Regular people like you and me do not get involved with people like them."

"So what should I do with the notebook?" she asked.

"Throw it in the trash with the rest of Gideon's shit."

"Okay," she said, and scurried up the stairs toward the bedroom.

Sherman was right behind her.

CHAPTER 24

GIDEON SQUINTED AT the mirror and slowly ran a brush through his dark, curly hair, looking for one of those rogue gray strands that had been popping up lately. Not a trace.

His brain wandered back to the woman with the sports bra and the FDNY baseball cap. "Timing is everything Andie," he said, playing to his image in the mirror, "and yours just happened to suck."

He left his apartment on West 84th and walked to the subway station at 86th and Broadway. He felt good about making his mother laugh. It's the least he could do after killing her husband.

He caught the number 1 downtown train and found a seat.

Gideon blamed himself for his father's death. Officially,

it was an accident—one he was positive never would have happened if he had kept his promise. He was supposed to watch the Super Bowl on Dad's new flat-screen, but two days before the game, he scored a pair of tickets on the forty-yard line, bailed out on his father, and flew down to Miami with Meredith.

It was the best weekend of his life—until his mother called him at halftime. After two beers, Roy decided to adjust the satellite dish on the roof. Maybe it had been four beers, maybe six. It didn't matter—a broken neck is a broken neck, and everybody said it was just as well that the fall killed him because he'd have been a vegetable anyway.

Gideon was racked with guilt. He should have been the one up on that roof. He swore he'd do whatever he could to make it up to his mother. Finding Sherman Frye to buy the flower shop helped a lot. Sherman made his mother happy, and that made Gideon happy.

He got off the train at the Chambers Street station, headed up West Broadway, then turned right on Duane Street toward the hottest bar in lower Manhattan— maybe even the entire borough.

Two years ago, three middle-aged criminal lawyers decided they'd rather get people drunk than get them acquitted, so they opened a sprawling bar on Duane only two blocks from the U.S. District Court for the Southern District of New York.

They christened it Don't Judge Me, and it quickly became the unofficial watering hole of the legal profession— a mecca for hordes of thirsty young attorneys—one of the few places in New York where you could say you were a lawyer and nobody would roll their eyes.

"Don't judge me either," Gideon said as he checked out his reflection in the frosted-glass window. The brass plaque on the front door read THE BAR NO LAWYER CAN PASS, and Gideon walked in.

The place was jammed, but Meredith must have had her eyes glued to the door because he heard her yell "Gid!" over the rest of the racket. She stood and waved, and he worked his way to the table where she was commiserating with the team of lawyers who had just lost the biggest case of their young careers.

Meredith, half-soused, completely devastated, but still beautiful, threw her arms around him. "I can't believe we lost," she said, not letting him go.

"I am so sorry," Gideon said, careful not to press his hips too close to her. Nothing says *insensitive jerk* like a guy with an erection trying to comfort a woman in pain.

"It wasn't you guys," he said, wiping a drooping hank of red hair from her face and planting a gentle kiss on her forehead. "The jury just bought into the defense team's bullshit."

She sat down, and Gideon took the chair between Meredith and her brother, Dave.

"Bad night," Dave said, pouring his best friend a beer from one of five pitchers on the table. "Real bad night for the justice system."

CHAPTER 25

"YOU GUYS ARE way ahead of me," Gideon said, picking up his beer. "I've got some catching up to do." He took four big swallows of the cold, crisp brew, set the mug down hard on the table, and let Dave top it off.

He scanned the room. The walls were peppered with TV sets, half of them tuned to *Monday Night Football*, the other half to *Post Mortems*, the popular CNN show that focused on the big legal news of the day. And in a bar filled with lawyers, nothing—not even the Hazmat Killer—was bigger than the Rachael O'Keefe case.

O'Keefe was a twenty-nine-year-old single mom living on East 71st Street with her five-year-old daughter, Kimi. By day, she was a phlebotomist, collecting blood, urine, sputum, and other bodily fluids for a private diagnostic lab on the Upper West Side. Most nights, desperate to escape from the tedium of her life, she'd put Kimi to bed at 8:00 and at 9:00 go downstairs to the bar across the street.

Kimi knew that if she woke up and needed anything, she could either speed-dial Rachael's cell or just pick up the intercom and buzz the doorman, who would run over to the bar and get Mommy.

Rachael knew it wasn't the kind of parenting Dr. Spock would approve of, but screw him—the men she met on the job stayed only long enough to have her stick a needle in their arm and fill a few test tubes. Nights were the only time she had to get out and meet a decent guy—or at least some badass who could take her up to her bedroom and put a smile on her face.

One Sunday night, something went wrong. According to Rachael, she came home at 2:00 a.m., fell into bed, and slept till 10:00. Kimi was usually awake by 6:30, so Rachael went to her room to see what was wrong.

The little girl was gone. And so was Mookie, the stuffed pink monkey she slept with every night. At 10:04 that Monday morning, Rachael dialed 911, and within twenty-four hours, Kimi O'Keefe was the most sought-after missing person in America.

Her body was found four days later in a landfill in Pennsylvania. She'd been smothered to death. There was no sign of the pink monkey, but the garbage pile she was found in was easily traced to the New York City sanitation truck that picked up at Kimi's building on Monday morning.

A month later, the DA charged Rachael with murder two.

Gideon remembered the night Meredith was assigned to the case. She came bounding into his apartment, squealing with joy. "I got it! I got it! I'm on the O'Keefe team!"

She wrapped her arms around him, and they fell to the sofa, kissing.

"That's fantastic," he said when he came up for air. "You're going to be a media star."

"Hardly," Meredith said. "There are nine of us. I won't even be in the courtroom. I'll be locked up on the seventh floor sifting evidence—it's mostly grunt work, but I do get to prep some of the witnesses. This is the biggest trial of my career, and if we win—"

"*When* you win," Gideon said. His hand found its way under her skirt and slowly, tantalizingly, made its way up her leg.

Sex with Meredith was everything Gideon had dreamed of when he was a kid. He and Dave never told her the truth about Enzo Salvi's murder, but in a weird way, Gideon always thought he had Enzo to thank for his good fortune.

It took two years before Meredith attempted to have sex again. It was a disaster. Meredith assured the guy it wasn't his fault, and then she made the mistake of telling him the truth. Instead of being empathetic, he put together beach party, booze, and sexy costume and came to a natural conclusion. *She had been asking for it.* The guy never actually said the words, but Meredith knew what he was thinking. After that, her sexual encounters were infrequent and unfulfilling.

And then came New Year's Eve 2009. Gideon and Meredith were at a party, dancing, when the ball dropped at midnight. He leaned in, pressed his lips to hers, and she kissed back. Their five-year age difference meant nothing to her at this point.

"I trust you," she said, kissing him with a ferocity and a passion that had been beaten out of her that night on the beach. Since then, the sex had been glorious. No shame, no guilt, and absolutely no "I love yous."

The first time Gideon said it, Meredith tossed it off. "Fifteen-yard penalty for violating the cardinal rule of friends with benefits—illegal use of the L-word."

That night, when she was on a high from being assigned to the biggest case of her life, Gideon tried it again. Lying on the floor, breathing heavily, surrounded by magazines from the overturned coffee table, Gideon, still deep inside her, whispered in her ear, "I love you."

He waited for her to remind him of the ground rules. And then he felt tears rolling down his cheek. Her tears.

"I'm sorry I made you wait so long," she said, lifting her head and lowering her lips to his. "I love you too."

Her body relaxed, and her breathing took on a familiar rhythm. "We're going to win this case," she said, drifting into sleep. "Right?"

"Mmmm...," he said, his eyes closed, his breathing in sync with hers. "You can't lose."

CHAPTER 26

"**I DON'T KNOW** why they're running that shit on CNN," Meredith said halfway through her fourth margarita. "It should be on Comedy Central, because the whole fucking trial was a joke."

The other lawyers around the table raised their glasses in solidarity.

"We had fifty witnesses who'd have gladly testified that Rachael O'Keefe was a barfly who would leave her daughter alone most nights," Meredith said, playing to the partisan audience. "Our mistake was that we only called five of them to the stand. And then we only called three who testified that Rachael felt trapped by Kimi—that she'd sit at the bar swilling white wine and telling anybody who would listen that she wished the kid had never been born. A day and a half of testimony, and did the jury even hear any of it? Yes! They heard just enough to find her guilty of endangering the welfare of a child. The Bad Mommy verdict. That's like finding O.J. guilty of getting blood all over the sidewalk and fining him for littering."

Meredith drained the last of her drink. Dave stood up and put his arm around his sister. "Time to sit down, sis."

She pulled away. "No. I'm still talking."

"How about you sit down, Dave," Gideon said. "She's had a rough couple of months. Let her talk it out."

Dave shook his head, but he didn't argue. He went back to his chair.

Gideon handed Meredith his beer. "Here you go, baby. Talk all you want."

"Okay, let's pretend I'm Rachael O'Keefe," she said, slurring her words. "It's two in the morning, and I am totally shit-faced."

"I'm convinced," Gideon yelled, and the group bellowed.

"NYU Drama Club," Meredith said, taking a little bow. "Where was I? Oh yeah, I'm staggering across the street to my apartment," she continued, slipping back into her Rachael character. "I look in on my daughter—because even drunk mothers look in on their kids—and poor Kimi, left alone in the dark for four hours, is crying. Damn kid is always crying, I think, so I grab a pillow and put it over her face. I don't want to kill her. I just want to shut her up. And I do. The kid stops crying. The silence feels so good that I hold the pillow there just a little longer. And then the kid stops breathing. Oops. I didn't mean to do that. I didn't mean to *kill* her."

Meredith stood up tall, smoothed out her skirt, and addressed the group. "Ladies and gentlemen of the jury," she said. "Rachael O'Keefe may not have *meant* to kill her little girl, but once she crossed that line, she did mean to *cover it up*. Who else would have wrapped her up all nice and neat in a blanket and put her in a garbage bag? Who else could have snuck out through the service entrance and left Kimi's body with fifty other garbage bags waiting for the morning trash? Bad Mommy? No. Rachael O'Keefe was always Bad Mommy. But that night, she became Killer Mommy."

"I'm convinced," Gideon said. "I vote guilty."

"Thank you," Meredith said, taking another slug of Gideon's beer. "You, my handsome friend, should have been on the jury. You know what their problem was?"

Gideon shrugged. "I'm going to go with brain damage."

Meredith laughed far louder and longer than the joke deserved. "No, the problem with that jury was that *nobody actually saw Rachael O'Keefe murder her daughter.* Twelve good men and true? More like twelve morons!"

Another swig of beer. "I have a question for you," she said to the group. "If you wake up one morning and your windows are wet and the sidewalks outside are wet, do you actually have to see or hear the rain to come to the inescapable conclusion that it rained last night?"

Head shakes and catcalls of, "No!"

"No," Meredith repeated. "We didn't have to see Rachael kill Kimi to know she did it. Nobody else was seen coming or going. Nobody else had access to the apartment. And most important, nobody else on the planet had a motive. Rachael O'Keefe murdered her daughter at two in the morning, waited eight hours until the body was inside the bowels of a garbage truck, then called the cops and reported her missing. The case was a slam fucking dunk. How the hell did we lose?"

"That's it," Dave said to Gideon. "Enough. She's just torturing herself."

Everyone knew how they lost. But nobody said a word. Nobody wanted Meredith to think they were blaming her.

Dave stood up, put his arm around her again, and sat her down next to Gideon.

"How the hell did we lose?" she said, burying her face in his chest. "How the hell did we lose?"

And then, as if the CNN gods had heard the question, they popped the answer on the screen.

The Warlock.

CHAPTER 27

ONE OF THE prosecution's key witnesses was Audrey Yeager, an unmarried, middle-aged legal assistant who lived in the apartment next door to the O'Keefes. Meredith had prepped her for the trial, and to her amazement, she was invited to sit at the prosecutor's table the day Yeager took the stand.

Audrey delivered. She testified calmly and articulately that numerous times in the past she had heard Kimi crying at night and that despite what Rachael said, Kimi did not always call Rachael's cell, or if she did, Rachael would not hurry home.

"There were nights when I could hear the poor little girl sobbing for hours," Audrey told the court. "It would start before I went to sleep, and then it would ebb and flow, from audible moans to soft whimpering, but because her bedroom was directly opposite my living room, I could hear everything clearly. It was very painful."

Her testimony was decisive. It painted a picture of Rachael O'Keefe as a sadly neglectful mother who would abandon her child night after night. Rachael's claim that she was just a short phone call away was riddled with holes. The reality, the prosecution maintained, was that most nights Rachael came home drunk and then was faced with having to calm down a hysterical child. But on that fateful Sunday night, Rachael didn't have the patience or the desire to comfort her daughter. She was overwhelmed by the burden of motherhood, and in her drunken state she put a pillow over Kimi's head in an effort to silence her.

It may not have been premeditated, but the intent to kill was without question. Murder two.

And then Dennis Woloch stepped up to the plate. Woloch was a legend. A defense attorney who consistently snatched victory from the jaws of defeat. A columnist from the *Daily News* once wrote that "Woloch has such an uncanny ability to cast a spell over juries that he should change his name to Warlock."

The moniker stuck, and Woloch reveled in it. By the time he turned forty, he took on only two kinds of clients—those with deep pockets who could add to his fortune and lost causes like Rachael O'Keefe who could add to his reputation.

"Ms. Yeager," he said as he ambled over to the witness, "let's start with full disclosure. We know one another, do we not?"

"Yes, sir," Audrey said.

"You work as a legal assistant for one of my colleagues, and we've met on numerous occasions," he said, smiling.

"Yes, sir," she repeated.

"Do you have any idea what I think of you?"

She cringed. "No, sir."

"Well then, let me go on record. Ladies and gentlemen of the jury," he boomed, "this woman is an absolute sweetheart. She's as caring and kindhearted and compassionate as they come."

Some of the jurors smiled. All looked puzzled. *Why would the defense attorney give a glowing character reference to the prosecution's star witness?*

Meredith didn't know either, but her mouth immediately went tinny, and her gastrointestinal system started to churn.

"Audrey," the Warlock said, "it must have been very difficult for you to listen to that poor child cry night after night."

"Yes, sir," she said.

Meredith nodded. *Just answer the question. Don't volunteer anything.*

"Did you ever talk to her mother about it?"

"No, sir."

"Why not?"

"It wasn't my place."

"Understandable," Woloch said. "Who among us wants to confront their neighbor and correct them on their parenting skills? You agree?"

Audrey nodded.

"So you just let poor little Kimi cry her eyes out night after night," he said.

Yeager didn't say a word. She sat there, stone-faced.

"I'm sorry," Woloch said. "I didn't hear your response. Maybe it's because I just made a blanket statement. Let me rephrase it as a question. Did you, Ms. Yeager, let Kimi O'Keefe, alone and afraid, cry her little heart out for hours on end while her pitiful excuse for a parent sat on a bar stool getting blotto, hoping she could find anyone in a pair of pants who would come upstairs and bang the crap out of her?"

"Objection!" the prosecutor yelled. "Badgering the witness."

"Sustained," the judge responded quickly. "Mr. Woloch, I will let you pursue this line of questioning, but I expect you to clean up your act and treat this witness more civilly."

"My apologies to the court," Woloch said. "And to Ms. Yeager. Audrey, I know you. You are made up of all those sterling character traits I described to the jury, and while I can believe you never spoke to Ms. O'Keefe about her substandard parenting, I cannot imagine you let that little girl suffer without doing something—anything—to help. Am I right?"

"Yes."

Meredith sat there, heart pounding, sweat coming out of every pore.

"Tell the jury what you did to help Kimi," Woloch said.

"One night I rang the bell," Yeager said. "I told her it was Audrey from next door. She knew me a little, and she opened the door. I went inside, and I calmed her down."

"How did you do that?"

"Oh, I'd read her a book, or we'd sing songs, or sometimes we'd play with her Barbies. We had lots of things we liked to do."

"So you visited Kimi more than once."

"Yes."

"More than five times?"

"Yes."

"More than ten?"

"Yes, sir."

"Let's not quibble about a number. Can we just say you went next door and kept Kimi company lots of times? Or should we say often?"

"Lots of times."

"Did her mother know?"

"Nobody knew," Audrey volunteered. "I told Kimi if she told anybody, they'd yell at me, and I would never be able to come back."

"Did you ever do anything to harm Kimi?" Woloch asked gently.

"Oh, God, no," Yeager said. "I...I loved her. I never had children. I couldn't stand to watch how her mother treated her." Her eyes welled up, and tears ran down both cheeks. "I was like a surrogate mommy. She called me Mama Audrey. She was...she was the best thing that ever happened to me, and that...that..."

Audrey Yeager was a lady, and whatever word was forming in her brain never came out of her mouth.

Woloch walked to the defense table and handed her a box of tissues. He waited until Audrey regained her composure. "Go on," he said. "Please."

Audrey took a deep breath. "Kimi was the best thing that ever happened to me," she repeated, "and Rachael murdered her."

"You may be right," Woloch said. "It's very possible that Rachael O'Keefe came home that night and murdered her daughter."

He paused and let the thought sit with the jury.

"*But!*" he screamed, and Meredith knew what was coming next.

"But," Woloch repeated softly, "Kimi was a love-starved child, willing—even eager—to open the door for anyone who heard her sobs and wanted to comfort her."

"Objection."

"Overruled."

"Maybe there was another compassionate neighbor. Or a not-so-compassionate neighbor who was tired of the incessant crying. Or a mentally deranged pizza deliveryman. Or any one of a thousand random strangers who could have wandered into the building while the doorman ran off for a quick bathroom break. So it *could* have been her," he said, pointing at Rachael and raising his voice again. "Or it *could* have been anybody. Am I right, Audrey?"

She shook her head.

"Speak up!"

"Yes, you're right."

He turned to the jury. "Yes, I'm right. It…could…

have...been...*anybody*. And Kimi, desperate for attention, would have opened the door and let that person in."

He walked slowly back to the defense table and pulled out his chair.

"And that, ladies and gentlemen of the jury—as Ms. Yeager, who is a legal assistant, can tell you—is what we call reasonable doubt. Very, very, very reasonable doubt," he said, and sat down.

The jury was mesmerized.

Once again, the Warlock had cast his spell.

CHAPTER 28

KYLIE AND I rolled up Third Avenue, both of us lost in our own heads. I was writing soap opera scenarios, all ending with Cheryl dumping me for Matt Smith. Knowing Kylie, I figured she was probably plotting how she could use her superpowers to save her husband from self-destruction.

We hung a right on 92nd Street and pulled up to a disaster area known as the Second Avenue Subway project.

The grand idea to bore a subway tunnel under Second Avenue from Harlem to the financial district was first proposed decades before I was born. They finally broke ground in 2007, and if they ever fund and finish the entire eight mile run, it will be long after I'm dead. In the meantime, Second Avenue from 63rd to 96th looks like Baghdad after the shock and awe.

We parked on First and walked back. Fall was in the air.

The temperature had dropped to the low forties, and the bars along Second were in full-scale Halloween promotion mode, their windows adorned with posters of goblins, ghosts, vampires, and Sam Adams Octoberfest beer.

Our first stop was the Foggy Goggle, which is typical of the cutesy bar names on the Upper East Side. When I was a kid, our local gin mill was Chop's Tavern, but nobody in this zip code is going to pay fifteen bucks for an appletini at a joint called Chop's.

Monday nights during football season are as busy as Fridays, and even though neither of the New York teams were playing, the place was packed with fanatics hoping to see the New England Patriots get clobbered by Miami.

We had flyers of Evelyn and started with our best bet—the smokers outside the bar. A few had seen her on the evening news, but nobody had seen her walk past the bar on Friday night. Nobody inside was any help either.

The next stop was Sticks and Balls, where there were almost as many people in the back room watching the Monday night pool tournament as there were rooting against the Patriots.

Kylie and I split up to work the room. At least half a dozen guys, their testosterone fueled by alcohol, thought they "just might know something" and offered to discuss it with Kylie over a drink.

Kylie had a stock answer: "Great. How about my place—Nineteenth Precinct. You can spend the night."

After ten minutes, we knew we'd struck out again and moved on to Not a Health Club. The name must have resonated with their target audience, because there were at least twice as many smokers outside as there had been at the first two bars.

One by one, they looked at Evelyn's picture and shook their heads. We had questioned about half of them when one of the smokers walked up to Kylie and said, "I'm Romeo. You been looking for me?"

He was five feet six, 250 pounds, with thinning, curly hair and a thick, unruly beard that made his moon-pie face even rounder. I seriously doubted if any woman was looking for him—especially if his pickup line was "I'm Romeo. You been looking for me?"

"Am I looking for you for what?" Kylie said.

"You're the cops, right? You're looking for information about her," he said, pointing at the flyer in Kylie's hand. "I'm the guy who called you. Joe Romeo."

"When did you call?" Kylie said.

"Tonight, right after I heard about this Evelyn Parker-Steele murder on the six o'clock news. I called the crime stoppers hotline number on your website. The one where they give you a two-thousand-dollar reward if my tip helps you nail the killer. Then I called them back at seven thirty and told them I can't hang around my apartment all night, and you could meet me here."

When there's a page-one homicide, our tip line logs hundreds of calls. Eventually the department follows up on all of them, so there was no sense telling Romeo his message was buried at the bottom of a slush pile.

"Oh, yes," I said. "We got both calls. Tell us what you know, Mr. Romeo."

"It was Friday night around eleven. I'm out here having

a smoke, and I see this Evelyn Parker-Steele walking up Second. I didn't know who she was at the time, but I was checking her out. I'm in the rag trade, and this woman knew how to dress. Gray pantsuit, burgundy silk blouse, Brian Atwood slingbacks—not cheap."

"Did you see where she walked to?" Kylie asked. "Did she turn the corner? Pop into another bar?"

"No, a car pulled up alongside her," he said, taking a drag on his cigarette. "A black SUV."

"Did you see the driver?" I said.

"No, but the guy in the backseat rolled down the window, and he called out to her."

The guy in the backseat? Kylie and I looked at each other.

"You're sure the man was in the backseat?" I asked.

"Yeah. I could tell she didn't know him. I figured he was just some douchebag hitting on random chicks, but she walked over to him. Now I'm totally tuned in, because I'm waiting for her to tell him to fuck off, but she listens for maybe ten seconds, opens the door, and gets in."

"She just got in?" I said. "He didn't step out of the car and help her in?"

He shook his head. "Nope. She just hopped in the back."

"But you're absolutely sure there were two men in the car," I said. Eyewitnesses who have been drinking are not that reliable, and I was pushing Romeo to see if he stuck with his story.

"No," he said. "I'm not sure there were two *men*. I never saw the driver. It could have been a woman or a trained monkey."

"Can you describe the man in the backseat?"

"He was white."

"What else?"

"I don't know. I never saw his face, but his hand was resting on the window. Hey, don't try to beat me out of the reward just because I couldn't see faces. I gave you the black car and a white guy. That's gotta be worth something."

"Absolutely," I said. "You've been very helpful. Thank you for calling it in."

Romeo stubbed out his cigarette, handed Kylie his business card, and waddled into the bar.

"He described the clothes she was wearing," Kylie said. "And the fact that he saw Evelyn get into a car backs up Matt's theory that she drove down Second and onto the Fifty-Ninth Street Bridge toward Queens before her cell signal went dead."

"Okay," I said. "Let's recap. We've got two suspects, one male, one gender undetermined, in a black SUV headed for Queens—and the male suspect definitely has a white hand."

Kylie couldn't help grinning. "Narrows it right down," she said.

CHAPTER 29

KYLIE AND I wrapped it up by 10:15. At 10:16, I called Cheryl at home. No answer. I didn't leave a message.

By 6:00 the next morning, I got to Gerri's Diner and sat at my usual table. Much to my surprise, Gerri herself waved off the waitress and was there in seconds, pouring me hot coffee.

"So, Zach," she said, "how's it going with the lady shrink?"

The diner is around the corner from the precinct, and Gerri Gomperts, who is a cross between a den mother and Dear Abby, makes it her business to know everybody else's business. The running joke at the One Nine is that if Internal Affairs needs to know anything about any of our cops, they walk straight past the precinct house and go directly to the diner.

Gerri had been following my relationship with Cheryl since before I even knew there was a relationship.

"It's going okay, I guess," I said, faking a smile.

Gerri faked a smile back. "That's so romantic. And yet you hardly ever hear any love songs with the lyrics 'It's going okay, I guess.'"

Cheryl showed up five minutes later and joined me. Gerri was right on her heels. "Good morning, Dr. Robinson," she said, pouring Cheryl some coffee.

"What?" I said. "No soy latte?"

They both gave me a look that let me know the dig had fallen flat on its face.

"I didn't get to those files before I left last night," Cheryl said as soon as Gerri left. "Can it wait till this afternoon?"

"Kylie and I are bouncing all over the city today. How about after five? And maybe dinner after that?"

"Good morning," said a familiar baritone voice before she could answer. It was Matt Smith, star of my soap opera fantasies. "Sorry I can't join you. I'm just grabbing a coffee. Captain Cates's email keeps crashing, and she wants it fixed first thing. How'd it go last night?"

"Fantastic," Cheryl said. "It was everything you said it would be."

"Actually, I was asking Zach," Matt said. "How did your barhopping go?"

"We got a lead," I said. "It looks like somebody—make that two somebodies—picked Parker-Steele up in a black SUV exactly in that spot where you said she dropped off the radar."

"Good show. That explains her quick trip to the Fifty-Ninth Street Bridge. I have her cell records. I'll check if anyone she called in the past six months owns a black SUV. I'll get on it as soon as I solve the captain's email issue. Still looking for the source of the choke pear."

"Thanks," I said.

"Don't thank me, mate. It's a pleasure to be on the team with you. As for you, Doctor," he said to Cheryl, "pop round my office at lunch. We can grab a bite, and you can fill me in on last night."

"Will do," she said.

I waited for Matt to go out the front door. "So, Doctor," I said, "what went so fantastic for *you* last night?"

"The play. I told you I was taking my parents to the theater for their anniversary. It's a new Off Broadway play that Matt recommended."

"Sorry. I've been busy. I guess I forgot. Glad it went well."

"Better than well. Matt is friends with the playwright. He arranged for me to take Mom and Dad backstage to meet him. Oh, my God, they flipped."

"Sounds...fantastic."

"Zach, you seem very out of it. What's going on with you, anyway?"

"It's personal," I said.

"Do you want to tell me what it is?"

"Are you asking me as a shrink or as a friend?"

"Either way, it will stay between the two of us. What's bothering you?"

For starters, you're popping round Matt's office for lunch.

But, of course, I couldn't say that. "It's Spence," I said, groping for something she would buy. "He's become addicted to painkillers, and it's affecting Kylie's reliability."

"It's obviously affecting you too."

"Well, he's my partner's husband. What happens to them affects me."

"Is that all?" she asked.

"That's all that's bothering me," I said. "Nothing more."

Cheryl rubbed her chin and nodded thoughtfully. "You, Detective Jordan," she said, "are delightfully full of shit. I just have one question—are you lying to me as a shrink or as a friend?"

Busted. I laughed out loud. "Both. And yet neither of you appear to be buying it."

"Zach, I don't know what's bothering you," she said, getting up from the table. "But even if I did, I wouldn't tell you. It works better if you figure it out on your own. Then I can help you deal with it. I've got to run. And yes, I'd love to have dinner tonight. If you want, we can pick this up then."

She left, and I sat there for another minute, sipping the dregs of my coffee. Then I got up and went to the front of the diner. Gerri was behind the register. She didn't say a word. She just frowned.

"What's on your mind, Gerri?" I said.

"Nothing."

"You seem judgmentally silent this morning."

"You know me," she said. "I have nothing but respect for personal boundaries."

"Since when?"

"Sweetheart, if you really want to know what I think, you'll ask me."

"Okay, Gerri. I'm asking. What do you think?"

"You sure you want to know?" she asked, toying with me.

I knew I'd regret it, but she'd tell me sooner or later anyway. "Feel free," I said.

"No questions asked," she said. "I'm just going to speak my mind. No discussion. I don't want to join the debating society."

"Fine. No questions. Just tell me what you think."

She stood up as tall as she could, which is still a foot shorter than me, and stared right into my eyes. "I think you should get your head out of your ass."

"Anything else?" I said.

"Yeah. A buck fifty for the coffee."

CHAPTER 30

IT WAS ONLY 6:45 when I got to the office, but Kylie was already at her desk.

"Good afternoon, Detective," she said. "Nice of you to stroll in."

"I'm guessing by your attempt at comic banter that you and Spence had a pleasant morning," I said.

"I was out the door before he woke up. It doesn't get any more pleasant than that," she said. "Cates is waiting on us for an update."

It took us ten minutes to bring Captain Cates up to speed on Evelyn. She interrupted us just twice. The first time was when we told her how both of Evelyn's computers had conveniently disappeared.

"And the doorman definitely saw Sykes walk out of the building with Evelyn's laptop?" she said.

"Technically he only saw her with a carrying case," I said, "but she gave him a hundred bucks to disremember what he saw."

"Another clear-cut case of obstruction of justice that won't survive our dumbass justice system," Cates said.

Her second comment came when we told her that Joe Romeo saw Evelyn get into a black SUV with two people on Friday night.

"So you think we have two Hazmat killers?" she said.

"The Hollywood on the Hudson killer had an accomplice," Kylie said. "Considering that Hazmat has some heavy bodies to lug around, we wouldn't be surprised if he had one too."

"You two pinpointed the spot where Evelyn Parker-Steele was abducted," Cates said, "and you found an eyewitness who saw her willingly get into a black SUV with at least two people inside. You came up with more viable information in twenty-four hours than Donovan and Boyle figured out in four months."

"Don't give us too much credit," Kylie said. "Those guys were nice enough to set the bar pretty low. The murder books they put together on the first three homicides are more like pamphlets. There's nothing to go on. Zach and I thought it would help if we backtracked on some of their investigation."

"If we can figure out where the other three victims went missing from, we might find a witness who can give us a better description of the car or the perps," I said. "We're going to start with the second victim, Sebastian Catt. He lived right around here—Eighty-Fourth and York."

"What's his story?" Cates asked.

"We don't have anything new on him yet," I said. "Just what's in Donovan and Boyle's pathetic little file."

"I'll be honest with you," Cates said. "I'm so caught up in all the political bullshit that I haven't had time to read any of the files—as skinny as they might be."

Kylie looked surprised. "Political bullshit?" she said. "First I've heard about it. Thank you for sparing us, Captain."

Cates cracked a smile. "And thank you for the laugh, Detective. With the mayor and the PC breathing down my neck, it very well may be my last. Tell me what you have on Sebastian Catt."

"He was a 'fashion photographer,'" Kylie said, using air quotes.

Cates knows cop-speak when she hears it, and she shook her head in disgust. "And who did he like to photograph? Little boys? Little girls?"

"Young women," Kylie said. "He'd find them on Craigslist, offer them a modeling career, then get them jobs doing webcam shows or modeling sleazy lingerie at private parties. Plus he was a sex addict. He'd get these kids—some of them underage—stoned, naked, and in the sack. He'd live with one or two, then rotate them out to make room for fresh meat."

"Hard to believe somebody would want to kill him," Cates said.

"He murdered one of his models first," I said. "Her name was Savannah Lee. She was nineteen, he was forty-nine, but this girl was different. He fell in love with her.

It lasted maybe two months, then one night Savannah was found stabbed to death a few blocks from Catt's place. Her knapsack was missing, and it looked like a robbery gone bad, but the cops didn't buy it. They suspected Catt, but there was nothing to connect him."

"Then a witness showed up—Hattie LaFleur," Kylie said. "She and her husband lived in the apartment next door to Catt. She was in her early seventies—managed the Daffodil Grill on York Avenue. She was a feisty old broad—everyone in the neighborhood loved her."

"You're talking about her in the past tense," Cates said.

"She was Catt's second victim," Kylie said. "Hattie would buy Savannah lunch at the restaurant a couple of times a week. She finally convinced the girl to dump Catt and get on with her life. The night Savannah was murdered, Hattie was out walking her dog. It was one in the morning, which was smack in the middle of the time-of-death window, and she swore to the cops that she saw Catt sneaking back into the building, all disheveled, and carrying Savannah's knapsack. He was arrested, made bail, then a week before the trial, Hattie was out doing her regular one a.m. dog walk, and she was knifed."

"Another so-called robbery gone bad," Cates said.

"Everyone knew who killed her," Kylie said. "Especially since Hattie's dog was never found. I mean, as long as you're getting rid of the woman who can put you away for murder, why not get rid of the annoying little dog who lives next door? But there was no hard evidence, and he got away with murder. Twice."

"And we know that for a fact," I said, "because Catt confessed to both murders on the video that got posted. He also admitted breaking the dog's neck and tossing it in the East River."

"Sebastian's body was dumped next to the International Center for Photography on West Forty-Third Street," Kylie said, "but we have no idea when he was kidnapped, or even where he was taken from. That's because he's the kind of guy that nobody missed when he disappeared. So we're going to see if we can nail something down. We're starting with Catt's next-door neighbor—Hattie's husband, Horton LaFleur."

CHAPTER 31

"**I HAVE TO** make a quick pit stop," Kylie said when we left Cates's office. "Get the car and meet me outside."

"It must be nice to have your own car and driver," I said, never missing an opportunity to do a little ballbusting. "Just like Police Commissioner Harries."

"Not really," she said. "I met the PC's driver, and he knows how to keep his mouth shut."

She headed for the ladies' room, and I was walking down the front steps of the precinct house when it happened.

Ambush.

He came from behind a parked minivan—Damon Parker, Evelyn Parker-Steele's brother.

If there were ever a contest for Most Hated Man in America, Damon Parker would enter, then campaign hard to win. When he was growing up, his heartless bastard of a father must have pounded home the message that nice guys finish last, because Damon had made a career in TV news as a guy who was anything but nice.

He was better known for his sneak-attack, in-your-face confrontations than he was for his journalistic integrity, and judging by the camera crew behind him, I was about to be his next victim.

"Detective Jordan," Parker bellowed—not so much at me as to the unseen audience who would watch him rake me over the coals later tonight. "The people want to know!"

That was his catchphrase and the title of his syndicated TV show: *The People Want to Know*.

My catchphrase is *I don't give a shit what the people want to know*, but the Public Information Office frowns on cops who blurt out what they're thinking on camera.

I kept walking toward the car, but Parker and his crew cut me off.

"The people want to know," he thundered as if he were a block away instead of thrusting a microphone in my face, "why their tax dollars are funding a police force of thirty-five thousand, and yet NYPD Red, Blue, or any other color have been unable to track down the monster who savagely tortured and murdered four innocent victims."

"No comment," I said.

"No comment is a comment, isn't it, people?" he barked to the faithful who tuned in to hear him rant on a nightly basis. "Of course he won't talk. He's been muzzled by the mayor. And do you want to know why? Because there is a fifth victim. A victim that Mayor Spellman in his desperate attempt to cling to a job he has failed at refuses to share with you. Can you at least comment on victim number five, Detective?"

Victim number five? The man was a master of manipulation. I'm trained not to get sucked in, and it was all I could do not to take the bait.

"I can't comment on an ongoing investigation," I said. Politely. Just the way I was taught.

"Then let me tell the people what the mayor doesn't want them to know," he said. "This fiend—this Hazmat ogre has been terrorizing New Yorkers to the point that many of them have barricaded themselves behind closed doors. I've been to Astoria, to Bensonhurst, to Kew Gardens, and the people are so afraid to come out at night that the small businesses in those neighborhoods are suffering. The restaurants go empty. Mom-and-pop stores that count on the locals have been forced to shut down. The fifth victim is the economy of the city of New York."

It was pure bullshit, but it was brilliant. He was campaigning for Sykes and using me as his stooge. I did my best to navigate past him without shoving. I'm sure he would have loved it if I got physical. Nice piece of police brutality footage if he could get it.

And then Kylie came through the front door of the precinct.

One of the things they teach you at the academy is this: *Sometimes the press will resort to desperate measures, attacking the officer or the department with inflammatory statements in an effort to provoke an emotional response. Do not react. Maintain your composure and continue to be assertive but polite.*

I've always done my best to steer clear of any confrontation with the media, but I'm sure that my partner, if she'd even heard the mandate, had decided that compliance was optional.

"Damon," she yelled from the top of the stairs.

Kylie and I travel in completely different circles. As the wife of a producer, she gets to meet a lot of people in the TV business, and it was clear that she knew Parker.

Parker turned, and Kylie charged down the steps. "What in God's name are you doing, Damon?"

The matador had waved the red cape.

The bull advanced cautiously. "What am *I* doing?" Parker said.

All that was missing was the sound of the crowd screaming, "Olé!"

"I'm seeking the truth," he said. "The people want to know the truth, Detective MacDonald, and I'm the one they depend on to bring it to them. That's what I'm doing. It's what I always do. Only this time it's personal. My sister was murdered, and I want her killer brought to justice."

He had used up his fifth victim crap on me, and suddenly he had morphed into the grieving brother.

"Are you even *looking* for my sister's killer?" he said, trying to drive one of his trademark verbal stilettos right through her. "Or have you been instructed to fan the flames of Evelyn's so-called confession and brand her as a murderer in an effort to tarnish the candidate that my dear sister so deeply believed in?"

It doesn't get much more inflammatory than that. Parker was pulling out all the stops. He had tried to piss me off, but I didn't bite. Kylie was another story. Kylie was a biter.

The cameraman spun around to catch her reaction, and she stared straight into the lens. Ms. MacDonald was ready for her close-up.

"You don't want justice. The *last* thing you want is for us to find out who murdered Evelyn. You're not after the killer. You're after the cops and the mayor. All you're doing is exploiting your sister's murder to boost your ratings. That's why you're standing in our way. I have one final question for you, Damon. How the hell can you live with yourself?" she yelled. *"The people want to know."*

She didn't wait for an answer. She bolted into the front seat and slammed the door. Parker was screaming at the camera as I peeled out.

Kylie is a rule breaker. Not only does she break them, but she seems to revel in the wreckage.

"So," she said, giving me a big-ass grin, "how'd I do? You think I have a future in television?"

"Beats the shit out of me," I said, heading up 67th to Park Avenue. "But after that public pissing contest, I'm just hoping you have a future as a cop."

CHAPTER 32

THE UPPER EAST Side of Manhattan is one of the city's most affluent neighborhoods. But unlike residents of LA's Bel Air, our rich folks don't have the room to build sprawling homes on magnificent grounds. New York real estate is vertical, so even a twenty-million-dollar apartment can easily go unnoticed when it's part of a forty-story highrise.

What does stand out is the not-so-affluent housing, like the five-story prewar brownstone on East 84th Street between First and York. It was flanked by a dry cleaner on one side and a two-hundred-unit apartment building on the other, and the fading facade was covered by one of those classic paint-flaked fire escapes that are mounted to the city's older low-rise, low-rent buildings.

That's where we found Horton LaFleur, a man who

was obviously bringing down the per capita income in his well-to-do zip code.

We rang the bell in the vestibule of his building, identified ourselves, and walked to apartment 1A—ground floor, front. The man who opened the front door was over six feet tall, gaunt, and pulling a portable oxygen tank cylinder behind him.

"Emphysema," LaFleur said, explaining it away in a grunt. "Come in."

The living room was compact. It had to be. Except for a tiny kitchen and bathroom, it was the only room he had. There was a daybed that doubled as a sofa, a dining table that doubled as a desk, and on the wall above it a framed Military Order of the Purple Heart award.

My eyes went right to it. "Thank you for your service," I said.

He nodded. "Nam."

That was all. Just a single syllable that let us know he was proud of the sacrifice he'd made for his country but had no interest in talking about it.

One corner of the room was cluttered with plastic bins filled with old telephones, wires, and a lineman's leather tool belt.

"I was a pole climber for the phone company," LaFleur said. "First it was New York Tel, then Bell Atlantic, then they became Verizon. Same shit, different patch on your shirt pocket."

I reached into one of the boxes and pulled out a pink rotary-dial Princess phone. "You don't see many of these anymore," I said.

"That's an early version of the 701B, very popular with teenage girls. It was so light that it would slide around when they would dial, so in the newer version we added a chunk of lead to weigh it down."

"Is it worth anything?" I said.

"Only to me. Don't go thinking I stole any of this crap. It's all junk, but that's how it goes with us phone monkeys. You have your hands on this equipment all day long, and when something gets phased out you just want to hold on to one or two. Hattie used to say all phone guys are pack rats. But it's part of my history. I used to have more, but I gave some of it up when we moved to this dump. I hate it, but it's all we could afford, and it was walking distance to her job."

There was a framed black-and-white photo of a bride and groom on the desk. It was Horton and Hattie, decades before the oxygen tank and the brutal murder.

Kylie picked it up. "She was beautiful. We're sorry for your loss."

"But somehow I doubt that's why you're here," LaFleur said, his voice devoid of emotion.

"We're investigating the murder of Sebastian Catt," she said.

"Why?" he asked.

"We're homicide cops. It's what we do."

"I know what you do, missy," he said. "But why are you doing it here? Some vigilante kilt him and made a video so the whole world would know that Catt deserved it. End of story."

"Not for us," Kylie said. "Catt was last seen at his photo

studio on Eighty-Seventh Street. His assistant says he went home at around six. His mailbox was empty, so we're pretty sure he came home that evening. There was evidence in his apartment that he made himself some dinner, but then he disappeared. You live next door. We thought you might be able to corroborate that you saw or heard him come home, or maybe you heard him when he left."

LaFleur shook his head. "I didn't."

"Are you sure you didn't hear *anything?*" Kylie said.

"My answer is I didn't," he said. "But even if I did, I wouldn't tell you. That pervert bastard murdered my wife. It was just nine days before our fiftieth wedding anniversary. Nine days. I told her not to agree to testify."

His breathing became labored, and he sucked deeply on his oxygen.

"We understand how you feel about Catt," Kylie said. "But withholding evidence is a felony."

He laughed. "You got no clue how I feel. As for your felony threat, that's the laugh. There's this Hazmat Killer on the loose, and you cops are supposed to find him. It's gonna look real good on your report cards if the only guy you arrest is a Vietnam vet whose wife was murdered, and who does the perp walk dragging this iron lung behind him."

He held out his hands. "Go ahead, missy," he challenged. "Cuff me."

Kylie pulled back. "Horton," she said. "May I call you Horton?"

He looked at her, his eyes blazing with rage. "No. You and I are not on a first-name basis."

"Fair enough," Kylie said. "Mr. LaFleur, we're not here to arrest you, but there is a vigilante killer out there, and—"

"How old are you?" LaFleur said.

"Thirty-four."

"You're not old enough to remember Bernie Goetz, are you," he said. "It was back in the eighties. He got beat up something fierce at a subway station by three punk kids. An off-duty cop jumped in and managed to grab one of them, but the other two got away. The kid that got arrested spent half as much time in the police station as Goetz. Half the time—and then, all they charged this little shit bucket with was criminal mischief for ripping Goetz's jacket. After that, Goetz applied to the city for a handgun permit. Went through proper channels, and guess what happened."

"His application was turned down," Kylie said.

"Right," LaFleur said. "A couple of years later, Goetz is on another subway, and *four* young hoods try to mug him again. Only this time, he's ready. Fuck the permit. Goetz has got himself a thirty-eight. Bang, bang, bang, bang—he shoots all four of them."

"It's a famous case, Mr. LaFleur," Kylie said. "I'm well aware of it."

"Then you know the ending," he said. "One kid winds up in a wheelchair. The other three all recover from their wounds and go back to a life of crime—robbery, rape, you name it. But Goetz—that poor bastard was convicted of criminal possession of a weapon and did time in jail. Now you tell me, Detectives—who's the bad guy, and who's the victim?"

We didn't answer. He really wasn't looking for one.

"Bernie Goetz was called the Subway Vigilante," LaFleur said, "and a lot of people vilified him. Not me. Me—I thought he was a hero. Same goes for the guy who killed Sebastian Catt. Believe me, if I was twenty years younger, and if I could breathe without this damn anchor I carry around, I'd have killed the bastard myself."

He picked up his wedding photo and stared at his wife of fifty years minus nine days.

"That's all I got to say," he said, jerking his head up and gesturing toward the door. "You can go."

Out of habit, I dropped my card on the spot where the picture had been.

It would probably be in the garbage before Kylie and I made it to the car.

CHAPTER 33

"HE KNOWS SOMETHING," Kylie said as soon as we were out of earshot.

"One thing he knows is how to get you to back off...*missy*," I said.

"I cut the crusty old codger some slack because he's a veteran and his wife was murdered," she said. "If he were forty years younger, I wouldn't have been so nice."

"And yet as nice as you were, you and Horton are still not on a first-name basis."

She shrugged. "Okay, I may have pushed his buttons a little too hard, but you have to admit he knows something."

"He knows a lot more than something," I said. "Did you see all that equipment—boxes of phones, cords, cable, wiring, installer tools? Maybe he really is sentimental about all that old crap, but there was more in those boxes than phone nostalgia."

"Like what?"

"Like when I dug my hand into that one box and pulled out the Princess phone, I saw a piece of equipment that didn't come from Ma Bell or any phone company he ever worked for," I said. "It was made by Shenzhen Adika, and they don't make cute little pink telephones for teenagers. They're in China, cranking out high-tech audio and video surveillance systems you can buy at any one of those spy shop websites."

"Son of a bitch," Kylie said. "He was bugging Catt's apartment?"

"Think about it. He's positive that Catt murdered his wife. How hard would it be for a guy like LaFleur who installed phones all his life to wire Catt's apartment, hoping he could pick up something that would connect Catt to Hattie's murder?"

"If you're right, we should search Catt's apartment," Kylie said. "We wouldn't even need a warrant. It's still sealed. It's part of the ongoing investigation."

"We can get in there easy enough," I said, "but we won't find anything. Whatever LaFleur put in there, he disassembled as soon as Catt disappeared. It's gone, and even if we did find a bug in that apartment, we can't prove LaFleur installed it, and we certainly can't get him to talk."

"Do you think he knows the guy—or the guys—who killed Catt?" Kylie said.

"No, but he probably could help us find out who did," I said.

"But he won't," Kylie said. "As far as he's concerned, the Hazmat Killer is every bit as heroic as Bernie Goetz."

"He's not alone," I said. "A lot of people in this city are rooting for Hazmat. He—they—who knows how many there are? All people know is that he's killing scumbags who got away with murder. Hell...they've even given him a fan page on Facebook. They love him."

"Then they sure as hell are going to hate us," Kylie said. "Because we're the ones who are going to bring him down."

That's the thing about Kylie. Nothing rattles her confidence. Certainly not a crusty old codger like Horton LaFleur.

CHAPTER 34

"WHERE TO NEXT?" I said, getting behind the wheel of the Interceptor.

"The two choices are at opposite ends of Manhattan," Kylie said. "Victim number one was Alex Kang—Chinatown. Or number three, Antoine Tinsdale—Harlem. Your call."

"Wherever we wind up, we're going to be closing in on lunch, and as much as I love Marcus Samuelsson's Red Rooster up in Harlem, I haven't had good dim sum since the Year of the Monkey."

"Done deal," Kylie said, giving me a thumbs-up.

"Whoever said police work was difficult?" I said, heading toward the FDR Drive.

"Speaking of monkeys, Chinatown is Donovan and Boyle's regular beat," Kylie said. "They've been working out of the Five for years. You would think that as sloppy as their reports were, their file on Kang would be the one they'd get right. But according to their notes, they only talked to one guy."

"I saw that. They probably talked to more, but they only named one in their report. Those two coppers are not big on paperwork."

"That would just mean they're lazy," Kylie said. "But did you see the name of the person they interviewed?"

I laughed. "Yeah, I did."

"It's not funny, Zach. They obviously didn't give a shit, and they probably never thought someone else would be taking over the case."

"I'll take the drive down to the Brooklyn Bridge exit," I said. "Give me the exact address in Chinatown."

"I can give you what they wrote in their report," she said. "Who knows if those numbnuts got it right? All they wrote down was 'CP Emperors gang HQ—Fifty-Eight Mulberry.'"

"And remind me again," I said, busting her chops. "What's the name of the guy they interviewed?"

She opened one of the files and pretended to look through it. "Let's see," she said, playing along and milking the situation for all it was worth. "Oh, here it is. According to their flawless record keeping, Detectives Donovan and Boyle interviewed a gangbanger named John Doe."

CHAPTER 35

THE CP EMPERORS headquarters was on the ground floor of a squat redbrick building in the heart of the Chinese community. It looked relatively innocuous, but clearly it was a fortress. The windows were barred, a rolled-up metal security gate spanned the front, and the entry door was solid steel. The only thing missing was a moat.

Kylie pounded on the front door. "NYPD," she yelled. Then she turned to me. "I think we should identify ourselves, just in case they can't figure out who the white couple pulling up to their building in an unmarked cop car is."

The door opened, and a sallow-faced Chinese gangbanger blocked our path. He was dressed in black, which is normally a slimming color, but it did nothing to hide his three hundred pounds. He filled the doorway.

"NYPD," I repeated. "Who's in charge?"

"You got a warrant?"

"Why would we need a warrant? We're just here to talk."

"We got nothing to talk about. Now get the fuck out of here."

And then we heard it coming from the other side of the door. Loud, clear, and unmistakable. *Click. Clack.* The distinct sound of someone racking the slide of a gun, most likely a semiautomatic.

Kylie didn't hesitate. She reached behind her right hip and drew her Glock. "Down on the floor!" she yelled. She didn't wait for a response.

She jerked her right foot straight between Fat Boy's legs and hit paydirt. He grabbed his balls, doubled over, and dropped like a canary in a coal mine.

I had no idea how many CP Emperors were in there, and I had no interest in finding out. I drew my gun and yelled from behind the door, "NYPD! Weapons down. Weapons down—now!"

I braced for the first shot to be fired and hoped the door was thick enough.

"Bullshit," said a voice from the other side. "You got no right to pull guns on us."

"Don't tell us what we can't do," Kylie yelled back. "As soon as that asshole racked the slide on that semi, we stopped needing a warrant. Exigent circumstances. Toss them. Now."

"All right, all right." I heard the gun slide across the floor. Then another. "I'm coming to the door. Move your fat ass, Rupert."

Still holding his crotch, the big guy slid out of the way, and a tall, long-haired Asian kid opened the door wide. He was about twenty-two, with a wispy mustache and a permanent scowl on his face.

"You in charge?" I asked.

"Most of the time," he said. "Except right now it looks like you're in charge."

"What's your name?" I said.

"John Doe," he said without disturbing the scowl.

"We already have plenty of guys named John Doe in the morgue waiting to be identified," I said. "How about your real name."

"John Dho," he repeated. "D-h-o. You're in Chinatown, dude."

So it turned out that Donovan and Boyle actually did know who they talked to. They just couldn't spell.

"This is a house of mourning. What do you want?"

"We understand, and we're sorry for your loss, but we still need to talk. Here or at the precinct?" I said.

"You can come in," Dho said. "The bitch stays outside."

"The bitch either comes in," Kylie said, "or she marches you out the door and parades you down Mulberry, screaming at you the whole way until we get to our car, which we parked two blocks from here."

"Bullshit. You're parked across the street."

"Then I'd have to march you back. I don't give a shit about your 'No girls allowed in the clubhouse' rules. I yelled 'NYPD,' and somebody in here locked and loaded a semi—which I'm sure you have a license for."

He stepped aside and let us in. "What do you want here?"

"We're looking for the person who killed Alex Kang," I said.

Dho was smoking a hand-rolled cigarette that smelled like the inside of a stable. He blew a lungful of smoke our way. "So are we," he said, "but we can do it without your help."

"Let's talk about it," I said.

The room was dimly lit and sparsely furnished. Two tumbledown sofas, a smattering of Formica-topped tables, and a mismatched assortment of folding chairs. One corner at the far end was a makeshift kitchen.

"Nice digs," Kylie said. "Clearly fit for an emperor."

"Tell us about the day Alex went missing," I said.

"He was hanging here till about eleven in the morning. He left to go visit his grandmother—she was in Beekman Downtown Hospital. When he didn't come back by two, we started calling him. No answer. I went to the hospital. His mother was there. She said he never came. We checked his apartment, all his usual hangouts—nothing. Six days later, he shows up in a Hazmat suit on a bench in the Canal Street subway station. I already told all this to those two doughnut commandos."

"Who are we talking about?" I said.

"*Defective* Donovan and *Defective* Boyle. They hassle the shit out of us all the time. Even when we're the victims."

"So you knew Donovan and Boyle before Alex was killed."

"Yeah, we all know them. They work this area. 'Youth Patrol.'"

"Did they have a beef with Alex?" Kylie asked.

Dho looked at her as though she were clueless.

"They're racists. They hate all the CPEs—only they shit on Alex even more because he was in charge. Do you really think those two cops are looking for the person who killed Alex?"

"I don't know about them, but I can promise you that these two cops really are looking for the killer. So as long as we're all on the same side, how's your investigation going?"

"It's none of the other gangs," Dho said.

"Are you sure?" Kylie said, asking the same question that got her in trouble with LaFleur.

Dho put his palms together and bowed his head. "Most sure, Honorable Detective. Our investigation very thorough," he said, purposely omitting the verb—a dead-on imitation of Charlie Chan, the classic Asian stereotype churned out by the Hollywood studios in the thirties and forties.

He stood up and dropped the act. "You cops are all full of shit," he said, the scowl firmly back in place. "When this Hazmat asshole killed Alex, you send in Detectives Dumb and Dumber. But now that he whacked some rich white lady, you're all over it like—how you round eyes say?—'white on rice.' You want to know who killed my best friend, Alex Kang? There's some freaky guy out there who thinks he's some kind of fucking savior, and he's doing his part to make this city a safer place to live. Here, you can read all about it in today's paper."

There was a newspaper on the table. He picked it up and shoved it toward me.

It was all in Chinese. The only thing I could understand was the picture of Evelyn Parker-Steele on the front page.

CHAPTER 36

"**I HAD CAUSE** to draw my weapon," Kylie said as soon as we were back outside. "As soon as I heard that semi—"

"Hey, no arguments from me," I said. "I was right behind you. I didn't agree with the way you handled Damon Parker this morning, but kicking Odd Job in the balls was spot-on. Nice work, partner."

She looked surprised. "Thanks."

"You really are a bitch," I said. "And I mean that in the nicest possible way."

We stood outside the building, absorbing the unique sights, smells, and sounds of Chinatown—this little enclave that is home to some and a tourist destination for many.

"I don't get it," Kylie said. "Alex Kang walks out of here at eleven o'clock in the morning. How does he just disappear? It's a little after eleven now, and look—there are people all over the street, cars are going in and out of the garage next door, somebody had to see something."

She looked right to left, slowly panning Mulberry Street.

"Don't strain yourself trying to pick out the surveillance cameras," I said. "This is gang territory. Whatever may have been here was probably vandalized long ago."

"Then maybe we'll have to rely on human surveillance," she said, pointing to the other side of the street.

Directly across from the gang's headquarters was Columbus Park. It's the only park in Chinatown, so of course the city named it after an Italian explorer. Even so, it's the CP in CP Emperors.

"The park is jumping," Kylie said. "The same people probably come here every day to read the paper, walk the dog, roller-skate. At the risk of repeating myself—somebody had to see something."

"Somebody did," I said. "The problem is going to be getting them to talk about it."

We crossed the street to the park entrance, where a dozen Chinese men from twenty-something to eighty-something were grouped in a semicircle, chain-smoking and watching two men hunched over a makeshift table. They were playing Go, the two-thousand-year-old Chinese board game.

I'm a gamer. My father got me started on backgammon when I was six. Then chess, and along the way, I got hooked on Go. The rules are so simple that anyone can learn the game in ten minutes, but the strategies are so infinitely complex that few can master it in a lifetime. And it's totally addictive, not only to play, but to watch.

I studied the two players—one in his sixties, the other a decade or more older than that. These were not men who could afford the traditional board made of seasoned wood cut from the kaya tree. They were playing on a piece of rough-cut plywood with hand-drawn squares. And instead of using the classic stones made of highly polished Japanese slate and clamshell, their black and white game pieces were a few bucks' worth of genuine Chinese plastic.

But the passion, the concentration, and, of course, the competitive spirit were genuine and authentic. One of the things that makes Go such a fascinating spectator sport is the wagering, and there were two ten-dollar bills on the table. I looked over the board, and clearly the older man had the edge. Within five minutes, he won the game and scooped up the money.

"You're good," I called out to the old man.

He bowed his head.

"I'm better," I said.

The crowd, who had not spoken a word of English, obviously understood enough of it to laugh out loud.

"You have money?" the old man asked. "Or you just have mouth?"

He put a ten-dollar bill on the table.

I opened up my wallet, pulled out a hundred-dollar bill, and laid it next to his ten. The crowd let out a collective guttural sound—the male Chinese version of *oooh*.

"*You* have money?" I said. "Or *you* just have mouth?"

The old man reflected for a few seconds, then dug

into his pants pocket and came up with a bunch of tens, fives, and ones. Not enough. He stuffed it back in his pocket and opened an ancient wallet with an equally ancient hundred-dollar bill inside. He unfolded the bill and placed it next to mine.

I sat down.

I was black and went first. There's an ancient Go proverb: *Play fast, lose fast.* And to his credit, the old man treated me with respect from the start. He played thoughtfully—not as if I were some loudmouthed white guy ready to be relieved of a hundred bucks, but as if I were truly a worthy opponent. After five minutes, he realized that I was.

The game lasted almost an hour. Neither of us dominated, and the highly partisan crowd went silent as we approached the endgame.

And then I made one bad move. Not just bad. Dumb. Really dumb. I knew it, the old man knew it, and he knew I knew it. His fingertips tugged at a few wispy gray hairs on his chin, and he stared at me, puzzled at first, and then it came to him.

I was throwing the game.

He snapped a white stone down on the board, and the crowd erupted with laughter, applause, and home team pride.

He won.

I stood up and turned to the platoon of smokers that had tripled in size since I'd set down the first stone.

"I am good," I told them. "He is better."

They clapped and hooted, and once again I bowed to

the victor. "This game has left me very hungry," I said. "Where would I go to get the best dim sum?"

The old man smiled. "Best dim sum? My mother's house. Guangdong Province. But I think I take all your carfare."

The group yucked it up again at my expense.

The old man reveled in it. "But if you willing to settle for not-so-bad dim sum, go to New Wonton Garden across street."

I bowed again, nodded to Kylie, and we headed toward the restaurant.

Like I said, I'm a gamer, and I had just invested a hundred bucks and an hour of Kylie's time and mine playing a mind game with an old man I'd never seen before.

Now I had to sit patiently in the New Wonton Garden, sipping tea, eating not-so-bad dim sum, and waiting to find out which one of us had won the game.

CHAPTER 37

TERESA SALVI TOOK off her robe and looked at herself in the full-length mirror. "Sixty-three years old and still a size four," she said. "Not bad."

Her closet was as big as a master bedroom, and there was a second one just like it. This closet was for daytime wear. She walked through the racks of dresses and pulled out a Dolce & Gabbana midi—charcoal gray. She had stopped wearing black years ago, but she was going to see Father Spinelli, and the dark gray would make the right statement—*still in mourning, but moving on with her life.*

The shoes and the bag were Prada, and when she finished dressing, she took another look in the mirror. Joe would approve. He wanted her to dress classy—not like those rich bimbo housewives on the reality shows.

She made sure her checkbook was in her purse. Father

Spinelli had asked her to join him for tea in his study, and that could mean only one thing. The church needed money.

"No more than ten grand," Joe told her as she was leaving the house. "It's October, and you know he's going to hit us up again at Christmas."

Teresa already had a higher number in her mind, so she just kissed her husband and said, "Don't worry. Whatever I give will be for a good cause."

Two good causes, she thought as she drove her beige Buick Regal the mile and a half to St. Agnes. Joe sometimes forgot the respectability factor. The newspapers always painted her husband like some kind of monster. But every time he donated to the church, Father Spinelli was out there spreading the word to the congregation about how generous the Salvi family was. It helped balance things out.

She parked in one of the visitor spaces, turned off the engine, and took the black rosary beads from her purse.

She loved this church, but sometimes she couldn't face going back. This was where Enzo was christened. And eighteen years later, this was where she'd last set eyes on his sweet face before returning him home to Jesus.

She prayed for Enzo's soul, then checked her hair and makeup in the mirror, locked the car, and walked toward the rectory.

The secretary escorted her to Father Spinelli's study, and he stood up as soon as she entered the room. He had been a strikingly handsome man when he'd joined the parish at the age of twenty-eight—too good-looking to be celibate, some women said. But now, having just turned fifty, he had evolved into the heart and soul of St. Agnes. People turned to him, respected him, loved him—none more than Teresa Salvi.

"Teresa," Father Spinelli said, giving her a warm, priestly hug. "I hope all is well with you and Joe."

The room was small, and the walnut-paneled walls, the heavy furniture, and the dim lighting made it feel even smaller—but intimate, not confining. Teresa took her usual seat on the well-worn leather chair on the other side of his desk.

"Joe and I are doing fine. And how are things here at St. Agnes?" She clutched her purse, ready to take out her checkbook.

"Everything is going remarkably well," he said, pouring her a cup of tea. "The plumbing, the heating, the electrical—all working, all up to code. It confirms my belief in miracles."

She put her purse on the floor. "Then why did you... why did you ask me to stop by?"

"Have I been that transparent? Only inviting you for tea when we are in need of a benefactor? Forgive me."

"Father, you never have to apologize for reaching out to my family on behalf of the church. How can we help?"

He poured half a cup of tea for himself. "Teresa, I didn't invite you here to ask for your help. It's my turn to help you."

She was confused. "With what?"

"I have something I need to give you. Something precious, something personal." He paused and took a sip of tea. "I know it will open up old wounds, but you're a strong woman, Teresa. I've seen it time and again, and I know your faith will see you through."

"See me through what?"

He opened his desk drawer and took out a brown manila envelope.

"This belonged to your late son, Enzo, God rest his soul," he said, passing the envelope across the desk.

Her hand trembled, and her heart raced as she took the envelope.

"Go ahead," he said softly. "Open it."

She tore the top off the envelope and removed the contents.

"It's Enzo's diary," she said, tears welling in her eyes. She ran her fingers gently over the dark red Moroccan leather journal bordered in gold filigree. "I gave it to him when he was thirteen. He carried it all the time. Where did you get this?"

"One of our parishioners brought it to me. She was cleaning house and found it among her son's things. I knew as painful as it might be for you to have this, it must be God's will that it turned up after all these years, and I hope you will find some comfort in having this little piece of your son returned to you."

What parishioner? Where did she find it? Teresa had a million questions. But she was well schooled in the family business. She knew not to ask a single one of them.

Run home. Talk to Joe. He'll know how to handle this.

CHAPTER 38

THE DIM SUM at the New Wonton Garden may not have been the best I'd ever eaten, but it was several notches up from the old man's description of "not so bad." Of course, I'd never been to Guangdong Province, so when it comes to Chinese cuisine, my Go buddy and I have two completely different sets of standards.

"There's one left," I said to Kylie, who had spent most of the meal sitting across from me, watching me eat.

"You finish it," she said. "I'm pretty full."

"Yeah. Three pot stickers can fill a girl right up," I said, and bit into the last shrimp dumpling.

"I'm not that hungry," she said, rubbing her thumb across the face of her iPhone.

"Do you want to call him?" I said.

"Who?"

"Kylie, I'm not trying to butt into your life, but yesterday Spence wound up in the ER because he was getting high on pills, and this morning you left before you saw him, so when I say 'Do you want to call him?' I'm talking about your husband, who you seem to be very concerned about. So, I repeat—do you want to call him?"

"No. My focus is on this case."

It was not a conversation I wanted to go any further, and as good fortune had it, the front door of the restaurant opened and the old man entered.

Kylie grinned. "You were right. He's here."

He walked to our table and sat down. "You crooked cop," he said.

"How do you know I'm a cop?" I asked.

The old man laughed. "How you know I am Chinese? You look at my eyes. I look in your eyes, and I know you a cop. A crooked cop. You cheat. Let me win."

With that he put my hundred-dollar bill on the table. Then he took his hundred and put it next to mine.

"I am happy to save face. But I can't take money I don't earn." He pushed the two bills toward me.

I stared at them for a few seconds, then slid them back across the table. "Then maybe you can earn it. Did you see Alex Kang the day he disappeared?"

The old man didn't hesitate for a second. He had done all his deliberating before he walked through the door. He knew what this was about, and he'd showed up to finish playing the game.

"Kang no good," he said. "He come out of clubhouse, two men in car waiting. One get out of car, talk to Kang.

Kang get in car. Last time anyone in Chinatown see him alive."

A witness. We had scored a witness. I stole a look at Kylie. She was stone-faced. She knew better than to utter a word. The old man would not be comfortable talking to a woman.

"Can you describe the men?" I asked.

"I only see one. White...big like you. Too far away to see his face."

"How about the car?"

"It was truck-car."

"Was it a truck or a car?" I said calmly.

"No," the old man said. He stood up and gestured for me to follow him to the front of the restaurant. Kylie stayed put.

"It was truck-car like that," he said, pointing out the window to an SUV parked on the street. "Only that one silver. The one that come for Kang is black."

We walked back to the table. I sat down, but he remained standing.

"Thank you. You earned this," I said, pointing to the two hundred.

He obviously agreed. He scooped up the money and gave us both a quick head bow. "Happy you get your money worth. Thank you. I go."

"One more thing," I said. "You've been very helpful. What's your name, old man?"

He grinned. "This Chinatown. You NYPD. Better you just call me old man."

CHAPTER 39

"SHOULD I WRITE this all down?" Kylie said. "Our witness's name is Old Man, and the gangbanger we interviewed was John Doe. We're almost as good as Donovan and Boyle."

The waiter cleared the table, then brought us the check along with fresh tea and a bowlful of fortune cookies.

"I guess any friend of the old man rates more than one cookie apiece," Kylie said. She picked one out of the bowl, cracked it open, read it, and nodded. "Hmm, very perceptive."

"What does it say?" I asked.

"Partner think he very smart cop, but you know better."

"Are you saying you don't appreciate my investigative genius?"

"No, I thought you were brilliant. I just think the cookie doesn't want it to go to your head."

I picked up the check. "I'll pay for lunch. I ate most of it."

Kylie snatched it from my hand. "You already paid a hundred bucks for the old man. I'll buy lunch."

We walked outside and stood in front of the restaurant. Neither of us was ready to get in the car.

"I don't get it," Kylie said, staring at the park across the street. "Two victims, Alex Kang and Evelyn Parker-Steele—polar opposites. In each case, two people pull up in a black SUV, and one of them—a white male—just says something like 'Get in the car,' and the victim gets in. We can't find a single common denominator between Kang and Parker-Steele, but they both must have known the guy who pulled up, because they both got in the car without an argument."

And just like that, a ton of bricks fell on my head.

"Holy shit," I said. "I'm an idiot."

"Two minutes ago you said you were an investigative genius. Now you're an idiot. When do I get to vote?"

"Shut up and listen. I think we've been looking for the wrong common denominator. We've got four victims—a gangbanger, a political heavyweight, a drug dealer, and a sex offender. We've been trying to figure out what's the connection—how do they all know the two men in the SUV? But what if the one thing they have in common is that *none* of the victims know these two guys?"

"Then none of them get in the car."

"You see that guy over there—the one with the jeans and the gray sweatshirt?" I said, pointing across the street to a young Chinese man on a park bench, tapping on his cell phone. "You don't know him, and he doesn't know you. Now, how do you get him to jump in your car—no questions asked?"

Kylie shrugged. "He looks pretty straight, so I don't know—take my top off?"

"Pretend I'm serious," I said. "*You*. How do *you* get a total stranger into your car?"

"Come on, Zach, I'm a cop. I just flash my—"

And then the ton of bricks fell on Kylie's head.

"Oh my God," she said. "They're posing as cops. Two guys in a black SUV. All they have to do is flash a phony ID or a fake piece of tin—who would even question it?"

"You think I'm right?"

"Detective Jordan, I not only think you're right," she said, "I'm going right back into this restaurant and find a fortune cookie that says 'My partner is a fucking genius.'"

PART TWO

THE CHOKE PEAR

CHAPTER 40

"**SHUT THE DOOR,** cowgirl," Cates said, glaring at us from her desk.

Apparently, our boss had heard about Kylie's run-in with Damon Parker.

We entered Cates's office, and Kylie closed the door.

"Are you under the impression, Detective MacDonald, that I don't have enough bullshit on my plate, and that I need you to generate more?"

"I'm sorry, Captain," Kylie said. "It's just that Damon Parker is such an asshole that I—"

"Damon Parker is a professional asshole," Cates said. "You behaved like an amateur. He's paid to get in people's faces. You're paid to avoid embarrassing the department on camera."

"It won't happen again," Kylie said.

"Of course it will," Cates snapped back. "Breaking the rules is in your DNA. But I'll tell you what won't happen again, and that's me cleaning up after your mess and letting you off the hook. If there weren't a serial killer on the loose, I'd chain you to your desk for a month."

She turned to me. "Jordan, fill me in. Start with Horton LaFleur. Did he cough up anything?"

"The poor bastard has emphysema," I said. "God knows what he coughed up, but none of it was information. He seems to be president of the Bernie Goetz Fan Club, so whatever he may know, he won't use it against a vigilante."

Then I took her through our visit to Chinatown. Her eyebrows arched slightly when I told her we had drawn our weapons at the gang headquarters.

Kylie jumped in. "Captain, they drew first. It was a clear-cut case of exigent—"

"They're bangers," Cates said, waving her off. "As long as you didn't pull your gun on Parker, I don't give a damn."

What she did give a damn about was my theory that the two killers might be posing as cops.

"I've seen it before," she said. "I was working Robbery out of the Three Two. One guy with a silver tongue and a fake piece of tin. He talked his way into sixteen apartments before we collared him."

"It's only a guess," I said. "But it would help explain how the kidnappers got both Kang and Parker-Steele into a car without a struggle."

"Talk to me about Hazmat victim number three—and no, I haven't read his file yet. Give me the executive summary."

"Antoine Tinsdale," I said. "African American, age thirty, a.k.a. the Tin Man. Some say it's a spin on his name, but most people think it was a *Wizard of Oz* thing—the Tin Man was the one who didn't have a heart. He was a drug dealer who liked to start them young. And the best way to hook a ten-year-old is to use ten-year-old runners."

Cates said nothing, but the anger in her eyes was palpable: she was an African American who grew up in Harlem.

"He had a network of underage kids working for him. The rival dealers warned them to back off, but the kids weren't street smart enough to be scared. Dope slingers are not known for their negotiating skills, so they whacked four of Antoine's baby-faced runners."

"And there's always a new crop just waiting to get in," Cates said.

"Tin Man kept so distant from these kids that it would be impossible to make any of their deaths stick to him. Even in his video confession he said, 'If these boys wound up dead because they got into a pissing contest over turf, it's not on me. A real jury would never convict me.'"

"He's right," Cates said. "A smart defense attorney would have beat it down to a cakewalk."

"That's probably what the killer thought, which is why Tinsdale wound up wearing a Tyvek jumpsuit under an exit ramp on the Harlem River Drive a half a block from a kids' playground. Kylie and I went there after school this afternoon."

Cates frowned. "And let me guess. The kids said even less than the old man with emphysema. Nobody heard nothing. Nobody saw nothing. Nobody knows nothing.

It's the code of the prepubescent black drug dealer. Growing up, I watched sociopaths like Tinsdale destroy young lives. I became a cop to get bastards like him off the street. And now a couple of vigilantes with a movie camera are doing it for me. You know what really sucks? It's my job to track these lunatics down and keep them from killing any more scumbags. These Hazmat boys got one thing right. There really is no justice."

There was a knock on the door.

"Come in," Cates called out.

It was Cheryl, looking every bit as beautiful as she had when I made an ass of myself at the diner this morning. "If you guys are having a group grope on Hazmat," she said, "can I join the group?"

"Absolutely," Cates said. "Jordan, give her your theory about the two men in the black SUV."

I spelled out my scenario of two killers luring their victims by posing as cops. "What do you think, Dr. Robinson?" I asked.

She smiled at me, and my brain jumped a few hours ahead to being alone with her at dinner, the wine warming us both. And then my testosterone took over, and my brain fast-forwarded to the two of us naked. She moaned and called out my name and said—

"What do I think, Detective Jordan?"

I snapped out of my fantasy.

"Right. That's what I asked. What do you think of my idea that the killers could be posing as cops?"

"I think it's a fascinating theory," Cheryl said, still smiling. "But I think you're wrong."

CHAPTER 41

GIDEON HAD BEEN the one who picked Alex Kang as their first houseguest.

A year earlier, Kang had tried to gun down Giap Phung, the leader of the rival Vietnamese gang NBK—Natural Born Killers. Kang had chased Phung into the Canal Street subway station and unloaded his Springfield nine-millimeter semiautomatic into the crowd. Phung got away, but Kang hit four bystanders. One of them, Jenny Woo, a beautiful young honors student at Hunter College, clung to life for ten days before she died.

Everybody knew Kang was the shooter. Jenny's parents begged someone—anyone—to come forward and identify him. But fingering a gangbanger was tantamount to suicide, so Kang walked.

Gideon convinced Dave that they should be the ones to avenge Jenny Woo's death.

"She was a college girl with her whole life ahead of her," Gideon said. "Just like your sister."

"I thought what we did was a onetime thing," Dave said.

"Maybe for you, but I've been thinking. We were sixteen when we killed Enzo. We had no idea what we were doing, and we were lucky that bastard didn't gut the two of us and feed our kidneys to his dog."

Dave nodded. It was his fault that Enzo had been able to pull a knife on them. If Gideon hadn't whacked him over the head with that bottle of vodka...

"Alex Kang is even more dangerous than Enzo," Gideon said. "He's what Enzo would have become if we hadn't killed him. But we're a lot smarter now, and this time we're not going to make any mistakes."

"I'm listening," Dave said.

Gideon laid out the plan.

"I really like the video confession part," Dave said. "Kind of wish we thought of that for Enzo. But scumbags like Kang don't confess in five minutes. We need a place to stash him. My cousin Todd has this old cabin he only uses in the summer. It's up in the Adirondacks."

Gideon shook his head. "When you're snatching someone like Alex Kang, you don't want to give him five hours in a car while you drive him upstate. Too much time for him to figure out how to get away. We need to keep him as close to home as possible. I'm thinking we can find something in Long Island City."

They spent a week scouting, driving past factories,

warehouses, and storage facilities, some occupied, some not. Then they found it—88 Crane Street—a graffiti-covered garage on a dead-end block that bordered the Long Island Rail Road rail yard.

It was not only an eyesore, it was an earsore, with diesel engines idling all day, drowning out any sounds that might remotely come through the thick walls.

"Not exactly a neighborhood that's going to attract people," Dave said.

It was six hundred square feet of cement block, mold, and rat droppings, with a corrugated metal garage door for vehicles and two wire-reinforced glass windows caked with decades of grime.

It had served them well for Kang and the three house-guests who followed. Now they were driving back to Crane Street to prep it for number five.

"You realize we're starting to cater to women," Dave said as they drove over the recently renamed Ed Koch Queensboro Bridge to Queens. "First Evelyn. Now Rachael O'Keefe. Looks like a trend. I think we should spruce the place up."

Gideon smiled. Dave was nervous, and the best way for him to cope was to make light of everything. Gideon played along. "Like how?"

"I don't know," Dave said. "I'm thinking lace curtains. Or maybe a mint on her pillow every night. Or how about a nice clean spackle can for her to shit in? Chicks dig those little amenities."

Dave could always make Gideon laugh, and today was no exception. "Enough comedy," Gideon said. "Let's get serious. The DA's office just let it leak that they're releasing O'Keefe tomorrow at noon."

"I thought they were going to turn her loose tonight."

"They are. The story they leaked is just bullshit to throw off the press and the picketers. Her sister, Liz, is picking her up at two a.m."

"Did Mer...did my..." Dave knew that Gideon was getting his information from Meredith. He hated the fact that she'd been dragged into it, but she was their only link to O'Keefe. The only way he could deal with it was to avoid talking about it. "Do you know where they're going?"

"Jersey. They have an aunt who spends half the year in Florida, and they're using her house."

"So we follow them, case the neighborhood, and figure out when to—"

"No," Gideon said. "There's no time for that. What happens if we're casing the neighborhood, and she packs up and moves to an undisclosed location—and I mean really undisclosed—one that Meredith can't point us to? The only thing we know for sure is where she's going tonight, which means we have to grab her tonight."

"Won't she have an escort on the trip to Jersey?"

"Definitely not," Gideon said. "According to my source, she has an escort as far as the front door, and then she's on her own. The city of New York won't spend another nickel on her. They're not bodyguards. As far as they're concerned, she's just some bitch who murdered her little girl and got away with it."

"Not for long," Dave said, a total convert to their mission. "Not for long."

CHAPTER 42

"WOULD YOU LIKE my take on the Hazmat Killer?" Cheryl asked. "Or as Zach pointed out—the Hazmat Killers."

"Cheryl," Cates said, "I'm happy to hear you even have a take. Shoot."

"Donald Li, the profiler Donovan and Boyle brought in, is a detective, not an analyst. Working with what he knew, he profiled the killer as white, male, strict parental upbringing, connected to fundamental religious principles. The killer expects God to punish wrongdoers, and when the offender slips through the cracks, our killer becomes the punisher. I have no argument with that, but it's pretty rudimentary, and won't get us very far.

"I have the advantage of working with two very smart detectives who figured out that these victims are not the type to simply jump into a car with two strangers unless it seems like they have no choice. Two men posing as cops could do it. But I think these guys did more than pose."

"Meaning what?" Cates said.

"Meaning they *think* like cops. They knew exactly how to track and kidnap their victims. They have a keen grasp of forensic techniques, and they know enough to leave no viable clues. They could be pretending to be cops, but they're so good at it, I think it's more likely that they're real cops. Or maybe ex-cops."

"Anybody who watches enough episodes of *CSI* has a keen grasp of forensics," Cates said. "It doesn't prove to me that real cops were involved."

"Captain, I can't prove anything. That's what your detectives do. My job is to study a pattern and come up with a profile. Based on the logistics of the crimes—kidnapping, torturing, transporting the victims' bodies—I agree with Zach and Kylie that this is the work of a team. Real cops work in teams."

Cates nodded. "I'm listening."

"I do a lot of one-on-one therapy sessions with cops—especially detectives. They bust their asses for months, even years, tracking down and locking up criminals who they are positive are guilty, and then for one reason or another, the bad guys go free. I don't have to tell you how frustrating that is to the arresting officer. I've done exit interviews with dozens of cops who resign or retire early because they're fed up with the justice system. More than a few have said to me, 'It was either quit the job, or one day I'm going to end up putting a bullet in the back of one of their heads.'"

"Most cops have thoughts like that," Cates said. "They don't act on it. If one bad guy gets away, they suck it up, go back out, and catch another."

"These killers don't think like that," Cheryl said. "They exhibit a brash level of confidence by leaving the body on public display. It's high risk, but they want the people of New York to know what they're doing. And then once they have our attention, they release the video. That to me is the key to their persona. The videos tell me that the killing is not their main goal."

"And what is their goal?"

"The confessions. Every video is telling John Q. Public that even though the police are smart enough to track down the murderers, the justice system will fail you and send them back on the street."

Cheryl stopped and took a deep breath. The more impassioned she had become, the louder she had gotten. "Captain," she said, lowering her voice and dialing down her excitement, "I hope for the sake of the department that these men are just a couple of impostors flashing a fake badge, but the more I think about it, the more I think they're the real deal. These men are not just killing people; they're making a statement. 'This due process shit doesn't work. It doesn't always punish the guilty. We do.'"

CHAPTER 43

IT WAS 8:30 by the time Cheryl and I got out of the office. I hailed a cab and told the driver to take us to 92nd and Madison.

"Where are we going to dinner?" she said.

"Paola's. Great Italian food," I said. *And hopefully I'll be so busy eating, I won't have time to put my foot in my mouth like I did at breakfast.*

The cabbie caught a light at 72nd, and Cheryl grabbed me and kissed me hard. "I've been wanting to do that all night," she said.

"I've been wanting to do that and a whole lot more," I said. "All night, and all this past weekend. So if you want to bail on the restaurant—"

"Sorry, I'm starved," she said, snuggling up against me. "How about you?"

"Kylie and I had lunch in Chinatown at one, so I've been hungry since two. Where did you have lunch?"

"Do you mean who did I have lunch with?"

"Damn. Was I that obvious?"

"Zach, I'm a shrink, for God's sake. You were like a neon sign."

"Did I ever tell you how annoying it is to date a woman who gets inside people's heads for a living?" I said.

"No, did I ever tell you how annoying it is to date a man who interrogates people for a living?"

Paola Bottero is not one of those larger-than-life chefs you see on reality TV. She's more of a quiet legend who has been feeding finicky New Yorkers for three decades. Her son Stefano welcomed me at the door. *"Signor Jordan, buona sera."*

"You've been here before?" Cheryl said as Stefano escorted us to a table.

"It's my go-to place for dinner whenever I act like an asshole at breakfast."

"Ahh...so you've been here often."

Paola's is a big, bustling, wide-open square room, and despite the soft lighting, it's a place where everybody sees everybody, and several people stole a glance at us as we walked by. I doubted they were looking at me.

Cheryl and I made a deal. We'd keep the chitchat light. No mind games till dessert. So I talked about my day, and she talked about the one thing we couldn't discuss when we were in Cates's office.

Cates.

"She's quite a role model," Cheryl said. "A strong woman of color who made her bones in a department that's dominated by white males. And for a cop who hates politics, she's figured out how to work the system. She'd make a better mayor than the one we have now, or the one who's running against him."

I ordered a bottle of Brunello di Montalcino and drank most of it. Then I ordered another glass. And when dinner was over, another.

"Are you taking the edge off because you had a rough day," Cheryl asked, "or are you fortifying yourself for our little talk?"

I sipped the wine, trying not to swill it down in one gulp. "I've never been great at relationship conversations."

"I'm fantastic at them," she said. "Unless the relationship is one of my own. Then I'm as bad as everyone else. So if you want to hold off, fine. Denial is the cornerstone of many relationships."

She rested her chin on one hand, drilled those dark brown Spanish eyes into mine, and waited. Part shrink, part devil, all hypnotic. *God, she was good at this shit. First she let me off the hook, and then she baited it again.*

I bit.

"Well, I cannot deny that I behaved like a jerk at breakfast. I apologize."

"I accept, but if dinner at this restaurant is payback, you can meet me at the diner tomorrow and be as big of a jerk as you want."

"Thanks, Doc, but I can't afford that kind of therapy."

I grabbed my wineglass again. Cheryl reached over and gently removed it from my hand. "How much liquid courage do you need to tell me what's bothering you?"

Say something, you idiot. Anything. You clam up and this whole night is over before you get to the good part. I had no idea which body part was giving me orders, but I'm pretty sure it wasn't my brain.

"What's bothering me," I said slowly, "is that you've been spending a lot of time with Matt Smith."

"Have you ever considered that it might be because Matt and I work together?"

"It feels like it's more than just work."

"It's the same as you and Kylie. You guys are joined at the hip fourteen hours a day. You're either knee to knee in a car, having lunch together, or camped out on an overnight stakeout. It's called working together."

"Kylie is different. She's married. Matt is single."

"And you're upset because I gave a single guy a book and he got me great theater tickets?"

"And a soy latte," I said.

"Which I realize in some parts of the world is considered a prelude to marriage. All I have to do to consummate the deal is ask my father to give his father six goats," she said.

"That's the trouble with you shrinks," I said. "You never take us crazy people seriously."

"Zach, I'm newly divorced, so you and I have been taking it slow. But do you really think it's my style to bring in another guy to compete with you?"

"No. I realize you didn't invite Matt to the party. He

horned in. And like you said, you're newly divorced, so you're beautiful, vulnerable, and available. That combination is a total testosterone magnet."

"Beautiful, vulnerable, and available," Cheryl repeated. "Based on what you told me about Spence's drug problem, that sounds like Kylie MacDonald any day now. I'm just curious. Is that tugging at *your* magnet?"

"That's not fair," I said. "You know Kylie and I broke up ten years ago."

"Technically, Kylie did the breaking up," Cheryl said. "She dumped you and married Spence. How ironic would it be if ten years later she left him for you?"

"Cheryl, I know you're a trained psychologist," I said, "but that scenario is...is...ridiculous—no, it's downright delusional."

"You're right," she said. "Kind of like the scenario you concocted about me and some guy in the next office who bought me a cup of coffee."

I opened my mouth to answer, but nothing came out.

Cheryl slid my wineglass back over to my side of the table. "At the risk of overmedicating you, drink this."

I sucked down the last of the wine.

"Wow," I said. "You're incredible."

"That's probably the wine talking, but thanks. You're not so bad yourself."

"And despite the fact that I've acted like an asshole at breakfast and dinner, please tell me that I didn't blow the whole relationship sky-high."

"Zach, you suffer from what we in the profession call 'the grown-man-dumb-as-shit syndrome.' But in your own crazy way, you were trying to save the relationship, and that makes me happy."

"Not to press my luck here, but how happy?"

She leaned across the table and kissed me softly. "Passionately happy."

"Then let's get out of here in a hurry," I said, "before some bloke shows up with a soy latte and screws everything up."

CHAPTER 44

LIZ O'KEEFE DROVE down the ramp from the George Washington Bridge, rolled down the window of her Honda CR-V, and inhaled deeply.

"You smell that, kiddo?" she said.

Her sister, Rachael, wrapped in an oversized gray sweat suit, slouched lower in the passenger seat. "Liz, it's Jersey," she said. "Close the window. I know what it smells like."

"Not tonight, honey. Tonight Jersey smells like freedom."

"Great," Rachael muttered. "Call Springsteen. Maybe he'll write a song about it."

"I thought that after eleven months in jail you might feel at least halfway good about getting out," Liz said, taking the Main Street exit toward Leonia.

"What should I feel good about? That Kimi is dead? That

I'm the most hated mother in America? Or that the jury found me not guilty, but if I try to walk around like a free woman, someone from the NRA or the Christian Coalition or maybe Rush Limbaugh himself will try to kill me?"

"You want to go back to jail? You think you'll be safer there?"

Rachael broke into a smile. "Hell, Lizzie, at least half of those women wanted to kill me. They'd look at me with this attitude like 'Hey, bitch, I might be a crack whore, but I was still a better mom than you.'"

"Well, guess what?" Liz said. "They're still in jail, and you're not. Another forty-five days and the judge will hand down his sentence on the endangerment charge, and you heard what Mr. Woloch said—it's probably going to be time served. Then you'll be free to really start getting on with your life."

"You mean my life without Kimi? Or you mean my life as a moving target every time I walk down the aisle in a supermarket?"

The Honda cruised along Fort Lee Road for less than a minute and turned left onto Broad Avenue.

"Look, the judge set down the rules. So whether you like it or not, you're going to be locked up in Aunt Pearl's house for the next forty-five days. After that, he'll probably cut you loose, and you can go where you want. But if I were you, I'd stay put till April when Pearl gets back from Florida."

"Are you serious? I'll go batshit crazy just hanging around an empty house doing nothing for six months," Rachael said.

Liz jammed on the brakes, and the CR-V stopped hard.

She spun around in her seat and grabbed her sister by both shoulders. "I don't give a shit how crazy you get. You're in hiding. You're a goddamn celebrity, Rachael, and not in a good way like Lady goddamn Gaga. How many death threats have you gotten in the past twenty-four hours? You think you'll be doing nothing? Staying alive isn't nothing. Besides, Mr. Woloch said he's already fielding book deal offers. You'll have plenty to do when you sit down with a writer every day and tell your story."

"Why bother? Nobody will believe me. They all think I killed Kimi."

Liz didn't answer. She checked her rearview for the millionth time since she'd picked Rachael up. Broad Avenue was deserted. She had stopped the car directly across the street from BonChon Chicken.

"Have you ever had that spicy Korean chicken?" she asked Rachael, pointing at the dark storefront.

"No."

"I'll bring some home tonight. It's to die for."

Rachael slouched back down in her seat. "Can't wait."

Liz put the car in gear, drove another four blocks, and made a right onto Harold Avenue. Calling Harold an avenue was overly generous. It was a dead-end, tree-lined street with only sixteen houses on it. A quiet middle-class patch of Bergen County, New Jersey, where one of America's most notorious accused child murderers could live in anonymity.

Aunt Pearl's house was the last one on the left. Liz pulled the car into the far side of the two-car garage, then keyed the door shut, and the two sisters walked through the breezeway into the kitchen.

"This place hasn't changed since I was a kid," Rachael said.

"Baby, this place hasn't changed since Aunt Pearl was a kid. It's all part of the joy of living in relative obscurity," Liz said, opening the refrigerator door. "I bought you a welcome-home snack—Mia Figlia Bella cheesecake and a bottle of Chardonnay."

"Sounds like you were expecting *The Real Housewives of New Jersey*. Give me a sliver of the cake and supersize the wine."

Liz grinned. *Supersize the wine*. That was the kid sister she knew and loved. She found the corkscrew and grabbed two cake plates and wineglasses from an overhead cabinet.

"Fuck them," Rachael said.

"Fuck who, sweetie?" Liz asked, cutting the seal around the rim of the bottle.

"Did you read this?" Rachael asked, picking up a copy of that morning's *New York Post* from the kitchen table.

The two-word headline practically filled the front page:

NOT GUILTY???

Rachael opened to page three and read out loud. " 'In a shocking turn of events in the Kimi O'Keefe murder trial, the jury brought back a verdict nobody expected. They found her mother, Rachael, not guilty. Judge Steven Levine sounded halfhearted and totally insincere when he thanked the jury for their service. It was as if His Honor, like virtually everyone else in this city, believed the jury got it wrong.' Well, that certainly sounds like fair and balanced journalism."

"Honey, a lot of people thought you were guilty," Liz said, turning the corkscrew so the wings spread to the sides. "Why do you think they snuck you out in the middle of the night? Whatever the verdict, there's always someone who says it's wrong. Look at O.J."

"O.J. was guilty," Rachael said. "I'm not."

Liz pulled out the cork.

"Did you hear me say I'm not guilty?" Rachael said.

"Of course," Liz said. "I was there when the jury brought in the verdict."

"Damn it, Lizzie, that's not what I'm asking. I said I'm not guilty, and you clammed up. Tell me the truth—do you believe I'm not guilty?"

"Rachael, I am so happy that you're free and not in jail," Liz said. "And *that* is the truth."

Rachael shook her head. "I don't believe it," she said. "My own sister. You think I'm guilty of murdering Kimi, don't you?"

"It's been a long day. A little wine will take the edge off," Liz said, removing the dead cork from the corkscrew and tossing it in the garbage. No sense saving it. The two sisters had never recorked a bottle in their lives.

"A little wine will not bring my daughter back," Rachael said, and she flung the newspaper across the room. "I asked you a question. Yes or no—*do you think I'm guilty?*"

The door between the kitchen and the breezeway crashed open, and two masked men stormed in, guns in hand.

"I do," one of them said. "Now get down on the floor. Both of you."

CHAPTER 45

LIZ STILL HAD the corkscrew in her hand. She lowered her arm and slowly let it drift behind her back.

"Drop it, bitch!" one screamed. "Do we look like fucking amateurs?"

The corkscrew clattered to the tile floor.

"Kick it across the room."

Liz studied the two men. They were dressed in black from head to toe. The one giving orders was about six two. His voice was slightly muffled by the mask, but it sounded young, white, and deadly serious. Nothing about him said amateur.

Give in, but don't give up, she thought as she kicked the corkscrew to the far corner of the kitchen.

"Both of you. Face down. Hands behind your back. Now."

The women stretched out on the floor, their hands behind their backs. The man in charge holstered his gun, knelt beside Rachael, put a zip tie around her wrists, and yanked hard. She yelped in pain.

The second man was still standing, straddled over Liz. He holstered his gun and reached into his pocket for a zip tie. Liz made her move. In one swift, fluid motion, she rolled over onto her back and jammed her knee into his balls.

He doubled over as Liz reached up, pulled him to the floor, and began scrambling for his gun. His partner sprang up and kicked at her hand. He missed, and Liz grabbed his leg, toppling him to the floor.

She clambered to her knees and pummeled the downed man with her fists, looking for a vulnerable point. His temple, his throat, anything.

A boot struck her on the back of the head, and she pitched forward. A pair of knees dug into her back. The man on top of her grabbed a handful of hair, yanked her head back, and wrapped his arm under her chin.

"Don't move or I'll snap your bitch neck like a twig!" he yelled.

She let her body go limp, but the man kept the pressure on, cutting off her air supply. She knew he had her in a death hold.

"Enough!" the other guy yelled. "She's not who we came for."

His partner relaxed his grip, and Liz sucked in greedy mouthfuls of air.

One of them grabbed her arms and the other her ankles,

and they carried her to the bathroom. The one who had almost choked her held her head over the toilet bowl.

"Any more shit from you, and I'll drown you right here, and my partner will piss on you while you die."

They laid her facedown on the floor, duct-taped her mouth, wrapped her legs around the base of the toilet, and zip-tied her ankles. Then they stretched her hands over her head and zip-tied them to a pipe underneath the sink.

One of them turned on the water and began filling the bathtub. Five minutes later, the other was back with every phone in the house, including her cell, and dropped them all in the tub.

"We should kill you just for harboring a child killer," he said.

They turned off the lights and shut the bathroom door behind them.

Liz lay there on the cold tile floor, her arms and legs stretched painfully wide, the zip ties cutting into her skin, and she listened.

She could hear them carry Rachael out the back door.

Then a car door opened. Finally it shut, followed quickly by two more car doors opening and closing.

An engine roared to life, and the car pulled out.

And then silence. She heard nothing. Nothing except for the agonizing sobs that emanated from her battered body.

CHAPTER 46

BRIDGET SWEENEY, THE housekeeper at St. Agnes's Church, was a large, robust woman with a bawdy sense of humor and an Irish brogue that was every bit as thick as it was the day she started working there forty-two years ago.

She had three responsibilities: cook for the priests, supervise the maintenance staff, and, most important, function as Father Spinelli's eyes and ears.

She was dusting the blinds in the rectory when she saw the black Cadillac Escalade pull up in front of the church. She hurried down the hallway to Father Spinelli's office. She didn't bother knocking.

"Father...," she said, winded from the brief journey, "you got company."

The priest took a quick look at his watch. "I have morning Mass in ten minutes. Who is it?"

"Eye-talian royalty," Sweeney said. "Take a gander."

She ushered Spinelli to a window, and the two of them watched as the driver of the Escalade got out and opened the rear door.

Joe Salvi stepped out. He was wearing a perfectly fitted dark gray double-breasted suit, white shirt, blue tie, and black wingtips.

"Will you just look at him now," Mrs. Sweeney said. "All dressed up spiffy like John Gotti and riding around in one of them big black SUVs like Tony Soprano. Is he thinking maybe we don't already know he's in the Mafia business?"

The priest shook his head. "Mrs. Sweeney, 'Thou shalt not go up and down as a dispenser of gossip and scandal among your people,'" he scolded. "Leviticus nineteen, verse sixteen."

She clasped her hands over her cheeks in mock penitence. "Mob boss Joe Salvi indicted on federal racketeering charges—*Daily News*, page one."

The priest chuckled. The old woman was incorrigible. But he'd be lost without her.

"It ain't Christmas nor Easter," she said, "so what in God's name is he doing here?"

"Not your concern. The Salvis are our biggest benefactors, so kindly hustle your aging Irish arse to the kitchen and bring us a pot of fresh coffee. Oh, and ask Father Daniel to take the Mass for me."

"Yes, Father," she said, taking one last look out the window. "But you gotta wonder what he wants at this hour of the morning."

"I have no idea," the priest said.

"Sure as hell he ain't here for confession," she said, cackling as she hustled her aging Irish arse out the door.

Spinelli stifled a laugh. *And good thing for me he ain't. I wouldn't have time to hear it all.*

Three minutes later, Salvi stood outside Spinelli's door. "Good morning, Father," he said. "I was hoping to catch you before Mass."

"Father Daniel is celebrating the Mass this morning, but if you're attending, I'll get my vestments."

"I'm flattered, Father, but Teresa does enough praying for the two of us. I just came here to make a donation to the church. Ten thousand dollars."

"Praise God," Spinelli said. "And if I may ask, what is the occasion for such joyous tidings?"

"My son Enzo's diary. It means the world to us," Salvi said without a trace of joy in his voice. "I want to thank you for finding it and bringing a little piece of our boy back into our lives."

"Joseph," the priest said, "we'd be more than grateful to receive your gift, but I can't accept it under false pretenses. As I told Teresa, one of our parishioners found the diary. She turned it over to me to pass on to you."

Salvi nodded as if he'd just heard it for the first time. He took a checkbook from his breast pocket. "In that case, we'll make it twenty thousand dollars, but I want the donation to be in her honor. Please tell me who she is so Teresa and I can send a note of gratitude."

"I'm sure she'd welcome that," Spinelli said. "Her name is Emma Frye. Let me go to my files, and I'll get her address."

Mrs. Sweeney entered, carrying a silver tray. "Good day to you, Mr. Salvi," she said. "And how's your lovely missus this morning?"

Salvi flashed his best benevolent community benefactor smile. "Wonderful. And you?"

He handed the priest a check, and Spinelli in turn handed him a three-by-five index card, which Salvi folded and tucked into his jacket pocket.

"I'm well. Thank you for asking," Sweeney said. "I brought you both some hot coffee and fresh-baked scones."

"I wish I had time," Salvi said, "but I must run. Peace be with you, Father."

"And with your spirit," the priest replied.

Salvi nodded politely at Mrs. Sweeney as he brushed by her and left the room.

I guess you got whatever it was you came for, she thought. *And 'tweren't no fecking scones.*

CHAPTER 47

WHEN I FIRST met Cheryl, I decided she was totally out of my league. She had a doctorate from Fordham University; I had a tin badge from the Police Academy. She was salsa; I was mayonnaise. And, of course, she was married to Fred Robinson, and I had a flat-out policy about not hitting on women whose first name was Mrs.

But that didn't stop me from fantasizing. And then her marriage crumbled. Still, I held back. I told myself she needed time to adjust, but I think it all went back to my first impression—she was totally out of my league.

Apparently Cheryl didn't agree, and three months ago she invited me to go to the opera with her. It was a magical evening, and even before the fat lady sang, it was clear that the door to a serious relationship was wide open. But I wasn't ready to commit. That very same week, my ex-girlfriend joined Red as my new partner, and despite the fact that Kylie was happily married, I was still pitifully hung up on her.

For the next three months, Kylie and Cheryl and I all lived together. The three of us shared cramped, unsafe quarters inside my twisted brain. I wanted them both, even though I was sure neither of them wanted me.

Had I manned up and told Cheryl what I was going through, I'm sure she would have diagnosed me as certifiably bonkers, but I kept my feelings buried, which is a basic tenet of my white Anglo-Saxon Protestant upbringing.

But when I woke up that morning after dinner at Paola's, everything had changed. I felt different. Good different. Fantastic different. It was more than the morning-after euphoria that warms you when a night that looked as if it were going to crash and burn ends in heart-pounding sex.

I felt something I hadn't felt in months. Centered. I finally knew what I wanted, and what I wanted was the bright, funny, incredibly hot, sexually adventurous woman lying next to me in bed, her thick black hair cascading over her smooth bronze shoulders.

I headed for the shower. Two minutes later, Cheryl, wearing nothing but a mischievous grin, joined me. One thing led to another, and I didn't question how lucky I was. I just accepted it.

Two hours later, I was in Matt Smith's office with Kylie.

"I pulled together a list of people Parker-Steele called on her cell phone, her landline, and her office phone,"

Smith said, "and I cross-checked to see if any of them owned black SUVs. A lot of her contacts live in Manhattan and don't even own cars, and of the thirty-seven who do, one drives a ten-year-old black Jeep Patriot. Her dentist."

"What's his name?" Kylie asked.

"*Her* name is Jo Ann Kinane," Matt said. "We're not looking for a female, and besides, the way the victim's teeth were mangled, do you really think her dentist would—"

Cates opened the door.

"Captain," Smith said, "we were just—"

"Save it," she said. "You people all know who Rachael O'Keefe is? She was accused of murdering her daughter, and the jury acquitted her?"

She didn't wait for an answer. Half the world knew who Rachael O'Keefe was.

"She was kidnapped last night at gunpoint. She was in Jersey with her sister. Two masked men stormed in at about three a.m. and took Rachael. They tied up the sister, and it was five hours before she managed to get loose. She was smart enough to call the Manhattan DA instead of the local cops. The DA called the commissioner, who called the chief of D's, who called me. We could be dealing with Hazmat. This one is different from the first four kidnappings—the other victims weren't taken by force, but if anyone sounds like a candidate for a couple of days of torture and a video confession, it's Rachael O'Keefe. I want you to get out to Jersey and interview her sister."

"It's not our jurisdiction," Kylie said. "You think we'll

piss off the locals or the Feds? It's a little early to be crashing their party."

"Well, well, well," Cates said, "look who suddenly wants to play by the rules. Do you think I have time to ask some police chief in Leonia, New Jersey, if I can trample through his sandbox? It's my job to worry about the political bullshit. It's your job to get out there before the locals or the Feds have it on their radar. I already have a CSI team on the way. I want you two to dig up anything you can that relates to the Hazmat case, then get the hell out fast."

"Who knew where Rachael was going once she was released?" Kylie said.

"Just a handful of people, but it was on a need-to-know basis. It was supposed to be a well-guarded secret, but secrets have a habit of leaking."

"Maybe the sister told someone."

"I don't think she'd be that dumb, but if she did, find out who and track them down."

Kylie and I headed for the door.

"And just in case preventing another homicide isn't enough incentive for you two," Cates said, "let me remind you that Election Day is only six days away."

CHAPTER 48

"DAMN," KYLIE SAID as we got into the Ford Interceptor. "I could kick myself."

"Because you were trying to suck up to the boss by pretending to care about the rules, and she called you on it?"

"I wasn't sucking up to her, and she already knows I'm not exactly a Girl Scout when it comes to following directions. But I figured if she tore me a new one because of Damon Parker, I should at least let her know that I'm aware of the rules I'm going to break. She's sending two New York City cops to investigate a high-profile kidnapping that happened across a state line. We're about to violate more jurisdictions in one morning than most cops do in their entire careers. It's not just the locals we're screwing with. Everyone is going to want a piece of this—the Bergen County sheriff, the Staties, and, of course, the Feds."

"Sounds like your kind of fun," I said. "So why are you kicking yourself?"

"Because I knew this was going to happen. I knew Rachael O'Keefe was going to be kidnapped."

"And when was this?" I said as I got on the FDR at 96th Street.

"Monday night when the verdict came down. Everyone on the planet knew O'Keefe was guilty, and the first thing I thought when the jury let her off with nothing more than a slap on the wrist was, *I'll bet the Hazmat Killer could have a field day with her.*"

"You should have said something."

"To who? And even if I did, what good would it have done?"

"Exactly. Nobody would listen to you, and even if they did, nobody would have done anything," I said. "So stop kicking yourself."

Kylie's cell rang. She looked at the caller ID and muttered two words. "Oh, shit."

She answered. "Hello, Shelley. What's wrong?"

For the next sixty seconds, she just sat there listening. I had no idea what was going on, but I knew who Shelley was. Shelley Trager was born in Hell's Kitchen and grew up to be one of the richest and most likable TV and film producers in the business. Over the years, Shelley's company, Noo Yawk Films, provided jobs for tens of thousands of New Yorkers who would otherwise have gone hungry or, worse yet, been forced to move to LA. One of his most successful protégés was Spence Harrington, Kylie's husband.

"Which hospital?" Kylie said into the phone. "No, I'll get there as soon as I can. Thanks for calling."

I pulled over to a narrow grassy strip on the left and stopped the car.

"It sounds like something happened to Spence," I said.

"Something did. He's in an ambulance on the way to Elmhurst Hospital. He was on the set, stumbled over a light stand, hit his head on the studio floor, and got cut up by the broken glass. Why are we stopping?"

"We're three-quarters of a mile from the George Washington Bridge. I don't have time to run you to Queens, but I can get off at 179th and drop you at the bus terminal. From there you can catch a cab to the hospital."

"I'm not going to the hospital," she said.

"You sure?" I said. "It sounds like Spence got hurt pretty bad."

"Drive," she said.

"Look, I can handle O'Keefe's sister on my own. You go check on Spence, and then we can catch up after you—"

"Zach, Spence didn't just fall. He was so high on painkillers he couldn't see straight, and this time he destroyed thousands of dollars' worth of equipment and put his life and the lives of others at risk. Spence has a problem, and my going to the hospital to hold his hand is not going to help it. I told you this on Monday, and I'll say it again. This is the best damn job in NYPD, and I'm not going to screw it up because of my drug addict husband. Now do me a favor."

"Anything. What?"

"Shut up and drive."

I shut up, pulled back onto the highway, and drove up the ramp for the bridge to New Jersey.

CHAPTER 49

DRIVING ONTO HAROLD Avenue in Leonia, New Jersey, you'd never know that this anonymous little patch of suburbia was a powder keg that would explode all over the next news cycle.

A black van was parked in the driveway of the last house on the left. It was pulled in tight against a clump of high hedges so that the gold letters that spelled out NYPD CRIME SCENE UNIT on the side panel were out of sight.

Our old friend Chuck Dryden looked up when he heard our car approach, and instead of burying his nose back in his work, he walked down the driveway to greet us.

"Detectives," he said with an uncharacteristic smile. "We meet again."

"I'm surprised to see you here," Kylie said. "There are no bodies to slice and dice."

"Ah, Detective MacDonald," he said. "I realize you think of me as a people person, but I have other talents you may not yet be aware of."

Kylie laughed as if it were funny instead of downright creepy.

"I've been told to sweep the place and make a hasty retreat," Dryden said. "I'll have a prelim for you in five minutes. The sister is inside."

Elizabeth O'Keefe, a recognizable face since Rachael's arrest and throughout her trial, was waiting for us in the kitchen. She was sitting on the only chair that was still upright.

"Don't come in," she said. "I just wanted you to get a good look."

We stood in the doorway and took in the mess. The room reeked of wine, and the floor was wet, slick, and covered with broken glass. The cabinet doors on one side of the room were splintered, and the lower half of the stainless-steel refrigerator door looked as if it had been rammed by a Toyota.

"There's some cheesecake over there," she said, pointing to a creamy yellow blob jammed against one of the downed chairs. "Take a slice back to the DA and tell him to shove it up his ass."

"Ms. O'Keefe," Kylie said, "we're here to help find your sister."

"I'm sorry," she said. "I'm just so effing angry. We asked the DA for police protection for Rachael, but a dozen death threats and the fact that the jury found her innocent wasn't enough to convince him."

"And yet when your sister was kidnapped, you called the DA's office instead of dialing 911," Kylie said.

O'Keefe stood up. Her jeans and her T-shirt were wet and covered with some of the same slop that streaked the floor. The left side of her face was bruised, there were cuts on her neck and chin, and her wrists and ankles were caked with dried blood.

"Ms. O'Keefe," Kylie said, "we can drive you to the hospital."

"Call me Liz. No, I'm fine. Let's get out of this mess."

She tiptoed through the broken glass, and we followed her into a small, cluttered living room that looked as though it had been sealed in a time capsule the day it was furnished back in 1960.

Kylie and I sat on a cushy sofa, and Liz, whose clothes were too wet for the fabric, sat on a cane-backed wooden chair.

"I didn't call the DA first," she said. "I called Dennis Woloch, Rachael's lawyer. He can't legally tell me *not* to call 911, but he said dialing it would get me the local cops, who would run right over as soon as they finished responding to a loud music complaint or a couple of teenagers smoking weed in the park. I know that's bullshit, but he also said if the news went out on the local police band, the press would turn the whole thing into another media circus."

"That part is not bullshit," Kylie said.

"Mr. Woloch said the DA released Rachael without any protection, and he might be embarrassed enough to call in this elite squad from NYPD, but I guess he sent you instead."

"Sorry to disappoint you," Kylie said, "but we are the elite squad."

"Oh...I was kind of expecting something more like the navy SEALs."

"Tell us what happened," I said.

"One second Rachael and I were in the kitchen talking, and the next second two masked guys with guns came through the breezeway door."

"Do you think they followed you from New York?" I asked.

"I was thinking somebody might, so I kept checking my rearview, but I never saw anyone. Even when I turned onto this dead-end street. Nobody."

"What happened once they broke in?"

"They made us get on the floor. One tied Rachael up. The other one holstered his gun so he could tie me up, and I kneed him in the balls. Do you know Krav Maga? It's an Israeli self-defense technique."

"We know it well," Kylie said.

"I've been studying it ever since I got mugged five years ago. If it had been just the one guy, I could've taken him, but they double-teamed me."

"And then what?"

"They carried me to the bathroom, tied me up, and disabled all the phones. A few minutes later, I heard them carry Rachael out and drive away."

"If their car was parked nearby, wouldn't you have seen it when you drove in?"

"No. I was worried about someone following me. I didn't check out the parked cars."

"Can you describe the two men?" I asked.

"They were dressed in black. One was maybe six two. The other was shorter. Both strong. Their voices sounded like they were most likely white guys, kind of young—they knew what they were doing, like they were military."

"Who knew you were bringing Rachael to this specific address?" I asked.

"Just me and Rachael's lawyer, Mr. Woloch."

"Did you tell anyone else?"

"No. Mr. Woloch had to tell the chief of corrections, but that's because Judge Levine is going to sentence Rachael on the child endangerment charge in forty-five days, and they have to know where she is."

"Detectives…" It was Dryden. "Can I see you outside, please?"

We followed him to the back of the house. The back door had been jimmied open. The wooden frame was cracked, and a small pane of glass had shattered onto the breezeway floor.

"You have prints?" I asked.

"They wore gloves. They left footprints when they tracked through the mess in the kitchen, and I can figure out which brand of sneakers they wore and what size, but I doubt if it will help. I wish I could do more, but these guys are pros, and I have to clear out of here."

He left, and Kylie and I stood there at the back door. Clueless.

"Do me a favor," she said. "Walk through the breeze-way, go into the kitchen, and close the door."

I did. Five seconds later, I heard glass breaking. I opened the breezeway door.

Kylie had her gun in her hand. "I broke another one of these windowpanes in the back door. Did you hear it?"

"Of course I heard it."

"So if Rachael and Liz were in the kitchen when these guys broke in, they'd have heard the glass smash," she said.

"But they didn't," I said.

"Because they broke in before Rachael and Liz got home," she said.

"According to Liz, nobody knew where Rachael was going to hide out," I said.

"Somebody knew," Kylie said. "And they were already inside the house, waiting for her."

CHAPTER 50

"LIKE FATHER, LIKE son," Jojo said, thumbing through his brother Enzo's leather-bound collection book. "He was only in high school and he already had a nice business going, shaking the other kids down. He even used the family numbering code."

Papa Joe Salvi smiled and tilted back in the very same desk chair that had been passed down by his father and his grandfather before that. He ran his thumb over the brass studs that held the green leather armrests to the ornate mahogany arms. "I taught him that code when he was only twelve."

"He never told you?" Jojo said.

"Told me what?"

"About the code. You taught it to *me* when I was twelve, but I had trouble with it, and I didn't want to tell you, so I showed it to Enzo. He figured it out in two minutes, and then he explained it back to me. He was a kid, only nine, but that was Enzo—smart as a whip."

"Oh, he was smart," Joe said, taking the book from his son's hands and stroking the soft red leather. Enzo, his youngest—named for his blessed father—Enzo was the one he'd always planned to pass the torch to. Enzo had a head for the business. He was a fox. His big brother was a bull.

"This Mrs. Frye who returned the book," Jojo said. "Is she white?"

"She's from St. Agnes," Salvi said. "What else would she be?"

"Pop, I'm just saying—I always thought the blacks from Ozone Park killed Enzo. They had a grudge from when he beat the shit out of one of their gangbangers."

Salvi shook his head. "You think this Mrs. Frye got Enzo's book from some black kid in Ozone Park? No. She found it in her house, and I'll bet her kid hid it there on the very night that Enzo died."

"So then this Frye kid—he killed Enzo?"

"Either him or he knows who did."

"So let me go have a little talk with him," Jojo said.

"In order for that to happen, I'd have to know who Mrs. Frye's son is and where to find him."

"No problem. Why don't me and Tommy Boy go over there and have a little chat with Mrs. Frye?"

Salvi rubbed his chin and took a deep breath. "Jojo, do you really think that sending over two muscle-bound *stunads* to scare the shit out of some old lady is the way to go?"

"I don't know, Papa. I didn't *think* about the whole thing. I was just trying to help."

"There will be plenty of time for you and Tommy Boy to help," Salvi said, patting Jojo on the knee, much the way he'd pat a dog on the head. "But for now, don't think. I know exactly how to handle it."

CHAPTER 51

"I'M DRIVING," KYLIE said when we got back to the car.

"As long as you asked so sweetly, sure," I said, tossing her the keys. "Just try to remember that it's a Ford, not the Batmobile."

"What is that supposed to mean?"

"It means I don't want to go on another suicide run like the one you did up Park Avenue on Monday."

"I'll drive like a little old lady," she said. "Just like you do."

She made a U-turn, drove to the top of Harold Avenue, and turned left onto Broad.

"I think you're right," I said. "The two guys who took Rachael were waiting at the house before she got home. This is a quiet little town. Liz said she kept checking her rearview, and at three in the morning there's no way anyone could have followed her without being seen."

"So how did they know where Rachael was going?"

"It would be easy if they're real cops."

"You and I are real cops," Kylie said. "We didn't know."

"But we could have found out easily enough. Just call a friend at corrections or the DA's office. That has to be where the leak came from."

"So between the two agencies, how many people do you think knew enough to disclose the undisclosed location?"

"A lot more than I feel like tracking down," I said, "but right now, it's the only lead we've got."

My cell rang. "It's Cates," I said, and picked it up.

"Where are you?" she said.

I told her.

"I need you and MacDonald ASAP," she said.

"We can be back in the office in—"

"I'm not in the office," she said.

She told me where to meet her.

"What's going on there?" I said.

"Just get here," she said, and hung up.

"What was that about?" Kylie said. "You didn't even fill her in on what we just figured out."

"She didn't ask. I think she's got something more important to deal with."

"Like what?"

"Like she didn't say. She just wants us to meet her in Queens."

"What's in Queens?" Kylie said.

"Silvercup Studios."

"Are you dicking around, Zach? Because if you are, it's not—"

I shook my head. "That's what she said. Meet her at Silvercup Studios."

"Is it Spence? Is he okay?"

"She didn't say anything about Spence. She didn't say anything about anything."

"Shit, shit, shit," Kylie said, whacking the palm of her hand on the steering wheel. "Of course it's about Spence. Why else would she want us at Silvercup?"

She flipped on the flashers and stepped on the gas, and the Batmobile lurched forward.

I buckled up my seat belt. The little old lady behind the wheel had been replaced by a crazy woman.

CHAPTER 52

WE BLASTED ACROSS the lower level of the GW Bridge into Manhattan and down the Harlem River Drive. "Cates is already pissed at me for my little run-in with Damon Parker," Kylie said as she merged onto the FDR and kicked the Ford up to seventy.

"You flat-out accused the victim's brother of exploiting her death for his own personal gain," I said. "I'm not sure the department would classify that as a 'little run-in.'"

"So if Cates chewed me out for that, what do you think she'll do now that she knows my husband has a drug problem and wound up in the ER twice in the past three days?"

"Who knows what Cates knows? She didn't say a word about Spence."

"She didn't have to. She told us to drop what we're doing and meet her where he works."

She got off the FDR at 53rd Street, turned right onto First Avenue, and shot up the ramp onto the bridge to Queens. We skidded into the parking lot at Silvercup fourteen minutes after Cates called.

A golf cart was waiting for us at the front gate. The man behind the wheel was Bob Reitzfeld, a former NYPD lieutenant who left the department after thirty years, then dodged what he called the "death by retirement" bullet by signing on as a night watchman at Silvercup. Two years later, he was running the entire security team.

"How's Spence?" Kylie asked as we climbed into the backseat.

"Short term, he'll be fine," Reitzfeld said as he navigated a narrow hallway between studios. "They're sewing him back together in the ER. But long term, your boy's got a problem, and Shelley can't cover for him much longer."

"How long has Shelley known Spence was using?" she asked.

"At least a month. That's when he first told me. But by now everyone in the cast and crew is aware of it. If he doesn't get clean soon, his career is going to be in the crapper."

"*His* career? How about mine?" Kylie said. "Right now I'm the lead detective on a high-profile murder case. Tomorrow morning Cates may have me hauling in sixth graders for spray-painting their names on schoolyard walls."

Reitzfeld eased the golf cart to a stop, turned around, and looked at Kylie. "Let me get this straight—you think

Cates is here because Spence got high and bowled over a couple of lights?"

"Why else would my boss show up at the studio an hour after my husband fucked up?"

"Kylie, I know I look like the guy in the blue blazer who drives the golf cart, but I was a precinct boss myself for a couple of tours, and I can promise you that Captain Cates didn't trek out here to Queens to make you pay for Spence's sins. Because if she did, she wouldn't have brought the mayor with her."

That caught both of us by surprise.

"The mayor is here?" Kylie said.

"Along with Irwin Diamond and Shelley. They're all waiting on you in Studio Five, and it's none of my business, but the last thing they need is a stressed-out cop, so I suggest you get your head together and put your game face on before you go in there."

He turned back around, and we drove the rest of the way in silence.

"Thanks, Lieutenant," Kylie said to Reitzfeld as he dropped us off in front of the studio. "I'll be fine."

"Don't tell me," he said. "Tell the guy you're walking into the room with."

He pulled out and left us standing there.

"Go ahead," I said. "Look me in the eye and tell me with a straight face that you're fine."

"Of course I'm not fine," she said. "As soon as I heard we were coming here to meet Cates, all I could think about was that Spence was about to wreck my career."

"Right now, there's only one person about to wreck your

career, and it's not Spence," I said. "Let me know if there's anything I can do to keep you from self-destructing."

"There is," she said. She dug her hand into her pocket and tossed me the car keys. "For starters, don't let me drive when I'm this crazy."

"Good call," I said, taking the keys. "Anything else?"

"Yeah…I know I haven't been the best partner these past two weeks. Do me a favor—set the clock back and give me another chance to make things right between us."

"You got it," I said.

What I didn't say was that I wasn't sure if I wanted to set it back two weeks or eleven years.

CHAPTER 53

STUDIO 5 IS one of the smaller studios under the Silvercup roof. Even so, it's at least fifty feet long and forty wide. Cates, the mayor, his *consigliere* Irwin Diamond, and Spence's boss, Shelley Trager, were waiting for us inside. They were at the far end of the room, standing in the living room set of a TV show I didn't recognize. Cates walked across the studio to meet us.

"Mayor Spellman is crazy as a shithouse rat," she said.

"Isn't that Muriel Sykes's campaign slogan?" I said.

In times of stress, inappropriate humor has always been the glue that binds cops together, so despite the difference in our ranks and the gravity of the situation, Cates laughed out loud. She quickly covered her mouth and turned the laugh into a cough.

"What's going on?" I said.

"Muriel Sykes is about to hold a press conference,"

Cates said. "Irwin dragged the mayor out here so they can watch it, videotape some kind of rebuttal, and get it on the air before his entire campaign spins out of control."

"That explains why *they're* here," I said. "Why are *we* here?"

"Because you're the lead detectives on the serial killer case that Sykes is using against him, and he's hoping you'll give him something to say."

"You want *us* to give him something to say? How about 'I concede the election and wish Muriel Sykes the best of luck in running the city that I couldn't'?"

This time she didn't laugh.

"Captain," I said, "you heard Irwin on Monday. The mayor is in a hole that he dug himself. NYPD wanted to investigate Evelyn Parker-Steele for the murder of Cynthia Pritchard, but Leonard Parker put pressure on City Hall. The mayor caved, Evelyn walked, and the vigilante serial killer who's been running loose in the city made her his fourth victim."

"Detectives!" It was Irwin Diamond. "Glad you're here. Captain Cates tells us you were out in New Jersey talking to Rachael O'Keefe's sister."

The mayor jumped in. "Is there a connection? Is her kidnapping related to the Hazmat Killer?"

"Sir, we have no proof that Rachael's kidnapping is connected to the other cases," I said, "but everything points to the fact that Rachael could be victim number five."

"Why is she *our* number five? Why isn't she New Jersey's victim number one?"

"She was taken from Jersey, but the information on where she was hiding may well have come from New York City."

"And not just from the city," Kylie added, "but possibly from a city official connected to the case. Detective Jordan and I were just on our way into Manhattan to talk to the chief of corrections and the DA's office to get a list of everyone who knew exactly where Rachael would be. The sooner we can get those names, the better."

To the mayor, I'm sure she sounded like a dedicated cop whose sole purpose was to get to Manhattan so she could track down the wrongdoer. To me, she sounded more like Mrs. Spence Harrington determined to get the hell out of Silvercup as fast as possible. It didn't matter. She was right on both counts.

"Is the word out yet that O'Keefe has been kidnapped?" Diamond asked.

Cates held up a hand to let us know she would take the question.

"Irwin, we're working way outside our jurisdiction," she said. "We're bending the boundaries because this kidnapping seems to be tied to the Hazmat case. Our people went in and got out under the radar, but the Jersey cops and the Feds will be on it in no time. And if you think Rachael O'Keefe dominated the airwaves during the trial, just wait till this breaks. The twenty-four-hour news cycle will be all Rachael, all the time."

"Understood," Diamond said. "But it's still under wraps?"

"For now," Cates said.

"Good," he said, "because Muriel Sykes is holding a press conference in two minutes, and at least she won't have this shit to fling at the fan."

CHAPTER 54

"SHE'S COMING ON," Shelley Trager called out. He had drifted away from the group and was standing in front of a large TV monitor that had been rolled in on a metal stand.

The rest of us gathered around, and the picture cut away from two NY1 news anchors to Muriel Sykes standing at a podium. There was a backdrop with her campaign logo behind her and two flags positioned strategically over her left shoulder—one, the Stars and Stripes; the other, the orange, white, and blue flag of New York City.

She was the picture of confidence—standing tall, smartly dressed, seemingly at ease despite the difficult road ahead. *Hello, Central Casting, send me a strong woman who looks like she could be mayor.*

I stole a glance at Spellman. He was stoop-shouldered

242 • JAMES PATTERSON

and world-weary. He looked more like the guy Central Casting would send over to play a bus driver at the end of a long day.

"Good afternoon," Sykes said directly to the camera. "For the past nine months you've all seen me aggressively campaigning for mayor. But this press conference is not about politics. It's about a sad personal loss, and I have asked my dear friend Damon Parker to make an opening statement. He is not here in his capacity as an internationally respected journalist, but as the grieving brother of my brutally tortured and murdered campaign manager, Evelyn Parker-Steele."

"What a crock of shit," Diamond said as Muriel moved to the side and Parker stepped up to the podium. "Evelyn hated that phony blowhard asshole."

"The murder of my sister, Evelyn, has shattered our family," Parker said in a somber voice. Gone were the histrionics and shouts of *The People Want to Know*. In keeping with his intro, the man put on his best internationally respected journalist facade.

"But even more devastating than her death," he said, "is this blatantly coerced video confession. It is nothing more than a fabricated atrocity created to tarnish our family name and to undermine the progressive reforms of U.S. Attorney Muriel Sykes's mayoral campaign. This is a personal and political attack that wounds my heart as her brother and aggrieves my spirit as a citizen of the greatest city in the world."

"I'm glad Muriel made it clear that this is not about politics," Irwin said.

Parker continued, "The tragic death of Cynthia Pritchard weighed heavily on my sister's heart every day of her life, and for a sadistic torturer…" He paused and choked up convincingly.

"And for a sadistic torturer to force my sister to spout these pre-scripted lies is almost too much to bear. Our family has received thousands of emails, letters, and phone calls denouncing this staged confession, and no words have been more heartfelt or more comforting than those that came from the woman for whom my sister gave her last ounce of energy and devotion—Muriel Sykes."

He placed his hand to his chest and turned reverentially to Sykes. They exchanged a brief hug, and she took his place at the podium.

"Talk about pre-scripted lies," Irwin said. "What a performance."

Sykes looked into the camera, her eyes filled with compassion. "My deepest condolences to the Parker and Steele families," she said. "The senseless killing of Evelyn Parker-Steele should never have happened. She was the fourth victim of a cold-blooded serial killer—a murderer who should have been brought to justice months ago. As U.S. attorney, I would never have tolerated the kind of misguided street vengeance that has been the hallmark of the sick individual who continues to stalk the streets of our city."

Irwin had a pen and a pad and was either taking notes, writing a rebuttal, or drafting the mayor's concession speech.

"I will not politicize Evelyn's death," Sykes said.

"Could have fooled me," Irwin called out, still scribbling.

"But I will politicize the need for the kind of bold leadership that will give our police—and our entire law enforcement community—the support and resources it needs to protect our city and its citizens from those who seek to do it harm," Sykes said. "Thank you. Are there any questions?"

Reporters started shouting, and Irwin stepped up to the television and turned it off.

"I don't want to watch Muriel Sykes answer a bunch of bullshit questions that Damon Parker planted with the press," he said. "The man's a powerhouse. He just endorsed our opponent, and it's only going to get worse. I have a script for a stopgap commercial the mayor can shoot immediately, but it's a Hail Mary. Once the public finds out that Rachael O'Keefe has been kidnapped, they'll forget that she's a child murderer, and Damon Parker will spin her into a martyr who was falsely imprisoned, found innocent, begged for protection from NYPD, and was thrown to the wolves by an insensitive, uncaring mayor. Nothing personal, Stan. I'm just trying to point out how they're going to skewer you."

"No, no, Irwin," Spellman said. "I'm convinced. I'm voting for Muriel."

Diamond gave his best friend a half smile. "We're not dead yet, Stan."

The mayor didn't look convinced. "What do you suggest?"

"I suggest that we find Rachael O'Keefe while she's still

alive, and bring in the Hazmat Killer—or as many of them as are out there."

He said "we," but he was staring directly at Kylie and me when he said it.

"Can you do it, Detectives?" Diamond asked about as casually as a guy asking his buddies if they could come over and help paint the garage. "Can you?"

"Sir," I said, "NYPD will do everything in our—"

"I don't care if you *can* do it!" the mayor erupted. "I only care if you can do it while I'm still in office. I need to be there for the victory dance, and it damn well better happen before Election Day, because after that, I don't give a flying fuck!"

He stormed out of the studio with Irwin Diamond right behind him.

Cates looked at us and shrugged. "Like I said—crazy as a shithouse rat. Keep me posted," she said, and followed them out the door.

Shelley Trager hadn't said a word to us since we came in. Now he walked over to Kylie and put a hand on her shoulder.

"I'm going back to my office," he said softly. "Meet me there in five minutes. We have to talk."

He too left the studio, and Kylie and I just stood there.

"I'll wait for you in the car," I said. "You go talk to Shelley."

"No," she said, looking as close to shell-shocked as I'd ever seen her. "Go with me. Please."

CHAPTER 55

"AT LEAST THE haystack is getting smaller," Kylie said as we walked past the carpenters' shop toward Shelley's office.

"I'm not up on all the hip cop talk," I said. "What's that supposed to mean?"

"It means we've been looking for a needle in a giant haystack. On Monday we had about eight million suspects. But this lead narrows it down to a handful of people who could have known where Rachael was going. It's a much smaller haystack."

"And we're looking for two needles," I said.

We entered Studio 1 and took the elevator to the fourth-floor production offices. Kylie led the way down the hall to Shelley Trager's corner suite. The door was open. "We're here," she said.

Shelley looked up from his desk. "We? Oh...Zach."

"Do you mind?" Kylie asked. "Whatever you have to tell me, you can say in front of Zach. He knows everything."

"Not at all. Come in. Both of you," Shelley said.

The room was big and bright, wrapped with eight picture windows—five on the 21st Street side and three on the Queens Plaza side. Directly outside, I could see the steel and stone of the Ed Koch Queensboro Bridge, a magnificent century-old New York City landmark that cantilevered across the East River, straddled Roosevelt Island, and finally disappeared into the skyline of midtown Manhattan.

"I was going to call and give you an update," Shelley said, "but when I heard you were coming here, I decided it's easier in person. Have a seat."

"How's Spence?" Kylie said as we sat in the two black leather chairs in front of Shelley's desk.

"Spence is okay, but he's in full-blown denial," Shelley said. "As much as I love him, I run a business, and I can't have him back in the studio until he cleans up his act. He's a major liability. And on the personal side, I hate seeing him do this to himself, so I'm happier if I don't have to watch."

"I understand," Kylie said. "I wish I didn't have to watch either."

"You don't," Shelley said. "We have a nice little apartment on East End Avenue. You can move in there for a while."

"*A nice little apartment?*" Kylie said. She turned to me.

"Zach, you should see it. Tenth floor, view of the river, and it's got three bedrooms."

"Two bedrooms and a conference room," Shelley explained to me, as if calling one of the bedrooms by another name would make it sound smaller. "It's a corporate apartment. We use it all the time when the big stars fly in to shoot here. It's nicer than a hotel."

"Zach, I've been there," Kylie said. "Trust me, it's nicer than most New York City apartments."

Shelley shrugged. "So it's nice. So it's big. If I had something smaller and not so nice, I'd be glad to give it to you, but this is all I've got."

It was classic old school New York charm, and Kylie smiled. "I don't know, Shelley," she said.

"Look," he said, "we're between celebrity guests, so the place is empty. It costs us a bundle whether it's being used or not, so if you move in for a few weeks, you'd be doing me a favor. What do you say?"

She didn't say anything.

Shelley threw up his hands and turned to me. "Zach, help me out here. Explain to your thickheaded partner that both she and her husband could use a little space for a while. Go ahead. Tell her."

I turned and looked at my thickheaded partner. "Kylie," I said, "please explain to your extremely generous friend that I'm only here as moral support, and you'd appreciate it if he didn't upgrade me to marriage counselor."

"Shelley, Zach's right. This is a decision I have to make with Spence."

"Honey, right now Spence isn't up to making decisions

about anything," Shelley said. "And if you don't get a couple of good nights' sleep, you won't be up to it either. It'll be a lot easier for the two of you to sort things out if you each take some time to decompress. Do me a favor. At least take the apartment for a few days."

Kylie looked at me for an answer. I shook my head. "Sorry," I said. "This one's your call."

She let out a sigh. "Okay," she said. "I'll give it a shot. One night. We'll see how it goes."

Shelley came around the desk and gave her a hug. "The doorman already has your name. He'll give you the keys, and I'll have the concierge stock the refrigerator."

"Thank you," she said. "I have no idea how I can ever pay you back, but I owe you one."

"You want to pay me back?" he said. "Go out and find this crazy Hazmat person. Then me and the rest of this *fakakta* city would owe *you* one."

CHAPTER 56

"TIENI I TUOI *amici vicino, ma i tuoi nemici più vicino,*" Joe reminded Teresa before he sent her off to thank Emma Frye for her act of kindness.

Keep your friends close, but your enemies closer—that, Teresa could live with. But *thank* her? She wanted to grab the Frye woman by the throat and scream, "How did you get my dead son's journal?"

Joe gave her instructions on how to play it. "Just be nice to her. Remember, you can catch more flies with honey," he said.

She loved her husband, but every time he laid that "more flies with honey" line on her, she wanted to say, "Is that how *you* win people over, Joe? With honey?"

Teresa didn't call in advance. She simply arrived at Frye's house. The woman almost peed her pants when she opened the door.

"Mrs. Salvi," Frye said, even though they'd never been introduced.

Of course she knows me, Teresa thought. *The Salvis are Howard Beach royalty.*

"I just came to thank you. Mother to mother," she added, letting her voice catch.

Emma Frye, of course, invited her in for coffee and apologized profusely that the house was such a mess. Teresa in turn apologized for showing up unannounced. They bonded like long-lost sisters.

After ten minutes, Teresa got to the crux of it all. "So how did you come to find my Enzo's journal?" she asked offhandedly.

"It was in my son's room," Emma said. "My husband and I are renovating, and I was collecting all of Gideon's old things when I found the journal."

"Gideon," Teresa said. "I remember a boy named Gideon, but not Frye."

"Oh, my first husband, Gideon's father, passed away two years ago. We owned the flower shop on Cross Bay Boulevard."

"Cross Bay Flowers? I've ordered from there many times."

Emma beamed. "I know. I'm the one who takes your orders over the phone."

"What a small world," Teresa said. "Now I know who your son is. The name Frye threw me off."

"I'm remarried now."

"How wonderful that you could find happiness so soon after your loss," Teresa said. "I had no idea that our sons were friends back in high school."

"Me either. You know teenage boys. They don't tell their mothers anything."

Irish boys, maybe. But Enzo told me plenty. Our sons were never friends. Ever.

Teresa sipped her coffee. "This explains how Enzo's journal wound up in your son's room. The boys were probably hanging out together."

Emma shrugged. "I guess so."

"And how is your Gideon doing these days?"

"Fine…" Emma hesitated.

"You say fine, but it sounds like something is wrong," Teresa said.

"No, no. I was about to say I only wish I could see more of him, but that's such an insensitive thing to say to a woman who can never see her son. I'm so sorry, Mrs. Salvi."

"No apologies necessary, and please, you must call me Teresa. All my friends do. But now I'm curious why you can't see more of Gideon. Did he move away?"

"Oh no, Gideon is living in Manhattan. But he's so busy saving everyone else, he barely has time for a phone call from his mother."

"So he's a doctor," Teresa said.

"If only," Emma said. "Then I wouldn't have to worry so much. Gideon is a New York City police officer. Very dangerous job, but he loves it."

Teresa's hand shook, and she set down her coffee cup before she dropped it. She forced a smile. "It's always good to see a boy make something of himself. I only wish I had been able to see my Enzo do the same, but thank you for bringing a little piece of my son back to his family. It's a great comfort to all of us."

Teresa stood up, the smile still plastered to her face. She thanked Emma one last time, then bolted from the house.

She couldn't wait to tell Joe that the Mick bastard who had Enzo's journal all these years—and the one who probably murdered him—was a fucking cop.

CHAPTER 57

MOMMY'S COMING, KIMI. *I'm sorry for what happened. Mommy's coming to make it better. Mommy loves you so much.*

Rachael O'Keefe knew she was going to die. She knew it as soon as they stripped her down and put her in a white Hazmat suit.

Then they gagged her, chained her to a pipe, and left her without food, water, or hope.

Talking to Kimi made it easier. Those two words— *Mommy's coming*—became her mantra. They were on a loop in her brain, and she chanted them silently, hoping they could lull her to sleep. But the blinding light, the damp cold, and the stench of mold made it difficult to sleep.

And the fear made it impossible.

Mommy is in a dungeon, Kimi. But don't cry. Pretty soon Mommy will...

The lights went out with a thunk that echoed off the corrugated metal door. Rachael inhaled sharply. *Were they back? Were the lights on a timer? What now?*

A hum. A motor. And then she felt it. Air. Warm air blowing down on her from above.

Thank you, Kimi, thank you, Kimi, she chanted. Her head dropped, and she let her body sink into the blessed warmth and darkness.

She was just crossing the sleep threshold when the barking began. She jerked awake. A second dog joined in with a low, threatening growl, and she screamed in terror, but the only sound that made its way past the gag was a muffled whine.

The barking grew louder and closer, and Rachael tried to wrench herself free. The chains around her wrists, ankles, and neck tore into her flesh as the room exploded with the sound of a pack of snarling, angry dogs. The silent screams continued, and then she lost control of her bladder, just as she had when she was attacked by her neighbor's pit bull at the age of nine.

Mommy's coming, Kimi. Mommy's coming, Kimi. Mommy's coming, Kimi. Mommy's coming, Kimi.

And then, a voice. "Are you ready to tell us the truth?"

The lights snapped on, and the barking stopped abruptly. Rachael looked around the room. No dogs. Just the two men in black.

The taller one—the leader—peeled away the duct tape and removed the ball gag from her mouth.

"Are you ready to tell us the truth?" he asked again.

Her wrists and ankles were bleeding, and her neck was

rubbed raw from the chains. "I did tell you the truth," she whimpered.

"No, you didn't," he said, opening a bottle of Poland Spring water. He tilted the bottle to his lips and gulped down half of it.

Rachael stared at the water.

"You look thirsty," he said. "The rest of this is yours. Just tell me who killed Kimi."

"I swear I didn't kill Kimi. I loved her. I would never hurt my only child."

"Oh yes. You were Mother of the Year," he said. "Here's first prize."

He held up the water bottle and turned it upside down.

Rachael sobbed as the water splashed onto the concrete floor. "The jury believed that I didn't do it. Why can't you?"

"Juries are stupid," he said. "And in a hurry to get home. We're neither."

The shorter one—the nicer one—pointed to a video camera on a tripod in front of her. "Just talk to the camera. Tell us what really happened, and we'll give you a hot meal, lots of cool, cool water, and then you can sleep."

"You mean then you can kill me," Rachael said.

"True," the leader said. "Death is inevitable. But pain and suffering are optional. Here—let me demonstrate."

He had a wooden box in his hand. It reminded Rachael of a music box her mother had when she was a little girl.

He opened it, and she almost expected it to play "Irish

Lullaby." But there was no music. There was just a strange metal contraption inside. She'd never seen anything like it, but she knew it was evil.

"It's called a choke pear," he said. "Some call it the pear of anguish. This one is from the sixteenth century. I bought it on eBay for twelve hundred bucks."

Rachael squeezed her eyes shut.

"Open them," he said slowly, "or I will open them for you."

She opened her eyes. The box was on the floor, and now he had the pear-shaped thing in his hands.

"Now open your mouth."

She shook her head.

He nodded to his partner.

The nice one pinched her nostrils and forced her mouth open, and the other slid the metal pear inside.

"Now here's the beauty of this little pear," he said. "The stem is really a corkscrew, and when I twist the spiral rod in the center—"

He gave the corkscrew two quick turns, and Rachael gagged and screamed at the same time.

"Relax," he said. "This is only a demo. It won't hurt. Not this time."

He twisted the corkscrew in the opposite direction and slid the pear from her mouth. Rachael gasped at the air.

The man in black smiled. "All I did was turn it twice," he said. "Like this."

He turned the corkscrew twice, and Rachael watched as the pear opened at the bottom and four spoonlike segments began to spread out.

"Now watch what happens when I turn it again. And again. And again."

The iron lobes spread out even farther, leaving no doubt as to what damage the device could inflict.

"How many was that?" he asked. "Five turns? You should see it at ten. Or fifteen. It's diabolical, but you know those crazy punishing medieval judges—they couldn't wait to use it."

"I didn't kill my daughter," Rachael said. "I swear."

"Hold that thought. I'm not quite finished."

He held the pear up to her face. "Here's the genius of this little beauty. It's a multi-orifice device. So if you were a blasphemous heretic, it would go inside your lying mouth. Male homosexuals were punished with the anal pear. And women who fornicated with Satan...well, like I said—it works in any orifice."

A cell phone rang, and the man patted his pocket.

"Something for you to ponder while I take this call."

CHAPTER 58

"HANG ON," GIDEON said into the phone as he walked behind the false wall they'd built to hide the audio equipment.

He had done his research well. He knew that Rachael would be petrified at the mere sound of dogs. And that was all it took to bring her to the point of hysteria—a cut from a sound effects library.

He stepped outside the rear door and put the phone to his ear. "Mom, what's up? I'm a little busy."

"I thought your shift would be over. That's why I waited till now."

"My shift *is* over. I'm busy with life." He still had the choke pear in his other hand, and he fondled it.

"Fine. I'll make this short. You'll never believe who came to the house today."

"Mom, can this wait? I'm really busy here."

"Teresa Salvi."

"That's great, Mom. I gotta— What? Who?"

"Mrs. Salvi. She told me to call her Teresa."

"What the fuck was she doing there?"

"Gideon. Language."

"Mom, Mom, I'm sorry. I wasn't focused. Just tell me again. Teresa Salvi came to the house? Joe Salvi's wife?"

"*Now* I have your attention. Yes, she did. She made a special trip just to thank me for returning her son's book."

There was a plastic milk crate behind the garage, and Gideon slowly lowered himself to it. "What book?" he asked. But, of course, he knew the answer before he even asked the question.

"Her son Enzo's journal. I found it wedged behind a desk drawer when I was cleaning up your room."

"That's...that's impossible."

"Is something wrong? Did I do something wrong?"

His brain was racing. His mother couldn't have the book because he had it. He could swear he had it.

That rainy night in 2001, he had read through every page. He remembered thinking, *If the people in this book knew I was the one who put Enzo Salvi out of the protection business, they would throw me one hell of a party.*

But he couldn't tell anyone. And he couldn't bring himself to burn it either. He was sixteen, and Enzo Salvi's leather book with the gold froufrous on it was a trophy. Over the years, he'd thought about destroying it, but he couldn't. It was a symbol of what he could accomplish when he was only a kid. Imagine how powerful he could become.

Sure, it was dangerous to keep, but Gideon never ran away from danger. He never told Dave he still had it. Dave would shit. But over the years, he'd had no regrets—he was happy he'd kept it. If he'd ever had any guilt about killing Enzo, the details in that journal were a living list of the scumbag's crimes.

A few years ago, when he'd moved out of his mother's house, he'd packed up everything he'd wanted to keep. He could swear he'd taken the journal. He'd been drinking that night, but still—he was sure he'd buried it at the bottom of one of those cartons that were stored in the closet of his new apartment. It had to be there. It had to.

"Gideon—are you listening?" his mother said. "I asked you a question."

"What, Mom? I didn't hear you."

"I said I hope I didn't do the wrong thing. The book had Enzo's name on it, so I gave it to Father Spinelli, who gave it to Mrs. Salvi. The poor woman's son was killed when he was only eighteen."

"No, Mom, you didn't do the wrong thing."

"I know those Salvis are mixed up in all kinds of shady nonsense. But not the mother. She's always going to Mass. She throws those big parties for the neighborhood. I thought the least I could do was let her have a little touchstone of her dead son. God only knows how his book wound up with your things."

"You did fine, Mom," Gideon said. "Thanks for telling me. I've got to go now."

"I know, I know, you're so busy with life, but maybe one night you can squeeze in a dinner with me and Sherman."

"I promise," Gideon said. "Love you, Mom."

He set down the phone and buried his face in one hand.

He didn't have to check the cartons in his closet. Somehow he'd screwed up. He had left Enzo's book at his mother's house, and she'd given it to the Salvis.

He stood up. *And now the Salvis are going to come after me and Dave.*

The back door opened, and Dave stepped out.

"Hey, Gid, what's going on?"

"Nothing," Gideon said. "Just the usual stupid Mom phone call. You know—'Who are you dating? Don't work too hard.' Nothing important."

"You did great in there with the choke pear. And the dogs—that was a good call. She's cracking."

"I think you're right," Gideon said. "She's on the edge."

"Let's give her another twenty-four hours in there," Dave said, "and come back mañana. At that point she should be ready to spill her murdering guts out."

"Good idea," Gideon said.

No sense telling Dave about the Salvis tonight. He'd freak. First we break Rachael, then I can deal with the Mafia.

CHAPTER 59

DESPITE THE FACT that we have the most sophisticated crime-solving technology at our fingertips, Kylie and I spent the rest of our day hoofing it through the bureaucratic roadblocks created by the New York County District Attorney's Office and the City of New York Department of Correction.

At 5:00 p.m., we reported in to Cates.

"Four people at the DOC knew where Rachael O'Keefe was headed when she left lockup," I said. "And at least eight from the DA's office."

"*At least* eight?" Cates said. "You can't get a hard number?"

"We tried," Kylie said, "but we're dealing with the justice prevention department."

"We interviewed and cleared everyone at the DOC and managed to track down six of the DA's people," I said.

"Then you have two left."

"Not quite. The ADAs went out on a group bender that night, and three of them admitted 'saying something to someone they knew they could trust,' so that brings us back up to five people we have to clear."

"How hard can it be to track them down?" Cates said.

"Tracking them down is easy. We've emailed, texted, and left phone messages—they all know what we want. Pinning them down for a face-to-face is the problem. They'd be happy to phone it in, but these guys lie for a living. We figured we had a better shot at getting the truth out of them if we confront them up close and personal.

"Two of them are coming up here tonight. A third just had an emergency appendectomy, and we can't talk to her till tomorrow. The final two on our hit list are Mick Wilson and one of his flunkies. And you know Mick—he has a bad habit of either not returning messages, or just not giving a shit."

"Make him give a shit. O'Keefe was taken fifteen hours ago. Hazmat's not going to keep her alive for long. Call me when you—"

"Captain."

It was Katina Hronas, a civilian employee assigned to our unit. Katina fielded hundreds of phone calls, emails, and faxes for Cates every day. She was tuned in to Cates's priorities, both personal and professional, and interrupted the boss only when it was urgent. Cates braced herself for the inevitable.

"This just came through from the chief of D's office," Katina said, handing Cates a single sheet of paper.

"Damn," she said, reading the small block of text in seconds. "It's out."

Kylie and I looked at each other. We both knew what "it" was.

"We kept the lid on it for nine hours," Cates said, "but the *Times* just issued an email alert—*Rachael O'Keefe Kidnapped Within Hours of Leaving New York City Jail.*"

"The *Times* doesn't print rumors," Kylie said. "Who corroborated it?"

"'O'Keefe's abduction was confirmed by her defense attorney, Dennis Woloch,'" Cates read. "Of course they don't say who leaked it, but I'd put my money on Hazmat himself. He loves ink, and the media will give him plenty of it."

"Which means our tip line will be flooded with hundreds of crackpot sightings," Kylie said.

"Not your problem," Cates said. "Commissioner Harries will give me all the manpower I need to deal with the wacko phone calls. All you have to do is find Rachael O'Keefe, take down the Hazmat Killer, and turn Mayor Spellman into a national hero before Election Day. Get on it."

"Best locker room pep talk I ever heard from a coach," Kylie said as we left Cates's office. "It's just what I needed to finally start giving a shit about this case."

By nine o'clock, two of the errant assistant DAs showed up and swore up and down that they never talked to anyone about Rachael's hideaway in Jersey. Neither one of them hedged, hesitated, or in any way held back. They were telling the truth.

"Three to go," Kylie said. "I move we adjourn for the night. All in favor..."

I was about to vote aye when the elevator stopped on our floor. Red has its own space on the third floor of the One Nine, and we don't get too much traffic—especially at this hour.

The doors opened, and out stepped the last two people I'd have expected to show up at our office. The ones John Dho called *Defectives* Donovan and Boyle.

They walked toward our desks, scowls still on their faces, chips still on their shoulders, and brooms still planted firmly up their asses.

"We figured you'd still be here," Donovan said.

"That's the thing about these serial killer cases," Kylie said. "You don't get to punch out early. What are you doing here?"

"What do you think? Catch us up."

"On what?" Kylie said.

He laughed. "On what? On the fucking case. Look, you may be calling the shots, but this has been our case from the get-go, and we're not walking away from—"

Boyle held up his hand. "Calm down," he said to his partner. Then he turned to Kylie. "I guess you can tell we're still a little out of joint, but it's not your fault. It's just politics, so let's start over. Okay?"

"Go for it," Kylie said. "It couldn't get any worse."

"Look," Boyle said, "me and Donovan were blindsided Monday morning. Hazmat was our case. We did the best we could, but let's face it—the first three victims were all scumbags, and nobody complained that we hadn't caught the killer. Then Parker-Steele gets whacked, and the case is page one. Now Rachael O'Keefe gets kidnapped, and the whole thing is going global."

"We don't have any proof that O'Keefe is connected to Hazmat," Kylie said.

"The *Post* doesn't have any proof either," Boyle said, "but they're going with it anyway—home page of their online edition. The point is, Hazmat is even bigger than before, and we don't want to be known as the two schmuck cops that couldn't crack it. Monday you said we were assigned to this so-called task force of yours. If we're still on it, catch us up."

"Fair enough," Kylie said. "We found a witness who saw Parker-Steele get into a car."

"Did they ID the car, or the driver?" Donovan asked.

"There were two suspects," Kylie said. "She got into the backseat with a man, but the witness couldn't see who was driving."

"*Two* suspects?" Boyle said.

"You sure?" Donovan said. "We've been looking for one."

"And we also have another witness who saw Alex Kang get into a car with two guys," I said.

They both looked bowled over.

"Son of a bitch," Donovan said. "You got lucky. We couldn't find a witness for shit in Chinatown. What kind of car?"

"A black SUV. No make, no model," I said.

"How about the two men?" Donovan said. "You get a description on them?"

"Just two average white guys like you and me," I said.

"How about O'Keefe? Anything on her?"

"Two guys took her, so the *Post* may be right. It's probably the Hazmat team."

"You closing in on them?"

"Not closing in," I said, "but getting closer. We just got some fresh evidence."

"Fresh evidence like what?" Donovan asked.

"The two who took O'Keefe left a trail. We're on it, but that's all we can tell you right now."

Boyle nodded. "Hey, I know we didn't get off on the right foot, but if you're closing in on these guys, you're gonna need backup, right?"

"Probably," Kylie said.

Boyle shrugged. He knew that "probably" was as much of a commitment as he was going to get.

"Hey, man, you've got our cell phones," he said. "Call anytime."

CHAPTER 60

DONOVAN AND BOYLE got on the elevator, and Kylie and I waited quietly as they rode to the ground floor.

"I didn't trust those two when they were trying to undermine us," she said as the elevator doors opened with a loud clunk that reverbed up the shaft. "I trust them even less now that they want to help."

"Technically, I think only Boyle wants to help," I said. "Donovan would probably be happier finding us stuffed into a couple of Hazmat suits. I can't believe they pulled a good cop/bad cop routine on us."

"I'm still trying to figure out if they're smart cops or stupid cops," she said.

"I vote stupid."

"We came up with more leads in three days than those bozos did in four months," she said, "so on the surface they come off as pretty lame."

"And you think there's something below the surface?"

"Let's just say Cheryl is right, and we're looking for real cops. If Donovan and Boyle are the doers, then they managed to set themselves up as lead detectives by committing the first murder in their jurisdiction. That's not just smart, it's brilliant."

"How do you explain the fact that they showed up tonight to pump us for details on the case? Don't they know that's the fastest way to move to the top of the suspect list? Sounds pretty dumb to me."

"It's only dumb if they know we're looking for dirty cops," she said. "Right now there are only four people who know we're thinking that the killers are NYPD. You, me, Cheryl, and Cates. These guys may be a lot smarter than they act. I think they threw a shit fit when we grabbed the case away from them, and they did everything they could not to help us. Then they realized that freezing us out freezes them out. So they decided that offering to be our backup is the best way to stay in the loop and keep tabs on the investigation."

"I don't care if they're dumb or smart. If they're keeping tabs on us, maybe we should keep tabs on them."

Kylie lit up. "Zachary Jordan, are you talking about tailing those guys?"

"Yeah."

"Do you think Captain Go-by-the-Book would approve of our putting a team on them?" she said.

"Maybe yes, maybe no," I said.

"Probably no."

"It doesn't matter, because I'm not asking her. Right now I don't give a damn what she says."

"Listen to the straight arrow talking," she said, giving me a big grin. "And I thought I was the only cop around here with a reputation for going off the reservation."

Long before she showed up at Red, Kylie was notorious for breaking the rules any time she felt they were working against her. And although the brass frowns on rogue cops, she always got the job done, so they always looked the other way. Donovan and Boyle smelled rotten, and I was ready to nail them—chain of command be damned.

"You heard the mayor this afternoon," I said. "Whatever we fucking have to do 'damn well better happen before Election Day.' Did that seem like a casual comment?"

"Hell, no. It sounded like a direct order from the top of the food chain. I love the way you think," she said. "Way to go, partner."

She picked up her desk phone and dialed. "Hello, it's Kylie. Oh man, I'm so glad you're still there. Can I swing by?"

Whatever the response was, it made her laugh. "Great. I'll pop round in a minute."

She bolted for the door.

"You mind telling me where you're going?" I said.

"Matt Smith's office. I'll be back in five."

And with that she was gone.

I just sat there fuming, as though the girl I'd brought to the dance went home with someone else.

Matt Smith? Way to go, partner.

CHAPTER 61

JOE SALVI STARED at the pot of spaghetti sauce on the stove. His mother would have dumped it in the garbage before she would have fed it to Papa. Then his eyes shifted to the woman who had just served it to him.

Teresa was standing at the kitchen counter, opening another bottle of wine. She stopped to kick off her eight-hundred-dollar five-inch heels. *Good idea, Teresa. A lady doesn't want to fall on her ass when she's swilling down her second two-hundred-dollar bottle of Bruno Giacosa Barolo.*

Forty-one years ago she had been the perfect wife, delivering on all three of the only characteristics his mother told him were important. Good in the kitchen, great in the bedroom, and Catholic.

Mama was gone now. And so was Teresa. They still shared a bedroom, but the sex was no longer spectacular. It wasn't bad. It just wasn't any good. Like the sauce.

She had drifted away slowly. She said it was because he was so wrapped up in his work.

His work? What did she think paid for all this? The house? The cars? The clothes? The jewelry? The charities? She gave his money away to whoever had a hand out, and they put her on a pedestal. Fine, if that's what she needed. But where did she think the money came from? It came from his work.

"Did I tell you she's remarried now?" Teresa said.

She had been droning on, but he had tuned her out.

"Yes, you told me," he said. *Twice.*

"She's so happy. She married the teacher from John Adams, and now they run their little flower shop together," Teresa said. "Her husband dies, and two years later another man is sleeping in his bed. Tramp."

She refilled her wineglass, staring him down as she poured from the new bottle, challenging him to say something about how much she was drinking.

"And she's so proud of her precious little pig cop son saving the world," Teresa said. "I'm glad, because it only means that when I get finished with him, it's going to hurt all the more."

He laughed. "When *you* get finished with him? Who died and left you boss?"

"Enzo died. That's who died. I've been waiting twelve years for payback, and now I'm going to get it."

"You going to take on the police department?" he said. "You going to go whack a cop?"

"*Two* cops," Teresa told him. "The other one whose name was in Enzo's collection book. The friend Dave. You always said it would take more than one to kill Enzo. You thought it was the blacks from Ozone Park, but it was those Mick bastards."

She gulped down half the wine in her glass. "Those people were our neighbors. We threw parties for them. We fed them. And this is how they show their respect? We welcomed them with open arms, and they turned around and stabbed us in the heart. Judas has been sitting at our table, Joe. Judas."

Salvi held up a hand. He hadn't seen her this bad since Enzo's funeral. "All right, Teresa, enough. I'll handle it."

"When?"

He stood up. "Now. I have a lieutenant who owes me a favor. He'll find out where these two cops work."

"And then what?"

"How should I know? Let me find them first. Give me some room to think."

"Don't think. Act. If not for me, then do it for your mother. Remember what she promised Enzo when she threw herself on his casket. *La famiglia fornirà giustizia.* An eye for an eye."

She lurched toward the counter, grabbed the bottle, and staggered out of the room.

Salvi took out his cell phone and called Bernice. "I'm coming over," he said.

That was all he had to say. He hung up and went to the closet for a coat.

Bernice worked for his accountant. Forty years old and never been married. Not pretty. Just a nice quiet Jewish girl who turned out to be a tigress in the sack. They'd been at it for seven years, and the woman never asked for anything. He gave her gifts, and she would say, "Thank you, Joe. You really shouldn't have." But there were no demands.

The sex was incredible. And on top of it all, she was a damn good cook.

Mama would have hated her.

She wasn't Catholic.

CHAPTER 62

KYLIE HAS ALWAYS had a knack for infuriating me. Tonight was no exception. Twenty minutes had passed since she'd yelled "I'll be back in five" and bolted out the door to talk to Matt Smith. No explanation. No invitation for me to come along. Just her signature I'm-in-charge-you-wait-here-for-further-instructions attitude.

I was working up a seriously unhealthy resentment when my cell rang. It was Cheryl. My slow burn dissolved into a warm glow, and I picked up the phone.

"Hey," I said, "you're not only beautiful and intelligent, you're also clairvoyant. How did you know I was in desperate need of a shrink?"

"And how did you know I was in desperate need of someone to tell me I was beautiful and intelligent? In real life, I'm sprawled on the sofa in my sweats, drinking wine, munching popcorn, about to subject my superior intellect to a movie I've already seen seven times."

"*Pretty Woman* with Richard Gere and Julia Roberts?"

"You know me well, Zachary. So why do you need a shrink?"

"Because I'm sitting here gathering dust while Wonder Woman toddles off to solve the biggest case of my career on her own."

"It's a tough time for Kylie," Cheryl said. "From what you've told me, her personal life is off the rails. Her job is the one thing she can control."

"Great. Except that her job is *my* job. I'm her partner."

"Then cut her some slack, partner."

"Is that your professional take on it? You want *me* to cut *her* some slack? I thought you'd be on my side."

"Professionals don't take sides. Come on, Zach— you've had some rough patches, and Kylie has always been there for you. Don't take it personally—she's not trying to cut you out. Diving into work helps distract her from her problem with Spence. Eventually, they'll iron it out, and you two will find your balance again."

"What am I supposed to do until then?"

"In the words of my illustrious colleague," she said, "suck it up, dude."

"And who said that? Dr. Freud?"

"Dr. Phil."

"Okay, you've successfully restored my mental health," I said. "Enjoy your wine, your popcorn, and your girlie movie. It sounds like you've planned an evening to re-member."

"It's only missing one thing," she said seductively.

Now I really felt restored. "Me?"

"Actually, I was thinking Richard Gere to take me shopping on Rodeo Drive, but sure—you'll do. Are you available?"

"Not immediately, but it's hard to turn down free wine and popcorn. Keep a light on for me. I'll be there in about two hours."

"The movie will be over in two hours," she said.

"You're a professional—I'm sure you'll find a way to help me cope."

Kylie walked through the door.

"Gotta go," I said. "Detective MacDonald has returned from her quest."

"Don't get snarky," Cheryl said. "Be nice to her."

"I will, I will, I promise," I said. "See you later. I blank you."

"I blank you too," she said, and hung up.

We still hadn't zeroed in on the best way to end a phone call. Neither of us was quite ready for *I love you*, but after three months, who were we kidding?

Kylie was grinning like a prospector who had just struck a mother lode.

"You're glowing in triumph," I said. "What have you got?"

"You were right on the money when you said let's tail Donovan and Boyle. Matt searched the DMV database to find out what kind of cars they each drive."

"And you wouldn't be this excited unless one of them owns an SUV."

"Detective David Donovan," she said. "A 2011 Toyota Highlander, and it is black as the hills of South Dakota."

"That's encouraging, but guaranteed he's not the only cop whose car fits the description."

"I know. Matt gave me the usual blah, blah, blah warning—don't jump to conclusions because there are two million vehicles registered in the five boroughs, and 15,811 of them are black SUVs. But still, if we're going to stick our necks out, it helps that Dave Donovan owns a car that matches the one used in the kidnappings."

"So now what?" I said.

"I agree with you that we can't ask Cates if we can tail two detectives on a hunch. Even if she says yes, it would create a paper trail, and if we're wrong, she'll look like an idiot along with the two of us."

"So we tail them without telling her," I said.

"Not 'we.' *We* have too much on our plate as it is. We need to recruit someone."

"You have anybody in mind?"

"I have a couple of thoughts," she said. "How about you?"

I'd had twenty minutes to think about it before Cheryl called, and I did have somebody I thought could tail them and keep it under wraps. I told her.

"Perfect choice," she said.

"Really? No counterproposal?"

"I know you have trouble taking yes for an answer, but I'm in violent agreement with you. Let's call their boss and see if they're available."

"We didn't call our boss. Are you really sure we want

to call theirs? I mean, why start going by the book now? Let's just call them direct. More Red, less red tape."

"An unauthorized tail," she said. "I'm proud of you, cowboy. You're finally learning how to bend a couple of rules."

"Yeah," I said. "That's because working with you is pretty much like taking a master class."

CHAPTER 63

WHEN I WAS fifteen, my mother got a regular gig doing makeup on *Guiding Light*. Every day I would stop by after school so I could pig out on the never-ending buffet of snacks that are always on hand for the crew.

It wasn't long before I realized that I was racing to the studio every afternoon because I was more interested in the twisted lives of the characters on the show than the junk food on the craft services table.

I was hooked on a soap opera—not an easy realization for a teenage boy to come to grips with, and I was sure there was something wrong with me.

Mom assured me that I was perfectly normal. "We all love getting caught up in other people's problems," she said. "It's human nature."

I can't speak for the rest of humanity, but it sure as hell

is my nature. Which is why as soon as Kylie said good night and hopped a cab uptown to Shelley's apartment, I hopped one going downtown and headed for hers.

Spence had been released from the hospital that evening, and I decided this was the perfect time to have a little heart-to-heart with him. I didn't tell Cheryl where I was going because she had already weighed in on the subject last night.

"Stay out of it," she'd said. "The man is an addict, and unless you know what you're doing, stay away. It would be like sending a traffic cop to handle a hostage negotiation situation."

Had we been at the office when she'd said it, I'd have argued with her. But we'd been in bed at the time, and I was still wrapped in the afterglow of postcoital bliss. Not the ideal moment to get into a discussion with my psychologist girlfriend about whether or not I was qualified to get involved in my former girlfriend's marital problems. Or why I even wanted to, which was a question I hadn't quite answered for myself. So I'd just whispered, "You're right."

But deep down, I knew Cheryl was wrong. I wasn't exactly a traffic cop.

Kylie and Spence lived in lower Manhattan in an eight-story factory that had been converted to eight incredible lofts with spectacular views of the Hudson River. There was no doorman—just a pair of thick glass doors and a wall-mounted video security system. I rang up.

"Zach?" Spence squawked over the intercom. "Kylie's not here."

"I know. I wanted to talk to you. You mind if I come up?"

"It's late, man. What do you want to talk about?"

The evils of drug addiction, but I was hoping we could have a beer and some guy talk before I jumped into it.

Clearly he wasn't buzzing me in. I had to make my pitch from the lobby.

I took a deep breath. "Look, Spence," I said, "Kylie told me what's going on. I know you've been having a few issues with the painkillers…"

"Oh, Jesus," he groaned. "So my wife asked you to take a break from chasing serial killers and start working narcotics?"

"She doesn't even know I'm here. This is personal—just between you and me."

"Personal? Bro, you're Kylie's friend, not mine."

"You're right, I'm not your friend, Spence. I'm just a casual acquaintance who risked his fucking life to save yours."

I stared defiantly into the camera. It took five seconds, but the buzzer finally rang, and I pushed my way in before he changed his mind.

I took the elevator to the seventh floor, and Spence opened the door. I expected he would look like shit, and he did not disappoint.

Until his run-in with The Chameleon, Spence Harrington had worked out in his home gym two hours a day. The Spence who stood at the front door had vacant eyes and a bloated face. I knew enough about his drug habit to know that lack of exercise was not the cause.

"Well, well, well," he said. "If it isn't the twelve-step Avon lady. If you're here to give me one of those Nancy Reagan Just Say No lectures, don't waste your time. I've been hearing them since I was smoking weed back in high school."

"Hey, I'm not here to lecture you. Just talk."

"I'm talked out, dude, so let me give it to you short and sweet. These painkillers I'm on—they're not like my coke habit. These are not recreational. They're prescribed by a doctor."

"From what Kylie tells me, you're taking a lot more than the doctor prescribed."

As soon as I said it, I wanted to take it back. He had pushed me right where I didn't want to go, and I was sounding like Kylie's drug enforcer. His eyes flared with contempt.

I looked down at his bare feet, which were a dozen different shades of red and purple. "I owe you an apology, Spence," I said, trying to backpedal. "If Kylie and I had caught the bastard who did that to you sooner..."

"Look, Nancy, I'm sure you mean well," he said, still barricading the door. "But go home. I already have a support group. I've got a program, a sponsor, meetings, and slogans up the ass. Right now, all Kylie and I need is a little space till I get this pain under control."

He started to shut the door, and I leaned into it.

"What pain, Spence? The foot pain? You and I both know that's long gone. The only pain you have now is knowing you're a junkie, but if you pop enough pills, you can make that go away. And if it doesn't, you'll be uptown at three in the morning looking for a coke dealer."

"Fuck you, Zach," he said, pushing hard on the door.

"Bring plenty of money, Spence," I said, pushing back, "because you're going to need a lot of coke once she walks. And trust me, she will. You think it hurt the last time she dumped you? This will be worse."

He eased up on the door and stuck his face in the opening. "Worse for who, Zach? The last time around, I got clean, and Kylie and I got married. If I remember correctly, you're the one she dumped."

My well-intentioned intervention had crashed and burned. I rammed the door hard and knocked him off his damaged feet. He hit the floor, and I stood over him.

"She was a twenty-two-year-old kid who wanted to become a cop," I yelled, "and the last thing she needed was a boyfriend who spent his whole day pounding blow. Yeah, she took you back, but don't count on her making the same decision again. Her job is even more important to her now, and she's not going to let a coked-up, pill-popping husband fuck it up for her."

He looked up at me, dumbfounded. He opened his mouth to speak, but nothing came out. I kept going.

"I don't have any Nancy Reagan lectures, Spence. Just think about this—what makes you feel better, the Percocet or your wife? Because you damn well can't have them both."

I stepped back from the door, and he got up on his knees and slammed it shut.

I stood there seething—filled with anger both at him

and at myself for being stupid enough to think that I was the miracle worker who could rehabilitate Spence and patch up his floundering marriage.

Obviously, I had seen too many soap operas as a kid, and they had completely screwed up my thinking.

CHAPTER 64

IT WAS 11:30 when I finally got to Cheryl's apartment.

"You look like you could use a drink and a hug," she said. "Not necessarily in that order." She wrapped her arms around me and pressed her lips to mine.

I scooped her up and held her tight, and my body went straight into sensory overload. All five of my senses were on point. I shut my eyes, turned off my hearing, and let touch, taste, and smell have themselves a field day.

Her mouth tasted like wine, her hair smelled like jasmine, and the feel of her body close to mine helped me block out the first twenty-three and a half hours of an exceptionally grueling day.

We stood there for at least a minute without uttering a sound. Finally she whispered in my ear, "You missed a fantastic movie."

"Was it as good the eighth time as the first seven?"

"Zach, I may be a grown-up scientist on the outside, but inside I'm still a little girl who believes in fairy tales. It was just as wonderful this time, and it will be just as wonderful every time I watch it. You're a man. You wouldn't understand."

She stepped back. She was wearing fitted black yoga pants and a hot-pink curve-hugging V-neck T-shirt.

"I thought you said you were wearing sweats," I said.

"I was, but watching Julia Roberts transform from a streetwalker to a lady inspired me."

"You both clean up well."

She led me to the sofa and poured me some wine.

"So how was your day?" she said.

"Not the best. It started with a violent kidnapping and ended with me flinging my partner's drug-addled husband to the floor. How was yours?"

Her mouth opened, first in shock, then it morphed into something resembling a puzzled smile. Or maybe it was a condemning frown. Whatever it was, it was a look I hadn't seen before. Certainly not from her.

"Run that drug-addled husband bit by me again," she said.

I had decided early on that win, lose, or draw with Spence, I wasn't going to hold back on Cheryl.

"Despite my doctor's best advice," I said, "I went to see Spence tonight. I guess you'd call it an intervention."

"No," she said. "I'm more inclined to call it a misguided, self-serving bad decision, but let me withhold judgment until I've heard the details."

"Sure, Doc," I said, taking a strong pull on my wine.

"Do you want me to lie down on the couch while you go and get a pad and pen?"

The joke fell flat. This time I knew a condemning frown when I saw one. "Please just spell it out," she said.

I launched into my story, starting off with my good intentions, working my way past Spence's initial resistance, and elaborating on his steadfast denial. She didn't say a word until I got to my dramatic ultimatum.

"*Your Percocet or your wife?*" She let out a hoot. "Brilliant technique, Doctor Jordan. Where did you get your degree—the Dirty Harry School of Addiction Therapy?"

"Do you want to hear the rest of the story, or do you want to sit around and critique my methodology?" I said.

"He just slammed the door in your face," she said. "I thought you were done. Is there more?"

"Yeah. I stood there feeling like crap. I realized I should have listened to you, but I didn't. Case closed. I walked back to the elevator, and before I could even hit the button, he opened the door and told me to come in. So I went back."

Her expression softened. "And then what happened?"

"Nothing. He just stared at me. I wasn't sure if he was going to take a punch at me or call Kylie and tell her what an asshole I was. And then he turned around and started walking toward his bedroom. Halfway there, he stopped and gave me a nod to follow him. So I did."

"Into the bedroom?"

"Through the bedroom and into his bathroom. He went to the medicine cabinet, took out a bottle of pills, opened it, and shook one out into his hand. Then another. And another. He stared at them, and I really thought he was going to pop them all into his mouth. But he didn't. He just held his hand over the toilet bowl and dropped them in. Slowly. One at a time. Then he turned the bottle over and dumped the entire lot of them into the water."

"Oh, Zach," she said, touching her hand to her chin. "That's amazing. And then what?"

"We both stood there. Neither of us said a word. I don't know how long, but it was a while. I didn't want to stare at him, so I just kept looking down at all those pills floating in the bowl. Finally, I looked up at him and said, 'Are you going to flush?' And he looked back at me with these big sad brown eyes, and he said, 'Give me a goddamn minute, will you? This ain't as easy as it looks.' Then he gave me this big bear hug, we broke, he flushed, and he went into his bedroom to call a rehab. My first intervention, and I'm batting a thousand. I'm thinking after this cop gig, maybe I should hang out a shingle and open a practice."

"What will it say—'World's Worst Therapist'?"

"Criticize all you want, Dr. Robinson, but you can't argue with results."

"You're right. Maybe the sign should just say 'World's Luckiest Therapist.'"

"I may not be classically trained," I said, "but you have to admit, I've got some redeeming qualities."

"I vaguely recall that you do," she said, taking me by the hand and pulling me up from the sofa. "But you're going to have to refresh my memory."

"You know, I think you're right," I said as she led me toward her bedroom. "Tonight, I definitely am the world's luckiest therapist."

CHAPTER 65

I WAS IN the office by 7:00 a.m. Kylie tumbled in ten minutes later, looking like a zombie on Ambien.

"If I didn't know better," I said, "I'd guess you spent the night sleeping in a homeless shelter."

"I wish," she said. "I spent the night in an eight-thousand-dollar-a-month apartment—not sleeping. I was crazy worried about Spence."

I wanted to tell her that I was pretty crazy worried about Spence myself, but it's never a good idea to tell a control freak that you tried to take control of her life.

"I finally dozed off at two," she said, "but I woke up at four and was awake the rest of the night, thinking how much I'd like to be out there tailing Donovan and Boyle."

"Not a great idea in your condition," I said. "Yesterday you almost got us killed driving the Batmobile into Queens, and that was after a good night's sleep."

We still had three people to interview who knew that Rachael would be in New Jersey. The one recovering from an emergency appendectomy was just a few blocks away at Lenox Hill Hospital. It took us less than half an hour to run over there and clear her.

Two to go—Mick Wilson, the stubborn-ass senior ADA, and the young lawyer assigned to work with him. According to Wilson's office, they were driving upstate to the Great Meadow Correctional Facility in Comstock to interview a prison snitch. It's in Washington County, a four-hour drive from the city.

I know Mick well. He was a rock star in the DA's office, and a front-runner for the top job when the current DA retired.

He didn't return my voice mails, so I texted him, explaining how important it was to talk to him and his junior lawyer.

He texted right back.

Was I not supposed to tell anyone where O'Keefe was holing up? I guess I should never have posted it on Facebook. Off the grid and won't be back till late tonight. You can arrest me then.

"Cute," Kylie said.

"It's Mick's way of telling me I'm an asshole for even questioning him," I said.

"How about the lawyer he's with? She's the last one on our list."

"I would hope that Mick would vet her on our behalf, but I'm sure he thinks anyone he handpicked to work with him is just as above suspicion as he is. We can try to contact her tonight, but I think we're coming up dry."

"Then Matt was right," Kylie said. "Last night he told me whoever kidnapped Rachael might not be connected to the DA's office. He said it would be easy enough for a pro to hack into the Correction Department's computer."

"How come you didn't tell me that last night?"

"I don't know. You were so down on Matt I decided not to—"

"Jordan! MacDonald!" It was Cates, using her preferred method of interoffice communication—yelling down the hall.

We went to her office, and she waved at us to shut the door and sit down.

"We may have a break," she said. "But it's a delicate situation. I have a friend, Alma Hooks. I've known her since she was a kid. She got pregnant at fifteen, had the baby, and worked hard to keep her life on track. She got a master's in library science from Pratt, and she's now an assistant librarian at the 125th Street branch of the New York Public Library. Alma is twenty-nine now, a single mom. Her son, Shawn, is thirteen, and she just called to tell me that the boy witnessed the Tinsdale abduction."

"That was over a month ago," I said. "And he's willing to talk to us now?"

"He's lucky he can talk to anyone. He took three bullets

the night before last. That's the delicate part," she said. "Alma has convinced him to tell us what he knows about the kidnapping, but that's it. We don't ask about the shooting, or what connection young Shawn may or may not have had to Tinsdale."

"The Tin Man was notorious for hiring baby runners," Kylie said. "You think Shawn worked for him?"

Cates ran two fingers across her lips, zipping them shut.

"Don't ask; don't tell," she said. "I promised Alma that all we care about is finding out what happened to Tinsdale. Those are the ground rules. You got it?"

"Totally," Kylie said.

"Good," Cates said. "Shawn's condition was just upgraded from critical to stable. He's at Harlem Hospital. Get over there before he changes his mind."

CHAPTER 66

JOE SALVI WAS sitting at the kitchen table, reading the *Daily News* and sipping his second cup of coffee. There were three cell phones in front of him.

"What are you grinning about?" Teresa said from across the room.

Joe hadn't realized he was smiling. But that was the way it was whenever he spent time with his *goomah*. Bernice always made him happy, and last night had been no different. Mama was right. Forbidden fruit always tastes the sweetest.

Last night, after they made love, Bernice curled up against him and whispered in his ear. "Joe...the sex..."

She let it hang there. He waited, but she didn't finish the sentence.

It was a tease. He took the bait. "What about it?" he said.

She nibbled on his ear. "It was age appropriately fantastic."

He belly-laughed so hard that tears came to his eyes. Bernice was the only one who could come up with something like that, much less say it. He had been reliving the moment when Teresa caught him smiling.

One of the cell phones vibrated, neutralizing her curiosity. "Pick it up," she said, as though maybe he wouldn't if she weren't there to give him orders.

He answered. "Good morning."

The voice on the other end said only one thing. A number.

Salvi repeated it. "You're sure," he stated clearly.

The caller knew it was a question. A brief pause, and then Salvi said, *"Grazie. Ciao."*

He tossed the phone to his son, who was standing at the sink. Jojo soaked the cell in cold water, then dropped it into the trash masher beneath the counter.

"You found him?" Teresa asked.

"Both of them," Salvi said. "They work together. Same precinct."

"So you want me and Tommy Boy to deal with them?" Jojo said.

At the sound of his name, Tommy Boy squared his shoulders and tugged at the sleeves of his Forzieri leather jacket. He was born Tommaso Benito Montanari, the same as his father, so they called him Tommy Boy from birth. Twenty-six years later, he was six feet eight and 275 pounds, but he was still Tommy Boy. His eyes locked in on Papa Joe for an answer to Jojo's question.

"No," Salvi said. "We're not ready to *deal* with anything. For now, you just follow them, and let me know what they do, where they go."

"What if they split up?" Jojo said. "Should we take two cars just in case?"

"*Two* cars?" Joe said. "Good idea. And while you're at it, get some horses, a brass band, and some of those big fucking balloons. What are you thinking? I said tail them, not start a parade. If they split up, stay with this Gideon. Scope him out and report back to me. But don't *do* anything."

"What if the opportunity presents itself? I could—"

"Did I say anything about opportunity? No. I said, do not do anything. *Non fare niente. Niente.* You clear on that?"

Jojo looked at Teresa and shrugged.

Salvi caught the exchange. "I don't give a shit what your mother asked for," he said. "His head on a silver platter, his balls in a glass jar—I don't care. I want him and his friend together, and then I'll decide where we go from there. You clear on that?"

"Yeah, Pop, I'm clear."

Joe turned to Tommy Boy. "These two you're following—they're cops. They got eyes in the back of their heads. So drive smart."

"Maybe I should take Mrs. Salvi's car," Tommy Boy said. "The Buick. It's beige. It won't stand out like the Escalade."

Joe tapped two fingers to his temple. "Now you're thinking. Get moving."

The two men went to the garage, and Tommy Boy moved the driver's seat in the Buick all the way back so he could squeeze in.

Jojo got in on the passenger side. "Maybe I should take Mrs. Salvi's car," he mimicked, doing his best to imitate Tommy Boy's deadpan delivery.

"Did I do something wrong?" Tommy said.

"My father pisses all over everything I say, so you have to act like some kind of consigliere? You're a soldier, Tommy Boy. Nothing more."

"Come on, man," Tommy Boy said, turning left onto Cross Bay Boulevard. "I'm almost thirty years old. I'm family. I'm too smart to be a soldier all my life."

Jojo spun around in his seat. "Listen to me, asshole. You're twenty-six years old, which doesn't count as almost thirty. You're married to my mother's cousin's daughter, so you're not blood family. And if you were as smart as you think you are, you wouldn't try to show me up in front of my old man."

Tommy Boy laughed.

"What's so funny?"

"You. It's the same thing every time with you, Jojo. Your old man treats you like crap, so you take it out on me. It's called transference."

"And you know what this is called?" Jojo said, sticking up his middle finger. "It's called shut up and drive to the goddamn police station."

"Sure thing, Jojo. Maybe when we get there I can run in and pick us up a parade permit."

CHAPTER 67

IF YOU'RE GOING to get shot in New York City, Harlem Hospital is one of the best places you can go. It's a Level 1 Trauma Center conveniently located only six blocks from where Shawn Hooks took three bullets.

It's also one of the most architecturally striking new buildings in the city. One entire glass facade—six stories high and a city block long—is covered with reproductions of colorful murals originally commissioned by the WPA during the Depression and painted by African American artists. It's a symbol of community pride on the outside, but I knew that the harsh realities of the street were waiting for us inside.

Alma Hooks was petite, no more than five feet at best. She was physically fit, but judging by the drawn face, the red eyes, and the clenched hands, she was emotionally whipped.

She stood up as soon as we entered the room. "Thank you for coming. Did Delia explain?"

"Yes, she did. And thank you for calling us," I said. "How's your son doing?"

"He's still in pain, but the nurse gave him another shot of Toradol an hour ago. He's a strong boy. The doctors say it'll take time, but he'll be fine."

"And how are you doing?" Kylie said.

"Me? I'm shell-shocked. I haven't slept since they called me Tuesday night. But I'm grateful."

"And you called because you think Shawn may have witnessed a crime?" I said.

"The Tin Man," she said. "Antoine Tinsdale. He was a drug dealer. He corrupted these neighborhood boys something awful. You raise them with good values, teach them to do the right thing, then he comes along dressed like a rock star, driving a Mercedes, and he promises them the moon, and they fall for it. They're just kids."

She didn't say whether or not Shawn was one of the kids Tinsdale had corrupted. She was simply underscoring what we already knew—these young drug runners were more victims than criminals. I was glad Cates had made a deal with her. I wouldn't have wanted to be the cop who dug into her son's past and possibly damaged his future.

"I'm not saying I'm sorry to see Tinsdale off the streets for good," Alma said, looking at her son rather than at us, "but kidnapping him and killing him is no kind of justice. Not the kind of message you want to send to your children."

"Can we ask your son some questions?" I said.

Shawn, who was under the covers, looked to be over six feet and close to two hundred pounds, but clearly the tiny woman at his side was in charge.

"Go ahead," she said, still looking at Shawn. "He's agreed to help in your investigation."

"Shawn, my name is Detective Jordan, and this is my partner, Detective MacDonald. Whatever you say is just between us. We'll try to make this brief. When did you last see Antoine Tinsdale?"

Shawn froze. Confessing to your mother is culturally acceptable. Talking to the cops isn't.

Alma sat on the bed and stroked his forehead. "Go ahead, baby," she said. "They're cool. They're friends of Miss Delia. Tell them when you last saw Antoine Tinsdale."

"The night they took him."

"Thank you," she said, and passed the torch back to me with a single tilt of her head.

"Who took him?" I asked.

"Two cops. They picked him up at 136th and Amsterdam."

"How did you know they were cops?" I said.

"They cuffed him. At first just one guy got out of the car and talked to him, but then the Tin Man, he started in with 'Whoa—wait a minute here—' like he didn't want to go. But then the driver, he comes around, cuffs him, and the two of them shove him into the back of their car."

"A squad car?" I asked.

"Unmarked. A black SUV."

"Make and model?"

"I don't know. It was dark. I could tell it was an SUV from the shape, but that's all."

"Did you see what these two men looked like?"

"White guys."

"Could you describe them?"

"Just regular white guys in suits. They were tall, but only regular tall, not like NBA tall. That's all I could see. I wasn't close enough to see anything else."

"Do you think if we brought you some mug shots, something might jar your memory?" I asked.

"I don't have any memory," Shawn said. "I told you. I didn't see faces."

"Was there anyone else with you who might have seen more?" Kylie asked.

The boy was done. He looked at his mother. She too seemed to be coming to the end of her civic responsibility rope.

"Detectives," Alma said, "my son has been forthright with you. He says that on the night Mr. Tinsdale disappeared, he saw two police officers take him into custody. It certainly didn't look like a crime to Shawn, so he didn't report it. That's all he knows. If somebody else saw something, they can volunteer just like he did. Do you have any more questions?"

"No, Mrs. Hooks," I said. "You've both been extremely helpful. If you think of anything else, please give me a call."

I reached into my jacket pocket to get one of my cards. My hand brushed against an envelope. Just before I'd left the office, I had decided to bring along some mug shots.

Four of them were random middle-aged white criminals that I pulled out of my files. The other two were the ones I hoped young Shawn would finger. I fished out a business card and handed it to Mrs. Hooks.

"That's not necessary," she said, returning it. "If I think of anything else, I'll call your boss."

My boss? I had to admire Alma Hooks. She was fiercely protective of her son, and once he'd given us all he was going to give, she dismissed us with a little reminder that Kylie and I answered to her buddy Miss Delia.

I shoved the card back into my pocket, next to the pictures of my two best suspects—Donovan and Boyle.

CHAPTER 68

"WHERE THE HELL do people park in Manhattan?" Jojo said as Tommy Boy drove the Buick past the precinct for the third time. "There are never any spaces on the goddamn street."

"The trick is to walk around first," Tommy Boy said. "Then as soon as you find a space, you get somebody to lay down in it, and you run out and buy a car."

Jojo didn't laugh. "You think this job is funny, TB?"

"I don't think anything, Jojo. I don't even know what *this* job is except we're tailing two cops. You want to fill me in? Are they dirty?"

"Dirty as it gets. They killed my brother."

"Son of a bitch. Cops killed Enzo?"

"They weren't cops back then. They were high school kids."

"So we find them, we tail them, and then what do we do?"

"Nothing. You heard my old man. We do the recon. He decides what to do after that."

"What the hell do you *think* he's gonna decide? He's gonna whack them. The only question is who gets to do it."

"You volunteering?"

"Maybe," Tommy Boy said, pulling into a space in front of a fire hydrant. "When Pacino whacks Sollozzo and that crooked cop in the restaurant, he takes off for Sicily for a couple of years. I wouldn't mind volunteering for that."

"Keep dreaming, Pacino," Jojo said, taking out his iPhone and plugging the white buds into his ears. "Now keep your eyes open and your mouth shut. I need a little Springsteen."

Three songs into the album, Jojo ripped the buds out of his ears. "The one in front is Gideon," he said, pointing at two men who came out of the precinct and headed toward a cluster of cop cars. They got into a black SUV and pulled out.

"Hang back," Jojo said. "Cops can spot a tail. Leave a little real estate between us and them."

Tommy Boy dropped the Buick back behind two cars. "Okay, let's just hope these guys don't go all lights and sirens on us, or we're fucked."

There were no lights, no sirens, no drama.

The SUV swung onto the Ed Koch Bridge, crossed the East River, turned right onto Vernon Boulevard, and stopped at San Remo, a tiny pizza parlor on the corner of 49th Avenue. Gideon went inside.

Minutes later, he got back into the car carrying a pizza box.

"You ever hear of this place?" Tommy Boy said. "Must be damn good if they drove all the way out here to pick up a pie at nine o'clock in the morning."

He followed the SUV onto Jackson. A quarter of a mile later, it hung a right onto Crane. It was a dead-end street.

Tommy Boy waited till the two cops drove to the end of the block, pulled into a graffiti-covered garage, and closed the corrugated metal door. Then he parked behind a battered van a hundred feet away.

Forty minutes later, the garage door opened, and the SUV backed out.

"What the hell are you waiting for?" Jojo said as the cops drove off.

"I'm waiting for them to get out of sight," Tommy Boy said. "Then we can go in and find out what they've got going on in there."

The SUV turned onto Jackson. "You're gonna lose them," Jojo yelled.

"We won't lose them forever. We know where they work."

"Follow them."

"Jojo, they didn't drive all the way out to a dump like this just to split a pizza. Your father is going to want to know what the hell is going on in there."

"My father told us to follow them. You heard him— nothing else—*niente*. Now either get moving or get out, and I'll drive."

Tommy Boy started the car and headed up the narrow street. "Okay, but I think you're making a big mistake."

"Well, guess what, asshole?" Jojo said. "You're paid to drive, not to think."

He tilted his seat back and put in his earbuds. He was listening to Bruno Mars when his cell vibrated.

"Mom?" he said, putting his face close to the phone. "I'm busy here."

"Did you find them?" Teresa asked.

"Yeah, they drove out to Long Island City to some dump."

"What kind of dump?" Teresa said.

"I don't know. Some old garage. A run-down cinder-block building on a dead-end street near the railroad yard."

"Why did they go there? What's in there?"

"How am I supposed to know?"

"How? As soon as they leave, go inside. Find out what they're up to."

"They already left. TB and I are following them now."

"Are you crazy?" Teresa barked. "Don't follow them."

"*Don't follow them?* What are you talking about? Pop told me don't do anything *except* follow them. Scope them out and report back to him."

"*Mannaggia!* You find the place where these two do their dirty business, and you decide *not* to check it out? What do you think 'scope' means?"

Jojo pounded his fist on the dashboard. "Mom, I can't check out the place and follow them at the same time."

As soon as he heard it, Tommy Boy eased his foot off the accelerator.

"So follow them tomorrow. Today you have a chance to find out what they're hiding in that building. Maybe it's guns. Maybe it's drugs from the evidence locker. Whatever it is, we know they'll go back, and that's when we settle accounts for Enzo. Or did you think you could just walk into a police station and take down two cops?"

Jojo rubbed his eyes and took a deep breath. "Let me talk to Papa."

"No. Stop running to your father and start using your brain. Think about it—that building is a godsend."

"Mom, it's a shithole."

"They left my son facedown in the mud. A shithole is better than they deserve. Now check it out before they come back. I'll deal with Papa."

And then, dead air.

Jojo couldn't believe it. She'd hung up on him.

"Hang a U-ey," he said. "We're going back."

Tommy Boy tried not to smile as he guided the Buick into a smooth U-turn at 42nd Road. "Whatever you say, Jojo. You're the boss."

CHAPTER 69

WHEN HE WAS twelve years old, Tommy Boy's parents sat him down and told him something they had been holding back for two years. He had an IQ of 147.

"So?" he said.

"So it means you're like Einstein," said Tommaso Montanari Sr. "Very smart. Smarter than everybody else."

"So?" he said again.

"So that's wonderful," his mother said halfheartedly.

"But it's gonna be a problem," his father said, "and you got enough shit to handle already. How tall are you now? Six one?"

"Six two."

"And you're only twelve," his father said. "So you're gonna stand out. Kids will make fun of you like you're some kind of freak."

Tommy Boy's eyes teared up. "You mean like calling me Big Bird?"

"Those assholes," Montanari said. "What are they all, like five foot nothing, eighty-five pounds soaking wet? They're jealous. They want you to feel like crap because you're built like a man, and they're not. You know why your mother and I didn't tell you about this IQ thing when we first found out?"

Tommy Boy shook his head.

"Because we wanted you to feel normal. Bad enough you're bigger than everybody else. Worse if they know you're smarter. People hate your guts when they think you're better than them."

The tears spilled over and trickled down the boy's cheeks. "So what do I do?"

Montanari looked at his wife. He knew the question would be coming, and his answer was simple: *Kick the shit out of the little bastards, and you'll see how fast they start showing you some respect.*

But that didn't fly with Angela. So, using all the parenting skills they had, they came up with another solution.

"Look, kiddo," he said, putting a hand on his son's shoulder, "you can't pretend to be short, but you can pretend to be dumb."

"Not *dumb*," his mother corrected. "Just not so smart. You'll fit in more."

It turned out to be not such bad advice, especially when he started working for Jojo. The man was clueless, but as long as Tommy Boy played the happy-go-lucky buffoon, Jojo felt superior.

Only one person figured out how smart he was. Papa Joe. Nothing got past him.

"You're dumb like a fox," he said one night when Tommy Boy was driving him to Bernice's place.

Tommy froze at the wheel.

"Don't worry," Salvi said. "Right now all I need is your muscle. But I like knowing you have a good head on your shoulders for when the time comes."

When the time comes. Tommy Boy had waited, and this was the time. Eliminating the two bastards who killed Enzo would make his bones with Joe Salvi forever. And the payback wouldn't be some bullshit two-year vacation in Sicily like he told Jojo. It would be a spot in the organization. A real spot. Then he could stop acting.

"You got a game plan yet?" Tommy Boy asked Jojo as he turned back onto Crane Street.

"Break the lock, go in, look around, take pictures with the cell phone if we see anything, then go back to Howard Beach."

"Good idea," Tommy Boy said. "Except maybe I could pick the lock instead of breaking it, so they won't know we were here."

"Of course we pick the lock," Jojo said. "That's what I meant. I just didn't think I had to spell it out for you."

They parked the car and walked to the back of the building. The lock was amateur hour, and Tommy had it open in seconds. The room was long and narrow, no more than four feet deep.

There were two mismatched chairs and a small folding table with a stack of audio equipment on it. Nothing worth stealing. Then Tommy Boy spotted the peep-holes.

"Over here," he whispered, pointing at the wall in front of them. "Whatever is going on in there, they watch from back here."

There were two narrow openings cut into the Sheetrock at eye level. Tommy Boy had to crouch down to peer through one of them.

Jojo didn't even bother to look. He waited for Tommy Boy to tell him if it was worth the effort. But the big man didn't say a word. He just stared at the woman in the Haz-mat suit who was chained to a pipe. The pizza box from San Remo was on the floor, most of it not eaten, and there was a video camera in front of her. He put it all together in a heartbeat, and when he did, he felt as if he'd just walked into King Tut's tomb.

"What the hell is so damn interesting?" Jojo said, press-ing his forehead against the second spy window.

"Holy fuck," he said. "What the—"

"Shhh. Don't let her hear you."

"These guys are cops? They got some real freaky shit going on," Jojo said in a harsh whisper. "What do you think we should do?"

Tommy Boy pulled his phone out of his pocket.

"Who you calling?" Jojo said.

"Nobody," Tommy whispered. "Getting pictures."

He put the phone up against one of the openings and started clicking. After he'd collected a dozen shots, he put the phone back in his pocket. "Let's blow this place," he said.

"Are you crazy?" Jojo said. "Are you looking at what I'm looking at? They've got some broad chained to a pole. Should we go in? Should we cut her down? We should at least find out who she is."

Tommy Boy stepped away from the wall. "I know who she is, dammit, and trust me, this is a lot bigger than me and you. We need to talk to your father."

Jojo went for his cell phone.

"Not now," Tommy Boy said. "And definitely not from here. You asked me what to do. I told you. Get the fuck out. Fast."

"How the hell do you know her?" Jojo said. "Who is she?"

"I'll tell you in the car. Trust me. Go." He took out a handkerchief and began backing out of the room, wiping down everything they had touched.

They were just about out the door when Tommy Boy saw it out of the corner of his eye. It was almost lost in the jumble of audio equipment on the table. "Hold on," he said.

"What now?" Jojo said.

"I'm not sure. Give me a second." There was a small wooden box on the table. He picked it up and opened it.

"What the hell is that?" Jojo said, looking over Tommy Boy's shoulder.

"I don't know, but I'm going to find out." He took the choke pear out of the box with his handkerchief, set it on the table, and clicked off some more shots. Then he tucked it back in the box.

"Now let's go," he said.

Tommy relocked the door, then wiped the lock, the knob, and the jamb. Minutes later they were on the Long Island Expressway, headed back to Howard Beach.

"I figured it out," Jojo said. "The white overalls. One of those cops is the Hazmat guy."

"Both of them."

"That's what I'm saying. But who's the girl?"

Tommy Boy told him.

"You sure that's her?"

"Her face was on TV every night."

"Not on ESPN."

"It was in the *Daily News*. Didn't you see it in the paper?"

"Probably. I can't remember everything I read. Was there anything about that weird corkscrew thing in the box?"

"No."

Jojo pulled out his cell phone. "I'm calling Pop."

"Make sure you call one of his burner phones. The Feds have ears on everything else," Tommy Boy said.

Jojo stopped dialing. It was as though he'd just remembered his father was a Mob boss and the FBI had had him under surveillance for years.

"Good idea. We don't want the *Federales* picking up on this one," Jojo said. "Y'know, you big ox, sometimes you're not as dumb as you look."

"Thanks, boss. I'm no genius, but I have my moments."

CHAPTER 70

OF ALL THE elite units in the department, Red is the toughest to get into. There are only seventy-five of us spread out across the city and at least a thousand more hoping to get in. But I've never met two cops more eager—or more qualified—to be part of Red than Casey and Bell, the two Anti-Crime detectives who saved my ass at the carousel on Monday morning.

They're skilled at undercover, fast on their feet, and, as Kylie pointed out, willing to break a few eggs to make an omelet.

When we asked them to tail Donovan and Boyle on the down low, they said yes. When we told them why, Bell asked only one question.

"Does IA know you're recruiting cops to investigate other cops?"

"No," I said. "And if IA finds out, they'll be investigating all of us."

"Don't worry," he said. "They won't find out."

He called me at 6:00 p.m. and said they couldn't wait to tell us what they came up with on their first day. I suggested an off-campus rendezvous at Uskudar, a hole-in-the-wall Turkish restaurant on Second Avenue. Logistically and strategically, it was the perfect choice. It was walking distance from our office, but nobody who knew us was likely to show up. The fact that I really liked their *musakka* may have also influenced my decision.

They were waiting for us at a table in the rear, and from the grins on their faces, I couldn't tell who was more excited—them or us.

We ordered drinks and a bunch of appetizers and got down to business.

"So, if we help you crack this case," Bell said, cutting to the chase, "do the two of us have a good chance of working for Red?"

"No promises," I said, "but I can tell you this—if we don't crack the case, the two of *us* have a good chance of *not* working for Red."

"So please tell us you have pictures of Donovan and Boyle shopping at a Hazmat suit store," Kylie said.

Casey laughed. "Nothing that exciting. We have bad news, good news, and great news."

"Start with the bad and work your way up," I said, popping a hunk of warm pita bread in my mouth and washing it down with cold beer.

"Eight thirty this morning," he said, putting his iPhone

on the table and bringing up a picture of Donovan walking out of a Starbucks carrying two cups wrapped with cardboard sleeves. "We put our keen detective minds together and concluded it was a coffee run."

"Two minutes later we ran into the snag," Bell said. "Our sergeant called us in. Some mope snatched a purse from a woman in the park. A couple of uniforms could have handled it, but the victim was a British nanny who works for a diplomat's family, so now it was all hands on deck, and we got pulled in to canvass the area. We were caught up in it for four hours, and we didn't get back to Donovan and Boyle again till one o'clock."

"They were having lunch at the Big Wong King on Mott Street," Casey said. "After that, they answered a robbery call at an optical store on Franklin, and then they got called to the Pu Chao Buddhist Temple on Eldridge."

"We didn't pick up on the radio what they were called in for, but they only stayed twenty minutes, so we figured it was no major crime," Bell said. "Maybe just somebody disturbing the enlightenment."

Kylie and I laughed. These guys were light-years more fun to work with than Donovan and Boyle.

Casey flipped through pictures of the restaurant, the optical store, and the Buddhist temple in a hurry.

"All those places are in the Five," Kylie said. "So basically they stayed close to their own precinct."

"Until around three this afternoon," Casey said. "Then they drove uptown to a storefront on East Fifty-Fifth Street."

He flipped to the next picture.

"Holy shit," Kylie said. "That's Muriel Sykes's campaign headquarters."

"Do you know if Sykes was there at the same time?" I asked.

Casey scrolled to the next shot. It was the three of them—Donovan, Boyle, and Sykes—walking out of the campaign office together.

"We have no idea what they talked about because we couldn't get close enough to hear anything, but whatever it was, they were in there with her for over an hour."

"If that's the good news," I said, "I can't wait to hear the great news."

Casey grinned and flipped to another picture on his iPhone. It was a pretty young woman with curly red hair. "She's the nanny whose purse got snatched. She gave me her phone number. Wants me to call on her day off."

I took the phone out of his hand and flipped back to the shot of Donovan, Boyle, and Sykes. "As impressed as Kylie and I are at your ability to hit on crime victims, we're even happier about this."

"It's a big help," Kylie said.

"We were hoping you'd say that," Bell said, "but we don't know enough about the case to understand why."

"Because the two cops who could be the Hazmat Killer are in cahoots with the politician who will most benefit if the murders aren't solved," I said.

"And I bet the reason Donovan and Boyle showed up to pick our brain last night is because they're reporting everything we know to Sykes," Kylie said.

"So they're like double agents," Bell said.

"You're being generous," Kylie said. "They're more like dirty cops. Zach is right. You guys did some great work in a big hurry. Thank you."

"You're welcome," Casey said, "but it goes both ways. We appreciate getting a shot to work with Red, so thank *you*, Detective Jordan. And thank *you*, Detective MacDonald."

"Hey—we're having beers and breaking bread here," Kylie said. "You don't have to be so formal. Call me Kylie. And he's Zach."

"Kylie and Zach it is," Casey said. "I'm Dave."

Bell raised his beer and toasted us. "And I'm Gideon."

PART THREE

LA FAMIGLIA FORNIRÀ GIUSTIZIA

CHAPTER 71

FRIDAY STARTED WAY too early. My cell phone rang at 3:02 a.m. I fumbled for it and focused on the name of the caller, glowing at me in the dark.

Delia Cates.

In my stupor, I could come up with only one reason my boss would call in the middle of the night. She'd found out that Kylie and I were playing fast and loose with the chain of command, and she couldn't wait till morning to get me started on my new assignment writing tickets to unlicensed street vendors in Jackson Heights.

I pressed the green button on my phone and mumbled something that sounded like "This is Jordan."

"The Rachael O'Keefe case just blew through the roof," Cates said. "I need you and MacDonald at Gracie Mansion in twenty minutes."

And just like that, I was wide awake. "What's going on with O'Keefe?" I said.

"I'll tell you when you get here. Call your partner. Repeat—Gracie Mansion. Twenty minutes. You got it?"

"Yeah, I got—"

She hung up.

I reached for the reading light on the headboard and flipped it on. Cheryl rolled over on her back, jet-black hair cascading over the pale blue pillowcase, caramel skin glowing in the lamplight.

I swung my legs onto the floor and sat on the side of the bed.

"Mmmm, don't go," she said softly, sitting up and letting the sheets slip below her breasts.

I couldn't believe that I was living in a universe where someone as beautiful and desirable as Cheryl would be lying naked beside me and I would leap out of bed and put on my pants. But that's exactly what I did.

"I have to," I said.

"Who called?"

"The police commissioner. He heard we've been sleeping together."

She gave me a drowsy smile. "And he's going to fire you?"

"Hell, no. He's giving me a medal. Go back to sleep."

I leaned over and kissed her. She wrapped her arms around me, worked her tongue against mine, slowly let one hand slide down my back, under my belt, and grabbed hold of my gluteus maximus.

She put her warm, soft lips to my ear. "Just stay ten

more minutes," she said. "I promise they'll be the best ten minutes of your day."

"You're killing me," I said, trying to pull away.

"I know," she purred. "But you'll die happy."

Her hand found a new resting place, and I stopped pulling away and leaned into it.

"I have a problem, Doctor," I moaned in her ear. "Something big just went down on the O'Keefe kidnapping, and Cates wants me at the mayor's house in twenty minutes. But then something big came up in my personal life, and I don't know what to do."

She pulled her hand away and sat up straight. "Are you serious? Why didn't you say something? Go."

"Thanks for understanding." I planted one more kiss on her lips. "I'll definitely be back to pick up where we left off."

Showing up for work wearing yesterday's clothes is a red flag for the gossipmongers, so I had one drawer at Cheryl's place just for times like this. I grabbed a clean shirt and called Kylie.

I told her what, when, and where, and I was about to hang up when I heard a man's voice in the background.

"Who is it? What's going on?"

It was Spence.

"Go back to sleep," I heard Kylie say just before she hung up.

I had to laugh. I'm sure she didn't want to get out of bed any more than I did.

At least the universe wasn't playing favorites. It was dicking around with both of us.

CHAPTER 72

I GOT TO Gracie Mansion at 3:26, three minutes past my ETA. Kylie was already waiting outside the guardhouse.

"How the hell did you get here so fast?" I said.

"I pride myself on punctuality. It's the hallmark of great police work."

"I deserved that," I said as we headed up the mansion's steps to the sprawling front porch.

"Also, did you forget I'm staying in Shelley's apartment? It's five blocks away. I strolled over."

I hadn't forgotten. But when I'd heard Spence's voice, I'd jumped to the conclusion that she had spent the night downtown in her own bed. But Spence must have made his way uptown.

Or maybe it wasn't Spence's voice.

Or maybe it was none of my damn business.

The four of them were in the mayor's office at a conference table—Mayor Spellman, Irwin Diamond, Captain Cates, and PC Richard Harries. Kylie and I sat down, and the PC started talking.

"Last night, a couple on East Seventy-First Street, Larry and Clare Bertoli, left their apartment at seven fifteen and went to the theater. Mrs. Bertoli got sick during the first act, so they left, went home, and walked in on a burglary in progress. They knew the perp. It was their doorman. He didn't try to run—just sat down on the couch and started bawling. Mrs. Bertoli called 911. The uniforms made the collar, took him in to the One Nine, and turned him over to the detectives to be debriefed."

I knew he hadn't gotten us up at this hour to talk about a routine burglary. Cates had already told me that the Rachael O'Keefe case had blown through the roof, and I was waiting for the bombshell. But I know Richard Harries, and he's painstakingly methodical. He needs time to land the plane.

"The lead investigator is Detective Sal Catapano," he said. "He's got twenty-one years, and as soon as he walked into the interrogation room, he knew he had a page-one case on his hands. The doorman's name is Vidmar, Calvin Vidmar."

Bombshell. I looked at Kylie. She knew it, too.

"You recognize the name," Harries said as soon as he saw our reaction.

"Yes, sir," Kylie said. "Vidmar was the doorman on duty the night Rachael O'Keefe's daughter was murdered. He testified against her in court."

He nodded. "It seems he's not the solid citizen the prosecution made him out to be. He's a thief. The tenants all leave house keys with the super in case of emergency. Vidmar would take one out of the storage box, enter an apartment, and help himself to something small—usually one or two pieces of jewelry, or if he found cash, he'd take some, but never enough to be noticed. And if it was, the victims didn't report it. They either thought it went lost, or in one case, a tenant fired her cleaning lady, thinking it was an inside job."

"Is there any evidence he was in O'Keefe's apartment the night Kimi was murdered?" I asked.

"Catapano got a search warrant for Vidmar's apartment in the Bronx and found several pieces of jewelry that he hadn't had time to unload. And this."

He put an eight-by-ten photo on the table. It was Mookie—the stuffed pink monkey, identical to the one taken from Kimi O'Keefe's bedroom.

"How long before we can get DNA to see if it's hers?" Kylie said.

"We don't have to wait. Catapano told Vidmar he'd be smarter to confess now rather than let the evidence hang him. He started crying again and then spilled his guts. It was a botched robbery. The girl woke up and started screaming. He panicked, put a pillow over her face, and you know the rest—he didn't mean to kill her; it just happened. He put the body in a trash bag, left her out for the morning pickup, and let the mom take the fall."

I felt as if I'd just been hit by the Hiroshima of bombshells. *The jury had gotten it right. Rachael had told the truth.*

"So maybe now I won't have to take the rap for turning a child killer loose," the mayor said.

"Mr. Mayor, if we release the news that O'Keefe is innocent, she's a dead woman," the PC said. "The men who took her plan to torture a confession out of her, but the minute they find out that Vidmar did it, they'll kill her on the spot."

"And if you think people hated you when O'Keefe beat the rap," Irwin said, "they'll hate you even more when it turns out that she's innocent, didn't get the police protection she asked for, and was murdered on your watch."

"Then where the hell are we on the Hazmat case?" the mayor said, looking right at me.

I couldn't let Cates know that we'd gone over her head and put an unauthorized tail on two cops. And I certainly couldn't tell the mayor that Muriel Sykes had spent an hour behind closed doors with our two prime suspects. I was groping for an answer when Diamond interrupted.

"The last time we spoke, you were getting a list of everyone who knew where O'Keefe was going when she was released. Did you question them all?"

"All but two from the DA's office," I said. "We plan to connect with them in the morning."

"The goddamn election is in four days," Spellman said. "I don't have time for you to *connect with them in the morning*. Talk to them now. Find out where they live and drag them out of bed." He turned to the commissioner. "Richard, we can't crap around anymore. Find her."

The PC is appointed by the mayor. If Spellman got voted out, Harries would get swept out along with him.

He turned to Kylie and me. "Who from the DA's office haven't you talked to yet?"

"ADA Wilson and one of his assistants," I said.

"Damn," Harries said. "Mick Wilson is a pain in the ass, and the last person I want to wake up in the middle of the night."

"So then, don't wake him?" I said.

"Hell, no. Just make sure he's last. Wake the assistant first."

CHAPTER 73

I'D BEEN SUCKER punched more than a few times in my career, but this one hit me the hardest. I never saw it coming. I was right there with the rest of the world, branding Rachael O'Keefe as the Worst Mother in America, and I wondered if my prejudice had any bearing on how hard I had been working to find her.

East End Avenue was dark, deserted, and eerily calming, and we drove without saying a word, both of us trying to process the news in our own way.

Kylie finally broke the silence. "That poor, poor woman. Her daughter was murdered. She had to be overwhelmed with guilt, and then when they accused her, nobody believed in her. Nobody. Including me."

She turned slowly in her seat and rested a hand on my knee. She had my undivided attention. "Zach...," she said.

That was all. Just my name. A single syllable that she

let hang in the air, wrapped up in a tangle of emotions—compassion, anger, and, above all, the trademark raw grit that makes Kylie MacDonald a woman you want at your side and a partner you want at your back.

I slowed down, caught a red light, and turned to face her. She lifted her hand from my knee. I couldn't tell for sure in the dark, but it looked as if my partner's eyes were a little on the watery side. My tough-as-nails, take-no-prisoners partner.

"I know what you're going to say, Kylie, and I'm there. Number one priority—we have to find her. Alive."

"Whatever it takes," she said. "I don't care how many stupid-ass rules we have to break."

But then I already knew that.

Mick Wilson's assistant lived at 47th Street and Ninth Avenue. There was a Starbucks directly across the street, but at 4:15 a.m., it was as dark as the rest of the city. Maybe if I'd had a cup of coffee or a few more hours' sleep, it might have dawned on me that the young lawyer we were going to interview had a familiar last name. But it's a common enough name—especially in the New York City Police and Fire Departments.

We identified ourselves over the intercom, took the stairs to the third floor, and knocked on the door. She didn't open it.

"I'm sorry, but I don't just let total strangers in," she said. "If you're real cops, you'll understand. I need an ID. Hold it up to the peephole."

Kylie went first, then I held up my badge and ID. But that wasn't enough.

"They look real," she said from the other side of the door, "but just tell me why you're here."

I recognized the syndrome. Somewhere in her life she'd been a crime victim, and she'd never gotten past the trauma. I mouthed three words to Kylie. *She's been mugged.*

Or worse, Kylie said silently. She waved me away from the door and centered herself in clear view of the peephole. "Meredith, we're sorry to barge in on you in the middle of the night, but we can't wait till the morning. You were part of the DA's team in the Rachael O'Keefe case. She was kidnapped, and we need your help."

A lock clicked. Then another. The door opened.

"Come in," she said. "Sorry if I got all paranoid on you. Mick told me what you'd been asking about. I told him to tell you that when Rachael got released, I knew where she was going, but I wouldn't tell anyone."

"Mick neglected to pass on the message," I said, "so as long as we're here, we'd like to get it straight from you."

"Sure," she said, conjuring up a smile that did nothing to hide her frazzled nerves.

I was frazzled, too, but I knew I couldn't come on like a storm trooper. "Meredith," I said in the calmest voice I could muster, "you just said you knew where Rachael was going, and you *wouldn't* tell anyone. We know your reputation, and we're sure you wouldn't."

"I'm an officer of the court," she said.

"And I'm sure if you're working with Mick Wilson, you're a damn good one. He's a pretty demanding guy."

She laughed. "That's a very generous way to characterize an unrelenting, perfectionist taskmaster, but yes, I'm thrilled to have the opportunity to work with someone of Mick's caliber."

"So let's get back to that night," I said. "What did you do after the verdict came down?"

"What do you think?" she said, forming her right hand into the letter C and tipping it toward her mouth three times.

Despite the hour and her state of mind, Meredith looked terrific without putting on makeup or brushing her thick red hair. It was a good bet that someone this pretty wasn't drinking alone.

"That's what I would do too," I said. "Find a bar and drown my sorrows. Who'd you go out with?"

"Just insiders. Colleagues. Some who knew where Rachael would be hiding out, some who didn't. It was a tough case to lose, so yeah, we all got pretty wasted, but we didn't talk about where Rachael was going. Mostly we just bitched and moaned about the Warlock."

"The what?"

"The Warlock—Dennis Woloch, the defense attorney. He totally worked his legal voodoo on the jury and convinced them that there was reasonable doubt. He did it pro bono. Rachael was lucky to get him."

Real lucky. If she'd had any other attorney, she'd have been convicted, stayed safely in jail, and not been kidnapped two days before the real killer confessed. Hats off to Mr. Warlock.

"Excuse me," Kylie said. She had been casually snooping around the small living room while I kept Meredith busy. "Who's this?"

She picked up a framed black-and-white photo from an

end table and brought it over to where I could see it. It was a cop in uniform. NYPD.

"That's my dad," Meredith said. "He was killed in the line of duty."

"I'm sorry," Kylie said. "What happened?"

"He was working undercover trying to bring down this gang of Russian gun runners. Somehow his cover got blown, and they killed him." She paused. "But not before he took two of them out first. They gave him the Medal of Valor."

I took the picture from Kylie. He was a handsome man in his mid-thirties and a dead ringer for the cop I'd had drinks with last night. I no longer needed coffee. My adrenaline was going haywire.

"What was your dad's name?" I said.

"David. David Casey."

I mentally kicked myself. "I know a Detective Dave Casey. He works Anti-Crime."

She smiled—clearly proud. "That's my brother. How do you know him?"

"He helped us out. Good guy," I said. "Do you think you might have possibly mentioned anything to him about Rachael?"

"No. I hardly talked to Dave that night. I went home with my boyfriend."

"Did you say anything to him?" Kylie asked. She tried to sound casual, but Meredith immediately went back on the defense.

"No," she said curtly. "I mean, I don't know. I was miserable. I wound up drinking myself into a blackout."

Kylie was on the attack now. "So you could have said something, but you don't remember?"

"You sound more like a lawyer than a cop. I could have said something...but it's highly unlikely."

"But it is *possible* that under the influence, something *could* have slipped out." Kylie smiled. "You know—unintentionally."

Meredith grabbed on to the lifeline. *Unintentionally.*

"Who knows? Sure, it's possible I might have said something to him *unintentionally*. But it's okay—he's a cop too. I've known him since we were kids. He's my brother's partner. If you know Dave, then you probably know him—Detective Bell. Gideon Bell."

CHAPTER 74

IT WAS THE second sucker punch in less than an hour, only this time it was personal. As soon as we got back into the car, I exploded.

"I'm an idiot," I said.

"Don't take all the credit," Kylie said. "I bought their bullshit too. We're both idiots."

"We've been chasing the wrong two cops."

"Zach, I know. I figured it out."

"I'm thinking back to the carousel. They told me they spent the entire night working undercover in the park, and my first thought was, *Lucky me. My partner isn't here yet, so the homicide gods sent two smart cops to bail me out.*"

"They *are* smart," Kylie said. "Do you think Meredith is in on it?"

"I doubt it. She gave up too much. If she had any clue

what was going on, she'd have clammed up tight. I think our new best friends played her the same way they played us. She told Gideon exactly how to find Rachael O'Keefe, and she was too drunk to even remember that she did it."

I still hadn't started the car. I pounded the heel of my hand on the dashboard. "Goddamn Starbucks!" I yelled at the darkened windows across the street. "Don't they know people need coffee at four thirty in the morning?"

"Get a grip," Kylie said. "There's a 7-Eleven on Forty-Second Street across from the post office. Calm down and drive."

"You know what really kills me?" I said as I headed down Ninth, breezing through one red light after another.

"Yes. You got snookered. I'm not happy about it either, but men really fall apart when another guy gets the best of him."

"I'm not falling apart. I just feel like such a fucking moron that I invited them into the inner circle and asked them to help us tail Donovan and Boyle. Talk about inviting the fox over to keep an eye on the henhouse."

"Look on the bright side," Kylie said.

"Point it out, will you?"

"We've been looking for the Hazmat Killer. I think we just figured out who it is."

I pulled up to the NO PARKING ANYTIME sign in front of the 7-Eleven. "How do we prove it before they find out Rachael O'Keefe is expendable and kill her? We can't arrest them. On what charges? That they might or might not have known where Rachael was hiding out?"

"What if we ask Matt Smith to trace the GPS on their

cell phones? Wouldn't that tell us they were somewhere close to Rachael's house when she was kidnapped?"

"These guys are too smart to leave digital bread crumbs. Even if they did, the fact that they were in New Jersey that night wouldn't be enough to nail them."

"Maybe we could convince Alma Hooks to have Shawn look at some mug shots," Kylie said.

"A thirteen-year-old black drug runner fingering two white cops. That ought to stand up nicely in court."

"I have an idea that I know you can't shoot down," Kylie said. "Let me get you some coffee."

"Good idea," I said. "That's one in a row."

She got out, and I tried to focus.

Unlike a lot of cop cars, the Ford Interceptor has an adjustable driver's seat, so I tilted it back and closed my eyes. All along, I had painted a picture in my head of Donovan and Boyle convincing Alex Kang, Antoine Tinsdale, and Evelyn Parker-Steele to get into their car. Now I had to go back and put Casey and Bell in their place.

Casey would have been the one driving down Second Avenue. Bell was better looking and would be the one in the backseat, calling out to Evelyn. She got in the car, they drove to Queens, and then...and then the picture went blank.

Strike one.

I tried the same scenario with Kang and Tinsdale. Bell's approach would have been different with those two, but all he had to do was play the NYPD card, and in the car they'd go.

But it didn't matter. Playing the situation in my mind's

eye with Casey and Bell instead of Donovan and Boyle didn't help. Strike two. Strike three.

And then it hit me. *I should be getting four strikes. I'd forgotten about Sebastian Catt.*

The car door opened, and I sat up.

"Sleeping on the job?" Kylie said, getting into the front seat and handing me a cardboard cup.

"Mulling on the job." I popped the lid and let the smell of fresh coffee work its way into my brain.

"Did you mull anything worth repeating?"

"Yeah, I think I've got something." I took my first sip. "No, I *know* I've got something."

I put the lid back on the coffee and started the car.

"Are you serious? You have hard evidence to connect Casey and Bell to any of these crimes?"

"I don't," I said. "But you and I know someone who does."

"We do?"

"Yes, we do, *missy*," I said, making a U-turn on 42nd Street and heading east. "Yes, we do."

CHAPTER 75

AT FIVE IN the morning, we flew across town and made it to Horton LaFleur's building on East 84th Street in ten minutes. I rang the doorbell to apartment 1A and stepped back.

"One ring won't cut it with this old bastard," Kylie said. "Lean on the bell till he answers."

I did. LaFleur didn't.

"Move over," Kylie said, and began pushing every doorbell on the panel.

Someone buzzed us in, and she stormed down the hall to apartment 1A and pounded on the door.

"NYPD!" she yelled.

"You got a warrant?" LaFleur hollered back from inside.

"I don't need a warrant. I have a foot. And unless you open this door, I'll kick it open."

It's not the way I would have handled it, but it worked.

LaFleur opened the front door and blocked it with his bony body and his rolling oxygen tank cylinder.

"What the fuck do you want now?" he screamed, jaw clenched, neck muscles straining. "You looking for a killer? You got him, missy. Here I am. I did it. I killed them all. Go ahead, arrest me. Come on—either arrest me or get the fuck out of my sight."

Some cops might have backed off. Not Kylie. Especially not now.

"We're not going anywhere," she said. "We have questions, and you can either answer them here, or we'll drag your sorry ass into the station."

"I already told you I got nothing more to say. You ever hear of the right to remain silent? It's one of the freedoms I took a bullet for, so get the hell out of here."

"Cuff him, Zach. We're taking him in."

"All right, all right...," LaFleur said, muttering some unintelligible profanity under his breath. "What do you want?"

"We want to hear the tape," she said.

On the outside, LaFleur looked like someone you'd see doddering around the halls of a nursing home, but inside, his brain was quick, nimble, and ready for the face-off with Kylie.

"And what tape would that be?" he said innocently. "The one of Sebastian Catt admitting that he murdered my wife? I don't have a copy. Why don't you look for it on the YouTube."

"I'm talking about the recording you made when you were bugging Catt's apartment."

LaFleur's eyes opened wide. "Me?" he said. "Bugging?" He looked surprised, almost horrified, at the accusation. "There must be some mistake. I never made any recordings, so if you don't have any more questions, I'm going back to bed. Have a nice life."

"Look," Kylie said, "we understand why you don't want to help us catch the man who murdered Catt."

"You understand?" he barked. "Then why the hell did you come back?"

Kylie squared herself off in front of LaFleur. "Because the man—no, make that the two men—who killed Sebastian Catt are about to kill an innocent woman. A woman as innocent as your wife. Hattie died doing the right thing. And if she knew you were standing in the way of our catching two murderers, she'd rip that oxygen line right out of your fucking nose."

Horton started coughing and didn't stop.

"Are you all right?" I said.

"No." He moved away from the door and wheeled the cylinder back into the room. He sat down at his dining room table/desk. "Get me some water, will you?"

I went to the sink and got him a glass of water. He drank it slowly, then took a series of big drags on the oxygen. The coughing stopped.

"Mr. LaFleur," Kylie said, "I know I pushed you hard, but the two men you're protecting are about to kill an innocent woman. We're racing against the clock to stop them, and right now, you're the only one who can help us."

"Who is she?"

"Her name is Rachael O'Keefe."

"The bitch who killed her kid?" he wheezed.

"That bitch was found not guilty by a jury of her peers—another one of those freedoms you took a bullet for—and the real killer was caught last night and confessed everything."

"The *real* killer? Nice try, missy, but I don't buy it. How dumb do you think I am? O'Keefe is big news, and I got nothing else to do but watch CNN all day. First they tell you O'Keefe is guilty, then they say she's not guilty, and then they say she went and got herself kidnapped. I can't keep up with this girl. And now you're telling me the *real killer* confessed? What a crock."

"It's true," Kylie said.

"Then it'd be all over the TV. I didn't hear nothing last night. Maybe it's on now." He picked up the remote.

"It won't be on TV," I said. "We're trying to keep it from leaking, because if it breaks, the two men who kidnapped her won't try to bleed a confession out of her. They'll cover their ass and kill her on the spot."

He dropped the remote and shook his head. "Cops lie all the time. Why should I even trust you?"

"I don't give a shit if you trust us," Kylie said, shaking a finger at him like an angry schoolmarm. "You either tell us what you know and help us stop an innocent woman from being murdered, or you can clam up, turn on the TV tomorrow morning, and spend the rest of your life trying to live with the biggest mistake you ever made."

The room was silent except for the sounds of a lonely old man sucking in bottled air. He needed time, and we gave it to him. The photo of him and Hattie on their wedding day was still on his desk. He picked it up and stared at it.

"I'd been bugging Catt for months," he said, not looking up from the picture. "It was easy enough to set up. Even in my condition. I was hoping he'd say something that might incriminate him, but he lived alone, so he didn't do much talking. Mostly phone calls, but nothing that would connect him to Hattie's murder."

He set the picture down. "But I didn't give up. It became my life's work. It's all I did, all I thought about. How to make him pay. I thought about killing him, but I knew what Hattie would say. Don't sink to his level. So I just kept at it. And then one night—it was around eleven o'clock—I heard someone ring Catt's bell and walk down the hall to his door. I put my headset on. It was two cops. At least they said they were cops."

"Do you think they weren't?" I said.

"Don't know; don't care," he said. "The one tells Catt that they want to take him in for questioning. He says, 'For what?' The other guy says, 'You're a registered sex offender. What do you think? Do you want to cooperate and come along nice, or do we cuff you and drag you out of here?'"

He turned to Kylie. "Sound familiar? Same bullshit, different cops. I was hoping he'd put up a fight so maybe they'd rough him up a little, but he went without a whimper."

"Did he ever come back?"

"Hell, no—and I kept my ears open. I also kept checking the news, hoping they nailed him with something big.

Nothing. Three days later, he's on the front page of the *Post* all decked out in his Hazmat suit. I'm thinking these two cops did what I would have done if I could. They didn't just kill him. I thought about that a lot. They got him to confess to Hattie's murder. Those two guys were my heroes. There was no way I'd turn them in."

"That was then. This is now," Kylie said. "Your heroes are about to murder an innocent woman. How heroic is that?"

LaFleur didn't answer. He just reached down and opened the bottom desk drawer. It was lined with row after row of audiotapes.

CHAPTER 76

THE BOXES OF old phones, wires, and installer tools Horton LaFleur had squirreled away may have been helter-skelter, but the surveillance tapes of his wife's killer were organized, dated, and coded.

We took them all back to the office but had to listen to only one to prove that Dave Casey and Gideon Bell were the last people to see Sebastian Catt on the night he vanished. They had identified themselves as NYPD, but there was no official record that they had arrested him, brought him in for questioning, or even been in his neighborhood.

"Now comes the hard part," I said.

"Arresting them?" Kylie said.

"Telling Cates."

Kylie scrunched up her face. "We've been doing pretty well with nobody looking over our shoulder," she said. "Do we have to tell her now?"

"No. We had to tell her two days ago, before we invited Casey and Bell under the tent. Let's not compound a bad decision."

It was only 5:45, but Cates had come straight to her office from Gracie Mansion. We told her everything and played the tape for her.

"And that's all of it?" she said.

"Yes, ma'am," I said. "The good, the bad, and the ugly."

"Ugly would be the two of you running the show on your own," she said, "but I'll deal with that another time. For now, let's focus on the good—you found the Hazmat Killer—and the bad—you don't have a case. You've got a surveillance tape made illegally by a man who admitted to you that he hated Catt so much, he thought about killing him. A first-year law student could get your evidence thrown out of court. And if you arrest Casey and Bell, they'll never tell us where Rachael O'Keefe is, and she'll wind up dying a slow, miserable death."

"She's innocent," Kylie said. "I thought these two guys were the champions of justice."

"She's the only victim who could possibly ID them. If it means saving their asses, they'll throw justice right under the bus," Cates said. "I don't know how much time we have left before Calvin Vidmar's confession leaks and the whole world finds out O'Keefe is innocent. We have to get Casey and Bell to lead us to her before it does."

"We'll follow them," Kylie said. "They must be feeding her. They fed all the other victims."

"You know where they are right this second?"

"No."

"You can't follow them until you know where they are," Cates said, "and if the news gets out before you find them, Rachael will be dead and buried, and those two will hang up their Hazmat suits, sit back, and watch the case go cold."

There was a reason Cates was a commanding officer at such a young age. I was glad to have her brain back.

"I have a thought," she said.

Really glad.

At 6:30 Friday morning—exactly four days after I thought I had met two perfect candidates for NYPD Red, I called Gideon Bell. By 7:15, he and Casey showed up at the precinct.

Kylie and I were all smiles when they walked through the door. We didn't have to fake looking happy to see them. We were. Sort of like the Wolf when Red Riding Hood shows up with a basket of goodies.

"Man, Zach, you sounded excited over the phone," Bell said. "What's going down?"

"My boss wants to be in on it," I said. "She'll tell you."

We walked down the hall to Cates's office. She stood up when they entered the room. Introductions all around, and then I shut the door.

"First, I want to thank you gentlemen for helping out," Cates said. "We have good news: 911 got a call from a woman who said she was Rachael O'Keefe. She said she was being held by two men. She was pretty incoherent, rambling on about being tortured. The dispatcher tried to get her location, and then the call dropped. She didn't call back, and we thought it was a hoax, but her sister, Liz, listened to the 911 tape and confirmed that it was Rachael."

"So she's alive," Bell said. "That's great news. Can you trace the call?"

"It was a cell—somewhere in Queens. We didn't get enough data to triangulate, but we're continuing to ping it. We may not be able to pinpoint the exact location, but as soon as we narrow it down to a manageable area, we'll go door-to-door till we find her. It could be a block of apartment buildings, so we need manpower. You wanted in, and Red could sure use your help."

"That's awesome," Bell said. "Thanks, Captain. We are totally in."

There wasn't a hint of a tell on his face. Casey, on the other hand, was forcing a smile, but he didn't look like a cop who had just gotten his big break to impress the boss of an elite squad.

Cates's phone rang. "It's our tech guy," she said, picking it up. "What's going on, Matt?"

She held the phone to her ear for five seconds and hung up.

"They're zeroing in on it," she said. "They need another twenty minutes."

"You guys grab these radios and start rolling," I said. "I'll call you as soon as we zero in on the target."

They each took a radio and headed for the door. Bell turned back. "Captain Cates, it's always been our dream to work with Red. Thanks again for the opportunity."

"And thank you," Cates said. "You've been a big part of this, and you deserve to be there when we find Rachael."

She waited for them to walk down the hall out of earshot.

"And thank you, Detectives Jordan and MacDonald, for letting me be part of your own private little police force. So," she said, raising her eyebrows, "how did I do?"

CHAPTER 77

"**HOW THE HELL** did she get her hands on a cell phone?" Gideon said as he got behind the wheel of the SUV and peeled out.

"I don't know, but this is falling apart," Dave said. "Just like with Enzo, only worse. This time we're really dead."

"Maybe somebody got in through the back door. Are you sure you locked it?"

"No, Gideon, I left it wide open so that anybody could walk in on her and call 911."

"Don't get all defensive. I'm just asking."

"Funny—it sounded more like you were just blaming."

"Sorry. This all came out of the blue. I'm a little freaked."

"That's the difference between you and me, Gideon. I'm a lot freaked."

"How about we stop panicking for a minute and start thinking," Gideon said.

"I'm thinking plenty," Dave said. "I'm thinking about what it's like to be a cop spending the rest of his life in Sing Sing."

Gideon maneuvered the car onto the Ed Koch Bridge. It was the start of rush hour, but the traffic leaving Manhattan was much lighter than the traffic pouring in from Queens. "Here's my take on it," he said. "Nobody came in through the back door. Nobody came in from anywhere. If someone was there, and they really did see Rachael, they'd have called back by now. Am I right?"

Dave shrugged. "I hope so."

"Plus, she's only wearing a Hazmat suit, so where was she hiding a cell phone? Even if she magically came up with one, she's in chains—what did she do, dial it with her teeth? It's all a hoax, Dave. Some crazy bastard called 911 pretending to be Rachael, and those idiot cops bought it."

"Which idiot cops? Jordan and MacDonald, or us? Once they said the sister identified her voice…"

"Come on, Dave. Use your head. The sister wanted it to be Rachael. The cops wanted it to be Rachael. So they bought it. But you and I know that she couldn't get her hands on a phone. It had to be a crank caller. Relax."

"*Relax?* Maybe if the son of a bitch made his crank calls from Brooklyn. But he didn't. Hoax or no hoax, he got them to zero in on Queens, so now I'm not relaxing until we move her as far away as possible. The sooner the better."

"I thought she'd confess by now," Gideon said, "but

she's tough. It could take days before we can get her on video."

"We don't have days," Dave said. "The garage is too hot. We can't keep her there. I hate to drive all the way up to the Adirondacks, but I think my cousin's cabin is the safest bet. I say we pack her up and head there now."

"Small problem," Gideon said. "It's a five-hour drive each way. Jordan and MacDonald will be calling us any minute to help them canvass whatever neighborhood they decide the call came from. We can't drop out of sight, and we can't exactly stash her in the back of the car."

"Well, we can't leave her in the garage."

"Sure we can," Gideon said. "We just can't leave her in the garage alive."

"So what are you saying—just kill her? Without the video?"

"I'd rather think of it as kill her without getting caught," Gideon said. "Hey, you can't win them all. She didn't crack, and we don't have time to wait. We have no choice. We have to kill her."

"When?"

"No time like the present," Gideon said as he came off the bridge and turned onto Vernon Boulevard. "We'll be there in five minutes."

"Just like that?" Dave said. "Just run right in and kill her?"

"What do you want to do? Stop off and bring her another pizza? Buy her some parting gifts? Dave, this isn't going to be a big production number like with Enzo. We know how to do this. We put a plastic bag over her head, pack up the equipment, and leave her there. They'll find her eventually."

Dave nodded, trying to adjust to the fact that they were going to kill someone in five minutes. He never got used to it. That was Gideon's thing. "Did anyone ever tell you that you are one sick motherfucker?"

"Yeah," Gideon said. "But tell me again. I never get tired of hearing it."

CHAPTER 78

IN THE TEN minutes that Casey and Bell spent being lied to by Captain Cates, Matt Smith had planted a GPS tracker and two bugs in their car. Then he used his geek magic so that Kylie and I could track their movements and listen to their conversation on an iPad.

In the thirty minutes before that, Cates had pulled together a twelve-man SWAT team and a helicopter whose NYPD markings were covered with ABC *Eyewitness News* logos. It was the perfect rush-hour cover for a cop chopper.

The entire operation was coordinated through the city's newest defense against terrorism—Monitor—a twenty-million-dollar electronic hub linked to more than a hundred thousand eyes and ears across all five boroughs. It was like Big Brother on steroids.

All those resources were being brought to bear to save one woman—a young mother whose criminal negligence had led to the death of her innocent five-year-old daughter and who only two days ago couldn't get the city to spring for a couple of cops in a patrol car to escort her to a safe haven.

That was then. Now Rachael O'Keefe had been upgraded from an anonymous fifteen-dollar-an-hour phlebotomist to one of New York's most important citizens. And the fact that the mayor's ass was on the line if she was murdered didn't hurt her cause.

Kylie and I put on Kevlar vests and NYPD windbreakers, and the instant Casey and Bell's SUV drove away from the precinct, we sprinted for our car. Kylie got behind the wheel, and the six SWAT vehicles that had been idling out of sight over on York Avenue barreled up East 67th Street and fell in behind us.

We moved out, and I tracked Casey and Bell, keeping us as close as I could, but always out of sight.

As expected, they headed for Queens, and it was clear from the verbal battle they were having in the car that we had found our Hazmat Killer.

Heads turned as our heavily armed convoy moved south down Second Avenue. "You've got to hand it to Cates," I said, "for pulling all this firepower together in no time flat."

"If you ask me, it's overkill," Kylie said when we were halfway across the Ed Koch Bridge. "Especially the clown car bringing up the rear."

The clowns she was referring to were Detectives Donovan and Boyle. Cates had called them in on the operation. No explanation. Kylie was not happy about it, but she knew better than to question Cates's judgment.

"What would you rather do?" I said. "Storm the castle in your designer camo with a gun in each hand and a nine-inch KA-BAR between your teeth?"

And then a bright orange fireball lit up the sky.

Like so many bright red dominoes, the taillights in front of us popped on, and Kylie slammed on the brakes to avoid plowing into the rear of a white van.

I radioed Big Brother. "Explosion on the Queens side of the EKB. What's going on?"

"We know. Our bells and whistles are going off. Hang on, I'm pulling up the traffic cams in front of you. There's a ten fifty-three—looks like a city bus slammed into an eighteen-wheeler, blew his fuel tank. People are pouring out of the bus, drivers abandoning their cars."

I checked the GPS. Casey and Bell were on the other side of the accident. They had just passed through Queensboro Plaza and were moving along at a rapid clip.

And then I heard Gideon come in over the wire. *"We have no choice. We have to kill her."*

"Monitor, this is Red Leader," I said. "We're parked. Can we get out of this box or not?"

"Negative. Everything is total gridlock. Hold on—you can skirt the accident if you're on foot."

Now *we* had no choice. "Red Team, this is Red Leader," I said. "Abandon your vehicles and move out. Now. Monitor, I can't track the targets when I'm on the run. Keep me posted."

Kylie and I jumped out of the Ford and started running along the steel roadway. The SWAT team was right behind us in full tactical gear. A few drivers rolled down their windows, yelling at us to run faster and get the goddamn traffic moving. You've got to love New York. There's always someone around to tell you how to do your job.

"Red Leader, targets just turned off Jackson onto Crane Street. It's a dead end, so that may be where the hostage is."

"How far is it from where we are?"

"One point three miles. Can you commandeer a vehicle once you get past the accident?"

"We're coming up on it now," I said. "It's total chaos. No first responders, but this whole stretch of roadway is a construction zone, and you have hard hats with fire extinguishers assisting. I can hear fire engines approaching, but negative on commandeering a vehicle, Monitor. Even if there were a troop transport waiting here, traffic is stretched all the way out to Queens Boulevard. This is the fastest way. I'm guessing ten to twelve minutes before the whole team is in place on Crane Street."

"Red Leader, I don't know if you picked up their last transmission. They plan to kill the hostage and run. I don't think you have ten minutes."

"Then I have to buy us some time," I said.

I stopped short. The elevated Queensboro Plaza subway station was overhead. I leaned against one of the graffiti-covered, steel-reinforced concrete pillars, pulled out my cell phone, and dialed.

Dave Casey answered on the first ring. "Zach. What's up? Did you find her yet?"

"No," I said, trying to keep my heavy breathing from giving me away. "But Calvin Vidmar, the doorman at Rachael's apartment building, just confessed to murdering Kimi O'Keefe. We found corroborating proof at his apartment. I thought you and Bell should know it. Rachael O'Keefe is innocent."

He didn't say a word.

"Dave—did you hear me? Did you process what I said?"

"Yeah...I heard you. Heard you just fine. Thanks for calling."

He hung up, and I broke into a run. Kylie and the SWAT team were already in front of me.

CHAPTER 79

"DID YOU HEAR the radio?" Gideon asked.

Dave shook his head, still trying to process his conversation with Zach Jordan. "No, I was on the phone. What's going on?"

"That explosion—a ten fifty-three on the off-ramp of the bridge. A bus hit a truck and blew the gas tank."

"Anybody hurt?"

"Dave, who gives a shit? The point is, the whole fucking bridge is shut down—we got here just in time. Let's do what we have to do and get moving."

Dave got out of the car, opened the garage door, and rolled the gate back in place as soon as the SUV was inside.

"Who called you just now?" Gideon said, stepping out of the car.

"Jordan."

"And?"

"He said O'Keefe is innocent. He said the doorman from her building confessed to killing the kid."

"Bullshit! He's playing us."

"What do you mean?"

"Put it together, man. Jordan, MacDonald, Cates— they're all playing us. First they call us in about this bogus phone call that we know was impossible for O'Keefe to make. Then we drive to Queens, and they follow us. They followed us, Dave."

Dave peered through one of the two grimy, wire-reinforced windows. "Then where are they?"

"They're on the other side of the goddamn explosion. They can't get here. That's why Jordan called you with another bullshit story. This time she's innocent? They're trying to buy time. Let's get our shit and get the hell out of here. You load the video equipment. I'll get the stuff from the back room."

"What about Rachael?"

"Same as before. She can identify us. We kill her. End of story, Dave."

"What if she really is innocent?"

"Dave, they're screwing with your head. She's guilty. We know she's guilty. You load the car. I'll take care of Rachael. Then let's get the hell out of here."

"Let's not," a voice said.

They turned, and a giant of a man had stepped out from behind the false wall at the far end of the building. Dave knew a lot about guns, and he recognized the Smith &

Wesson 5946 nine-millimeter pistol as soon as he spotted it. This one was fitted with an eight-inch Infiniti silencer on the business end.

"We're cops," Gideon said. "Put the gun down. Now."

The big man laughed. "*Put the gun down?* You got balls, man. How about *you* get on your knees, put your weapons on the floor nice and easy, slide them here, and then put your hands behind your head. You know—just like in the movies."

Dave lowered himself to the ground and slid his gun across the room. Gideon didn't budge. "You're making a mistake," he said. "We're NYPD."

"Well, that explains why you don't listen. Now either get down while you still have knees to help you down, or I'll cap one of them and let gravity do the rest. Right or left—your call."

Gideon knelt down next to Dave. "If you think you can just walk in and rob a couple of cops," he said, sliding his gun across the cement floor, "you're crazy."

He laughed. "Is that what you think? This is not a robbery."

"Then what the hell do you call it?"

"I'd call it Judgment Day," said the silver-haired man who stepped out from behind the wall. He had a gun in his right hand—a black Beretta 85 fitted with a five-inch suppressor. In his left was the choke pear.

"Jesus," Dave said. "Joe Salvi."

"And son," Salvi said.

With that, Jojo Salvi swaggered out from behind the wall, a satin nickel version of his father's Beretta in his hand.

"Over there," Salvi said to Jojo. "Opposite Tommy Boy."

Jojo took his position, and the three men stood there in silence—an ominous triangle of guns and muscle.

Finally, Salvi spoke. "Ingenious," he said, holding up the choke pear. "Easy to operate, extremely effective—every smart businessman should have one. I think I'll keep it." He tossed the pear to Tommy Boy.

Salvi stared at them with the same dark, menacing eyes that had scanned a church filled with people at his son's funeral. But now he had found what he was looking for. "Your partner looks confused," he said to Gideon. "But you expected us, didn't you, Gideon?"

Dave's head snapped to the left. "Gideon, what is he talking about?"

Gideon stared straight ahead.

"Let me make this easy for you," Salvi said to Dave. He reached into the breast pocket of his jacket and pulled out a dark red Moroccan leather journal, bordered in gold filigree. "Look familiar?"

Dave couldn't quite put the pieces together fast enough. "Where did...how..."

"Shut up, Dave," Gideon said. "Salvi, don't be an idiot. We're cops. I don't care what you think is going on, but you can pull a shitload of jail time for this. Put the gun down now, and we'll drop the whole thing."

"Oh, you're cops?" Salvi said, lowering the gun and bringing his arm out to his side. "Why didn't you say something?" He turned to Rachael O'Keefe, still chained to a pipe, her mouth sealed with duct tape.

"Look, lady—the cops are here. You want to go with them?"

Rachael shook her head violently and let out a muffled scream.

"Bad news, boys," Salvi said. "You're striking out with the ladies. I guess nobody has any respect for cops these days. Even a damsel in—" Without warning, he brought the butt of his gun down hard against Gideon's jaw, shattering bone, ripping flesh, and exploding capillaries.

Blood spattered across the room. Gideon doubled over but managed to stay on his knees.

Salvi turned to Dave. "I'm sorry, Detective Casey. I got distracted. Did you have a question? Oh yes, how did I get my son's journal? Funny thing—Gideon's mother found it and was kind enough to return it to the family. Lovely woman. Took care of most of the flower arrangements for my son's funeral."

Dave turned to Gideon. "Your *mother?* You said you burned it. Why would you keep—"

"Shut up," Gideon said, spitting out blood and chunks of teeth.

"You knew your mother gave it back to them?"

"Of course he knew," Salvi said.

"I just found out about it," Gideon said. "I didn't want you to freak out while we were in the middle of this, but I swear I was going to tell you as soon as we finished here."

"So you *spared* me the fact that the Mob was gunning for me?"

Gideon looked away.

"There's no talking to him, Dave," Salvi said. He walked

over to the video equipment. "Nice little setup you got here. You like to tape confessions? So do I. We've been here a while, and I think Jojo's got the hang of it. Jojo, turn on the camera."

Jojo didn't move.

"You deaf?" Salvi said. "Turn on the camera."

"I don't know, Pop," Jojo said. "We have to do what we came to do, but videotaping it—I don't know if that's such a good idea—"

Salvi held up a hand. "Don't think," he said, his voice a menacingly low whisper. "Your mother has been waiting twelve years. Now turn on the fucking camera."

"Okay, okay," Jojo said, tucking his gun in his belt. He stepped behind the camera and pointed it at the two men on their knees. He pressed the red Record button and a red light blinked on. "Whenever you're ready, Pop," he said.

"Okay, then," Salvi said. "I guess I'm the director of this little movie. This is going to be the big confession scene—the one everybody's been waiting for."

He stood eight feet away and pointed the gun straight at Dave's head. "Now, start confessing."

"This place is going to be swarming with cops any minute," Dave said.

Salvi laughed. "You *are* cops. You came to torture this woman. What did you do—call for backup?" He lowered his voice to a whisper. "Look, Dave, you seem like a reasonable man, so tell me—whose idea was it to kill my son?"

"Your son raped my sister," Dave said.

"I don't care if he fucked your grandmother, chopped her up, and fed the pieces to his dog. You both killed him. I know that. Now I want to know which one of you planned it."

"What's the difference? You're going to kill us both anyway."

"The difference? The difference is that one of you pulled the strings. The other is just a soldier—a follower. One of you made the decision to bash my boy's head in and hold his face underwater until he drowned. There's always a leader." Salvi pointed his gun at Gideon. "Was it him? He acts like he's in charge."

Gideon, dripping with blood, stared at Salvi defiantly.

Salvi stared back. "But he's not," he said, kicking Gideon in the ribs hard enough to hear bone crack. "He's not in charge of anything."

Gideon collapsed to the floor and yowled in agony.

"Aw...does it hurt? Bad news—it's not the first hit that hurts the most. It's every breath you take from now on. The good news is you don't have that many breaths left." Salvi waved a hand at Tommy Boy. "Pick this piece of shit up."

The big man grabbed Gideon's collar and yanked him to his knees.

Dave looked away, and then he saw it—a shadowy figure popped up and peered through the grimy window.

It was Kylie MacDonald.

CHAPTER 80

THREE MORNINGS A week, I try to work out at the precinct gym—weights, treadmill, elliptical. Once a week, I see a yoga instructor. So I'm in good shape—not as good as the SWAT team, but they were weighed down with so much tactical gear that I was able to catch up with the pack.

"We're not going to make it," Kylie said as I fell in place alongside her. "Our five minutes are up, and we've still got three-quarters of a mile to—"

My radio interrupted. "Monitor to Red Leader."

I answered it on the run. "Go ahead, Monitor."

"I've got you on traffic cam. There's transport on Twenty-First Street a block ahead of you. It's all yours."

Sure enough, there it was—a big, beautiful blue-and-white NYPD bus.

"Thank you, Monitor," I said as the team piled in. "What's the twenty on our target?"

"Our eye in the sky saw them pull into a garage at Eighty-Eight Crane six minutes ago."

"We're rolling," I said as the bus moved out.

Twenty-First, which runs under the el, is a narrow two-way street, but the driver managed to maneuver his way through morning traffic quickly. I just wasn't sure it was quick enough. If Gideon kept to his five-minute deadline, Rachael would be dead before we got there.

I briefed Alan Rowe, the SWAT leader, on the latest. We Google-mapped 88 Crane, and by the time the bus stopped at the top of the dead-end street, Sergeant Rowe had a plan.

He split the team into three—one to breach the garage door, a second to come through the rear, and two men to cover the side of the building next to the railroad yard.

Every building on Crane Street was covered with graffiti, and all of them looked to be abandoned, including the four-story warehouse in the middle of the block.

We ran almost noiselessly to the end of the street and took our positions. Kylie and I followed Rowe to the front of the garage.

The garage door was about eight by ten feet and made of corrugated steel. "No problem," Rowe said. "I just heard from the team in the rear and there's a small door in the back that's much easier than this one. The breacher is running detcord around each door. On my command, he'll blow the back one as a diversion. A second later, he'll take down the garage door."

"Jordan and I will go in first," Kylie said.

"Not a chance," Rowe said. "You know the drill. Entry team secures the room. It's what they do."

"Fine, you go first," she said. "Do you know what you're walking in on?"

"No idea."

"You should." With that she plastered herself against the side of the building, got down on the ground, and crawled to one of the two almost blackened windows.

"What the hell is she doing?" Rowe said.

"My best guess would be intel," I said. "Whatever it is, there's no stopping her."

Kylie raised her head high enough to look through the grimy window. Five seconds later, she dropped down and made her way back to us.

"It's a whole new ball game," she said, taking out a pad and pen. She drew a box. "Here's the room."

She put an X in the middle of the box. "Here's Rachael. She's chained up, but she's standing, so it looks like she's still alive.

"And here," she said, adding two more X's, "are Casey and Bell. They're on the floor on their knees, and there are three men pointing guns at them." She added three more X's.

The curveballs just kept coming. "Three men," I repeated.

"Yeah," Kylie said. "And one of them is Papa Joe Salvi."

CHAPTER 81

"**LET ME REPEAT** the question," Joe Salvi said. "Who came home from high school one afternoon and told the other that you both had to murder Enzo? There's always a leader. There's always a follower."

Salvi's words reminded Dave of his father. "There are chiefs," his dad would say, "and there are Indians. The problem with NYPD is that there are too many damn chiefs and not enough good Indians. I'm an Indian, Dave. I get an order, and I get the job done."

And that's what Dave had tried to do. Sure, it was all Gideon's idea, but once Dave signed on, he gave it all he had. Enzo, Kang, Catt, Tinsdale, Parker-Steele—every one of them got what they deserved. He only wished he'd had the time to take down more.

But all he had left was twenty seconds. Kylie MacDonald wasn't out there alone. She and Jordan would be backed up by a SWAT team hell-bent on saving Rachael. They'd blow the garage door, and an army of cops with ballistic shields and assault rifles would storm in.

Twenty seconds. Just enough time to take down one last scumbag.

"I did it!" Dave screamed at Salvi. "Gideon is all mouth and no balls. Enzo raped my sister, and I vowed to kill him. I'm the one who cracked his greasy Guinea head with a bottle of cheap shit vodka. Then I dragged him down to the water, and the whole time he was squealing like the little pussy that he was."

Dave could see Salvi tighten his grip on the gun. He willed him to squeeze the trigger.

But Salvi held back. He still needed one more push.

"All you Salvis are such hot shit when you have the upper hand," Dave taunted, "but when the tables are turned, you're all like Enzo—calling out for his fat whore of a mother—"

Salvi's gun exploded.

Blood, bone, and gray matter from Gideon's skull sprayed across Dave's face.

"You know, Dave," Salvi said, "you're not only a lousy cop, you're a lousy liar. I don't know why you'd want to take a bullet for that asshole. He fucked you over. I admire you for your loyalty, but I'm going to kill you anyway."

He was leveling his gun at Dave's head when the first explosion rocked the room. The back door imploded, sending a shower of smoke and debris through the rear wall. The three mobsters wheeled around. An instant later, a second blast ripped a wide, gaping hole in the metal garage door, and men in helmets, goggles, and tactical vests poured in.

Tommy Boy reacted instantly, firing blindly into the horde of uniforms rushing toward him.

For a smart man, it was a dumb way to die. A barrage of bullets from six different assault weapons tore through Tommy Boy's body, and he crashed to the floor like a boulder.

"Hold your fire, hold your fire!" Joe Salvi yelled, raising his hands in the air.

"Drop the weapons, face down on the ground, hands behind your head," a voice barked.

A half smile crept across Dave Casey's face. The cop giving orders was Kylie MacDonald. Jordan was right there with her.

Two Berettas clattered to the floor, and Salvi and Jojo lowered themselves to the ground. Four cops cuffed them, patted them down, and pulled them up to their knees.

"Hey, take it easy," Salvi said. "We just captured the Hazmat Killers. My driver shot one of them."

"Plus we rescued the baby-killing bitch," Jojo said.

"Really?" Kylie said. "That's not the way I saw it through the window."

Joe Salvi looked at her incredulously. "What? You looked through a wire-mesh window that has a hundred years of crap on it, and you think you're going to be a believable eyewitness? My lawyer will have a field day with that."

"I don't think the DA will be needing my testimony, Mr.

Salvi," Kylie said. "There's a much better eyewitness who was in the room with you the entire time."

"Who? Him?" he said, gesturing at Dave. "A disgraced cop turned psychokiller? Or how about her? I'm sure she'll make a fine witness after being chained up and tortured for the last three days."

Salvi laughed. Jojo joined in.

"No, Mr. Salvi," Kylie said. "I think we've got an unimpeachable witness that will convince any jury what went down here no matter what your lawyers say or do."

"And where is this so-called witness?" Salvi said.

"It's right here," Kylie said, resting her hand on the video camera and pointing at the blinking red light. "And it's still rolling."

CHAPTER 82

DAVE CASEY WAS waiting for us in the interrogation room. For a cop who murdered a black drug lord and a Chinese gangbanger and was about to spend the rest of his life locked up among their homeboys and *péngyous*, he looked remarkably at peace.

"Thanks for coming," he said as soon as Kylie and I walked in. "Did you watch the videotape?"

"Not yet," I said. "We came straight here. Are you sure you don't want a lawyer or a union rep?"

"You've already read me my rights. No thanks. The only ones I want to talk to are you."

"Then it's just the three of us," I said, sitting across the table from him. Kylie stood.

"Right. The three of us, plus how many behind the two-way?" he asked, pointing at the large mirror set inside the far wall.

"Seven and counting. Dave, you know how big this is. You're going to pack a room. Now, should we ask questions, or would you rather just talk?"

"Oh, I'm ready to talk, but first I have a question of my own."

"Go ahead."

"That last phone call you made to me. You said that the doorman confessed to murdering Kimi O'Keefe. Was that bullshit?"

"No. It was the real deal," I said. "We knew you were about to kill Rachael, and we wanted to head you off."

"Thanks. I couldn't live with myself if we had..."

He paused, groping for a better phrase than *murdered her in cold blood.*

"If we had...followed through."

"But you were okay killing the other four," Kylie said.

"The other five," Casey said. "Twelve years ago, back when we were still in high school, Gideon and I killed Joe Salvi's youngest son, Enzo. He was a vicious, sadistic little punk who terrorized the neighborhood, and we knew it was only going to get worse. Then it did—he raped my sister, Meredith, and Gideon convinced me it was up to the two of us. I'm not blaming Gideon. I was with him all the way."

Just when I thought I'd seen my last curveball, Dave Casey smoked one right past me. I looked up at Kylie. Her mouth was open, but nothing was coming out.

"From the look on your faces, I'm guessing Salvi didn't explain why he and his crew were there," Dave said. "He wouldn't. It's family business. He's been looking for whoever killed Enzo all these years, and he just stumbled on the truth a few days ago. Totally blindsided us."

"That explains why a guy as high up the food chain as Salvi didn't send in a hit team," I said.

"It's all on the tape," Casey said.

"That's the one thing that doesn't compute," Kylie said. "Guys like Salvi wrap themselves in secrecy. If there's a camera in the room, they smash it. Did he not know the tape was rolling?"

"Salvi's the one who told Jojo to turn it on. All he wanted was to record me and Gideon confessing to Enzo's murder and bring it home to his wife. I doubt if he planned to pull the trigger on tape, but that's the funny thing about video cameras—you get distracted, you forget it's on."

"What distracted him?" I said.

Dave cracked a smile. "Just watch the movie. I don't want to ruin the ending for you. By the way, you probably want to send a copy up to the One Oh Six in Howard Beach. They've got a twelve-year-old cold case I'm sure they'll be happy to close."

I was positive that someone on the other side of the looking glass was already doing just that.

"Dave," Kylie said, "you were kids when you killed Salvi's son. It was a personal vendetta. What about these other random killings?"

"They weren't random. We were cleaning up a city that couldn't or wouldn't clean up after itself. Are you telling me you never felt like doing anything like that?"

"Feeling like it and going ahead with it are worlds

apart," Kylie said. "We're cops, not vigilantes. We work within the system."

He smiled. "You two—especially you, Kylie—only work within the system when it's working for you. Then you blow right through to the other side and do whatever the hell you want. Don't forget, you're the ones who had me and Gideon running an illegal tail on a couple of innocent cops."

Kylie looked over her shoulder at the mirror. I could pretty much guess what kind of a look she was getting from the other side.

"A lot of people supported the Hazmat Killer," Casey said. "I know you don't condone what we did, but don't pretend that you don't understand."

"Help us understand it a little better," I said. "Take us through it from the beginning."

"It all started with a simple question," Casey said. "Do you think Hitler was a nice guy when he was in high school?"

He talked nonstop for the next two hours. When he was finished, he looked directly into the camera and said, "Well, that's my video confession. None of it was coerced. All of it was voluntary. I just want to add that my sister, Meredith, never had a clue that Gideon and I killed Enzo or anyone else. Yes, she did tell Gideon that Rachael O'Keefe would be holed up at her aunt's house in Jersey, but that's only because Gideon got her drunk and pried the information out of her. We were cops. She trusted us. A lot of people trusted us, and, in fact, Detectives Jordan and MacDonald also shared confidential information with us. Meredith was just one of the many people we duped. She played no part in any of our crimes and shouldn't have to suffer any of the consequences."

He folded his hands and rested them on the table. "I think I'm done, but I have two more questions."

"Go ahead," I said.

"What's the status on Rachael O'Keefe?"

"She was taken to the trauma center at New York–Presbyterian," Kylie said. "Her sister is with her, and there's round-the-clock NYPD protection to keep away the press, the crazies, and the usual assortment of bottom-feeders who want to exploit her ordeal."

"Tell her I'm..." He stopped. "No, there's nothing I can say that she wants to hear." He shook his head, trying to clear away regrets that no doubt would haunt him the rest of his life.

"What's your second question?" Kylie said.

"What do you think will happen to the Salvis?"

"The DA's office screened the videotape, and they're one hundred percent positive they can convict Joe Salvi."

"The tape is definitely admissible?" Dave asked. "The courts won't throw it out? They like to do that, you know."

"Not this time," Kylie said. "The DA confirmed that Salvi knew the camera was there. He says something at the very top about being the director of the movie. And the lens was open wide enough to catch him gunning down a cop. That's life without parole. And Jojo will get at least twenty-five years as an accessory."

"You know, my father was a cop, and deep down inside,

Gideon and I were always cops. And even though we went off the rails, we managed to take down an entire Mafia dynasty. Joe Salvi and his two sons. Gid would be pretty goddamn happy about that."

"I imagine a lot of people in Howard Beach will be pretty goddamn happy about that," I said.

"You don't know the half of it," Casey said. "Everybody lived in fear of them. It's the end of a sixty-year reign of tyranny. Nobody in Howard Beach will miss the Salvis."

He paused, and an eerie smile crept across his face. "Except maybe on Thanksgiving, Christmas, Fourth of July, and Halloween."

HAZMAT'S FINAL VICTIM

CHAPTER 83

IT WAS THE Wednesday morning after Election Day, and I bounded up the stairs of the precinct with a shopping bag in one hand and a newspaper in the other. I was surprised to see Kylie at her desk.

"I thought you were driving Spence to rehab," I said, setting the shopping bag on the floor.

"He can't check in till three p.m., so I figured I'd come in here and give him some alone time. I'm sure by the end of the day, he'll have had more than enough of me."

"I know the feeling," I said, and held up a copy of the *Daily News*. "Did you see this?"

There were two photos on page one—a jubilant Muriel Sykes making her acceptance speech and a forlorn Mayor Spellman watching the returns on TV. There was a one-word headline above each photo:

SYKES!!! YIKES!!!

"Zach, I know who won. We all know. The networks all called it for Sykes last night an hour after the polls closed."

"Yes, but only the *Daily News* mentions us," I said.

That got her attention. I turned to page three. "'Despite the fact that one of the Hazmat Killers was shot down in cold blood by Mob boss Joseph Salvi, and the other was apprehended in a daring raid by NYPD's elite Red unit, the two serial murderers have claimed one final victim—the political career of Mayor Stanley Spellman.

"'For four months Hazmat terrorized our city, but Spellman refused to call in his powerhouse Red team. Only when his political opponent's campaign manager became the latest homicide did the Mayor call in the finest of New York's Finest. The effort, led by Detectives Zach Jordan and Kylie MacDonald, cracked the case in only four days. Exit polls confirmed that Spellman's failure to harness the Red team sooner was a key reason why so many voters pulled the lever for Muriel Sykes.'"

"Powerhouse Red team...finest of New York's Finest... I'm guessing Damon Parker didn't write the piece," Kylie said. "What's in the shopping bag?"

"It's a Go board, handmade out of a seven-hundred-year-old kaya tree. Plus, a box of authentic Yuki stones. It's for the old Chinese guy in Columbus Park. He's too good to be playing on plywood."

"You bought him a gift?"

"No big deal. It cost less than I would have paid a CI

for the same information. Didn't you ever do something nice to thank a witness?"

"No."

"Well, maybe you should start by taking that short fat guy, Joe Romeo, out for dinner. He was angling for some kind of reward."

She punched me in the shoulder just as the elevator doors opened, and out stepped a tall woman in a tailored blue business suit, accented by a red, white, and blue Hermès scarf.

It was Muriel Sykes.

"You should see the looks on your faces," she said, walking toward us. "Like a couple of schoolkids who got caught roughhousing in the classroom by the new principal. Take me to Captain Cates's office."

We walked her down the hall. Cates's door was open and Sykes walked in. "You too," she said to us. "Inside."

We followed her in, closed the door, and stood there clueless.

Cates, on the other hand, is a political pro. Her face brightened, and she stood up, came around her desk, and shook Sykes's hand.

"Mayor-Elect Sykes," she said, the perfect mix of bubbles and bullshit. "Congratulations. This is an honor. What can I do for New York City's first female mayor on this historic day?"

"Thank you, but this is more about what I can do for you," Sykes said. "I know there were people involved in my campaign who trashed NYPD Red."

"Not people," Cates said. "Just Damon Parker. He said he'd like to turn Red back into Blue."

386 • JAMES PATTERSON

"I know. Damon can behave like a total ass, but that's politics, and now that the election is behind us, I want to assure you that I'm your biggest supporter."

"That's good to know."

"I'm grateful for what you did, Delia," Sykes said. "I've known Detectives Donovan and Boyle since back in my U.S. attorney days. They are definitely not Red material, but they are fiercely loyal, and they've been my go-to guys for years. The fact that you brought them in for the collar after they bungled the case for months meant a lot to them and to me. So thank you."

"Anytime."

"City government has been male dominated long enough," Sykes said. "I've made it a priority to find smart women I can count on."

"If I come across any," Cates said, "I'll send them your way."

Sykes laughed and turned to us. "As for you, Detectives, congratulations on your brilliant police work. I can see why Irwin Diamond handpicked you for the case. Nobody gets anything past you. Including me," she said.

And that, I knew, would be the one and only reference she would ever make about the fact that she had violated every statute in the book by hijacking Evelyn Parker-Steele's laptop.

"Not only did you solve the Hazmat case, but you rescued an innocent kidnapping victim, and on top of that, you nailed the most notorious Mob boss in the city on a charge that is guaranteed to stick."

We both thanked her.

"I just wish we had the death penalty in New York," Kylie added. "Nobody deserves it more than Joe Salvi."

"I agree," Sykes said. "Which is why first thing this morning I put in a call to Fred Pearson. Fred replaced me as the U.S. attorney for the Southern District. New York can't execute Salvi, but the Feds can."

"We knew that," Kylie said, "but there's a difference between 'can' and 'will.' It almost never happens."

"You're right," Sykes said. "*Almost* never. But the Feds have struck out before, trying to indict Salvi on RICO charges. Fred Pearson is a protégé of mine, and I know he'd be thrilled to have a video of Joe Salvi murdering a police officer in cold blood."

"But Salvi knew that Bell was a crooked police officer," I said.

"True, but it doesn't negate the fact that Bell was with NYPD and on duty at the time. Also, Salvi killed him because of a personal vendetta, so he can't exactly claim he was on a public service mission. No promises, but the Feds would love to burn that bastard, so don't be surprised if Joe Salvi winds up on the wrong end of a lethal injection before I run for reelection in four years."

"Thank you for your support, Mayor-Elect Sykes," Cates said. "If there's anything we can do, just let us know when your reelection campaign starts."

Sykes inhaled and rose to her full impressive height. She stared straight on at the three of us and said, "It just did, Captain. It just did."

CHAPTER 84

WRAPPING UP THE paperwork on the average homicide investigation can take days. But this case was anything but average. Two cops were the killers, someone from the DA's office had leaked confidential information, and one of the victims had been the campaign manager for our new mayor. Kylie and I were drowning in official procedure.

"I think we just passed the point where it's taking us longer to finish filing these reports than it did to solve the crime," Kylie said as she got up from her desk at noon. "Sorry I can't stick around for the rest of the fun, but Spence and I have to be on the road to recovery in thirty minutes. I'll see you tomorrow."

She left, and thirty minutes later, I got a text.

What in the world is more interesting than me? C.

I'd forgotten my lunch date with Cheryl.

I hit Save on my laptop and ran around the corner to Gerri's Diner.

Gerri was at the register. "Hello, handsome," she said. "I heard you have a new girlfriend."

"I'm fifteen minutes late, so the current one may be pissed at me, but why would you think I have a new one?"

"Rumor has it that our new mayor came a-callin' on you this morning. None of my business, but Muriel Sykes is old enough to be your mother."

"None of your business? Gerri, everything that happens at the One Nine seems to be your business. And don't worry about the new mayor. If I ever start dating women my mom's age, you'll be first on the list."

"Promises, promises," she said. "Now hustle over to that booth before that British computer guy steals Dr. Cheryl right out from under your nose."

I hustled. My lunch date was halfway through a small salad, and Matt Smith was sitting opposite her.

"Mind if I join you?" I said.

Matt jumped up. "I'm not staying," he said. "Just keeping your seat warm, and making sure none of these randy cops hit on your girlfriend."

Cheryl stopped eating and looked up from her salad, but she didn't say a word.

I sat down. "My what?" I said.

"Come on, mate—I know you think it's a well-guarded secret, but I don't have to be a bloody genius to see there's something happening between you two. More power to you. You're a fantastic couple." He looked at his watch. "I guess Kylie is on her way up to the rehab with her husband."

"Sit down," I said.

He sat next to me.

"You are a vast storehouse of personal information," I whispered. "How the hell do you know about Spence?"

He shrugged and leaned in, keeping his voice low. "Information is what I do. What do you think the 'I' in IT stands for? I promise I won't breathe a word of it. I just brought it up because I knew that the two of you knew. This is not Spence's first rehab. Do you think he'll make it?"

I looked at Cheryl to see if she'd take the question. Not a chance in hell.

"Yes," I said. "He knows that if he doesn't, he's going to lose the best woman he ever had."

"That's precisely what I was thinking, and if Kylie MacDonald ever winds up single again..." Matt took a long, thoughtful pause into fantasyland. "Hell, mate," he said, "I don't have to tell you how fantastic she is."

"No, you don't," I said, trying to keep my eyes away from Cheryl and my head as far away from the past as I could and even further away from the future. "No, you don't."

"Well, enjoy your lunch, you two," Matt said, getting up. "And I know I've said this before, Zach, but brilliant job on the Hazmat case."

He headed toward the door. Cheryl stared at me without saying a word. Ten seconds into the silence, she burst into a girlish giggle, and I immediately started laughing with her.

"Well, that certainly gives new meaning to the phrase *embarrassingly awkward social situation*," she said. "You thought he had the hots for me, and it turns out he has the hots for Kylie. How do you feel about that?"

"I feel like it's something I don't want to talk about," I said. "Certainly not now, and absolutely not within a hundred yards of Gerri's Diner."

"How about a hundred miles from Gerri's Diner?"

"I don't understand."

"I think I'm ready to take this relationship to the next level," she said.

"Okay..."

She slid her iPhone across the table. "I know I've mentioned it, but I've never even shown you a picture."

I looked at the screen. It was a picture of a white house, its roof, front yard, and driveway covered with snow.

"It's even prettier in the summer when the flowers are out, or in October when the leaves are turning," she said.

"Is that your house in Woodstock?" I said.

"Half the time. The settlement says that Fred and his child-bride-to-be have it the other half, but..."

"But what?"

"They won't be using it for a while. The soon-to-be-next Mrs. Fred Robinson is pregnant."

"Hmmm," I said, stroking my imaginary beard. "And how do you feel about *that?*"

"I feel like it's something I don't want to talk about," she said. "Ever. So, would you like to drive up to Woodstock this weekend, rake some leaves, breathe some country air, lie by the fireplace, and drink wine?"

"It sounds like it could be almost as much fun as the paperwork I've been grinding out."

"You'll love it. That house was once a very joyful part of my life, and then one day it wasn't. I'm finally ready to go back there and find the joy again, and I'd like it to be with you. So, what do you say? This weekend?"

"Are you kidding? I was wondering if you were ever going to invite me."

"Well, now you can stop wondering."

Me? Stop wondering? Never happen. Even now I was wondering if Spence would make it through rehab, and if he didn't, would Kylie leave him, and if she did, would Matt ask her out, and if he did—

Cheryl smiled at me, reached across the table, and, without caring who was watching and who wasn't, took my hand in hers.

I smiled back, covered her hand with mine, shook all the other baggage out of my head, and wondered, *How the heck did I get to be this lucky?*

ACKNOWLEDGMENTS

The authors would like to thank Undersheriff Frank Faluotico and First Sergeant Alan Rowe of the Ulster County NY Sheriff's Office, NYPD Detective Sal Catapano, Dr. Lawrence Dresdale, Bob Beatty, Mel Berger, and Jason Wood for their help in making this work of fiction ring true.

ABOUT THE AUTHORS

JAMES PATTERSON has created more enduring fictional characters than any other novelist writing today. He is the author of the Alex Cross novels, the most popular detective series of the past twenty-five years. His other bestselling novels feature the Women's Murder Club, Michael Bennett, Private, and NYPD Red. Since his first novel won the Edgar Award in 1977, James Patterson's books have sold more than 300 million copies.

James Patterson has also written numerous #1 bestsellers for young readers, including the Maximum Ride, Witch & Wizard, Middle School, and Treasure Hunters series. In total, these books have spent more than 330 weeks on national bestseller lists. In 2010, James Patterson was named Author of the Year at the Children's Choice Book Awards.

His lifelong passion for books and reading led James Patterson to create the innovative website ReadKiddo Read.com, giving adults an invaluable tool to find the books that get kids reading for life. He writes full-time and lives in Florida with his family.

MARSHALL KARP has written for stage, screen, and TV, and is the author of *The Rabbit Factory* and three other mysteries featuring LAPD Detectives Mike Lomax and Terry Biggs. *NYPD Red 2* is his third collaboration with James Patterson.

BOOKS BY JAMES PATTERSON

FEATURING ALEX CROSS

Hope to Die
Cross My Heart
Alex Cross, Run
Merry Christmas, Alex Cross
Kill Alex Cross
Cross Fire
I, Alex Cross
Alex Cross's Trial (with Richard DiLallo)
Cross Country
Double Cross
Cross (also published as *Alex Cross*)
Mary, Mary

London Bridges
The Big Bad Wolf
Four Blind Mice
Violets Are Blue
Roses Are Red
Pop Goes the Weasel
Cat & Mouse
Jack & Jill
Kiss the Girls
Along Came a Spider

THE WOMEN'S MURDER CLUB

Unlucky 13 (with Maxine Paetro)
12th of Never (with Maxine Paetro)
11th Hour (with Maxine Paetro)
10th Anniversary (with Maxine Paetro)
The 9th Judgment (with Maxine Paetro)
The 8th Confession (with Maxine Paetro)
7th Heaven (with Maxine Paetro)
The 6th Target (with Maxine Paetro)
The 5th Horseman (with Maxine Paetro)
4th of July (with Maxine Paetro)
3rd Degree (with Andrew Gross)
2nd Chance (with Andrew Gross)
1st to Die

FEATURING MICHAEL BENNETT

Burn (with Michael Ledwidge)
Gone (with Michael Ledwidge)
I, Michael Bennett (with Michael Ledwidge)
Tick Tock (with Michael Ledwidge)
Worst Case (with Michael Ledwidge)
Run for Your Life (with Michael Ledwidge)
Step on a Crack (with Michael Ledwidge)

THE PRIVATE NOVELS
Private India: City on Fire (with Ashwin Sanghi)
Private Down Under (with Michael White)
Private L.A. (with Mark Sullivan)
Private Berlin (with Mark Sullivan)
Private London (with Mark Pearson)
Private Games (with Mark Sullivan)
Private: #1 Suspect (with Maxine Paetro)
Private (with Maxine Paetro)

THE NYPD RED NOVELS
NYPD Red 2 (with Marshall Karp)
NYPD Red (with Marshall Karp)

STANDALONE BOOKS
Invisible (with David Ellis)
Mistress (with David Ellis)
Second Honeymoon (with Howard Roughan)
Zoo (with Michael Ledwidge)
Guilty Wives (with David Ellis)
The Christmas Wedding (with Richard DiLallo)
Kill Me If You Can (with Marshall Karp)
Now You See Her (with Michael Ledwidge)
Toys (with Neil McMahon)
Don't Blink (with Howard Roughan)
The Postcard Killers (with Liza Marklund)
The Murder of King Tut (with Martin Dugard)
Swimsuit (with Maxine Paetro)
Against Medical Advice (with Hal Friedman)
Sail (with Howard Roughan)
Sundays at Tiffany's (with Gabrielle Charbonnet)
You've Been Warned (with Howard Roughan)
The Quickie (with Michael Ledwidge)
Judge & Jury (with Andrew Gross)
Beach Road (with Peter de Jonge)
Lifeguard (with Andrew Gross)
Honeymoon (with Howard Roughan)
Sam's Letters to Jennifer
The Lake House
The Jester (with Andrew Gross)
The Beach House (with Peter de Jonge)
Suzanne's Diary for Nicholas

Cradle and All

When the Wind Blows

Miracle on the 17th Green (with Peter de Jonge)

Hide & Seek

The Midnight Club

Black Friday (originally published as *Black Market*)

See How They Run (originally published as *The Jericho
    Commandment*)

Season of the Machete

The Thomas Berryman Number

FOR ADULTS AND TEENS

Witch and Wizard: The Lost (with Emily Raymond)

Confessions: The Paris Mysteries (with Maxine Paetro)

Homeroom Diaries (with Lisa Papademetriou, illustrated by
    Keino)

First Love (with Emily Raymond)

Confessions: The Private School Murders (with Maxine Paetro)

Witch & Wizard: The Kiss (with Jill Dembowski)

Confessions of a Murder Suspect (with Maxine Paetro)

Nevermore: A Maximum Ride Novel

Witch & Wizard: The Fire (with Jill Dembowski)

Angel: A Maximum Ride Novel

Witch & Wizard: The Gift (with Ned Rust)

Med Head (with Hal Friedman)

FANG: A Maximum Ride Novel

Witch & Wizard (with Gabrielle Charbonnet)

MAX: A Maximum Ride Novel

The Final Warning: A Maximum Ride Novel

Saving the World and Other Extreme Sports: A Maximum Ride Novel

School's Out—Forever: A Maximum Ride Novel

Maximum Ride: The Angel Experiment

FOR YOUNGER READERS

House of Robots (with Chris Grabenstein, illustrated by Juliana
    Neufeld)

Treasure Hunters: Danger Down the Nile (with Chris Grabenstein,
    illustrated by Juliana Neufeld)

Middle School, Save Rafe! (with Chris Tebbetts, illustrated by
    Laura Park)

Middle School, Ultimate Showdown (with Julia Bergen, illustrated
    by Alec Longstreth)

I Even Funnier (with Chris Grabenstein, illustrated by Laura Park)

Treasure Hunters (with Chris Grabenstein and Mark Shulman, illustrated by Juliana Neufeld)

Middle School, How I Survived Bullies, Broccoli, and Snake Hill (with Chris Tebbetts, illustrated by Laura Park)

Middle School, My Brother Is a Big, Fat Liar (with Lisa Papademetriou, illustrated by Neil Swaab)

I Funny (with Chris Grabenstein)

Daniel X: Armageddon (with Chris Grabenstein)

Middle School, Get Me out of Here! (with Chris Tebbetts, illustrated by Laura Park)

Daniel X: Game Over (with Ned Rust)

Middle School, The Worst Years of My Life (with Chris Tebbetts, illustrated by Laura Park)

Daniel X: Demons and Druids (with Adam Sadler)

Daniel X: Watch the Skies (with Ned Rust)

The Dangerous Days of Daniel X (with Michael Ledwidge)

santaKid

Manga and Graphic Novels

Daniel X: The Manga 1 - 3 (with SeungHui Kye)

Daniel X: Alien Hunter (with Leopoldo Gout)

Maximum Ride: The Manga 1 - 8 (with NaRae Lee)

Witch & Wizard: The Manga 1 - 3 (with Svetlana Chmakova)

Zoo: The Graphic Novel (with Andy MacDonald)

For previews of upcoming books and more information about James Patterson, please visit JamesPatterson.com or find him on Facebook or at your app store.

WHEN A BILLIONAIRE'S SON IS
KIDNAPPED BY A BRUTAL KILLER,
NYPD RED'S DETECTIVES MAY
HAVE TO PAY THE ULTIMATE
PRICE...

Please see the next page
for an exciting preview of

NYPD RED 3

"THERE'S MONEY TO BE MADE"

ONE

EVERY DECEMBER 31ST Hunter Hutchinson Alden, Jr. made the same two New Year's resolutions.

1. Be worth X dollars by the end of next year.

2. Quit drinking.

This year's goal was 5 billion, and considering the fact that his current net worth was 4.86 billion, getting there was a slam-dunk. But forty-five minutes and three glasses of Pellegrino into his father's New Year's Day party, he knew #2 was doomed to failure. Again.

He crammed himself into the corner of a blue calfskin Himmel settee at the east end of the Great Room so he could avoid eye contact with the swarm of well-heeled narcissists who were strutting around Hutch Alden's Fifth Avenue triplex flaunting their glorious *Christmas-in-Saint-Bart's* tans.

It was the same crowd every year—the A-list of the Rich and Shallow—and Hunter was there for only one reason. He was duty bound to charm the hell out of his old man's guests.

But not yet. Right now he was too pissed to be charming.

He glared at his iPhone, willing it to vibrate, beep, chirp, or in any way show some sign of life. One of them would call eventually. Knowing his son, the kid wouldn't have the balls to man up, so he'd pass the buck to Peter, who would apologize profusely and blame himself for Tripp's bad behavior.

The first note of his ringtone erupted from the phone, and he hit the green *Accept* button the instant it blossomed onto the screen. "Where the hell are you?" he growled, not even knowing if he was dealing with Tripp or Peter.

"Is that any way to talk to a lady?" a sexy female voice drawled.

"Sorry. I was expecting a call from the most irresponsible eighteen-year-old on the planet. Or at least from the driver I sent hours ago to bail him out of trouble."

"I'm none of those, but I'm blond, I'm hot, and you seem to be extremely agitated. Perhaps I can do something to calm you down."

"I'm sure you could."

"Are you available?"

"Technically I'm married, but I'm not a fanatic about it."

"Good," the blond said. "Ditch her. You're exactly the kind of man I've been looking for."

"What kind is that?"

"A lifelong challenge."

"But worth the effort," he said. "Where can I find you?"

"The same place Romeo found Juliet."

Hunter looked up at the sweeping balcony on the west side of the room. There was his wife Janelle, waving. "Stay where you are, Romeo."

Hunter hung up and watched as the former Miss Alabama sashayed down the marble staircase and breezed across the room, a natural-born ambassador, greeting guests on the fly, a flurry of blond hair and pink silk.

Pink was Janelle's color. She wore it often in honor of sister Chelsea, who survived breast cancer at the age of twenty-six only to die at thirty when the twin towers fell.

Hunter met Janelle a year later—September 11, 2002. He was one of the thousands of mourners who filed into the gaping hole at Ground Zero to remember the dead. And there, in the middle of the sea of somber gray and funereal black, was this golden-haired, angel-faced vision in pink.

She was the polar opposite of his late wife. Marjorie had been Yankee bred, Harvard Business School trained, and Wall Street ruthless. Janelle was Heart of Dixie to the core, never took a business course in her life, yet she had raised millions for charity simply by using her abundant charm.

She sat down on the settee and rested a hand on his knee. "I'm going home. Early day tomorrow."

"I'll go with you. We haven't had sex all year."

"Not so fast, cowboy. You're wanted up top," she said, pointing toward the balcony. "Hutch has someone he wants you to shake hands with."

"He's got a house full of people he wants me to shake hands with."

"But only one is the new mayor of New York, which is why she's having a drink with Hutch in his private sanctuary while the rest of them are forced to wander aimlessly around the castle. I'll see you at home."

"How are you getting there? Peter is still off the grid."

"I'm sure he's busy fixing Tripp's car."

"He's not a damn mechanic, Janelle. He's our driver. I specifically told him to leave Tripp's car where it is and just bring the kid home. Not keeping in touch is Tripp's MO. Now he's got Peter doing it."

"Sweetie, Tripp *did* keep in touch," Janelle said. "He texted to say he needed help, you sent help, end of story. Now stop micromanaging and don't worry about me. Hutch already arranged for Findley to drive me home. Now why don't you practice what you preach?"

"What's that supposed to mean?"

"Be a good boy and don't disappoint *your* father. He expects you to go upstairs and make nice to our new mayor. Do it." She gave him a quick kiss and headed for the door.

Hunter stood up and took a deep breath. The room smelled of money—*publishing* money, *cosmetics* money, and, of course, *money* money, the kind that comes from making canny investments when the rest of the world is betting the other way. He downed his fourth Pellegrino, turned on his handcrafted smile, and glided into the clowder of fat cats.

"Hunter!" It was Damon Parker, the despicable TV journalist who once described Hutch Alden as a folksy

Warren Buffet who tragically spawned a son as ruthless as Rupert Murdoch.

Parker advanced on him, all smiles, hand outstretched, but Hunter bounded up the stairs into hallowed ground—Hutch's five-million-dollar command center where none could go unless summoned.

"There you are," his father said, striding toward him, arm in arm with Muriel Sykes, the tall, athletic woman whose face had been on page one of every newspaper in New York that morning. "Say hello to our guest of honor."

"Madam Mayor," Hunter said. "I'd shake your hand, but you don't have a free one."

It was a standing tradition at Hutch's New Year's party to provide his guests with a taste of Old New York, and the mayor had a half-eaten hot dog in one hand and a chocolate egg cream in the other.

She turned one cheek, and Hunter planted a kiss. "Happy New Year and Happy New Administration," he said. "How's it going so far?"

"Crazy day, but I'll give you the highlights. This morning the President called to wish me well, and tonight your father treated me to the single best New York hot dog I've ever had in my life."

"That's my Dad," Hunter said. "True to his roots."

"I hate to eat and run," Sykes said, "but they've spent the entire day moving me into Gracie Mansion, and I'm dying to kick off my shoes and stretch out in my new digs. Happy New Year."

"You've been checking your phone all night," Hutch

said as soon as Sykes was out of earshot. "What's so important?"

"It's Tripp. He had car trouble—up in Harlem of all places. Peter went to rescue him, and I haven't heard from either of them for hours."

"Relax. Harlem is Peter's stomping grounds. He's probably showing Tripp a good time. Those Haitian boys sure know how to party...if you catch my drift."

"*Haitian boys*? Yes, Dad, I catch your extremely politically incorrect drift."

"What are you talking about? I'm as politically correct as they come. Hell, I just spent a small fortune helping that goddamn broad get elected mayor."

Hunter laughed. "That's fiscally correct. I'm sure she'll come in handy if you ever need her."

The strapping white-haired man put one arm around his son's shoulder. "If *we* ever need her," he corrected. "As they say in español, '*mi mayor, su mayor*.' Now are you ready to go downstairs and show these rich old farts how charming you can be?"

"Dad, there's nothing I'd rather do than go downstairs, rub a couple of elbows, and shake a couple of hands," Hunter said, putting on his game face. "Except maybe track down Tripp and Peter and wring a couple of necks."

TWO

HUNTER HAD HATED his father's New Year's Day soirees ever since he was a kid, but if this bullshit made the old man happy, what the hell? It was part of his birthright.

He spent the next two hours working his way through the crowd, clasping hands, bussing cheeks, and tossing off honey-voiced banalities. They were nothing more than empty platitudes, but personalized just enough to give people on the receiving end the impression that he actually gave a shit. What they didn't know was how much he actually knew about them.

Hunter Alden's entire financial engine was fueled by information. He spent millions putting eyes and ears in place around the globe. His intelligence network had infiltrated governments, businesses, and regulatory bodies. And because the rich have more dirty little secrets than most, he made it his business to dig deep into the personal lives of almost everyone in the room. He was willing to use it against them, and he had.

By ten p.m., his glad-handing done, he slipped quietly out the door and took Hutch's private elevator to the lobby.

Nils, the short, squat night doorman, was on duty. "Pretty nippy out there, Mr. Alden," he said. "Nineteen degrees. Twelve with the wind chill factor. You sure you don't need a coat?"

Why the hell would I need a coat? Hunter thought. His world was climate controlled. Even the canopy outside the building had been outfitted with heat lamps to warm the wealthy walked the twenty feet from the lobby door to their waiting limos.

"Don't worry, Nils. I'll be fine," he said.

His father's black Cadillac was idling at the curb. Findley St. John, Hutch's long-time driver, saw him and spread both arms open wide.

Findley was one of the few people to penetrate the wall Hunter had built around himself. He sang songs with Hunter when he drove the boy to his first day of kindergarten; he pummeled three young thugs who'd mugged Hunter in middle school; and he'd almost gotten himself fired when he swore that the vodka bottle in the back of the Caddy belonged to him and not Hutch's fourteen-year-old son.

"Happy New Year, Sport," he boomed, wrapping his arms around Hunter.

"Same to you, old man. I see you're still driving this piece-of-shit American car."

Findley put a gloved hand on the rear door handle, swung the door open, and shut it as soon as Hunter was in, leaving almost no time for the preheated air to escape into the cold night.

"Piece-of-shit car?" Findley said, getting behind the wheel. "You know what your daddy says. 'If it's good enough for the President of the United States, it's good enough for me.'"

"My father is too old and too rich to settle for 'good enough.' Nothing is more reliable than German engineering."

The *mano-a-mano* verbal sparring between the two men had been going on for decades, and Findley was thrilled to have another go at it. "And yet," he said, looking over his shoulder at Hunter, "that reliable German car of yours had to be bailed out by this piece of shit from Detroit."

"It wasn't the car that caused the problem," Hunter said. "It was my unreliable Haitian driver."

Findley let out a throaty laugh. He was from the same village as Peter. "I just drove Miz Janelle home, and she didn't say nothing about no unreliable Haitians. Sounded more like the problem was that footloose teenager of yours. The apple sure don't fall far from the tree."

The ride up Madison gave them less than five minutes to catch up before Findley turned left on 81st Street. "Good news," he said as he pulled the Cadillac up to Alden's four-story Beaux Arts limestone townhouse. "Light's on in the garage, so it looks like Peter is home."

"Son of a bitch," Hunter said, jumping out of the car

before Findley could get to the door. "Why the hell didn't he call me?"

"I'm not hanging around to find out," Findley said, putting the limo in gear. "Don't be too hard on him, Sport. It's New Year's."

Hunter headed straight for the garage. He flipped the keypad cover and tapped in the code, more excited to see his dream car than to confront Peter.

His Maybach 62 S had been built at the Center of Excellence in Sindelfingen, Germany. It was, in the words of the personal advisor who worked with Hunter during the entire fourteen-month period from commission to delivery, "a one-of-a-kind automotive masterpiece, thoughtfully designed and flawlessly hand-crafted to mirror the style and personality of its owner." And to Hunter, worth every penny of the 1.1 million it cost to build it.

The garage door opened, and the room lit up even brighter. The space was wide and deep and empty. Hunter sucked in a lungful of the crisp January air. His car wasn't there. The only thing on the silver pearl and slate-gray Swisstrax floor was the bright yellow molded polyethylene box that sat in the middle—Tripp's camera case. For Hunter, it was a bit of a relief. At least his son was home.

And then he saw it. At first it looked like random red markings on the yellow case. He got closer. The brownish-red lines were not from a marker. It was dried blood. And the haphazard strokes were actually letters—HHA III—Hunter Hutchinson Alden III, Tripp's initials.

Hunter dropped to his knees, snapped the stainless steel butterfly latches, and opened the case. Nestled on top was a Ziploc bag with a cell phone inside. He removed the bag and jerked back in horror at what was underneath—a severed head, cushioned by the case's thick foam lining, blood-soaked viscera hanging from the stump of its neck, the whites of its eyes staring up at Hunter.

It was Peter.

A single piece of paper was wedged between his lips. Hunter unfolded it and stared at the message. Five words, neatly typed.

There's money to be made.

His chest clenched, and he could barely fill his lungs with air. It was impossible, inconceivable, but there it was. Somebody somewhere had found out about Project Gutenberg.

Shaking, Hunter Alden closed the garage door and headed upstairs to pour his first drink of the New Year.

PART ONE

THE SINS OF THE FATHER

CHAPTER 1

I HAD JUST had the best New Year's Day of my life, and when I opened my eyes on the morning of January 2, the euphoria continued.

In front of me was a captivating panoramic view of Central Park, still dotted with patches of last week's white Christmas. Above me, the ceiling was adorned with hand-painted cherubs and half-naked women frolicking in a wooded glade. And curled up next to me on our zillion-thread-count sheets was a totally naked woman who could put every one of those Roman goddesses in that Bacchanalian fresco to shame.

"I could get used to this, Zach," Cheryl said. "You definitely should start taking more bribes."

Two nights ago Cheryl and I had checked into the Steele Towers on Central Park South for a mini New

Year's vacation. The room I booked was something I could afford on a cop's salary, but when we got there, the desk clerk apologized. There was a maintenance problem in our room.

He waited just long enough to register the look on our faces, and then he said, "But don't worry, Detective Jordan. We'll upgrade you to a slightly better accommodation."

His version of "slightly better" was an 1,800-square-foot penthouse suite, the top of the line in this world-class, five-star hotel.

"Oh my God," Cheryl said when the floor concierge escorted us to our new digs. She looked at the pricing chart on the back of the door. "And only sixty-five hundred dollars a night."

"Happy accidents happen to the nicest people," the concierge said.

Not for a second did I think this was an accident. I knew exactly what it was—a silent gesture of gratitude from Jason Steele, the man who owned the hotel. His wife had been murdered a few months ago, and my partner Kylie MacDonald and I had cracked the case.

I stood in the doorway of the suite, called my boss, Captain Cates, and explained the problem.

"It's not a problem," she said. "You're there as a private citizen, not a cop."

"But the desk clerk called me Detective Jordan. He knew I was a cop."

"Zach, you're one of a handful of detectives assigned to NYPD Red. You've made two front-page arrests in the past six months. You better get used to the fact that people are going to recognize you. Now, you called me for a ruling. Here it is. Hotels upgrade all the time. Shut up, take it, and you and Cheryl have a Happy New Year."

Boy, did we ever. But now it was time to go back to reality. I got out of bed. "I'm going to take a shower," I said.

Cheryl stretched like a cat in the summer sun, and the sheets slipped below her breasts.

"On second thought," I said, "I'm hopping back in bed."

She smiled. "Just hop to the shower. I'll be right behind you."

"Behind me, in front of me...I'm sure we can work out the best arrangement once we're all wet and slippery," I said.

Cheryl's cell rang. "It's probably my parents wishing me a happy New Year," she said. "We played phone tag all day yesterday. I kept missing them. I'll be right there."

There were three bathrooms, and Cheryl and I had experimented with shower gymnastics in every one of them. I headed for our favorite.

I dimmed the lights, dialed up some slow jazz, stepped into the double green granite-tiled shower, and turned on the water. It was heaven.

Despite the fact that my job keeps me in daily contact with New York City's wealthiest citizens, rarely do I get to live like one. I lost myself in the pulsating rhythms of the six perfect pressure shower heads, closed my eyes, and thought about the dark-haired, caramel-skinned, drop-dead beautiful, and kick-ass smart Latina I was rapidly falling in love with.

I'd met Cheryl Robinson four years ago. She was an NYPD psychologist, and I was a candidate for the department's most elite unit. It took her three hours to evaluate me. I, on the other hand, only needed three seconds to evaluate her. I'd never seen a cop or a shrink this desirable, and if it weren't for that gold band on her left hand, and the fact that she stood between me and the best job in the department, I would have thrown myself at her feet.

I got the job, and six months ago, shortly after her wedding ring came off forever, I got Cheryl. I'd only been in love once before. Eleven years ago I had a torrid twenty-eight-day affair with a fellow recruit at the police academy: Kylie MacDonald. But she dumped me and went back to her old boyfriend. A year after that, she married him.

Ten years later, the Department of Let's-See-If-We-Can-Drive-Zach-Jordan-Crazy decided to test my emotional resilience and put Kylie back in my life. Not as my girlfriend, but as my partner in crime solving. And for the past six months, Kylie and I have been inseparable—except for the part where she goes home to her husband, Spence Harrington, every night.

Fifteen minutes into my bathroom revelry, Cheryl still hadn't made an appearance, and I was starting to shrivel up in more ways than one.

I toweled off, put on a thick white terry robe, and went back to the master bedroom.

She was still on the phone.

"Be strong," she said. "I'll be there as soon as I can. Tell her to feel better and give her my love."

She hung up. "Zach, I'm sorry. Family emergency."

"Is your mother sick?" I asked.

"No. It's Fred's mother."

Fred? Fred was Cheryl's ex-husband. "That was Fred who called?"

She nodded. "He's devastated."

"I thought Fred was out of the picture."

"He is. But his mother is dying. I told you I was planning to drive up to Bedford next weekend for Mildred's birthday. It looks like she's not going to make it till then. I'm going to run into the office, wrap up a few things, and catch a train up to Northern Westchester Hospital as soon as I can."

She got out of bed and threw on a robe. "I'm sorry, sweetie, but I'm going to shower, and it's going to be short and solo." She headed for the bathroom. "Oh, I almost forgot. Your phone rang while I was on the phone with Fred. I saw it was Kylie, so I picked up and told her you'd call right back."

Kylie wanted me, which meant work. Fred wanted Cheryl, which meant I would have something to obsess about all day besides work.

I called Kylie. "Happy New Year," I said.

"Not for everybody," she said. "We have a headless body in Riverside Park."

Decapitations were standard fare for Mexican drug cartels, but rare in New York—even rarer for our unit. "Are you sure it's for Red?" I asked.

"The body is wearing a chauffeur's uniform," Kylie said, "and there's a big-ass black limo in the parking lot. License plate ALDEN 2. Which means this homicide is about as Red as you can get. Where are you?"

I told her, and she said she'd pick me up outside the hotel in ten minutes.

My New Year's euphoria was officially over.

CHAPTER 2

NOT TOO MANY New Yorkers know it, but Riverside Park was conceived by the same guy who designed Central Park. And while it's not Frederick Law Olmsted's most famous work, the four-mile strip that hugs the Hudson River between 72nd and 158th Streets is the most spectacular stretch of natural beauty and recreational possibilities in the city.

Kylie took the Henry Hudson Parkway north, swung around under the George Washington Bridge, and headed back south on the Parkway until we spotted the 151st Street entrance to Riverside Park.

The parking lot was empty except for a dozen assorted police vehicles and one shiny black limo that looked as out of place as a debutante at a biker rally.

We spotted the one guy we were looking for—Chuck

Dryden. Chuck is a brilliant criminalist with all the charisma of a wet bathmat. He'd been dubbed Cut and Dryden because he was all business, no small talk. His emotional content ranged from ho to hum, but I'd discovered that there is one defibrillator that could jumpstart his dispassionate heart. Like a lot of men before him, he was totally smitten by Kylie. So as soon as we saw him, my partner took the reins.

"We're in luck, Zach. It's our favorite CSI. Happy New Year, Chuck," Kylie said, tantalizingly putting on a pair of latex gloves as if she had something else in mind other than preventing the contamination of a crime scene.

He looked down, muttered a quiet "same to you," and immediately went into his observations. "The victim appears to be Peter Chevalier, age fifty-five, from Cité Soleil, Haiti, American citizen since 1988, resides on East 81st Street."

"*Appears* to be?" Kylie asked.

"There was a wallet in the victim's pocket," Dryden said. "Normally the headshot on his license would help me get a positive ID, but as you can see, this man's head is nowhere in sight."

He peeled back the tarp that covered the body, gave us ten seconds to take in the mutilation, then discreetly covered it back up.

"As the vanity license plates would imply, the vehicle is registered to Alden Investments, which is owned by Hunter Hutchinson Alden, Jr. There's no evidence of a struggle inside the car. Judging by this pool of blood, Mr. Chevalier was standing outside when he was decapitated."

"Time of death?" I asked.

"Somewhere between 7:52 and 8:11 last night."

"How the hell did you come up with such a narrow window?" I said.

Dryden almost smiled. "It was well below freezing last night," he said. "Even colder here at the river's edge than the rest of the city, so I can't give you a definitive time frame till I get him to the lab and run a thorough check on blood pooling, stomach contents, rigor—the usual indicators. However, we retrieved a cell phone from the ground under the driver's side door, and it appears that the victim was composing a text to Mr. Alden when the killer came up behind him."

He held it up so we could read it.

cant find tripp. do you want me to

"The text is unfinished and unsent, so I can't tell exactly when he wrote it," Dryden said. "But then there's a flood of incoming texts, all from Alden, all basically saying 'call me—where the hell are you.' Since all of Alden's previous texts were answered promptly, a logical conclusion would be that the time of death was somewhere between Mr. Chevalier's last reply at 7:52 and Mr. Alden's text that followed at 8:11."

"Cause of death?" Kylie asked.

"Excellent question, Detective," Dryden said. "Many cops would hesitate to ask what killed a headless man, and they'd be wrong. There are no bullet wounds or puncture marks on the body, but there is a fresh bruise on his lower back consistent with the classic knee strike delivered in conjunction with a garrote attack. However, since his head was removed with a rope saw, which is quite messy, I can't find any visible ligature marks in the field, so a garrote is only an educated guess. It's also possible that he was strangled with the rope saw, and then the killer kept cutting. Either way, decapitation was post mortem."

"I'm a city girl," Kylie said. "What in the world is a rope saw?"

We knew that Dryden had a treasure trove of weaponry in his cerebrum, and we'd always suspected that he might have quite a few of them in his basement.

"A rope saw is a jagged-toothed carbon steel chain attached to two handles. It affords the user all the benefits of a chain saw without the noise."

"Thank you, Chuck," Kylie said. "You are, as usual, incredibly thorough."

He nodded. "I'll call you from the lab once I have further findings. And needless to say," he added, "if you come across *la tête de Monsieur Chevalier*, make sure you send it my way."

"Sure thing," Kylie said. She waited till we were twenty feet away before she whispered out of the side of her mouth. "He probably needs it to complete his collection."

CHAPTER 3

"**I HAD MATT** Smith run Peter Chevalier's name through the system," Kylie said. "Over the years he's picked up hundreds of parking violations for Alden Investments, which is no surprise. People who ride in the back of limos would rather pay a fine than walk half a block. Otherwise, he was an upstanding citizen."

"Upstanding citizens don't usually have many enemies," I said. "His boss, on the other hand, is one of the richest, most ruthless bastards on Wall Street."

"And as good fortune would have it," Kylie said, "rich, ruthless bastards are our specialty. Let's go have a chat with Mr. Alden."

We double-parked on East 81st Street and were about to get out of the car when the weathered bronze front door opened. Hunter Alden was standing there with another man who was about to leave.

"Holy shit," Kylie said. "The short one in the coat is Silas David Blackstone."

"You know him?"

"Oh yeah—smarmy little bastard. He's the head of SDB Investigative Services. If you have a legal matter you want done, Silas Blackstone will do it. If it's illegal, he'll do it for more money. Let's find out what he's doing here."

We got out of the car. The two men saw us immediately.

"Kylie?" Blackstone said. "Kylie MacDonald?"

He bounded down the steps and let us in the front gate.

"What a pleasant surprise," Blackstone said. "I've been following your career, and you are just burning up a trail at NYPD, aren't you?"

"This is my partner," she said, ignoring the question. "Detective Zach Jordan."

"Silas David Blackstone. Jordan, you are one lucky devil," he said. "I'd kill to ride around town all day with this woman. Only with me, it would be a much better car."

He extended his arm, and it was hate at first handshake.

He turned back to Kylie. "How is your husband doing these days? I heard he was ill."

Smarmy was an understatement. He must have known that Spence was in rehab because he put air quotes around the word "ill."

"He's on the mend, thank you," Kylie said. She pulled out her shield and held it up. "NYPD. Hunter Alden?"

"That's me," Alden said. "Come on up."

Kylie and I walked up to the doorway with Blackstone right behind. "Detectives Kylie MacDonald and Zach Jordan," she said. "If you've been consulting with Mr. Black-stone, you must know why we're here."

"Yes, Peter's been missing since last night. I was concerned and called Silas."

"And I picked up the One Eight Seven on the scanner. I came here to break the bad news to Mr. Alden."

"How did you pick it up?" I asked. "The victim's name wasn't on the air."

Blackstone's lips curled, transforming his phony plastic smile into a genuine contemptuous sneer. "Yes, Detective, but there was a description of the car. Not many May-bachs on the road. They start at about 400 grand. Plus, this one is tricked out with armor plate, bulletproof windows, and a complete—"

"That's enough, Silas." It was Alden.

"I just want them to know that's a million-dollar car they've impounded, and we'd appreciate it if they returned it to you sooner rather than later. By the way," Silas said, turning back to me and Kylie, "it's pronounced My-Bock, not May-Back. I guess your dispatcher is more used to Hondas and Toyotas."

Alden raised his voice. "Enough, damn it."

"I was just leaving," Blackstone said. "Wonderful to see you again, Kylie. Remember, there's always a job opening for you at SDB."

He took the first three stairs, then turned back to his boss. "You're in excellent hands, Mr. Alden. These two cops are not just NYPD, they're with NYPD Red, which is as good as you're going to get..." He arched his eyebrows and shrugged. "...from the public sector."

CHAPTER 4

HUNTER ALDEN ESCORTED us into one of those grand foyer entryways most people only see in movies. I've learned enough to know that directly ahead of us was what they call a butterfly staircase. Or as us poor folks say, the curved kind where you can walk upstairs from either side.

I could see by the grain that the floor was wood, but it gleamed like the ebony keys on a piano. Overhead was a crystal chandelier suspended from an intricately carved paneled ceiling. To the left was a pair of ebonized wooden doors inset with silver grillwork and beveled mirrors.

The only contrast to the monochromatic tones of black and gray was a glorious Christmas tree that was the seasonal focal point of the room. It towered past the iron-forged balcony railing on the second floor and looked like it would be as at home in the White House as it was here on 81st Street. It was like stepping into the holiday edition of *Architectural Digest*.

"Sorry about Blackstone," Alden said as he closed the front door. "He's a bit of an abrasive little asshole, but he's good at what he does."

"And what exactly is that?" Kylie asked.

If there had been a tour of the Alden estate in our future, it was abruptly cancelled. Hunter Alden stopped right there in the entryway.

"And what the hell business is that of yours, Detective? My family is in the middle of a devastating tragedy. Peter has been with us for twenty-three years. I'm told you're the best cops the department has to offer, and you lead off with an irresponsible question that is nothing more than a breach of my privacy."

Some cops might have apologized, but Kylie was born with a seriously defective *I'm Sorry* gene. She came right back at him. "Mr. Alden, that wasn't my intended opening question, but when I see an 'abrasive little asshole' like Blackstone at the home of a murder victim, I want to know what he's doing here. Now, I'm sorry for your loss, but since we'd both like to know who killed Peter Chevalier, let me start off with a different question."

"I have a few questions of my own." He turned away from her and looked squarely at me. "Tell me," he said, adjusting his voice to the more respectful tone reserved for the guy who plays Good Cop, "was it a robbery? I hope he didn't get killed trying to protect my car. Was he shot? Stabbed?"

"No, sir," I said. "It appears Mr. Chevalier was choked to death and then decapitated."

That was something Blackstone couldn't have told him, and Alden took a step back. "De...I...I don't know what to say."

"You can start by telling us about Peter. Did he have any enemies?"

"He had a reputation for being a bit of a skirt chaser. He probably pissed off more than a few husbands and boyfriends in his life."

"Enough to kill him?"

"Detective, I'm his employer, not his drinking buddy. All I know is what I just told you."

"Did he ever borrow your car for his own personal use?"

He looked at me like I'd spat in the punch bowl. Clearly he thought I was clueless about the boundaries between upstairs and downstairs. "Absolutely not," he snapped.

"Then he was working for you when he was murdered. Can you tell us what he was doing all alone in an empty parking lot off the West Side Highway at that hour of the night?"

He repeated the question, a sure tell that he'd rather not answer it. But I'd painted him into a corner. "I have no idea" was not an option.

"Simple explanation," he said. "Around 6:30 last night I got a text from my son Tripp that his car broke down, so I sent Peter to pick him up."

"Then Tripp must have been one of the last people to

see Peter alive," Kylie said now that she could smell that Alden was on the defensive.

"No, they never connected," he said quickly. "Tripp called me late last and said Peter never found him. He eventually got one of his friends to pick him up and spent the night at the kid's house."

"What kind of car does your son drive?" Kylie asked.

"One of those useless hybrids. A Prius—blue, maybe green—I don't really remember."

"There was no car matching that description in the area," I said.

"Have you been to Riverside Park?" Alden said. "It's huge. I'm sure it'll turn up. Is that all, Detectives? I'm rather pressed for time."

"That's all we have right now," I said. "But we'd like to talk to your son."

"You can't reach him now. He's a senior at Barnaby Prep, and the school has a strict no-cell-phone rule. But I'll be glad to leave him a message."

He took a cell from his pocket. "I realize Silas didn't broach the subject with any tact," he said as he tapped his speed dial, "but I really do need my car back as soon as possible. Can I count on you to expedite—hold on, I got his voicemail. Hello, Tripp. Something happened to Peter last night, and the police are here to discuss it. They have a few questions they'd like to ask you. Call me when you can, and I'll arrange a meeting with them."

He hung up. "If you leave me your number, I'll contact you as soon as I hear from him."

I gave him my card. "One last question. You said your

son first called you about his car problems at 6:30. At that hour, the park was dark, empty, and bitter cold. What was he doing there so late?"

"Tripp is a film nut," Alden said. "So I hired him to make a surprise video for my father, who is turning seventy in March. I think he decided to go get some footage of the old neighborhood where my father grew up."

"Exactly where is that?" I asked.

Alden hesitated.

"Think hard," I said. "If your father is anything like mine, he dragged you there more than once to show you where he lived as a kid."

His memory came back fast. "You're right. It's 530 West 136th Street."

"That's in Harlem."

"I know," Alden said. "Your rags-to-riches story doesn't get any better than that. I can't wait to see the look on my father's face when he sees this video."

He reopened the front door. "Give me a buzz and let me know the status of my car. It's not just transportation. It's my mobile office. I'm lost without it."

He smiled as he saw us out. He seemed to have bounced back nicely from his family's devastating tragedy.